The Courtesan's Pirate

The Courtesan's Pirate

A Venice Beauties Mystery

Nina Wachsman

To my late brother Stuey who loved to play pirates

Contents

Praise for The Courtesan's Pirate   iv
Cast of Characters   vi

I   The New World

Chapter One: Belladonna   3
Chapter Two: Belladonna   9
Chapter Three: Belladonna   13
Chapter Four: Belladonna   15
Chapter Five: Isaak   19
Chapter Six: Isaak   22
Chapter Seven: Belladonna   25
Chapter Eight: Isaak   29
Chapter Nine: Isaak   33
Chapter Ten: Isaak   37
Chapter Eleven: Isaak   43
Chapter Twelve: Belladonna   46
Chapter Thirteen: Belladonna   49
Chapter Fourteen: Isaak   57
Chapter Fifteen: Isaak   62
Chapter Sixteen: Belladonna   68
Chapter Seventeen: Belladonna   73
Chapter Eighteen: Isaak   78
Chapter Nineteen: Isaak   83
Chapter Twenty: Belladonna   89
Chapter Twenty-One: Isaak   93

Chapter Twenty-Two: Belladonna   97
Chapter Twenty-Three: Isaak   99
Chapter Twenty-Four: Isaak   102
Chapter Twenty-Five: Isaak   106
Chapter Twenty-Six: Isaak   109
Chapter Twenty-Seven: Isaak   112
Chapter Twenty-Eight: Isaak   116
Chapter Twenty-Nine: Isaak   119
Chapter Thirty: Isaak   122
Chapter Thirty-One: Isaak   126
Chapter Thirty-Two: Isaak   129
Chapter Thirty-Three: Isaak   133
Chapter Thirty-Four: Isaak   138
Chapter Thirty-Five: Isaak   142
Chapter Thirty-Six: Belladonna   148
Chapter Thirty-Seven: Isaak   150
Chapter Thirty-Eight: Isaak   154

II   The Old World

Chapter Thirty-Nine: Belladonna   161
Chapter Forty: Diana   166
Chapter Forty-One: Belladonna   170
Chapter Forty-Two: Belladonna   175
Chapter Forty-Three: Belladonna   178
Chapter Forty-Four: Belladonna   181
Chapter Forty-Five: Diana   184
Chapter Forty-Six: Belladonna   187
Chapter Forty-Seven: Diana   190
Chapter Forty-Eight: Diana   194
Chapter Forty-Nine: Belladonna   198
Chapter Fifty: Belladonna   201
Chapter Fifty-One: Belladonna   205

Chapter Fifty-Two: Diana   209
Chapter Fifty-Three: Belladonna   214
Chapter Fifty-Four: Diana   220
Chapter Fifty-Five: Belladonna   222
Chapter Fifty-Six: Belladonna   227
Chapter Fifty-Seven: Belladonna   231
Chapter Fifty-Eight: Diana   235
Chapter Fifty-Nine: Belladonna   238
Chapter Sixty: Diana   242
Chapter Sixty-One: Belladonna   245
Chapter Sixty-Two: Belladonna   249
Chapter Sixty-Three: Belladonna   254
Chapter Sixty-Four: Belladonna   257
Chapter Sixty-Five: Belladonna   262
Chapter Sixty-Six: Belladonna   269
Chapter Sixty-Seven: Diana   276
Chapter Sixty-Eight: Belladonna   282
Chapter Sixty-Nine: Diana   287
Chapter Seventy: Diana   290
Chapter Seventy-One: Belladonna   294

Author's Note   299
Acknowledgements   302
About the Author   303
Also by Nina Wachsman   304

Praise for The Courtesan's Pirate

"Join Belladonna and Isaak on a Caribbean quest filled with rich history, dangerous risks, and suspenseful intrigue. Will the couple be reunited? Can Belladonna save her love and her soul? If you like an atmospheric adventure story, you'll love *The Courtesan's Pirate*. Witty and engaging!"—Kelly Oliver, author of The Fiona Figg & Kitty Lane Mysteries

"*The Courtesan's Pirate* is a thrilling cinematic adventure featuring a remarkable and resourceful woman. The third book in the Venice Beauties Mystery series shows that you can take Belladonna out of Venice, but you can't take Venice out of her. It was a bold move for Wachsman to move her protagonist along with a few supporting characters to the other side of the world, but with meticulous research and writing talent, she pulled it off. I highly recommend *The Courtesan's Pirate*—both the book and the man."—Lane Stone, author of the Big Picture art thriller trilogy, Member of Curators of Crime

"*The Courtesan's Pirate* is a delightful swashbuckler that spans the Atlantic with strong women who not only survive, but thrive, among the danger of 17th Century pirates in the New World and intrigue in the Old."—M. A. Monnin, Agatha Award-nominated author of the Intrepid Traveler Mysteries, Member of Curators of Crime

"From the pirate-infested waters of the Caribbean to the silken-clad intrigues of Venice, Nina Wachsman vividly recreates life, and particularly the dangers faced by Jews, in the turbulent 17th century. Exciting and richly textured, with strong, admirable female characters."—Alyssa Maxwell, author of The Gilded Newport Mysteries

For the series:

"If you like fiction served on a platter of historical realism, with colorful characters and page-turning intrigue…get to know author Nina Wachsman."—*New Jersey Jewish Link*

"This historical tale reads like a thrilling adventure that includes spies, lost treasure, and romance."—*King's River Life Magazine*

"Readers enticed by dazzling, enigmatic Venice of this era, with its beautiful women, romance and conspiracies will enjoy this book."—Historical Novel Society

Cast of Characters

- *Belladonna* – a former elite courtesan of Venice, and the fiancé of Isaak
- *Isaak* – Belladonna's one true love, the captain of the pirate ship, *Sabato*, and the son of the chief rabbi of Venice
- *Mariella* – the widow of Roderigo, Belladonna's long lost brother, and the owner of a plantation in Jamaica
- *Moises* –son of Mariella and Roderigo, nephew of Belladonna
- *Hernando* –former first mate of the *Sabato*, blown off the ship by the hurricane and washed up on the surf of Jamaica
- *Ahmad* – *Sabato*'s ship surgeon , with training from the great Arabic physicians

The pirate captains:

- *Captain Ross* – young English pirate captain
- *Captain Glover* –another English pirate captain, formerly of the English navy
- *Captain Williams* –an English pirate captain from Cornwall
- *Captain Marcel Olivante* – a French pirate captain
- *Captain Hendriksson* – a Dutch pirate captain

In Curacao:

- *Yehuda* – a Jewish pawnbroker- dealer who has ties to the Brethren
- *Menachem* – Yehuda's son, and a dealer in ship refitting and repair
- *Brethren*- the alliance of Jewish pirates in the New and Old World

In Venice:

- *Bardon Morosini*—a Venetian aristocrat and powerful member of the Council of Ten
- *Council of Ten* – ten members of the governing Senate who become magistrates and are considered the most powerful men in Venice
- *Niccolo Contarini* –Morosini's rival and a Venetian aristocrat who is a leading member of the Council of Ten
- *Foscarini* – a nobleman assigned to procuring all that is needed for the visit of the Duke of Mantova
- *Josef of Constantinople* – a leading trader and nephew and poerful matriarch who sits by the throne of the Sultan
- *The Turk* – an importer in Venice, of any desired item for the right price
- *Mattia Correr* –A portrait artist in Venice
- *Diana* – the scholarly widowed daughter of the chief rabbi of Venice
- *Zebulun* –Diana and Isaak's youngest brother, an adventurer and ship captain
- *Rabbi Leone di Modena* – chief rabbi of Venice and father of Diana, Zebulun and Issak
- *Sarra and Jacob Sullam* – a wealthy and generous couple in the Ghetto who are also great patrons of the arts
- *Isabella* – an influential courtesan of Venice
- *Avigdor Marguiles* – a Jewish importer and trader who is building the new port of Venice
- *Duke of Mantova* – a noble visitor to Venice, and the brother-in-law of the Holy Roman Emperor

Florida
Gulf of Mexico
gulf of campeche
Yucatan
Yucatan Strait
Cuba
CARIBBEAN SEA
North Atlantic ocean
Cayman Islands
Jamaica
Hispaniola
caribbean sea
North Pacific ocean
cabo gallinas
Curacao
Orinoco
Trinidad

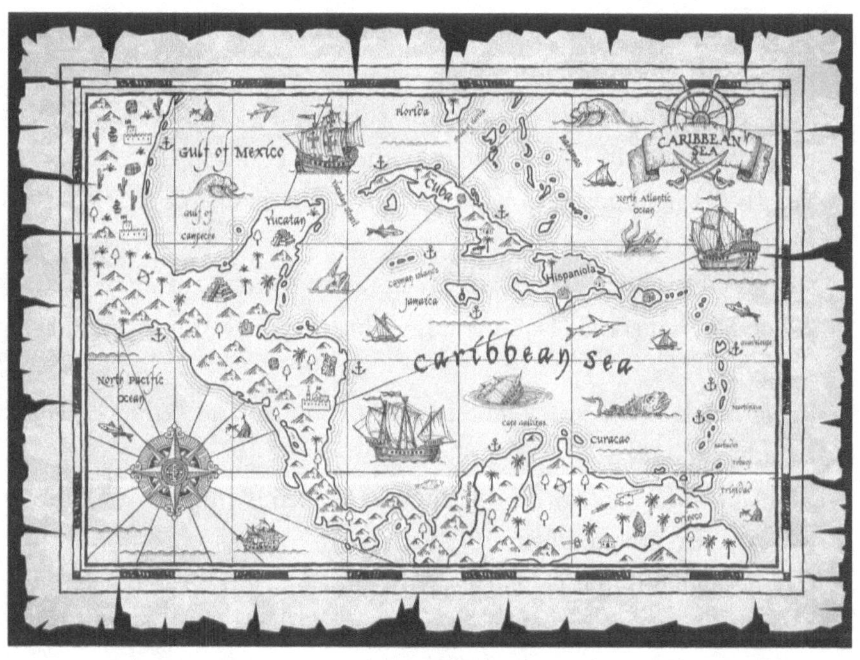

Hispaniola

I

The New World

Chapter One: Belladonna

THE ISLAND OF JAMAICA, The fifth of NOVEMBER, 1614

"Just a short trip to Curacao," Isaak said as he stood beside her on the dock, "I will return shortly, I promise."

Belladonna wondered how many women had heard the very same words from their fathers, sons, and lovers and how many had returned to their families as promised.

"Why must you go?" Belladonna had waited so long and given up so much to be with Isaak. She secretly believed their union was at risk every time they were away from each other.

"Despite our efforts to attract the English to Jamaica, the Spanish have moved faster, and the heirs of Christopher Columbus have been bought off. We need to find somewhere else to settle," Isaak said, wrapping his arms around her.

She raised her eyes skyward to keep the tears from rising. "Then my brother died for naught."

"We cannot change the past, but we must try to find the way to our future, for you and I and for your brother Roderigo's family. Curacao has been abandoned by the Spanish and will soon become part of the dominion of the Dutch West India Company."

Belladonna wanted to believe his promise, but after a life tossed about at the whim of Fate, it seemed like random interventions could foil any plan they made for the future.

Isaak caressed her cheek. "It is also a port of call of the Jewish Brethren. Under the Dutch, we have little to fear. The Dutch are the only nation that does not force its Jews to live separately in a Ghetto. We will soon formalize our union. There lies our potential future."

Belladonna sighed. "In Curacao, do you believe no one will care about our origins- if we are Jew or Christian?"

Like her sister-in-law Mariella, she had begun life as the daughter of a New Christian landowner who had sought freedom in the New World. In a terrible twist of Fate, on a visit to Recife, Brazil, the Inquisition murdered her parents because of their Jewish heritage, turning her into a refugee. Luck had found her, and she had been rescued by Isaak from Barbary pirates. Thanks to Isaak, she had been taken to Venice, but he had soon set sail once more, on a mission to save others from captivity.

When Isaak returned to Venice to reunite her with her brother Roderigo, feelings between the courtesan and the corsair were rekindled, and Belladonna made her decision to sail with Isaak. Giving up her palazzo, her wealth and servants had gone against her usual cynicism, but for once, she had chosen love over security.

"It is worth the chance," said Isaak, and then he pulled her close, "You must stop nourishing your guilt over the death of Roderigo. You have come here to take care of his family as you promised. And we have accomplished the impossible: we are together at last."

Belladonna acknowledged her satisfaction with her decision. "Over the past year in Jamaica and with you, I have discovered the comfort of family, which had been missing from my life for so long. Why dare Fate to disrupt our happiness once more?"

Isaak looked beyond her towards the sea. "There is a storm coming, which will provide us with a distraction to sail by Spanish warships gathering along the coast." He lifted her chin and brushed her lips with a last kiss. "Both the storm and the Spanish ships represent a bad omen. But do not fear. I am a seasoned captain and have sailed through worse brews than this. But my senses tell me our idyll in Jamaica is bound to come to an end. I must go to Curacao."

Belladonna did not want to let him go, but he kissed her and gently disengaged from her. She ran to the edge of the wooden dock and leaned as far forward as she dared. He waved one last time as he boarded his ship. She reasoned that the fierce winds should be good for sailing and would speed Isaak's journey. Squinting, she tried to see his figure on the bridge, imagining him making his farewell to Jamaica and to her.

Isaak's fears about Jamaica were not unfounded. The Spanish were becoming bolder in establishing their dominion over the island, even though it officially remained under the sovereignty of the heirs to Christopher Columbus. The end of Jamaica's independence was near, and once the Spanish took over, both she and Isaak, as well as her newfound family, would be in danger because of their Jewish blood.

"Senora, we must go. Big storm is coming, and we must prepare. The sky do not look good. Horses do not like it." The coachman peered up at the amassing dark clouds and then gave her a pleading look.

Reluctantly, Belladonna turned away from the sea towards the mountains. "Let us go."

Adjusting his hat so it was firmly placed on his head, the driver flicked his whip, and the horses responded by taking off at a gallop, as if they were as eager as the driver to find shelter. Belladonna craned her neck, still looking towards the dock as they drove away.

The coachman kept the horses going at a fast gallop, so she had to hold tight to both sides of the carriage to avoid toppling forward. The wind kicked up the dust of the roadway, flinging it through the bushes and trees, shaking loose leaves and petals, swirling through the air and into their faces.

"Hiyah!" the coachman shouted again at the horses, using his whip to make them gallop even faster. Used to traveling by boat in Venice, she knew little of carriages and put her faith in the coachman to get them home safely.

Lurching from side to side in the speeding carriage, she closed her eyes to shut out the frightening views of a careening landscape. She dared open them only when the carriage slowed and the wails of the wind were softer. They had entered the sheltering thickness of the mangrove forest adjoining her brother's land. The trees here were very thick and though their upper boughs still rustled in the wind, she felt more protected. The respite from the wind did not last long, and soon, the carriage emerged from the mangrove trees into a slashing rain. The downpour swamped the open carriage, soaking her completely and making it even more difficult to move forward. Though it seemed like an eternity in the wind and rain, the coach soon drew to a sharp halt. Safe.

Her brother's plantation house stood two stories tall, surrounded by trees, which the wind lashed against the closed shutters. Assailed by wind and rain, it did not seem to be the safe haven it had seemed several months ago when she first arrived on the island. After over a year at sea, when she first stepped onto the grand veranda, it had conjured long-ago memories of home. Though not as grand as the palazzo she possessed in Venice, it did have many rooms furnished comfortably with bright island fabrics on sofas and chairs. There were flowers in abundance, and island paintings and pottery similar to her childhood home on the island.

That home and her family had been torn from her when the Inquisition came to Recife, Brazil, where they had been visiting relatives. Her parents were New Christians, having been born Jews but then baptized, like many others who had come to the New World, and easy targets for accusations of heresy and the fires of an auto de fé. Both she and Roderigo had escaped capture, but each did not know the other survived until very recently when they had found each other in Venice. Their reunion was short-lived, and Roderigo's dying request was for Belladonna to find his family in Jamaica and make sure they were cared for.

After securing the door behind her, Belladonna stood in the entry hall, water dripping from her gown and pooling at her feet.

"Mariella!" she shouted, hoping her sister-in-law was in the house and could hear her above the howling wind.

Mariella and Moises, her son, bounded down the stairway from the upper floor, each carrying armfuls of clothing and possessions.

"We do not have much time," Mariella shouted back to her above the rattling of the shutters and the wind, "We must go. Take what you need."

"We cannot stay here?"

Moises answered for his mother. "When the wind is this strong, the house is not safe. We must go to the Cave."

Cave? Belladonna shivered in her wet clothes at the thought of it. Mentally, she checked off what she needed to take, including the small leather sack of jewels that had been with her since Venice. Hurrying up the stairs with her water-heavy skirts, she raced to her room. She quickly shed her wet clothing for dry ones, then pulled up a few select floorboards and retrieved the leather sack. She stuffed it into a bundle of clothing she had grabbed and was heading for the stairs just as the shutters of her room banged wide open. Rain and wind invaded as Belladonna ran, skirting the flying debris of a large tree that had crashed through.

Her wet feet slid on the polished wood floors where she landed from her flight down the stairway, but neither Mariella nor Moises were in sight. She called out both their names and let out a breath of relief when Moises emerged from behind the door to the servant's area and beckoned to her.

She followed Moises below the stairs to the servants' dining area and the kitchen. The servants' quarters were protected by bushes and were on a lower level, so Belladonna assumed they could take refuge there. The few servants huddled together on plain wooden benches.

"Ready to go?" asked Mariella, Belladonna's sister-in-law, who had taken full charge. "We have taken some food and supplies. The storm is growing more severe, and it is best we go now, or we will not be able to make it to the Cave."

"What is this Cave?"

"The Cave of Christopher Columbus. It is on the highest point on the island, safe from flooding, and deep enough to avoid the damage of the wind."

"That is not the same cave from the map that Roderigo—"

Mariella held up a hand and did not allow her to continue. "Yes, it is. But there is no time for talking or explaining. It is imperative we leave this house now before another tree crashes down."

A whimper from a maid was the only other comment as the servants were instantly on their feet, each clutching a bundle of belongings.

Mariella wrapped a shawl around her head and handed another to Belladonna to do the same. As soon as the outer door opened, the wind swept them into its maelstrom. Clustered together, they braced themselves as best as they could and faced the storm.

Chapter Two: Belladonna

THE ISLAND OF JAMAICA, The fifth of NOVEMBER, 1614

Belladonna unwrapped the wet shawl plastered across her face. They had fought their way through an onslaught of wind and rain to the shelter of the cave. Inside, the temperature had dropped drastically, causing Belladonna to shiver uncontrollably.

Moises noticed. "You will be warm once we can light a fire."

The coachman lit a torch and proceeded to lead the way. They descended along a declining path growing ever narrower until they reached a wide slit in the rock. Like Mariella, she maneuvered her sodden skirts through it, surprised to find herself in a larger cavern. Shadowy forms moved, revealing themselves to be more refugees who clustered together for warmth and comfort.

Torches in the wall illuminated their way as they moved deeper into the cavern. Many people were huddled here, but the cathedral-like chamber was large enough to accommodate many more. Belladonna sniffed the air. Besides the odors of sodden clothing and too many people, she caught a whiff of wood smoke and savory cooking.

"Come closer to the fire," the coachman said, and she followed him towards the warmer air.

Rocks had been piled up into a mound that glowed red in the darkness. Hands were held out to grasp at the warmth, hands of all shapes, sizes, and colors. As Belladonna joined the circle and basked her cold hands in the heat, she asked Moises, "How is it that the rocks here glow with such warmth?"

It was Mariella who answered her question. "This cave has been a refuge for generations, and those who came before us built the oven-like structure you are now using to warm yourselves. The Brethren keep this cave well stocked with wood chips and food stuff, in case the need for a quick retreat from the Spanish marauders who plague both the land and the sea."

Belladonna squinted at her sister-in-law in the dimness. Isaak and his crew were members of the Jewish Brethren, a fleet of Jewish pirates who patrolled the seas, attacking mostly Spanish ships that had kept captured Jews in their galleys or holds. It was the Brethren who had transported Roderigo, Mariella's husband, to the Old World on his mission to save the Jews of Jamaica, and it was Isaak who had taken him to Venice to be reunited with the sister he had thought lost, Belladonna.

"Will it be safe with the rising tide and waters?"

Mariella nodded. "Most caves are beneath the tide line, but this one was discovered high in the face of one of the tallest mountains and is fed by an underground spring."

Her life was now in Mariella's hands, and in this situation, she was sorely lacking in experience or resources. Belladonna's assessment of Mariella changed over the course of the several months since they arrived from Venice. When Belladonna and Isaak suddenly appeared at her home bearing the news of her husband's death, Mariella collapsed. Belladonna had supposed her sister-in-law had led a pampered life, unused to adversity. But it seemed she had misjudged Mariella, for after the seven days of mourning had passed, Mariella had resumed control of the plantation and had tended to her guests with crisp self-confidence. Riding out to the fields to oversee the harvest of the sugar cane, only a furrowed brow and the hard line of her lips betrayed her pain and sorrow.

With the threat of a great storm, Mariella demonstrated her courage and pragmatism in ensuring they all found a safe haven. Belladonna would be sure not to underestimate Mariella again.

The fire was beginning to chase the chill from her bones, and Belladonna held her hands as close as possible to feel the warm air. Looking around at mounds of rock and niches of darkness, Belladonna wondered if they would provide her with enough privacy to remove some of the clothes that had gotten soaked, so she could lay them by the fire to dry.

The cathedral-like chamber had rock piles that rose from the floor to meet stone tendrils descending from the ceiling like rocky icicles. Beneath their feet was firmly-packed earth, scattered with pebbles of flint and shale which crunched underfoot. Belladonna, Moises, and Mariella, exhausted from their battle against the wind, dropped their bundles at their feet as they stood basking in the warmth of the fire-fueled oven. Moises's shoulder was closest to her, so Belladonna nudged him to get his attention. "What lies over there in the darkness?"

"We have always been told to avoid going beyond the glow of the torches," her nephew answered, "so I do not know."

Mariella had overheard her and said, "If you need privacy for relief, one of the women servants will lead you with a torch to the next chamber, which has been allotted to such needs of the women."

Belladonna raised her eyebrows, wondering how often women had needed to take refuge in this cave and if it was always due to stormy weather. She shifted the bundle with her dry clothes to her shoulder as Mariella signaled to one of the maids to guide her.

When she returned, she found Mariella and Moises cradling rough wooden bowls, steaming and smelling of cooked spices. Belladonna's stomach growled, as she had forgotten to eat anything when she had dashed to the docks earlier in the day to see Isaak before he sailed. As she gratefully accepted a bowl from Mariella and ate, she felt better.

Warmed and fed, exhaustion finally overtook her, and Belladonna dropped off to sleep. In the midst of a turbulent dream, she instinctively reached for Isaak, and his absence by her side awoke her. *Isaak, where are you? Do not leave me!*

Now, sheltered from the ravages of the wind and rain, she feared for Isaak, despite his earlier reassurances. What happened to a sailing ship assaulted by such winds? Had Isaak sailed through it unscathed as he promised, or had the storm smashed his ship into the rocks?

Chapter Three: Belladonna

THE ISLAND OF JAMAICA, The sixth of NOVEMBER, 1614

Belladonna ached to leave the cave but had no idea if it was day or night, or if the storm had ended. The fire still burned, keeping the area warm, and though the torches had burned low or had gone out, the shapes of sleepers were visible around her. She rose, unable to sleep any longer, and searched for another wakeful member of the group, preferably someone with a torch. Searching through the darkness, another pair of eyes met hers. The coachman.

She stepped carefully over the slumbering forms to stand before him. "I should like to venture out of the cave. Can you guide me?"

He stared back at her in silence, a resentful expression on his face.

Belladonna persisted. "How long should this storm last? We should check to see if it has abated."

Shambling to his feet slowly, the coachman reached for a smoldering torch and removed it from its bracket. Bringing it closer, he blew on it, releasing glowing embers and ash, causing it to flare brighter as the flames licked at new areas of wood.

With the torch held high, he led her out.

Outside the mouth of the cave, it was still dim, so it was not yet dawn. Belladonna inhaled the rich smell of rain-soaked earth. The rain had stopped, and the wind had grown mild. Coconuts littered the path, and she kicked them out of her way. Further from the cave, the path was littered with tree branches and uprooted tree trunks.

At the sight, the coachman shook his head. "Bad, very bad."

Belladonna gingerly took careful steps among fallen branches, leaves, and coconuts. The trees rippled as the wind whistled through them.

The coachman pulled her back. "Not yet, not safe."

"Is it not over?"

The man squinted at the pearly grey sky. "We now in the center, so it is quiet. But only temporary. Soon, the wind will shift and swirl, and it will all begin again."

Chapter Four: Belladonna

THE ISLAND OF JAMAICA, The seventh of NOVEMBER, 1614

Two more days passed before the wind ceased and the waters receded. They ventured from the cave tentatively, minding the debris in their path. They came upon the house, which no longer had its roof or many of its walls and was filled with branches, dirt, and sand. There were no animals about since they had opened the stalls and released them at the start of the storm. Now, the stables no longer stood, marked only by a clutter of uprooted trees and pieces of wood. Belladonna clasped her hands together tightly and felt her insides clutching. Taking deep breaths, she hoped to relieve some of the anxiety steadily coming over her as she worried about becoming a refugee. After a decade of making her home in Venice, she had thought never to repeat the sense of powerlessness that had overwhelmed her after her escape from Recife.

The coachman had salvaged a single wheel from the carriage, and as he held it up to her, his face was marked with sorrow.

"There is enough left of the house to provide us shelter," Mariella said, disturbing the coachman from his reverie to engage him in helping her salvage whatever she could. Mariella stood tall and with hands on hips, was a commanding presence. Belladonna admired her sister-in-law's ability to look beyond the devastation and to focus on the practical steps necessary for their survival.

How had Isaak's ship fared in the storm? She chased aside the image of Isaak flailing, striving to keep his head above the waves. Had he gone overboard? Had the *Sabato*, his ship, been tossed against the rocks and destroyed? A small voice growing louder was declaring Isaak dead. Belladonna wanted nothing more than to hurry down to the bay to discover the whereabouts of Isaak and his ship, but she could not leave. There was no horse, no carriage to take her, and she could not make her way down to the town alone. All hands were needed to help Mariella, who could not spare anyone to accompany her. It would take hours to reach the bay, if it was possible at all, and they had much to do to clean up the damage and make the house habitable again. She made every attempt to quash the voices and the doubts that scared her and returned her focus to helping her sister-in-law arrange a shelter to keep them dry and warm.

"We can work for a few hours, but then we will have to return to the cave for the night," said Mariella, confirming Belladonna's expectations that the cave would remain their refuge.

For the next few days, they worked as long as they could at clearing the debris from the kitchen and lower level which was less damaged. The floor and walls were stone, so had withstood the winds, and the trees which had fallen on the upper parts of the house had not crashed through the thick timbers of its ceiling. The oven could work once its chimney was cleared, and then they could have hot food and warmth, and with furniture salvaged from the floors above, it could become comfortable.

Despite the hard work during the day, Belladonna had trouble falling asleep, as her thoughts were plagued by different scenarios of Isaak's fate.

Had his ship been smashed to smithereens by the storm, or had it been blown out to sea? Had Isaak been drowned as a great wave deluged the deck, or had he navigated his ship through the storm to safer waters?

After tossing and turning for hours, Belladonna awoke with the others and struggled to get herself ready for the day. Her clothes were rumpled but dry, and she had managed to fashion a thick rope belt around her waist, under her skirts, to hold the leather sack of jewels and the dagger she was never without. Remnants of her life in Venice—the jewels had been designed and gifted to her by her many admirers, as had been the dagger filled with poison, which she relied upon for defense. Another small pouch of gold coins, the currency of escape everywhere, was hidden in her bodice. The rest of her belongings were left in the cave when she went on her forays to the house.

Belladonna and Mariella left very early in the morning ahead of the others, and they were still on the path when they heard the sound of hoofbeats. Irrationally, Belladonna imagined it signaled the approach of Isaak and his crew and was set to run out to greet him when Mariella pulled her back. Mariella raised a finger to her lips and gestured to Belladonna to crouch low under the cover of the scrub and watch without being seen.

Soldiers on horses came into view, cursing at each other in Spanish as they dismounted. One man without a helmet, marking him as their leader, ordered the men into the house. The bareheaded man noticed the partially cleared stairway and peered down into its depths. While he descended, Mariella gestured to Belladonna to turn and retreat back to the cave.

The two women ran through the thicket of trees and scrambled up the mountainous path. Meeting the others on their way, Mariella raised a finger to her lips and motioned them to return to the cave.

Once inside, nearly breathless, Mariella gasped, "It is as we feared. The Spanish have come, and we must go. They are focused on looting and capturing women now." Turning to Belladonna, she added, "You are in the greatest danger. Once they discover you have been baptized and now live among Jews, you will be condemned as a Judaizer and a heretic and consigned to the fire. Moises and I have not been baptized, but since we are Jews, our property will be confiscated, and we will be banished from the island."

Belladonna frowned. "What is our best course? We cannot remain in this cave forever."

Most of the others who had sought refuge in the cave had departed after the weather cleared, so only Mariella and her servants remained. At one look from Mariella, the servants began to pack for departure. "We had prepared for this. Along the other side of the island are hidden boats, if they survived the storm. It should be possible to sail to the western coast of Hispaniola, frequently traversed by French and Dutch ships which can take us the greater distance to Curacao." She gave Belladonna a questioning look. "But we will have to make it through the mangrove swamp first to get there."

Belladonna swallowed but met her sister-in-law's eyes with a boldness she did not really feel. "There is no time to waste, then. Let us go."

Belladonna had her belongings and took a sack of provisions for the journey. That was all. Though usually fastidious about her dress, she knew more bags would only bog her down.

"We must take care to leave no trace of this cave," Mariella whispered to the coachman once they were on the path. He nodded and hung back, taking care to brush away footprints and to push fallen trees and debris across it.

Belladonna braced herself to face the dangers ahead.

Chapter Five: Isaak

ATOLL IN THE CARIBBEAN SEA, EAST OF THE ISLAND OF JAMAICA, The seventh of NOVEMBER, 1614

Isaak awoke to voices speaking in rapid Spanish. Sand in his mouth, and his throat was dry. A stab of pain as a boot prodded his middle, and then rough hands flipped him over on his back like a newly caught fish. Men were dark silhouettes against a bright blue sky, temporarily blocking the baking rays of sun that streamed around them.

"Ahh, he lives! Speak devil, from where do you come?"

The boot was aiming for his side again, but Isaak grabbed it and twisted and was gratified to hear a yelp of pain. Isaak was able to speak flawless Castilian Spanish and answered in their language. "I was washed overboard during the great storm."

"What ship?"

Isaak thought of the sailors drinking and boasting in the taverns of Jamaica, fresh arrivals from Spanish ships. Though Jamaica still was under the dominion of the heirs to Christopher Columbus, the Spanish roamed the island as if it already belonged to them.

"*La Roqueta.*"

There was a grunt from one of the men above him. "Your position?"

"Navigator."

An order rang out that gave Isaak some hope. "Fix him up and get him on board."

* * *

After purging the seawater from his gut and gulping down a strengthening dram of rum, Isaak felt recovered. Remembering the storm and the winds and waves that had tossed his ship across several leagues of sea, Isaak shuddered as he recalled the giant wave that swept him off the bridge. Had his ship survived its onslaught, or had the *Sabato* plummeted to the bottom of the sea? By God's grace, he escaped drowning, but was this initial salvation only to result in his capture by his sworn enemies, the Spanish?

Perhaps God had taken pity upon him at the last moment, inspiring him to answer the Spanish captain's question with 'navigator.' For after hearing it, the captain had instructed his men to lift the weakened Isaak onto their shoulders. Claiming he was a navigator, he had secured his safety and a spot on the bridge beside the first mate. Otherwise, the Spanish would have left him on the spit of sandy reef where they found him.

With the wind rifling and knotting his long hair, he faced the horizon, his eyes peeled for the sail of a pirate ship. The pirates in these waters were likely to be English, the sworn enemies of the Spanish, and he preferred their company to these men. From the grumblings Isaak had heard below decks, food was scarce, men were hungry, and the spit of an island where they had found him had yielded little to replenish their stores. A raid on one of the larger islands or a merchant ship, preferably Dutch, was required, or there would be bad blood and violence. The Spanish captain was shrewd enough to perceive the unrest and cruel enough to look forward to any bloodshed as long as it was not his own.

"Navigator!"

"Yessir," said Isaak immediately, and he stood, ready for orders.

"Take us to Jamaica."

Isaak saluted and then squinted from the brightness of the setting sun to the compass in his hand. He raised his face to oppose the wind and turned to the first mate. He did not want to be accused of sailing the ship into a storm. "There are storms in the East".

El Capitan scowled at Isaak for challenging his orders, so Isaak promptly corrected himself. "As you say, El Capitan, likely the storm should have passed by now."

Isaak hoped there was something left of Jamaica after the storm. Had Belladonna found shelter with Mariella and Moises? How could they survive? He could not afford to dwell on such thoughts while the captain and first mate watched him, ready to toss him overboard should they deem him valueless.

He shouted the coordinates to the mate at the helm, "Forty-five degrees, East!"

The mate grasped the big wheel and wrenched it hard to the left, causing nearly everyone standing to lose their footing. There were curses and thumps, which led to a scowl from El Capitan and then a warning. "You had better know where you are taking us, Senor Navigator, or there will be one less mouth to feed after tonight."

"I am taking us to the west side of the island, where there is a cove that runs into the mangrove swamp. Far away from the guns of the fort and the safest place to land our men and take the fort by surprise." He had to keep his voice steady, careful not to betray his fear the storm may have destroyed too much of the island and the needed food and supplies would be gone. If such were to happen, Isaak had no doubt the Capitan would direct his men's fury towards him. The only glimmer of hope was if the Brethren had come to Jamaica, and he would be able to escape to join them.

El Capitan looked hard at Isaak. He must banish any thoughts of uncertainty, or his face might betray insecurity. The Capitan surprised Isaak by saying, "You are a clever man. You think like a Capitan and know how to navigate." He pointed from his eyes to Isaak's, "But I will still keep my eyes on you.'

Isaak would have to be very wary of El Capitan. He was no fool, and he had just demonstrated his judgment of men was as keen as Isaak's own. To quell the anxiety building within, Isaak shifted his glance to the horizon and prayed a pirate ship would arrive before El Capitan discovered more about him.

Chapter Six: Isaak

THE CARIBBEAN SEA, NORTHWEST HISPANIOLA, The seventh of NOVEMBER, 1614

When the first mate dismissed him from the bridge, Isaak wasted no time to go below, hoping to find other survivors of the storm. He navigated his way through the hold, aiming for the galley. In his early days of piracy, Isaak had been captured by a Spanish warship off the coast of Morocco and had spent two months in hell, chained to the oars with fifty other captives. It was that experience that had spurred him to further acts of piracy with the unstated mission to raid Spanish ships and free their galley slaves.

He was in no position to do so now and would have to think of a plausible excuse to convince the guards to let him enter the galley. Isaak's strategy for survival was to always take full stock of his situation, which included possible allies among the galley slaves. If the ship was attacked by pirates, as he hoped, freed prisoners attacking from the inside could ensure a pirate victory.

The stark contrast between the brightness of the deck and the darkness below blinded him at first. As his eyes acclimated, he made out a few dark figures hanging in hammocks that looked like cocoons, sleeping in preparation for the next shift on deck. Isaak made his way around them, but counted the sleepers to get a better idea of how many would need to be dealt with below deck. Following the sounds of the thudding hammer, which kept the beat for the oarsmen, he descended another few stairs to the lowest regions of the ship.

The stench of human waste, sweat, and despair nearly overwhelmed him, bringing back his own memories of the incessant beat, the desperate need for water, and the sting of the lash on his back. The thuds came at short intervals, and he winced at every strike, knowing the demand it placed on the poor fellows chained to the oars, charged with building speed to follow the course he had set for the ship.

A thick door, with bars and locks to keep it in place, stopped him. A small latched window would provide him with a quick view of the galley without having to challenge the guards, who would stop him if he attempted to open the door.

Isaak grasped the small knob of the latched window and lifted it. He had only a partial view from this angle, but the men he could see were dark-skinned, and most did not look European. The Spanish were notorious for making prisoners of the local islanders, most likely after raping their wives and killing their families. It did not matter to Isaak who they were or where they were from, since he was certain these men hated their Spanish captors and would not hesitate to attack them once they were free.

As quietly as possible, Isaak lowered the window and backed up to the staircase. When he turned to ascend, he found himself staring into the face of the first mate.

"What do you think you are doing here?"

Isaak forced himself to remain calm and his voice to remain assertive. "My job."

"Eh?" the man backed away as Isaak pushed his way up the short ladder. The two men confronted each other, hands on hips.

"All is well. At this pace, I expect we will arrive at our destination before nightfall," said Isaak without backing down.

"How do you know?" asked the first mate, one eyebrow raised and one hand on the short sword in his belt.

"Mathematics, dear fellow. I calculate the number of pulls on the oars based on the beat and the percentage of nautical miles each pull will achieve.

Then I calculate the number of pulls needed to achieve a nautical mile, which I then divide into the nautical miles needed to be covered." What Isaak said was pure nonsense, but the technicality of his answer would be enough to confuse the first mate.

Isaak's strategy worked its magic, and the first mate backed away, grumbling that Isaak should be back on deck where he belonged. Isaak took his time ascending the ladder to the deck, as any disgruntled seaman would do, though he wished to escape the horrors of the galley and the suspicious first mate as soon as possible.

As he felt the cool wind and the cleansing scent of the salty air, Isaak could have danced a jig on the creaking floorboards of the galleon as he heard the man on the rigging call out, "Sails!"

Chapter Seven: Belladonna

THE ISLAND OF JAMAICA, The tenth of NOVEMBER, 1614

Belladonna had tied up her skirts and the bottom of her shift to preserve it from the filthy bogs she kept stumbling into. Glancing at Mariella and Moises, who were less muddy, Belladonna assumed they had been through this swamp before and were aware of its pitfalls. She tried not to focus on the creatures slithering beneath her feet or latching onto her skin and kept her face forward and her chin high. Belladonna had been lucky enough to survive the murderous grasp of the Inquisition and the ruinous intent of the Barbary pirates and strongly believed her determination to survive would prevail, even in this hellish swamp.

Mariella's servants had decided not to leave their island and to take their chances with the Spanish, so only a small party of Belladonna, Mariella, Moises, and their coachman kept pace together, plowing through razor-sharp sawgrass and sloshing through water that ran as high as their waists. They kept silent and paused for a few moments as they progressed, listening for any sounds of pursuit. There were none.

She rested against a thick mangrove tree, only to have a large snake appear at her shoulder. Belladonna could not stop herself from screaming, but her scream was cut off by Mariella, who clamped a hand across Belladonna's mouth. The coachman swiftly flicked the snake away from Belladonna with a thick branch, and Belladonna nodded to Mariella, who removed her hand.

"Are you settled?" asked Mariella softly, then she gestured with her head to the path forward. "Not long before we reach the cove. Do you feel the breeze?"

Belladonna stepped out of the leafy structure of the banyan tree. Faint as it was, a breeze stirred the wisps of hair not pasted by sweat to her forehead. She swiped the back of her hand across her brow and strode forward.

Moises, the first to spot the clearing beyond the mangroves, ran ahead, zigzagging through trees and reeds. The end was in sight, and the three adults followed Moises towards it. The cooler air and the smell of the sea urged them on, but as soon as they emerged from the swamp, they realized their troubles were not over.

A large, curved sword, like those of the Barbary pilots, was raised above Moises, held by a bare-chested muscular man with wild hair and beard, a red scarf wrapped around his neck. Moises had fallen to one knee, cowering beneath the raised sword, his arms held protectively above his head.

Before the coachman could stop her, Mariella strode boldly to the swordsman and shouted, "Stop! He is just a boy, and you have no business threatening him!"

The swordsman, who seemed equally surprised at being ordered by a woman, responded to her request and lowered his sword. "I am sorry, senora, he took me off guard. This reaction was natural for a man such as me. Now, maybe instead of the boy, I should—"

He had stepped closer and peered at them from beneath the strands of curly, greasy hair. He exclaimed, "Belladonna!"

Belladonna arched an eyebrow, wondering who had recognized her. As if reading her mind, he continued, "It is I, Hernando! I sail with Captain Isaak for many years."

At the mention of Isaak's name, Belladonna felt the pounding of her heart and took a step closer to get a better view of his face. Mariella pulled Moises to his feet and stood by Belladonna's side. "You know this man?"

Belladonna squinted to see through the unruly hair which half hid his face. She only recognized a handful of Isaak's men, but this man was one of them. He was Isaak's second mate and was frequently found at his captain's side. "Hernando, is the ship… have the Spanish…where is your Captain?"

Keeping her voice from trembling, it was difficult to form the words to describe scenarios she dreaded.

Hernando sheathed his terrible sword and grinned. "It is not so easy to sink a ship like the *Sabato,* especially since our captain has the brains to outwit a maelstrom. He ordered us to lower all but one sail and use it to fly into the wind like a great kite, so we were pushed away from the shore out to sea instead of being smashed to bits. It was only a trick of the sea that got him—and me. A great wave came suddenly over the port side and washed us both overboard. Luckily, I was tossed by the waves back to these shores, but the captain..."

Belladonna gasped and bit her lip before stammering. "Wh-wh-what happened to Isaak?"

He shook his head and sighed, "I have not seen him since."

Belladonna took a deep breath to hold in a wave of grief. But then, smacking a hand into her palm, she willed herself not to believe she had lost him. "Isaak is a strong swimmer. I am certain, like you, he must have been washed ashore. We will find him. Alive."

Mariella folded her arms across her chest. "As long as he is not found by the Spanish."

"I have not seen any Spanish ships along this side of the island. They keep to the bay and the docks where the taverns are. I have been walking this shore for the past three days, hoping to see a sail or a donkey to take me away from here." Hernando's eyes flicked from one of them to the other. "Why have you been in the mangrove swamp?"

Mariella unfolded her arms and, waving her hands for emphasis, described the advance of the Spanish and their need to escape. "The storm is over, and already the Spanish are looting our homes. Roderigo anticipated the need to escape if the Spanish should come. He said they would not venture into the mangrove swamp, so it was our planned escape route to take us to this side of the island, where, as you have discovered, few ships will anchor. There are small boats hidden here, and if they survived the storm, we could use them to set sail."

Hernando raised an eyebrow at the mention of hidden boats and stroked his beard. "You have been smart to plan for such an escape, and the boats should be strong enough to land us on the northwest coast of Hispaniola, where we will find friends." He put a protective arm around Moises, who grimaced but did not openly protest. "And your first bit of good luck, my friends, was finding me. Now, you have the navigator to get you there."

Mariella's coachman shifted from one foot to the other, and he looked up sheepishly at his mistress. "This man can help more than I can."

Mariella took both of hands of her loyal servant in her own. "You do not have to come with us. Go back to the house. Find the horses and keep them. They should be yours, not the Spaniards."

The coachman nodded to Mariella and bowed his head deferentially to Belladonna.

Belladonna nodded back. Hernando and Moises had already gone in search of the boats. Fate or God was offering them salvation, and she was grateful for the intervention.

Chapter Eight: Isaak

SOMEWHERE ON THE CARIBBEAN SEA, EAST OF THE ISLAND OF JAMAICA, The seventh of NOVEMBER, 1614

El Capitan pulled out his spyglass and aimed it in the direction the lookout had pointed. Isaak held his breath as he awaited the captain's orders. It would do Isaak no good if it was a Dutch or French merchant ship, since either would be easy to plunder. There would be more prisoners for the oars and no chance of escape for Isaak.

Isaak prayed it was a pirate ship. If it was, El Capitan would order the helmsmen to spin their ship around, the tempo would increase to life-threatening speed as their ship would try to make its escape.

El Capitan lowered his spyglass and squinted at Isaak as if he did not recognize him. Then he spun around and began barking orders, "Away, away, men! What say you navigator, one eighty degrees south, or shall it be north, eh?"

Isaak's heart beat faster, his prayers were answered. Without hesitation, he said, "South," knowing full well it would not matter. Pirate vessels were built for speed, while Spanish vessels were built for cargo and guns. They would not be able to outrun the pirates, so now it was up to him to delay to expedite this ship's capture. It would help to have a map to refresh his memory of the waterways to prevent the discovery of his ignorance of these waters.

"El Capitan, if I can get the map to refresh my memory. I seem to recall a hidden cove—"

"Get to it, man, now! There is not much time, they will soon be upon us," El Capitan's voice was hoarse as a bear's growl.

Isaak raced towards the captain's cabin, where he knew to find the map. He was hoping to round up a weapon as well, which would come to good use in the galley. The best plan for Isaak was to keep below-ship during the attack and keep out of the fighting on deck. He could then seize the opportunity to free the galley slaves at the oars. Once freed, they could join the fray on deck and make the difference to ensure the Spaniards would fall.

El Capitan's voice carried down below to the crew, who knew the kinds of cruelties the captain could unleash if they did not move fast enough to his command. Pounding feet and curses flew as some men bolted up the stairs and others towards the cannons, another level below. Isaak kept to the space under the stairs, where it was darkest.

A loud crash and the boat shook, shivers of pitch falling from above. The ship had been hit. The first mate thudded down the stairs, shouting, "Fire those cannons, you slow-witted fools!"

Isaak waited until the first mate was safely past and headed to the captain's cabin. He would grab a pistol and the map, and perhaps other papers that could be of future use to the enemies of Spain. The ship angled and rocked, and Isaak fell through the door of the captain's cabin as soon as it opened. The room was large and lavish, fit for a galleon transporting the riches of the West Indies to the treasuries of Spain. He marveled at the canopied bed, which seemed to have no place at sea, and then headed to the large desk cluttered with maps.

A quick glance assured Isaak the map on the very top of the pile was the one he needed, and he folded it up quickly, placing it inside his shirt. Then he headed towards a long cupboard, which looked like a place where weapons were stored. Locked. Isaak began searching through the desk's drawers until he found the key and was able to unlock it.

As he had hoped, it held the captain's cache of weapons. Isaak selected a long knife and a short sword. Another crash and the sound of screams.

A man, aflame, fell past the large window of the cabin. The floor shook beneath his feet. Time to go.

As he descended to the lower level, there was no thudding sound of the mallet keeping the time. The oars had stopped. Sunlight poured in from a gaping hole in the side of the ship. Timber and bodies were strewn around a blackened floor. The first mate was no longer shouting orders, but lay amid the debris and the ruins of a cannon, which seemed to have backfired and exploded. Isaak leaned into the breach and peered out, catching sight of the grappling hooks swinging towards the ship's railing from the attackers. The hooks must have caught hold since the floors tilted as the two ships listed towards each other. The door to the galley hung open. The first mate must have ordered the soldiers topside to fight, leaving only one man to guard the galley slaves.

Isaak rushed in and thrust his sword into the surprised overseer, who toppled to the floor. Sweating, beaten backs straightened, and dead eyes came alive with hope.

Isaak found the keys on the guard and hurried over to unlock the chains of the men in the first row. "Hurry, pass it along, and as soon as you are free, come with me aloft."

The first man freed of his chains rubbed his wrists, before eagerly accepting one of Isaak's knives. "Who are you?" He spoke in English.

Isaak answered in the same language. "A friend and a former galley slave. Now, take whatever you can find as a weapon. It is time we taught these Spaniards a lesson!"

Isaak went first, heading towards the ladder up to the next level. He stepped cautiously through the broken bodies and listened for any other shouts or footsteps. There were none. "All clear!' he called out to the freed oarsmen as they crept out of the room that had been their prison for so long.

Isaak cautiously moved towards the hatch to the deck. Thuds of bodies slammed against the floor, the clang of metal on metal as swords clashed. He gestured for the men behind him to follow. Some held pieces of the broken hull as weapons as they ascended into the light and the fervor of the battle.

Chapter Nine: Isaak

*SOMEWHERE ON THE CARIBBEAN SEA, EAST OF THE
ISLAND OF JAMAICA, The seventh of NOVEMBER, 1614*

The battle was raging on deck amid fire and gaping holes where the cannon had hit. When the men Isaak had freed launched themselves into the attack, it was with a fury that could not be stopped as they unleashed their hatred. It did not take long for El Capitan to present his sword to the leader of the pirates, a youngish man with long hair and beard whose doublet was stained with blood.

The young captain of the pirate ship placed his fingers to his lips and blew a loud, low whistle. At the sound, swords about to thrust and necks held by their collars were lowered. Isaak followed, waiting for the next order. Would they kill all the prisoners and scuttle the ship?

"Huzzah!" shouted one of the freed oarsmen, raising a fist high. It triggered an immediate response from the invaders, who echoed their shout. Isaak had never uttered the word before, but noticing that the only ones who were not shouting were the Spanish, he let out the same cry. "Huzzah!"

Isaak climbed over the dead and dying Spanish to join the cheering men below the bridge where the young captain stood, hands on hips.

"Shall we scuttle her, Cap'n, and leave this sorry lot to the fate they have doomed many an Englishman?" called out a tall, thin man in English, who sported a large golden earring in one ear and a long black beard.

"Scuttle her! Scuttle her!" chanted several of the ragged former galley slaves in the same language, eager to have their revenge.

The young captain seemed to notice these sweaty half-naked men for the first time. He gestured to the two mates by his side. "Who are they? Not ours, I reckon."

Isaak stepped forward. "Galley slaves, captives. Some of them Englishmen. I freed them."

As he suspected, all eyes turned towards him. The Captain raised an eyebrow. "Is that so?"

He put his question to the ragged English-speaking men. "Is it so?"

The first man Isaak had freed spoke out for him. "Aye, it is. He killed the guard and took the keys to unlock our fetters."

El Capitan, kneeling on the bridge before his conqueror, spat at Isaak, an impotent gesture. The young captain laughed and invited Isaak to come up on the bridge and strike a blow at the Spaniard in retaliation. Without hesitation, Isaak gave the rogue the back of his hand and sent the Spaniard sprawling beneath his feet.

The first mate clapped Isaak on the back. "Bet that felt good, mate!"

"Much as I would enjoy seeing this ship at the bottom of the ocean with all these devils with her, our ship is full to the brim, and we have no room for any more," said the Captain. "Shipwright! Go tend to the damage, and make sure this tub is seaworthy. Botsworth!"

The second fellow by his side, burly with a red face and yellow hair, responded. "Aye, sir!"

"You take charge of this ship with these good men. As for the Spaniards, chain them to the oars and see how they like it!" The young captain barked out a laugh, and the rest of the company, save El Capitan, laughed along with him.

"Where we headed?" asked the yellow-haired Botsworth, "Jamaica?"

The captain rubbed his chin and, with a twinkle in his eye, snapped his fingers as if the idea had just occurred to him. "I expect Tortuga might be a better place to refit. There are enough hunters there to victual the ship with plenty of flesh for our additional crew."

Before Isaak could step back to join the other men, the man called

Botsworth grabbed his shoulder and held him back. "Just a minute, you. You look like a Spaniard but can speak English. Where does your allegiance lie?"

All eyes fixed upon him once more, Isaak placed his hands on his hips. "I am from Venice, but recently arrived in Jamaica in time for a great storm, which separated me from my ship. I was found by the Spanish and talked my way onto this ship as a navigator."

"How did you do that?" asked the young captain, leaning over his knee.

"I am a trained navigator, and they found themselves in need of one."

The captain slapped his knee. "By my reckoning, you are attempting to do the very same now. What do you have to offer us?"

Isaak liked the young English captain, who introduced himself as Captain Ross, a daring but not foolhardy leader and a man Isaak thought trustworthy enough to share a variation of his true story. Isaak did not identify himself as one of the Jewish Brethren, for he was unsure how the English viewed members of his faith. From his father's friend, Sir Henry Wotton, the English ambassador to Venice, Isaak was stunned to learn there were no people of the Hebrew faith in all of England, since the Jews had been banished from the kingdom since the thirteenth century. The captain warmed to Isaak's proclaimed mission to free all those enslaved or taken prisoner on Spanish galleons, for the captain had once been captured and had felt the whips and chains of the galley himself.

"I am half inclined to believe your fantastical story," said Captain Ross, "but whether storms have cast you asunder or your mutinous shipmates, it matters little to me. We share the same enemy, and therefore, you can be part of our crew."

The captain pointed to a spot on the map east of their current location. "Tortuga is where we are bound. We are filled to capacity with booty, and the men want to cash in." He slapped Isaak on the back, "Now that I know your capabilities, I trust you to navigate our Spanish prize ship there."

"Port Royal is far closer than Tortuga." Isaak still hoped to find his ship and Belladonna.

"That goose is already plucked. After that storm, with plenty of Spanish around, it holds only danger for us now."

Isaak's fists clenched, and the captain must have noticed since he said, "I, too, hate to shy away from a fight with the Spanish, but we saw too many sails as we passed that way. We were lucky to get by them but could not resist the temptation to pick off the ship you were on. We find it difficult to pass a Spanish galleon without checking to see how much loot she may hold."

"My ship was outside of Jamaica, my men—"

The young captain patted his shoulder, interrupting him. "You can search for your men after we unload and replenish ourselves in Tortuga."

The conversation was over, and Isaak nodded in agreement, resigning himself to taking the helm on the conquered Spanish ship and delaying his quest for his ship and Belladonna.

* * *

Those that remained alive in the Spanish crew were now chained to the oars below. There were a half dozen Englishmen and even more natives who could sail the damaged galleon towards Tortuga. Isaak took the wheel on the bridge, and the wind on his face freshened his spirit as he straightened his back in the familiar stance of command. He thanked God for his salvation and prayed silently that Belladonna had not perished in the storm nor fallen into the hands of the Spanish.

If what they dreaded had come to pass and the Spanish had used the storm to take over the island, the Jews would be threatened with the Inquisition once more. If his ship was still intact, his men would be combing the seas, searching for him while trying to avoid any Spanish ships. Once in Tortuga, Isaak was determined to try again to steer the captain west, promising to attack Spanish ships along the way and then retreat to the pirate island of Curacao and relative safety.

Chapter Ten: Isaak

IN THE BAY OF TORTUGA, AN ISLAND IN THE CARIBBEAN, The ninth of NOVEMBER, 1614

Once they had entered the pirate-ridden waters around Tortuga, the men on the ship became jovial, singing as they went about their chores or basking in the warm sun, as if they had never risked their lives or been fired upon.

Isaak was surprised Captain Ross tolerated their behavior; on the *Sabato*, under his command, Isaak's men would never be so lax. For Isaak believed renegade pirates and corsairs should always be vigilant; there was no respite from enemies once joining the lawless. Perhaps Captain Ross was still too young to know the true nature of the devils he sailed with.

Isaak raised the spyglass and scanned the island that lay before them. Even at this distance, he could see high peaks, higher than he had seen on any other island in the Caribbean. The men pulled at their ropes with gusto to bring the ship into the bay. As soon as it was securely anchored, most of the men leapt into the long boats and dipped their hands into the warm, placid waters of the wide bay. The oars were pulled without hesitation or pause, speeding the landing party towards shore. Even the usual snarl on the first mate's face had softened; he seemed as eager as the others to reach the island.

The water was so clear Isaak could see fish scurry away from the prow, more colorful and plentiful than in the bay of Jamaica. As he trudged up the sandy beach, the smell of roasting meat assailed his nose and made him quicken his steps as his mouth watered. Freshly roasted meat would claim much gold from any man who had been living on hard-salted beef tack for months.

"Come along, now. There are men I would like you to meet." Captain Ross placed an arm across his shoulders and guided him forward.

Gold was tossed to native vendors by grizzled sailing men dressed in odd assortments of looted clothing. A ragged-looking fellow, getting fitted with a new peg leg, flashed a pouchful of coins when he paid the carpenter. There were guffaws and spitting and bursts of loud laughter from men lying, standing, pacing, and leaning on each other. Isaak followed Captain Ross into a large hut, leaning precariously, as if it was reeling from drink.

The noise was amplified inside, with music of some sort being played on pipes, accompanied by a chorus of shouts and laughter, which made Isaak wince. Captain Ross wove his way through the carousing pirates to a studded wooden door. Looking as if it had been salvaged from a sinking ship, the formidable door was further barred by a big man, standing frozen like a statue with folded arms and a dangerous-looking short sword. At Captain Ross's approach, he thawed and immediately bent over to pull the handle, which opened the door with a loud creak.

It was not a room as much as a large veranda, open to a wall of dark trees. The men nursed tankards, which they held in their laps, but unlike their companions inside, none of them seemed drunk. Isaak was immediately on guard; this was to be a meeting, not a celebration, and Captain Ross had plans for him, or Isaak would not have been invited in.

A thick-set man rested a large, booted leg on the rail of the veranda. He gave a loud snort on their arrival. "Well, well. Better late than never, Ross. Although many of us had imagined it might be never."

"Did you miss me, Glover? Or just worried over my return with the lucre?" Captain Ross tossed a bundle of coins in the man's direction, which he caught and tucked into his doublet.

"Who is *he?*" asked a man in thickly accented English, resembling a devil with a pointy mustache and beard.

"Another prize I liberated from the Spanish ship." Captain Ross gestured to Isaak, who nodded and raised a hand to the brim of his hat as a salute.

Eight pairs of eyes shifted in his direction. Captain Ross sat down, took off his hat, and gestured to Isaak to do the same. The young captain pointed to the large man. "Captain Glover, commander of the *Zephyr.* Formerly of His Majesty's navy."

On to the dark-haired man who resembled the Devil. "Captain Marcel Olivante, commander of the *Beau-Marais*, originally from Marseilles, but a veteran of these islands."

Olivante did not acknowledge the introduction, glaring equally at Isaak and Captain Ross from beneath black-arched eyebrows.

Ross pointed to a grey-haired man who had the look of an old soldier seated beside the Frenchman. "Hendriksen fought the Spanish outside of Flanders and had the pleasure of wresting one of their prized brigantines, *El Dona Maria,* from them. He now commands it but has dubbed it *The Helena.*"

"No demmed Spanish name for my ship," said Hendriksen, grunting after his pronouncement.

The last man in the room was fair-haired and sported a boyish grin, though in years, he looked much older than Captain Ross. He took it upon himself to make his own introduction. "Williams is the name," his accent was very different from Ross's. "I hail from Cornwall, a way off from these gentlefolk. And who might you be?"

As disarming as his disposition seemed to be, Isaak noted the man's fingers were around the dagger he wore at his waist, ready to send it flying. He must keep his wits about him with this gang. At a whim, they would kill him.

"Isaak, formerly of Venice, most recently of Jamaica. I was blown off my ship in the great storm and was picked up by the Spanish. I then became the reluctant guest of El Capitan Cortega until our encounter with Captain Ross." Isaak had straightened his back, and pasted a relaxed grin on his face, hoping to disarm the tension gathering around him.

The French Captain's eyes bored into his, as if searching for a sign of weakness. "Venice? Are you not in the wrong waters? Venetians have a stronghold on the trade routes to the East, so what has drawn you to the West Indies? Perhaps you are a—a—trader?"

"No, a corsair. Spanish treasure ships are the fodder for my ambition, and they are quite plentiful in these waters." Isaak's thoughts raced to anything he could leverage to abate their distrust. He decided to bank on the truth, with the omission of a few details best kept unknown.

"An English Lord promised treasure, which caused many of us to set sail for the Caribbean. I encountered him in Venice, where he was after a map of said treasure, brought from the New World by a man from Jamaica."

Captain Ross eyed him. "And who would this English Lord be?"

"Sir George Villiers. Paid me handsomely, too."

There was a bark of laughter that was cold as ice from the jovial-looking Captain Williams. "Villiers! You poor fool. That preening peacock is an ebb-water, with little coin ever flowing into his pouch and a great deal flowing out of it."

"Villiers did well at the gaming tables one night. I demanded quick payment on the next. I do not concern myself with the status of his finances."

Captain Williams seemed to accept Isaak's explanation. "Well, I hope you collected all you could from him. Villiers is a man destined to die with his boots on."

Captain Ross cut in, "Let us not discuss any more of this. We all have tales about how we came to these waters, but we are assembled here tonight not to talk about the past, but the future. I brought Isaak here for a purpose: he has demonstrated he has the wit to survive, and I believe he can help us succeed in taking Havana."

Isaak's eyebrows rose at that last word. *Havana?* The main port of the Spanish Caribbean and the main stop for all galleons sailing from the New World to the Old. A prize of a city for looting and about to be the most fortified of all the Spanish settlements.

No one challenged the young captain's statement, and instead, shoulders relaxed, and Captain Williams' fingers had meandered away from his belt to his drink. The French captain must have noticed Isaak's look and leaned forward, his mouth curled into a snarling half-smile, as he added his own commentary. "You think of us as either bold or fools, eh? Well, we are tired of chasing after the minnows when the big fish sits in our path. Now, all is quiet, but soon—Boom! We will destroy a fort of sixty cannons, a threat to every pirate who sails in that direction."

Even though Isaak was a newcomer to the Caribbean, he was well aware of the stronghold Spain had created at the narrow channel between Havana and the mainland of America. "El Moro is the fort being built at the eastern entrance to Havana Bay. It has only twelve cannons now, but I suppose there are more to come. Now, it is not too much for a large, well-armed fleet to handle, but when El Moro is complete…"

Captain Ross slapped his thigh. "There you have it, my friends. Isaak gets right to the heart of the matter."

Isaak could see the last of the sneering mistrust fade away. They were now comrades. Captain Williams continued, "The fleet is returning from Recife with a major load of silver and is bound to anchor in Havana, joined by ships stocked with salt, pearls, and sugar from Punta Araya."

Captain Hendriksen's nostrils flared as he muttered a string of profanities against the Spanish and banged his fist on the ramshackle railing. "Such rich prizes must be wrested from the Spanish, who do not deserve such bounty."

Captain Williams cocked his head in the Dutchman's direction as he explained, "Hendriksen was a soldier in that infernal war between Spain and Netherlands, which has filled the canals and waterways with blood. Now, the Spanish have decided to bring the battle here and have blockaded the Dutch settlements from getting salt, wood, and even food, forcing old warriors like Hendriksen to turn to pirating. What about you? What score do you have to settle with the Spanish?"

Before Isaak could respond, the Frenchman waved his hand as if to brush all the talk away. "We all have scores to settle with the Spanish, *mon amis,* which is why we are here. I do not care to discuss our vengeance, but to plan it." He rose and took a few steps around Isaak, regarding him with a disdainful eye. "There is something about you, Capitan Isaak. You are not like the rest of us. Aha! I see it now," he placed a hand on his hip and gave a mocking bow, "You are not here for the treasure, no. You came to Jamaica on a mission. Ah, you are a man of conviction. No doubt all you wish is to be done with us, to find your ship and your crew, and exact your own revenge. An eye for an eye, *eh bien?*"

"I do not care if his heart is with us, Marcel. All we need is his mind. He managed to survive aboard that Spanish ship and free the English prisoners besides, and I believe he can command one of the Spanish galleons we have captured." Captain Ross stood eye to eye with Olivante, daring him to disagree.

With a shrug, Olivante backed down. "*C'est la vie.* If that is what you all agree, I will not oppose you."

Captain Ross raised his eyebrows as he looked at each captain. When no one shook their head or muttered a curse, he grinned at Isaak. "Congratulations, Captain Isaak. You are now the master of your own ship."

Chapter Eleven: Isaak

*THE ISLAND OF TORTUGA, CARIBBEAN, The ninth of
NOVEMBER, 1614*

Isaak listened carefully as the four captains unfurled the map and their plan of attack on Havana. His mind raced over the possibilities for counterattack and for any happenstance that could turn all their plots to dust. His face must have betrayed some of his concerns, and Captain Ross noticed. "You are scowling, my friend. Is there something that does not seem right to you?"

The Frenchman intercepted Isaak's response. "The plan, it is perfect. Every possible defense from Havana has been taken into account. The fort is not yet complete, and we will surprise them."

"But one or two of our ships are bound to be hit. I suppose you have already decided that *my* ship will be first into the bay." Isaak glanced at each captain in turn.

Captain Williams grinned. "You *are* a clever boy. One of us must be first, and by unanimous decision, we chose you."

Olivante grinned and placed a hand on his heart, and in a mocking tone, said, "The cannons that they have, they will not get to fire, *je vous promets.*"

Isaak narrowed his eyes. "Despite your promise, Olivante, what if there is a better way? A way that will also ensure every ship sails away with as much treasure as it can carry."

The Dutchman leaned forward. "We are all ears, captain, though we know these waters better than you. Every angle of attack has been considered."

Isaak pointed to Havana on the map. "Ah, but you consider only the direct approach of attack. All those ships bound for the Old World, like those from Punta Aroya, carrying a fortune in sugar and salt, stop at Havana. They come through here," he traced a nearly straight line on the map across the vast open waters from south to north, "past the northwest coast of Hispaniola, loaded with silver from Recife. But they also must pass through this way," he drew the invisible line with his finger to illustrate the journey, "by the west coast of Hispaniola." He jabbed another finger at Santo Domingo, which was adjacent to Hispaniola, and trailed it along a similar path to Havana. "All this bounty traversing the same waters. *What do you think?* Gentleman, every captain in the Caribbean knows the northwest coast of Hispaniola has been abandoned by the Spanish since 1605, leaving it ungoverned and open to the likes of us."

Isaak sat down and placed one leg atop the other, looking at each captain in turn. Captain Williams squinted at him, and the Dutchman flattened his lips into a hard line. The French captain took a swig from his bottle and wiped his mouth roughly on his sleeve. It was Captain Ross who was the first to challenge him. "What are you suggesting?"

Leaning forward, Isaak said, "Imagine a much greater surprise for the fort in the bay of Havana. Suppose we target Spanish treasure ships in the waters of Hispaniola, empty their holds into our own, remove their crews, and replace them with ours. We sail these ships, with their Spanish flags and fittings, boldly into the bay of Havana without raising alarm. In the meantime, we also send out a clandestine party in small boats to approach the fort by land. The fort is still under construction, which means there will be plenty of gaps and openings to allow us entry. Once our ships are in position in the bay, they will unleash cannon fire from the sea while our land party attacks the fort from within."

The Dutch captain's lugubrious long face lit up. "That is a plan I support. We blast them to smithereens on the outside while we sneak inside to slit their throats."

Captain Williams, his eyes on Isaak, added, "Thus minimizing the loss, but gaining more treasure because we take it in advance." He gave a nod. "I like this plan."

The French captain hurled his bottle against the wall. *"Eh bien*, I christen this our new plan. But," he pointed to Isaak, "you must still sail the first ship into the bay of Havana."

Isaak shook his head. "Alas, I will not be aboard that first ship, as I will be leading the group by land to raid the fort."

Captain Williams scowled. "Explain."

Isaak leaned back and rested a leg on the rail. "The fort, once completed, will have a formidable number of guns, correct? And every single gun will be pointed towards the sea, vigilant and ready for an attack. The land side of the fort? Under construction and under guard, providing the best opportunity for us to slip in unobserved." He paused.

"You come by land first and sabotage those guns pointing out to sea," said Captain Ross. He nodded to the other captains and then pushed a bottle of rum in Isaak's direction. "You have earned yourself a drink."

Isaak accepted it and felt the burn of the rum as it traveled down his throat. "And that will be my final act. After we take Havana, I will depart."

A look flashed between each of the four captains, but it was Captain Williams who asked, "Why are you in so much of a hurry to be off?"

"A ship and a woman I left behind." Isaak hoped the truth would satisfy his newfound allies.

"We have given you a new ship, and there will be many more women if our plan succeeds," said Olivante with a dismissive wave of his hand.

Isaak grinned but did not say more. He wondered whether his plan would succeed and, if it did, how he would extricate himself from his new partners.

Chapter Twelve: Belladonna

ON THE CARIBBEAN, HEADED FOR HISPANIOLA, The fifteenth of NOVEMBER, 1614

Mariella had demonstrated her mettle by leading them boldly through the dangers of the mangrove swamp but was unused to the rolling of boat among the waves and lay moaning at the bottom. Belladonna had no such troubles and sat forward on the prow, relishing the wind blowing through her hair as the little boat plowed its way forward. She was able to follow Hernando's directions to keep to their course with a hand on the tiller when he needed to rest. Though she had spent many days by Isaak's side on the bridge of the *Sabato*, but she was no navigator and was grateful to rely on Hernando's navigational skill.

Moises's eyes followed Hernando as he jumped up to manage the sails as he steered them towards Hispaniola. When the sea grew calm, Moises unfurled a paper he had hidden in a round container, pulled out a bit of dark chalk, and began to sketch. Belladonna caught a glimpse of his drawing before Moises could cover it up. In a few graceful strokes, Moises had artfully captured the wind-filled sails and the figure of Hernando at the helm of their tiny craft. Sadly, such talent would be wasted, for as a Jew, Moises would find no apprenticeship nor gain admittance to any art academy. Belladonna shrugged. They were thousands of miles from Venice, and with their very survival uncertain, why worry about such things now?

With a hand raised to shield her eyes from the blazing sun, Belladonna strained to see into the distance. Could she make out the welcome shape of the land? Not yet. Spray splashed her face, offering cool relief from the heat of the sun. Up and down, tossed by the waves, Hernando fought to pull their craft forward. Mariella was not faring well with the deep dips and high rolls and was gagging over the side. Moises had his head in his hands. Perhaps sips of water would help, since there was little food, and neither Mariella nor Moises looked like they would have much of an appetite.

Belladonna placed all her trust in Hernando, relying on him to get them to land and safety. He had the skills to navigate them to Hispaniola, and he had been Isaak's right hand on the *Sabato*, and therefore, she could trust his loyalty. But experience had taught her the unpleasant fallacy of assumptions of loyalty, and her survival depended on maintaining a constant wariness.

It was her hope that Hernando would disprove her worst fears and was truly navigating their boat towards the northwest coast of Hispaniola and not to the waiting arms of the Inquisition.

Hernando must have sensed her suspicion, for he abandoned the prow and took the seat beside her. "If the wind holds, I suspect we will sight land by nightfall."

Belladonna licked her dry lips. "How will we be able to navigate to shore in the dark?"

Hernando patted her hand. "There is always a Dutch or French brigantine anchored in the harbor, and their lights should illuminate it enough for us. Besides, I know that coast well, and could guide us in without any torchlight." Noticing her dry lips he added, "Take some water, we should have enough to last us all 'til we land. In the glare of this sun and the buffeting of wind, you might need it more than you think."

Her confidence in Hernando was confirmed when smudges of dark grey appeared on the deepening blue of the horizon.

"Is that land?" asked Moises, his voice climbing higher with hope.

"That it is, my lad. The island of Hispaniola, right there, as promised," Hernando cackled, as if he had made some clever joke.

"How can you tell we are on the right side of the island?" Mariella interjected. Her head emerged from its cocoon of wrapped shawls, and she squinted into the dimness for a sign of ships.

Hernando tapped the side of his nose. "I can smell the difference. On the south side, where the Spanish devils have taken up residence, there is always the stink of ash on the wind. Those fellows are always finding something to burn, whether the homes of their enemies or the heretics of the Inquisition. The north side, where we are headed, you smell the welcome scent of smoking meat and fish, from the French and Dutch provisioning their ships."

Moises rubbed his belly. "Smoking fish? I would not mind a nice helping of that."

"Aye, we will be sure to get our share of provisions, supposing we have the means to pay for it." Hernando raised an eyebrow at Mariella and Belladonna. Belladonna's nostrils flared, as well as her naturally suspicious nature at the mention of payment. Rather than respond to Hernando's challenge, she chose to change the course of the conversation. "Do you think it possible someone here will have news of the *Sabato* or the Captain?"

Hernando pointed to a flicker of light in the distance. "That will be a ship's lantern. This is the closest island to Jamaica, and I warrant some ship shall bear tidings of what happened after the storm."

Hernando, true to his boasts, expertly navigated their craft around the rocky approach to shore and found an inlet that opened up to a hidden cove where two brigantines were moored. Torches flared on their decks, providing enough illumination to guide their small boat to shore.

Chapter Thirteen: Belladonna

ON THE CARIBBEAN, ON THE SOUTHWEST BAY OF HISPANIOLA, The fifteenth of NOVEMBER, 1614

They pulled their boat to shore amid the chirping of bats and insects. There was the sound of human habitation in the distance; shouts and laughter, faint music. Thick vegetation bordered the beach, and Hernando headed towards the lights and voices beyond the scrub, forging a path for them to follow.

Trees bordered the entrance to a rundown town. It must have once been populated by the Spanish settlers, with neat little houses laid out in rows with well-stocked stores alongside them. After being ravaged too often by the attacks of marauding pirate ships, the Spanish decided to retreat to the strongholds on the other side of the island, burning most of the town as they departed. What was left of the town were makeshift shelters, their walls and roofs fashioned from whatever could be salvaged. The once neat streets were now cluttered with refuse. Ragtag groups of sailors gathered in the main square, smoking pipes, shaking dice, and speaking French.

Belladonna straightened her posture and smoothed her hair into a semblance of order. Inhaling the delicious aroma of roasting meat, she followed her nose to the fire and the spit tended by a portly man. He prodded the meat with a large knife, cursing at everyone who came close. His curses revealed he was a Frenchman. As Belladonna and her companions approached, it seemed to grow very quiet, and a quick side glance revealed they were surrounded, with all eyes fixed upon them.

It was time to use her femininity to full advantage, at least to disarm them. Raising a hand to her forehead, she faltered a few steps and swooned. Hernando, taking the cue, caught her as she fell. The portly man dropped the large knife and ran to an open barrel, then scurried to Belladonna with a scoopful of water.

Belladonna drank deeply and opened her eyes. Mariella, arms wrapped protectively around Moises, came closer. Belladonna gestured to the portly fellow to share the water with her companions. They both drank the cool, fresh liquid and gave appreciative sighs.

"You are too kind," said Belladonna. It was time for some play-acting. "Where are we? What is this place?"

"Hispaniola," said a burly man with one arm in a sling.

Belladonna gasped loudly and widened her eyes. "We are on Spanish territory!"

"The Spanish are long gone, lady," perked up a man with a less grizzled face that betrayed his youth.

Belladonna tilted her head and narrowed her eyes as she regarded him. "The Spanish are likely to return. I fear it would not be safe here if they do."

The burly man, who seemed to be their spokesperson, sounded annoyed. "Those Spanish fools came to the northwest side and forcibly relocated all their kind to the other side of the island. There they shall remain, poor devils, to rebuild the forts destroyed by the natives. Which leaves us to claim this territory, free and unencumbered."

He gestured over his shoulder at the cluster of wood and rush huts. "Burned most of their homes in the settlement, but left enough to salvage."

Hernando took his turn at a question. "We saw two ships in the cove. From which do you hail?"

It was a thin man with lanky long hair who answered, "*The Zyderzee*, from Curacao, bound for Amsterdam."

Hernando cocked his head towards the others. "All of you from the *Zyderzee*?"

"Not all of us," said the leader. "I was first mate on the *Falcone*, but what is left of her are the walls of several of these dwellings. Battered by a Spanish man of war a year or so ago, her last voyage was to these shores."

Belladonna sat up and pointed to the man's sling. "A year ago? Then how did you come about your wound?"

Her question caused the man to shift from one foot to another and his eyes to avoid hers. "Er—it is but a trifle I received from a little scuffle. Not every man aboard all the ships that come here behave as they should. I had to teach a few fellows a lesson."

"And one they will not soon forget!" said the young man, puffing out his chest, "A good many of those Frenchies are not going to make it back aboard ship when it comes time to sail."

Belladonna eyed the assortment of men, some in uniforms and some in rag-tag garb. "I suppose a great many ships stop here for provisions?"

In response, the leader rattled off the names of ships in different languages, although one of them was familiar to Hernando.

"One moment. Did you say *The Golden Bough* has stopped here? How long past?"

The leader rubbed his chin, "Mebbe, a week ago. Time goes by slowly sometimes, quick at other times. Depending on when we get to sail. Why are you asking about the *Golden Bough*? You know Captain Ross?"

Hernando sat down on a pile of rocks and said, "Not personal-like. But I have heard of him. He started young killing Spaniards, which is all right by me."

The leader looked squinty-eyed at Belladonna and Mariella. "What of these women? Though I heard her speak French, the other speaks Spanish, I wager."

Hernando slapped his thigh. "They come from Jamaica, as I first told you! They had no choice but to leave after the storm, and those thieving Spaniards came to steal what was left of this lady's home. Ran away through the swamps, and lucky for them, I found them, or they would not be here today, for cert."

"That one does not look as if she were an island girl. Too proud by half, I would say," the lanky one pointed at Belladonna.

Belladonna lifted her chin high as she said, "I was born in Jamaica, but have lived in Venice. Along the way, I escaped not only the Spanish but the Barbary pirates."

Belladonna moved her hand to the dagger hidden beneath her bedraggled skirt. She pressed its tip, releasing the poison onto the blade. The playacting was over. Whoever attacked her would not live long enough to regret it.

"Venice? I have heard of this city. A marvel it is, with no streets, no horses, only boats to get about," said the younger man to the leader in English, not expecting her to understand.

While Belladonna's attention had been focused on the leader, a dark man in a gaudy crimson vest had come from behind to grab Mariella by the waist. Moises cried out and was pounding on the man's thick arms to prevent him from dragging his mother away.

Fueled by anger and frustration, Belladonna sprang onto Mariella's assailant. The dagger was out, and she swiped it across the bare arm secured around Mariella's waist, drawing blood. With a curse, Mariella's assailant released her, and she scrambled behind Belladonna.

Nursing his wound, the attacker began to sway, clawing desperately at his throat. When he fell, his eyes were bulging and his mouth frothing, until at last he lay still.

"I am from Venice, the capital of poisons, and be assured, I know how to protect myself and my friends." Belladonna feinted a jab with the bloodied and poison-tipped dagger at the nearest man, and he backed away, hands raised defensively.

A new man, wearing a hat with a large feather, stepped forward from the men encircling them. "You have made your point. No one will molest you or your companions. But enlighten us, what has brought a Venetian lady to these shores."

He spoke in English, so Belladonna answered formally in the same language. "A lady does not reveal her cards unless she knows the gentleman who addresses her."

The fellow doffed his hat and gave her a deep bow. "Jeremiah Stone, once of Bristol, now of Tortuga, and Captain of the *Gilded Lily*, at your service.

My ship is moored in the cove, beside the *Zyderzee*."

Belladonna curtsied. "Belladonna. We are from Jamaica, refugees from the great storm and marauding Spanish."

She gestured to Hernando to introduce himself, which he did, with heavily accented English. "I am first mate of the *Sabato*, originating in Amsterdam, most recently moored at the bay of Jamaica, until the storm took over. Both I and my captain were washed overboard. Our goal is to find the *Sabato* and sail far away from these Spanish-infested waters."

Captain Stone tucked his thumbs in his thick belt, very close to his weapons, but his stance was relaxed, and he did not seem ready to use them. His eyes were focused on Belladonna when he asked, "How is it you speak English so well?"

"I had been in the company of an English nobleman, Sir George Villiers, who paid the captain of the *Sabato* to provide him transport to your country. I confess, Villiers charmed me, and I had agreed to accompany him to his estate in England."

The captain threw back his head and laughed. "You are not the first to get sold a bill of goods from that devil. At least you were able to get that rogue to pay for your passage; there are not many women who fared half as well. But I fear any lingering hope of being with Villiers is destined to remain unfulfilled." He lowered his eyes and placed a hand on his chest, "May he rest in peace."

"He is dead?" asked Belladonna. Understanding dawned. Villiers' death was the reason the English king did not follow through with the plan to take Jamaica.

"Very. A duel with a former soldier he had bilked."

"When did this happen?"

"Several months ago." At this, the man removed his hat, revealing his fair hair and handsome and clean-shaven face, marred by a fearsome scar that went from eyebrow to jaw. He pointed to the scar. "My souvenir from my encounter with Villiers. He had gotten the King to endorse some half-baked scheme of his to arrange the marriage of the young prince with the Infanta of Spain. Needless to say, the trip to Madrid went terribly wrong.

My men were slaughtered while Villiers escaped without a scratch. I was disappointed to learn of his death, only because I was not the cause of it."

Formidable, this Captain Stone. A few of the men still had the temerity to leer at her, but it was evident he had them under his control. She decided it would be best to humor him. "You must either be a very clever man or a very lucky one."

Captain Stone grinned. "A little of both, I presume." He nodded to Hernando. "I seem to recognize you from a brief but memorable encounter with the *Sabato* after months on the oars of a Spanish galleon."

"Then we share a similar history and enemy. I owe a debt to the captain of the *Sabato* for rescuing me from Berber pirates many years ago." Belladonna had sheathed her dagger, and Captain Stone offered her his arm as if they were about to go into dinner.

Accepting the captain's invitation, Belladonna beckoned for Mariella and Moises to follow her, and the men cleared a path for them. The men did not follow the procession but kept their distance because Captain Stone had waved them away.

As they walked, Belladonna asked, "How did you find yourself in these waters?"

"After my freedom, I had found I had a taste for piracy and an ache to take revenge on every Spanish galleon that crossed my path. I followed a Dutch captain heading to the Caribbean to capture ships loaded with silver from Mexico and Recife. These waters are filled with Spanish treasure ships just right for the picking."

Belladonna winced at the name of the settlement in Brazil where her parents had met their death at the hands of Spanish Inquisitors. Her companion must have noticed her reaction and paused, his eyebrows in an unspoken question.

Belladonna considered it would be to her benefit to reveal some of her true story. "My family was killed during a Spanish raid on Recife, and I escaped on a ship which was then captured by pirates. I had no family, no home, when Captain Isaak, the captain of the *Sabato*, rescued me, brought me to Venice, where I started a new life."

The English captain pursed his lips, nodding. "The captain from *Sabato* is from Venice. No wonder he is such a master of the sea. It is in the blood of Venetians; they have married themselves to the sea."

"You are referring to the *Festa della Sensa*, a great celebration when the Doge tosses a gold ring into the lagoon, as a sign of the covenant between Venice and the sea."

"It must be quite an event. One day I should hope to see it. Perhaps with you as my guide?" Captain Stone patted her hand with his. Belladonna raised an eyebrow and smiled, intending to be only mildly encouraging, enough to satisfy his ego.

They had arrived at a large hut comprised of salvaged planks of wood with a roof made of palm tree fronds and rushes. The rich smell of roasting meat and the sizzle of fat on the fire made her stomach growl. Captain Stone gestured to them to take a seat among the driftwood benches filled with men chomping on shanks of roasted meat. When Belladonna hesitated, he laughed and slapped the backs of a seated group, who took the hint and vacated their seats for the captain's guests.

"Please," he gestured for Belladonna, Mariella, and Moises to take the seats beside him. A roasted pig was turning on a spit. Moises held back, looking at the meat not with hunger, but revulsion. Belladonna pulled him towards the table, but with his eyes still on the roasting meat, he would not sit.

His mother spoke to him rapidly in Spanish. "When you are facing starvation, it is permitted to eat forbidden foods, even pig meat. You must know that."

Moises shook his head. "I cannot. I would rather starve."

Mariella was about to protest when Belladonna took her hand and squeezed it. She spoke softly to them in Spanish. "Not now. I will do what I can, but, if necessary, pretend to eat. We do not know how these men will react if they know your origins."

She turned to the captain. "As a gentleman, can you not indulge a lady and fulfill a little request? The meat you are offering may be delicious, but I confess to a craving for fish."

The captain sat comfortably with Hernando by his side. He laughed and shook his head but then shouted some orders to the servers. Belladonna and Mariella were gratified when a plate of charred fish was brought to them. Belladonna, conscious of the captain's eyes on her, tried to eat the fish as delicately as possible, though her desire was to grab its flesh with both hands and stuff it into her mouth. Mariella and Moises grabbed the fish and began eating as soon as it was passed to them.

The company was intent on devouring their roasted meat and guzzling down watered wine. The wine was served in golden goblets, which must have come from Spanish booty, and Belladonna relished every drop of it. After they all had eaten their fill, Hernando brought up the *Sabato* once more. "Now that we have shared a meal together and have become good friends, tell me, have you seen or heard anything of the *Sabato* or of Captain Isaak?"

The captain answered Hernando's question with one of his own. "How strong is your captain?"

Hernando puffed out his chest. "He is the bravest and shrewdest of men."

The captain shifted his gaze to Belladonna as he said, "I have heard a man was washed ashore by the storm and taken aboard a Spanish ship. This ship has a constant need for more slaves because its captain is a brutal man, and neither his crew nor the galley slaves survive for very long. If your man has been taken—"

Belladonna interrupted him. "Do you know the name of the ship?"

He nodded. "The *El Conquistador*."

Belladonna's nostrils flared, and she gave Hernando a look as if she were a dragon ready to breathe fire. "Then we must take the *El Conquistador*."

Chapter Fourteen: Isaak

ON THE CARIBBEAN, ON THE ISLAND OF TORTUGA, The first of DECEMBER, 1614

For the past few weeks, Isaak had needed to keep his focus on refitting the *El Conquistador*, now renamed *The Pelican,* to be ready for Havana. Captain Ross's ship had damaged the galleon's hull, and the main mast was cracked. It looked as if a strong gust of wind could make it split and fall.

He found a ship's carpenter, and the man knew his woods, for under his gnarly hands, progress was being made on the repairs. There was still more restoration to be done before the hull and the mast were ready for sailing. Isaak paced the deck while the stricken mast was being secured with yards of strong rope to keep it standing. If the shaft could be restored by the carpenter, it would be possible to get underway in a few days. If they were forced to replace the mast, the work could take several weeks.

Barrels of water and provisions were hoisted onto the ship, while sailors carried out the Spaniards' cache of sugar and spices from the ship's hold. The goods would be sold to brokers, and the proceeds distributed to the crew. From the amount of precious cargo they found on the *El Conquistador,* they now had ample coins to spend.

The men stomped their boots and clogs to different tunes from far-off lands, including the exotic chanting of the Moors and the raunchy ballads of the English. It reminded Isaak of Venice, its different cultures and people clustered among their own, in *campos* filled with the food, the music, and the dress of their kind.

He had escaped the Ghetto by going to sea, but its sounds and smells and traditions would never leave him. The fate of the Jews of Venice was always precarious, but where in this world was it not?

Isaak could not risk his origins becoming known. Though the Jews had been banished from England for centuries, he suspected the Englishmen would view him with suspicion, a bias from medieval times when Jews were blamed for the Black Plague. With the Dutchmen, he would have less to fear since Amsterdam's Jews lived freely among other citizens and were not forced to live in ghettos. As for the Frenchman, he did not believe Olivante would ever come to a comrade's aid, regardless of his origins.

Unconsciously, Isaak had been pacing. He stopped and assumed a casual stance, leaning on the rails. Not healthy to show signs of worry or uncertainty when in command of a ship, especially when preparing to execute such a bold attack on Havana. He had to appear fearless and convey an unshaken belief of invincibility, or this mission would fail.

"Captain!" a shout came from below, calling for his attention. Peering over the side, Isaak recognized the distinctive large ostrich plume of Captain Ross's hat. His eyes followed the bobbing feather of the English captain as he strode up the gangplank and joined him on the prow of his ship. Shading his eyes from the bright sun, Ross turned around to observe the status of the repair work.

"Pull, men, pull! Come now, give it what you got!" shouted the first mate. The crewmen he addressed were struggling to gain enough leverage to move forward, with the ropes pulling taut against their shoulders.

"Will it work, do you think?" asked Ross.

"It has to."

The two captains stood side by side, watching the men pulling on the ropes and the binding and hammering of the carpenter as he aimed to keep the mast pointing skyward.

"Ho!" shouted Captain Ross along with the men, raising his fist to commend their work. Suddenly, a loud crack, then a scream, and a man fell from the crow's nest. There was a collective gasp as his falling body hit the sea with a great splash.

Springing into action, Captain Ross removed his coat, hat, and shoes, and leapt from the deck into the sea. Isaak rushed over to the side, gripping the rails and craning his neck for a sight of the two men. The head of the would-be rescuer broke the surface, gasping for breath, but without the fallen man in his grasp. Taking a great gulp of air, Captain Ross dived again below the surface, but returned once more empty-handed.

"Sank like a stone, he did," murmured the first mate, who leaned over the rail beside Isaak. "A bad sign, that is."

"Go about your duties," ordered Isaak to the mate while he waited for Captain Ross to swim back to the ship and climb on deck.

"Pity," said the young captain, water streaming from his sodden clothing. He sniffed and picked up the clothing he had left behind on the deck. "If you will permit me, I would like to go below to dry off. In the meantime, order the carpenter to see to the damage to the crow's nest."

Isaak's jaw tensed as he followed Captain Ross below, uncertain of the young captain's purpose in his cabin.

Captain Ross had squeezed the excess water from his shirt before descending and now hung it on a railing to let it dry. The chart of the sea around the island to the Port of Havana was marked, and maps of the island of Hispaniola overlay it. Bare-chested, he leaned over the chart and traced a path with his finger.

"You were quick to go over the side. That surprised me," said Isaak.

Captain Ross paused and looked up at Isaak. "If you want unswerving loyalty, you have to demonstrate you care."

"Do you?"

"Not really."

"You seem older beyond your years."

Captain Ross stood up straight. "I am a captain, the son of a captain, and the grandson of a privateer who sailed with Drake on the *Golden Hind*. I have been at sea since I was a lad. Probably longer than you." Ross pointed to the map. "Have you been studying the routes?"

Isaak nodded, and Ross continued, "Tell me, the ships from Mexico will most likely have to pass directly across the northwest of Hispaniola, right into our parlor, so to speak?"

Isaak agreed. "Now that the Spanish have likely taken full control of Jamaica, Spanish ships will not hesitate to take that route. It is the shorter way to Havana."

"From Cartagena, would you say the most logical route would be along a similar path?"

"What are you suggesting?"

Captain Ross placed a hand, not gently, on Isaak's shoulder. "We will have to split up—divide and conquer. Are you following?" Ross removed his hand and pointed to the southern area on the map. "For the ships coming from Punta Araya, on the mainland, loaded with sugar and chocolate, they will pass along the islands here; Curacao is close by. The Dutch pirates roost around that island so I will suggest Hendriksen sail there. There should be other ships, loaded with silver, coming from here," he pointed to another large Spanish settlement near Punta Araya, "with no need to go westward toward Havana. Instead, they will head to San Juan for provisioning and set off on a more direct route to Spain. They will consider this safer, passing by Spanish-held islands. More ships with better cargo. We will have to take them while avoiding the Spanish guns. A tough challenge but for a very lucrative reward."

"A very astute assessment of the potential," Isaak said, intending to encourage the captain to reveal more of his plans.

"I will suggest to the others that *our* ships take *these* waters to capture the galleons loaded with treasure before they make the port at San Juan." Ross traced a path with his finger from the southeast to the northwest of the Caribbean. "This would be the path from Cartagena. Right through the waters where my ship—and yours—will be waiting to relieve them of cargo and crew."

"The *Pelican* and *The Golden Bough* would intercept all Spanish ships from Cartagena and Mexico, while Williams, Glover, and Olivante stalk the waters around Jamaica." Isaak was beginning to understand this man's game.

"Exactly."

"Why intercept the ships from Cartagena? They grow no tea or chocolate, do they?" There must be something else Ross was after.

"Emeralds, my friend, the best in the world are from Cartagena. Why should they not fill our pockets instead of the Queen of Spain's?"

Isaak stroked his chin. "I see. The route from Columbia is wide open, not many islands along the way. We will come from the West—while the Spanish captains will have their spyglasses searching the eastern horizon. We will fly a Spanish flag until we are close enough for the grappling hooks. Have you salvaged some Spanish helmets and armor?"

Captain Ross grinned. "Of course! We keep a few men on deck dressed like Spaniards until we draw close enough to board and take her."

"Then on to Hispaniola, where we unload cargo and prisoners, and we are off to take Havana."

Ross grabbed Isaak's arm. "Why should we have to drag every ship's cargo to Hispaniola?"

There is no loyalty among thieves. Isaak thought it best to play along. "Yes, if we stick to the plan. However, there is probably another place to keep it. I warrant a clever man could find a nice little island to hide what we gather and keep it secure."

"I see we understand each other."

"Perfectly," said Isaak. He would have to watch out for Captain Ross, for it was clear the man did not like sharing the loot with all of his partners. If only he could find a boat, slip away, and sail off! He had no desire for treasure or emeralds, but only to find the *Sabato* and be reunited with Belladonna.

Chapter Fifteen: Isaak

ON THE CARIBBEAN, ON THE ISLAND OF TORTUGA, The fifteenth of DECEMBER 1614

The repairs to the *Pelican* were nearly completed and all the cargo from the Spanish ship had been sold, the proceeds dispensed to the crew. Eager to celebrate their new prosperity, the men were awash with wine and rum as they settled into the many taverns on Tortuga. A comfortable haven for pirates of any nationality or allegiance, Tortuga was always busy with pirate ships arriving and departing its shores. Crews mingled, captains toasted each other's victories, and gossip was traded like currency.

Isaak mingled with the French, English, and Dutch crews, hoping to gain insight from the boasts of their successes and the whispers of their failures. To attempt an attack on Havana was like slipping between the jaws of a lion, and Isaak wanted to know the type of men he sailed with and to what extent they could be depended upon.

"A drink, my friend?" Isaak asked one of the Englishmen freed from the Spanish galleon. The fellow's eyes narrowed, but he pushed out his grog cup towards the serving girl as Isaak paid for the refill.

"How was it you came to make the acquaintance of *El Capitan*?" Isaak asked to start the conversation. It was important to know whether it was the weakness of the captain or the cowardice of the crew that led to his capture. "What happened to your ship?"

His question elicited a scowl, but after gulping down a bit of grog, the Englishman seemed to recover himself to answer Isaak's question. "Fool of a captain thought it would be easy to take the *El Conquistador*. Too many guns, I told him, but his greed got the better of him, as it did to many of my mates." He wiped his mouth with the back of his hand and pointed to the ground. "They are down there, at the bottom of the ocean now, and I would still be chained to the oars of our enemy if Captain Ross had not come around."

"Out-gunned?" Isaak asked.

"And out-maneuvered. *El Capitan* may not be the best navigator but he was bloody sharp as a tack when it came to counter-attack." The Englishman squinted at Isaak. "I hear you may be the new captain to sail the *El Conquistador* out of the harbor."

"News travels fast," said Isaak, looping his thumbs through his gun belt. "The ship has a new name, it is now the *Pelican*."

"You have need of a second mate?"

Isaak stroked his chin as he regarded his companion through half-lowered lids. "Perhaps I do, since I like to sail with men who have the courage to stick to their guns."

He took Isaak's hand and gave it a vigorous shake. "You did me a good turn in freeing me from that hell-hole. I owe you my life and my loyalty."

"Then, welcome aboard the *Pelican*, mate. Finish your grog and go sign the articles," said Isaak as he downed the last of his own drink.

* * *

Isaak avoided the clusters of men around the fires with roasting meat on spits, since it made his stomach roil. He was not observant of the religious rites of his upbringing, but he could not bring himself to eat the forbidden roasted pig or boar. Instead, he squatted down to watch men carving pieces of driftwood into whimsical shapes like mermaids and sea serpents. They, too, were a good source of information since they kept their ears open and themselves sober.

"Where did you gain such skill?" Isaak asked an older man with flowing grey locks and beard.

The man looked up from his carving and squinted at Isaak. "Waiting. You can learn much about anything when you are becalmed and waiting for the wind. Or when peering at the the horizon for the next ship when you are hungry and thirsty and have been on some god-forsaken island for too long."

"Not here, surely? This is supposed to be paradise for men like us."

Grey-hair snorted a laugh and shook his head. "Paradise, is it? A far cry from that, I will wager. And as for the men here…" He held up his knife. "This here is good for more than whittling."

Isaak took a seat beside him and rested both elbows on his knees. "You come from the Dutch ship, my friend? Captain Hendriksen must be a tough man to follow."

The man stopped the scraping of the wood and turned to him. "He is a good captain. Knows what he is about, steady on what he must do. I got no bone to pick with him."

Isaak raised his eyebrows. "But you do of the others?"

His companion brushed his straggling grey curls from his face. "Many an honest man should think twice about sailing with the Frenchman, or Captain Ross for that matter. They have gold fever, the blood rushing to their heads and getting them giddy with greed. If I were looking to ship out, Captain Isaak, I would stick with Hendriksen."

The man knew his name. Isaak clenched his fists. "You look somewhat familiar. Have we met before?"

"Aye, we have. When I was chained to an oar, and you had the courtesy to set me free before you sent another Spanish ship into oblivion." He reached out a calloused hand and covered it over Isaak's fist. "I would be some scurvy dog to forget you, or your ship. But do not fear. I will not share my knowledge with these fellows. It would do you and me both no good."

Isaak gave him a nod. "I appreciate your help and can use it to keep ahead of this bunch." When the man resumed his whittling, Isaak relaxed his shoulders as he asked his companion about the island, the men, and the other ships.

"All three English captains are good commanders but attract the worst rogues, who are enticed by the promise of booty and controlled by the threat of a few strokes of the lash. The Frenchman is a two-faced liar, drinks too much, and is overfond of women."

"Are they good fighters? What of the gunmen?"

"They will fight like the very devils for the opportunity to loot a Spanish treasure ship, and as to the gunmen, they know their work. But for captured passengers, pity them if they have no worth for ransom, for these brutes and the captains care little for their welfare." He shook his head. "A far cry from your fellows of the Brethren."

Isaak bit his lip, taking in all the man said. "You have not heard anyone talk of the *Sabato?*"

The grey-haired man lowered his head over his whittling and was careful to respond in a low voice. "One of the carpenters mentioned a strange vessel he had encountered recently on Hispaniola. He was an Englishman and spoke of an odd crew speaking many languages he had never heard. It also seemed there were two women aboard. Could not stop blathering about them."

Isaak felt his throat grow numb and swallowed to restore it. "Two women, you say?"

"Yes, he remarked on their beauty. One dark, and the other fair. He asked where they were from, as one of them spoke his language. They had come from Jamaica, escaping a great storm."

Isaak rose to his feet, unable to stay still in light of this news. The description seemed to fit the *Sabato*, Belladonna, and Mariella. He saluted the grey-haired man. "Thank you for your conversation; it may be worth my life."

The grey-haired man shrugged. "You saved my hide, so I am bound to save yours. Such is the way of things. Have they given you a ship?"

"The very same Spanish galleon, formerly the *El Conquistador,* from which Captain Ross liberated me along with its other prisoners. Now it is *The Pelican* and it is crewed by its former galley slaves."

"That is not too bad, then. Since you freed them, they owe you. Besides, they hate the Spanish and are likely to be drooling for revenge. They will fight with all their might. You may have a chance of surviving after all."

* * *

When he entered the tavern, Captain Olivante had a woman in one hand and a tankard of rum in the other, so he did not look Isaak's way. The back room served as headquarters of the pirate captains. Captain Ross was playing dice with Captain Williams, by turns laughing or cursing with every throw. Glover and Hendriksen had tankards before them but seemed completely sober, and they beckoned Isaak to join them. Glover had unfolded a map and spread it across the rough plank of a table.

"The Spanish treasure ships from the south set sail from Cartagena and pass by the eastern side of Jamaica on their way to their final stop at Havana. Ross suggests Hendriksen and I take the ships here," said Captain Glover, pointing his thick finger at a spot midway in mid-ocean, southwest of Jamaica. "We take the cargo, then sail to the west coast of Hispaniola, where it is safe for us to unload the goods and whatever is left of the Spanish crew."

"Then the treasure fleet coming from the west, from Santa Cruz, where the Spanish have their viceroy, will sail across the Gulf of Mexico towards Havana. There is nothing to stop you and Captain Ross to take them there." Glover pointed to a spot midway between the mainland and far enough from Havana. "It is not far from there to Barataria Bay, a pirate haven on the Great Continent, where you can empty your ships and sail unimpeded under the Spanish flag towards the port of Havana."

"I see," said Isaak. "Though it would be best to have another crew standing by on that atoll of islands northwest of Jamaica. I plan on landing with a chosen few on the southwest coast of Havana. I know that atoll. I was blown there by the storm, and I know the waters around the southwest of Havana. It would be better if I sailed along with you two rather than with Ross. Captain Ross and Olivante should have enough firepower to take down the biggest of those galleons."

"You make a good point," said Captain Glover, raising an eyebrow as he studied first the map and then Isaak. "I will support this plan of yours. What say you, Hendriksen?"

The Dutch captain did not even look up from the map. "I would rather have this man leading the land attack than Williams."

Isaak was curious at his comment. "Why is that?"

Hendriksen glanced at Glover, who gave him a slight nod. "Williams commands a bloodthirsty crew who often get carried away during an attack. He cannot always control them, nor does he usually want to."

"Especially when taking a fort like *El Moro*. We do want to create havoc on land, but we still want to make sure we are protected on the sea. Otherwise, those cannons will keep firing on us while Williams and his men forget to dismantle them, if they are too busy looting and slaughtering." The big man shook his head. "I, like Hendriksen, am an old soldier and value discipline. Williams does not. Though he be clever and daring, he is wild and ruthless. I do not trust him on such an attack."

Isaak grinned. "I take it that you have decided to trust me."

Glover held out his hand to Isaak, who shook it. "Though I be a pirate, I like a man with morals who places limits on himself and on his men. The men you rescued on the *El Conquistador* say you risked your own neck to free them. You earned my respect when you earned theirs."

Isaak pulled up a stool and took a seat between his new comrades. "Captain Ross has different plans, you know."

"The devil take Captain Ross! He is still a pup. Let him sail with Olivante. Now, we are asking you straight, Captain Isaak, are you with us?"

Isaak quickly weighed the possibilities of aligning himself with these two captains, and the danger of going against the greedy Captain Ross and the drunkard Captain Olivante. It did not take him long to agree. "I am."

Chapter Sixteen: Belladonna

ON THE CARIBBEAN, ON THE SOUTHWEST BAY OF HISPANIOLA, The twentieth of NOVEMBER, 1614

The days passed slowly for Belladonna in the heat and humidity that settled on the island of Hispaniola. In a makeshift shelter, out of the worst of the sun and winds, they had little space and an uneasy rest. She was faced with a decision she did not like to make: either stay and do nothing but wait for news of Isaak or the *Sabato* or take passage aboard the Dutch ship the *ZyderZee* to Amsterdam to enlist the help of the Brethren. Practically, there was little she could do by remaining in Hispaniola, but if she sailed to Amsterdam and enlisted the help of the Brethren, there would be a greater chance of success in rescuing Isaak. Emotion tangled the threads of reason, and she could not help feeling that by leaving the Caribbean, she was abandoning hope of ever seeing Isaak again.

Unsettled and undecided, Belladonna appealed to Mariella for her opinion. "After all," she concluded after reciting her fears about staying and her concerns about leaving, "you and Moises should be a part of the decision. We must stay together whether in the Caribbean or if we sail to Amsterdam."

Mariella had become quiet and distant since they arrived in Hispaniola. Her forehead was puckered with worry, and she jumped at every sound or movement around them. When Belladonna mentioned sailing to Amsterdam, it was as if Mariella had awakened from a stupor. Her eyes lit up as she asked, "We have the chance to leave this terrible place and sail to

Amsterdam?"

Moises added his voice. "Aboard a big ship? Oh, can we?"

The reaction of both of her companions left Belladonna with no doubt that Mariella and Moises would be brutally disappointed if she were to stay in Hispaniola. Her brother's dying wish was for her to take care of his family, but now, how could she leave the Caribbean without feeling like she was abandoning Isaak? Her loyalty to Isaak challenged her loyalty to her dead brother. She held her head in her hands as she tried to massage away the pain of a throbbing headache.

"How are we to leave?" asked Mariella.

That was a question she was prepared to answer. "A Dutch ship and a sympathetic captain who has agreed to give us passage to Amsterdam."

"When can we go?" Moises began to collect his belongings.

How could she tell him she was unsure of whether to accept the Dutch captain's offer?

"Moises, there is still time. You do not have to be ready to depart now. The ship is gathering provisions and will not depart for a few days."

Mariella's eyes narrowed as she studied Belladonna's face. "Will you be ready to depart?"

Again, Mariella had surprised her by understanding her conflict. "I do not know," she answered truthfully.

Moises began to protest, but Mariella stopped him and addressed Belladonna, "You must think it through for yourself. We will not go without you."

But it would be highly unlikely they would be sail on the Dutch ship without her. Belladonna had offered the Dutch captain substantial payment for their passage, but she suspected the captain had agreed to take her aboard because he had plans for her. Managing such expectations was an art in which Belladonna excelled. She was certain the captain's benevolence would not be extended to Moises and Mariella without her.

She feared for Mariella, whose spirits had flagged greatly since their departure from Jamaica. Faced with a violent storm and a perilous trek through the swamp, her sister-in-law had demonstrated both courage and leadership. Now, Mariella spent most of her day in silence, occasionally strumming a guitar she had found, singing sad melodies. Her music seemed to charm the men around them, who requested songs, and Mariella's voice was haunting and sweet and could lull her listeners into a peaceful half-sleep. The authority of the two captains kept these outlaws and cutthroats at bay, and Mariella's singing kept them quiet—at least for now.

Belladonna, like Mariella and Moises, was tired of the dirt, the drunkenness, and the lack of decent food. Each day passed like the one before it, yet Belladonna had the energy to climb to the top of the rocky hill behind their camp daily to get a clear view of the bay. Shading her eyes from the sun, she searched the horizon for the tiniest white triangle that heralded the approach of a new ship and, with it, the possibility of news of Isaak or the *Sabato*.

Mariella seemed just as lackluster, managing only to reach for the guitar to play woeful melodies. Moises kept himself busy with sketching and asked every evening if tonight was the night he should be packing up his bundle to prepare for a journey. Belladonna changed her mind daily, deciding they must leave one day, to the conviction it was better to wait the next.

She had spoken to Hernando of her dilemma. He was definite about her next course of action. "There is nothing to be gained by you remaining in Hispaniola. Isaak would not wish you to. By seeking the help of the Brethren, you may be the most successful in saving his life."

His argument was rational but could not assuage her feelings of guilt at abandoning the search for Isaak. "The *Sabato* is in these waters, and I have only to wait—"

"If the *Sabato* comes, do you think it would be best for Isaak if you were to join in their search? Out of consideration for your safety, there would be less enthusiasm to search in Spanish-infested waters, no?"

Again, Hernando had made a strong point. Belladonna sighed. "We will be in the way."

Hernando took her hands and wrapped them in his own. "Whether you stay or go, I will remain, and when we do find Isaak, and I am certain we will, I will let him know where you are. I will not have to explain why you had to leave, for he will understand and be grateful you did."

Belladonna found her eyes were filling with tears, and she blinked several times, for she did not like to be seen crying. She looked down, so Hernando should not see and nodded. Thanks to him, she had made her decision.

Captain Stone predicted the Dutch ship would be ready to sail in three days. If the *Sabato* did not appear by then, they would board the Dutch ship.

When she told Mariella the news, her sister-in-law nodded solemnly. "We will be leaving the Caribbean, then. Perhaps forever."

"Do you fear the journey or finding a new place in Amsterdam?"

"Perhaps both."

"And you?" asked Belladonna of Moises.

Moises paused; his chalk held up in mid-stroke. Then, he lowered the chalk and made large bold swashes. "I am sad to have left our home, but I have no sorrow in leaving this place."

Belladonna nodded. "In that, I agree. The cave was a palazzo in comparison."

Moises perked up, his eyebrows raised, his eyes wide. "Did you live in a fine palazzo in Venice? With looking glasses and paintings on the ceilings?"

Belladonna laughed lightly. "Yes, my home in Venice was a beautiful place. But how did you know of paintings on the ceilings and such things?"

The boy shifted in his seat and tilted his head to consider. "Isaak once spoke of the beauty of the city on water, with beautiful ladies and palazzos, and artwork and beautiful glass in every room."

Belladonna blinked several times at the mention of Isaak. "I am glad Isaak spoke to you of these things. I will take you to Venice, and you shall see such wonders as the sparkling of the sun's rays on the rippling waters of the canals and glass of every color and shape reflecting the light of candles in chandeliers and sconces along the walls of elegant salons."

"Are we to go to Venice, then?"

Belladonna smoothed down her hair, as if she were preparing to enter a salon, and said, "Yes, you shall see Venice, I promise."

"I cannot wait!" said Moises, putting down his drawing. "When shall we go?"

Belladonna patted his chalk-smudged hand. "Soon, perhaps in a few weeks. The Dutch ship is nearly ready to sail."

Chapter Seventeen: Belladonna

ON THE CARIBBEAN, ON THE SOUTHWEST BAY OF HISPANIOLA, The twenty-fifth of NOVEMBER 1614

Belladonna snuck away in the early morning to the waterfall she found when climbing up an outcropping of rock to get a better view of the bay. She wanted one more good wash before she would spend so many long days aboard ship. She stripped off her bodice, which was ragged but intact, and the outer skirt, which had suffered more tears but had been mended by Mariella. Wearing only her shift, she slipped into the waterfall between the rocks, thrilled by the cold of the water on her hair and shoulders. The force of the cascade rinsed the grit from her hair, and though she had no perfumes or soaps, she believed it cleansed her shift and her body.

It was still early, and the heat was not at its peak, but it was warm enough for her shift to dry thoroughly as she lay in the sun atop a large, flat rock. As she lay across the sun-warmed stone and closed her eyes, her hair and skin dried. A shadow came over her. Shading her eyes, she propped herself onto her elbows and recognized the English Captain Stone.

Wits about her, she greeted him. "Captain, I did not expect you to come calling so early."

He stretched out a hand which she took and pulled her to her feet, but he did not relinquish his grip and pulled her close, too close. She arched her back and tilted her head, ignoring his hot breath as she regarded the

Englishman through half-lowered lids. Thankfully, from this high point above the trees, she had spotted a most wished-for sight. A ship was entering the harbor.

"I appreciate your gentlemanly attention, but I did not expect my charms would be adequate to distract you from the advent of a new ship entering the bay."

The captain released her at once and turned to look. "You have sharp eyes and good sense. I beg your pardon, but as a 'gentleman,' I must leave you to dress."

Belladonna gave him a mock curtsy as she reached for her bodice and skirt. The captain was already halfway down the summit as she finished dressing and tying back her hair. The ship had gotten closer, and her heart quickened. She did not know much about ships, but it did seem as if the newcomer had the look of the *Sabato*.

* * *

The arrival of any new ship sent a flurry of activity among the rag-tag colony. In the camp-like town, vendors appeared, natives hawked the local fare, and would-be sailors smartened their appearances, hoping they could get aboard as shipmates. The women in the ramshackle tavern were agog with excitement. They were bored with men who already spent their money and were drunk all the time.

Captain Stone and the Dutch captain were among the welcoming committee assembled on the northern shore, awaiting the approaching long boats. Hernando stood close by Belladonna's side, and she was glad to see he was grinning.

"With the sun glaring it is difficult to see, but I believe it is the *Sabato*. Once the boats come in, we shall see, madam." Hernando kept his hand on his belt, resting on the hilt of his big knife.

As soon as the boats landed, Hernando raced forward, knocking the island men out of his way. When he reached the boat, he grabbed the first man and hugged him to his chest. That was all Belladonna needed, and lifting her skirts, she sped after him.

The *Sabato,* at last. She did not need to ask the question when she saw it was the first mate who led the men and not Isaak. Her shoulders sagged as Belladonna looked back to the assembly on the beach. Mariella and Moises lingered under the shelter of the scrub. Captain Stone and his entourage stepped forward, hands at rest on the weapons in their belts as the men of the *Sabato* disembarked.

He looked from Belladonna to Hernando.

Hernando pounded his chest with his fist. "My ship has come. They have found me."

"How fortunate," said the Englishman, his eyes narrowed and his hand poised at the hilt of his sword in his belt. "You recognize these men?"

Belladonna looked boldly into his eyes. "I do. They brought me here from Venice."

"And your captain?" he addressed his question to Hernando.

"Lost in the storm, perhaps captured by the Spanish. Just as we told you. Now that the *Sabato* is here, we will go after him." Hernando gestured to the new arrivals.

Captain Stone kept his legs apart in a belligerent stance, signaling he was ready to fight. The leader, a man as fair as the Englishman, ignored the scowling captain and introduced himself with a smile as he held out his hand. "Ben Markham. Taken by the Spanish off the coast of Cadiz. Freed by Captain Isaak, and it is only fair I do the same for him."

After a moment's hesitation, Captain Stone took it and said, "Welcome, and we will help you any we can. Any enemy of Spain is a friend of ours."

Belladonna exhaled as she felt the tension in the group dissipate. After more introductions on both sides, Captain Stone led the newcomers from the beach to the camp-like structures of the town.

Besides the first mate, Belladonna was relieved to see the ship's surgeon, a tall, gentle Moor from Cairo, who had studied the medicines of the master Arabic physicians and was adept at keeping the wounded alive. The Moor, like the other dark-skinned crew members, walked proudly with swords and scimitars at their sides and not with bowed heads and the humility of the natives on the nearby islands.

The crew of the *Sabato* hailed from so many different countries and spoke many languages, all bound together by having once been slaves in a Spanish galley and freed by Isaak. Just as she had been long ago.

At the tavern, they shared food and stories, the common thread of Spanish captivity, and their hatred toward an enemy that knew no bounds. Mariella played her guitar and sang in her low, sultry voice, and though her songs were in Spanish, the men were quiet until she finished and then clapped and whistled to convey their appreciation.

Belladonna, conscious of Captain Stone's unremitting stare, sat beside Hernando, a pewter tankard of watered-down wine beside her. Captain Stone called everyone's attention to her, which made her take a long gulp of her drink.

"Now that we have all shared our tales, we are most curious about the lady who calls herself Belladonna." He pointed a finger at her, and the flickering candlelight made him look sinister; his eyes hollower and the lines around his mouth deeper. "You have named yourself after a poison, and you carry a deadly dagger which you are skilled to use, as we have seen firsthand. You must tell us your story."

All eyes were on her. Hernando patted her hand and the men of the *Sabato* gave her a cautious nod. Treating them all to her most charming smile, she began, "I, too, am a survivor of the Spanish. In a raid on Recife, they murdered my family, though I managed to escape aboard a Dutch ship bound for the Netherlands. I was captured by pirates in the Mediterranean and bound for slavery in Constantinople when the captain of the *Sabato* found me and freed me. He took me to Venice, where I found a new home." She toyed with a stick, drawing circles in the sand as she lowered her eyes. "Until twelve months ago, when a man from Jamaica arrived in Venice, courtesy of the Captain of the *Sabato*."

The fire crackled, and a few sparks shot out. Belladonna decided to skim over the whole truth and highlight the points that would win their sympathy. "The man turned out to be my brother, who I thought long dead, but had survived Recife and had settled in Jamaica, outside of Port Royal.

He learned of my whereabouts from Captain Isaak, who sought to reunite us. Unfortunately, Spain once again came between us."

"My brother was an envoy whose mission was to encourage England to take Jamaica before it could be annexed by Spain. To prevent him from negotiating with the English, the Spanish sent an assassin after my brother, who disappeared shortly after he arrived in Venice. Captain Isaak foiled their plans, but by the time I had located my brother it was too late, he was wounded and deathly ill. On his deathbed, he extracted a promise from me to find his wife and son." She gestured to Mariella and Moises. "After coming to Jamaica and fulfilling my brother's wish, I was caught in a deadly storm, nearly captured by the Spanish, trudged through a mangrove swamp, and, thanks to Hernando, managed to make our escape to this island."

Captain Stone cleared his throat. "Quite a tale, and not an uncommon one when it comes to the Spanish. And Captain Isaak? He seems to have stuck out his neck quite a bit for you. Is he another member of your family?"

Belladonna stuck out her chin and leveled her eyes so they bored directly into his. She would enjoy his reaction to what she was about to announce. "Not yet, for you see, I am to be his bride."

Chapter Eighteen: Isaak

ON THE ISLAND OF TORTUGA, The sixteenth of DECEMBER, 1614

On the island of Tortuga, the dawn cracked open a new day without much protest from the pirates and their ladies, who were tousled over each other in exhausted sleep. Only Isaak was witness to its beauty and the way the light peaked through the darkness of the trees and hills like it was tiptoeing into the town, cautious of waking its residents.

Isaak had slept only a few hours, but he had slept deeply, dreaming of Venice. In his dream, he had been walking the narrow *calles* of the Ghetto, looking for a way out. No matter which direction he took, he was thwarted—each passage ended in water. He awoke at dawn, expecting old stone to greet his eyes and to be lulled by the gentle lapping of the canal waters. Instead, it was the shifting of large fronds from the palm trees and the chirping of unknown insects which jarred him awake and shook him from fantasies of Venice.

Today should be his last on this island sanctuary with its odd assembly of bandits and refugees who now considered themselves buccaneers. Their pirate captains would assemble to finalize their plans for the assault on Havana, then disperse to their corners of the sea to lay in wait for Spanish ships carrying all types of treasures.

Isaak got to his feet, brushing off sand and errant leaves and buckled his sword belt in place. He was headed to the stream in the clearing to give his face a bracing wash and shave off yesterday's grizzle. He encountered no one on the path through the trees and felt comfortable removing his doublet, shirt, and weapons for a more complete wash. The coldness of the water on his face and hair banished the last of the early morning sluggishness, and he felt new vigor as he pulled his shirt back over his head. Reaching for his doublet, he heard thrashing and sharp cries of someone crashing through the path. Isaak skipped donning the doublet and, instead, opted for his sword.

Isaak had it drawn and ready when a young girl burst forth and splashed into the stream, with the French captain in hot pursuit. Olivante's hair and eyes were wild as he lunged at the girl, grabbing her, tearing away a swath of her bodice. The girl screamed and struggled to keep the cloth together to cover herself. She squirmed backwards as Olivante came towards her. Suddenly, another figure emerged from the trees and leapt onto Olivante's back, knocking him to the ground. Olivante rolled over his attacker, and the two grappled in the shallow water.

"Stop!" Isaak called out, but the men continued to pound each other, rolling out of the stream and into the brush. There was a cry, and Isaak grabbed his short sword.

Olivante emerged from the bush, a knife glistening and dripping blood. He seemed to see Isaak for the first time, and smirking, he said, "Put it away, *mon ami*. There is no cause for alarm. It is merely the way with *la femme*, you know. This fellow thought she was his, but she is mine. He should respect a captain, no?"

The girl, eyes round and filling with tears, clasped her ruined bodice to her chest. Isaak gestured to her with the point of his sword, "She does not seem to be as taken with you as you think."

"*C'est mon affaire.* Now go away if you know what is good for you." Staggering as he stomped into the water, which swirled at his ankles, he progressed towards the girl.

The girl was a native and very young, and she whimpered as she crawled away from Olivante. Isaak angled the tip of the sword closer to the Frenchman. "Leave the girl alone."

Nostrils flaring, his lips pulled back in a snarl, Olivante flicked the blood-stained knife at Isaak, who easily ducked out of its way. Cursing, the Frenchman was now unarmed, and Isaak feinted at him with his sword. Olivante snickered. "What do you intend to do, run me through?"

"You just killed a man," said Isaak, gesturing to the body in the bushes.

"I kill so many men, *mon Capitan*. What is one more?"

"A life for a life. I should kill you."

"Why? For him, who you do not even know? Or for a girl? How do you think the others will take to that?" Olivante wiped his hand across his breeches. "It is over now, and my passion has cooled. We will both forget this ever happened, *n'est ce pas?*"

The Frenchman retrieved his knife and waved a hand dismissively at Isaak, then went off down the path in the direction of camp.

Once the Frenchman was gone, Isaak sheathed his sword and went to examine Olivante's victim. The man was also a native, and from his resemblance to the girl, he could be her brother. Blood was seeping into the ground from a wound in his neck. His eyes stared, unblinking, at the sky.

Isaak extended his hand to the girl to help her up. The girl did not take it and instead scrambled away, crashing through the thick foliage and out of sight. Isaak retrieved the rest of his clothing and, realizing there was nothing more he could do, headed back to the tavern. He doubted he could count on the other captains to support a confrontation with Captain Olivante. For the sake of expediency, they would probably take Olivante's side and justify the murder as self-defense.

The town was just waking up when he returned. The grey-haired carpenter was already at his usual spot, methodically scraping at a spindle of wood. He gave Isaak a quick salute and inclined his head towards the tavern. Isaak saluted the older man and kept his right hand on his sword hilt as he entered. Only a few men were drinking at this early hour, and they gave Isaak a suspicious eye before returning to focus on their rum.

The big man placed as sentry let Isaak pass into the private area where the captains convened.

Three of the captains stood around a map on the table before them.

Olivante was sprawled in the corner, his feet up, his eyes bleary, staring at the wall. Captain Ross yawned, but winked at Isaak when the others were focused on the map.

"Come here, Captain Isaak. We are finalizing our rendezvous spot now," said Captain Glover, beckoning him to stand alongside him. Isaak complied, but kept an eye on Olivante, wary of a sudden burst of malevolence from the Frenchman.

"We will meet here, on the northwest bay of Hispaniola," said Glover, pointing to the island closest to Tortuga.

Captain Williams explained, "We have traders there who can unload the ships while we make any needed repairs."

Isaak pursed his lips but nodded.

"You will then sail the *Pelican* around the southwest coast of Hispaniola, keeping your distance from Santo Domingo, where the Spanish are, to anchor beyond the southwestern coast below Havana," continued Captain Glover, tracing the path on the map with his finger.

"With Spanish flag flying, right under their smug Spanish noses," said Captain Ross, as if they were speaking of a childish prank.

"If they attempt to engage and they learn who we really are, they will come out full guns blazing," said Isaak, glancing from one captain to another. They grinned. "Ah, I see. The *Pelican* sails boldly into Spanish turf. If we go unnoticed, we then make the approach to *El Moro* by land, but if luck has it and the *Pelican* is unmasked, why we draw the attention of the Spanish gunships to us, and it is clear sailing for you all into the bay of Havana."

Captain Ross cocked a thumb in Isaak's direction. "You see, I told you he was a clever fellow." Then, turning to Isaak, "We have every confidence in you to turn the tables on the Spanish in either case. After all, that is how you came to be here today, in command of the *Pelican*."

Isaak placed his hand on his hip. He had his part to play, and these men would brook no refusal from him. "If I am to be the sacrificial lamb, I suppose it should be reflected in my share of the treasure on this big adventure?"

For the first time, Olivante voiced his opinion, "Your share, *mon ami,* is your life. Which Captain Ross granted you when he took the *El Conquistador*. You have sailed like one of us. But make no mistake, if not for your role in this 'adventure,' I would have run you through as you stepped through this door for your earlier interference."

Captain Williams glared at Olivante. "Your private squabbles have no bearing here, Olivante, so save your belligerence for the Spanish."

Hendriksen added, "We sail together as a unified force, and we will do our best to defend each other. We all risk our lives, and we all share in the profits. It is the same for you."

"Let us now get down to business. We must discuss provisions, weapons, and men," added Captain Glover.

With a loud grunt, Olivante rose, and, glaring at Isaak, stalked out.

"Where are you going?" Captain Williams called after him.

"To sea, and blast you all!" came the shout back, followed by a string of curses in French.

"You should not have interfered with his woman," said Captain Ross in Isaak's ear.

Isaak did not answer.

In a lighter manner, Ross added, "No matter. Women will be the death of him. He had better be sober enough to keep his men under control and his guns aimed at *El Moro*."

Chapter Nineteen: Isaak

ON THE ISLAND OF TORTUGA, The eighteenth of DECEMBER, 1614

Isaak was surprised to find the grey-haired carpenter at the gangplank of the *Pelican* at dusk as the last of the provisions were being loaded aboard.

Busy supervising the crew as they prepared to make way, Isaak spared a few moments for his newfound friend. "Have you come to wish me luck?"

"No, sir, I am here to come aboard and join the crew if you will have me," the grey-haired man shifted a small sack from one callused hand to another.

Isaak did not hesitate to welcome him. A man he could trust would be essential aboard ship. "You can, but first, you must tell me your name. You know mine, but never revealed your own."

"Bennett, sir. Caleb Bennett, of Bristol, England."

"Go below, Caleb, and see the first mate to sign on and claim your place. We do not have a ship's carpenter, though, Faith, we should not have need of your services."

It was not long before all was loaded, and the ropes and gangplank were secured. The sails were lowered and billowed with the wind. A good omen. Isaak signaled the first mate to pull in the anchor and make out to sea. He stood behind the navigator, who had taken the wheel, and confirmed the coordinates—heading slightly south in the waters west of Jamaica. He gave a silent prayer they would meet the *Sabato* in these waters, so he could abort this mission in favor of finding Belladonna.

He kept a watchful eye on his first mate, Brockton, who had been one of the men he had freed from the cruelty of the galley on the *El Conquistador*. Isaak hoped he could rely on the Englishman's loyalty, but it was never good to assume the best of one's fellow man. Still, he had to wager on the men he had freed from the Spanish as those he could count on, versus the rest of the crew, the wastrels and layabouts who had joined them from Tortuga. Regardless, Isaak knew it was good policy to address the men now before they encountered any ship and ordered the mate to assemble the crew on deck.

"Men, many of you know me from the *El Conquistador,* where I, too, was subject to the cruel whims of *El Capitan.* He ruled his ship with the brutality of the whip and the threat of the sword and, therefore, failed when he tried to inspire his men to fight his battle. I will not bludgeon you into following me, but I demand your unquestioning loyalty, which I promise will lead us to victory. The Spanish have earned retribution, and you must swear to deliver it. Unleash your revenge with cannons and sword! Are you with me?"

"Aye!" came the shout unanimously.

"We may have to fly their flag, but it is only to trick them. They have many guns, but they are slow. We are smart, and we are swift. Have no fear, for we will take them and relieve them of the heavy gold that weighs them down, eh?"

"Aye! Huzzah! Huzzah!" fists punched the air, and voices shouted in unison. A quick survey of the crowd revealed no furrowed brows or grimaces of dissent. A good sign. It was not long before their enthusiasm would be put to the test.

As the horizon radiated an orange tint, there was a first sighting of a ship. Isaak had just come on deck and when he heard the call from the crow's nest. He signaled the men to raise the Spanish flag. The First mate called all hands on deck.

Though it was early, and they had been awakened from sleep, the men took to their places with alacrity, displaying an eagerness for action. Isaak had the spyglass to his eye, and as the ship on the horizon drew closer, he squinted, trying to determine its flag.

"Is it Spanish, sir?" asked Brockton, the first mate.

"I believe so." Isaak handed the spyglass to him. The first mate looked and nodded in confirmation.

Isaak gave out a packet of orders, adding, "Tell the gunners to be prepared, but to fire only when I give the word. Not before. We must wait until we are closer and can see how low she rides the waves. If she is low, she will be well loaded, and in these waters, headed for Havana, it could be with gold. We would not want to sink her too fast then, would we? At least until we got what she is carrying into our hold."

"Right, you are, Captain." Brockton picked up the spyglass again. "She looks like a low rider to me, sir." He grinned and tapped his fingers on the spyglass, restless with excitement.

In full sail, the ship glided with the wind to close the gap between the approaching Spanish craft. It was a galleon, but they must have spotted the Spanish flag, and its gun ports were closed. Closer, closer, the lack of bustle on its deck seeming to indicate their presence had raised no alarm.

Isaak had initially planned on firing all cannons and then boarding, but upon seeing how quiet and unsuspecting their prey was, he had another thought. "The Spanish uniforms are still below, are they?"

"Aye," Brockton said, stroking his chin, giving Isaak a puzzled look.

Isaak pointed at the galleon. "You see, there are oars, so there are men down there. I would rather not blast them to the bottom of the sea. Assemble ten of our best and get them dressed. Then I will join them in the long boats."

"Aye, Captain," he tapped the spyglass with enthusiasm. "I will meet you there."

Isaak grabbed Brockton's arm, holding him back. "No, you must stay here. While we gain the bridge, move closer alongside, attach the grappling hooks, and launch the rest of the crew to board her."

Now, the first mate's grin widened into a full-tooth smile, "Aye, aye, sir."

Isaak, leaning over the side rail, cupped his hands to his mouth and called out in Spanish, "Hail! We have need of some assistance. Can we board?"

An affirmative shout in Spanish, and Isaak was off to join the men, first donning the heavy iron helmet of the former commander of the *El Conquistador*. Isaak was relieved to recognize the faces in the longboat as the former galley slaves, all wearing the helmets and breastplates of their Spanish tormentors, their faces grim with determination. "Keep silent, and allow me to do the talking since I know their language. Four of you keep yourselves around me while the rest of you stay on the main deck, and when I attack, make sure to secure the hatch so the men below cannot come up."

He handed a reed whistle to the second mate, "As soon as we attack, blow this to signal to Brockton on the *Pelican*. When the men come alongside, we will take this ship without firing a single cannon."

Things do not always go as planned, so Isaak had his pistol, fully loaded and ready, at hand.

"Remember, not a word, I will do all the talking, and in Spanish. Watch for my signals and wait for my orders."

The men nodded. After Isaak called out in Spanish, the rope ladder was lowered, and knives at ready, they vaulted on board.

"Greetings, Captain, and thank you for welcoming us onto your ship," said Isaak, bowing and touching his helmet in an informal salute.

The captain had the red eyes of a man who had little sleep and the reddened nose of a man who had had too much to drink. His voice was gruff and impatient as he asked, "What do you want?"

"I have come to ask your assistance, after a run of bad luck. You see, we sailed through the devil of a storm and lost a few men to the sea. Then, we lost half of the galley slaves to some sort of sickness. In summary, we are short of men and wondered if you could spare a few—slaves will do."

"Why should I?" the grizzled jaw of the Spanish Captain jutted towards Isaak, challenging and belligerent.

"Because if you give us a few men, we will be happy to unburden ourselves of a few crates of silver and precious objects collected by the Viceroy in Vera Cruz that might not make it all the way to Spain." Isaak knew the Spanish ship captains and crew were underpaid and were always looking for ways to profit.

It was clear Isaak's offer had made its impact when the captain's eyebrows shot up, as did those of the men who stood nearby. The Spaniard's grizzled cheeks widened as he smiled. "How many crates would that be? Slaves are valuable and worth more than one crate of silver."

Isaak threw himself into the negotiation, knowing it was a part that must be played. "What say we make a trade? Two crates for eight men."

The Spaniard shook his head, "No, no, no, *amigo*. I know the value of the men but have no guarantee of the value of the silver. Let us say four crates for four men."

"Are you a robber baron by birth, or did you come about it naturally?" Isaak thought it wise to take a bantering tone during the negotiations. "Come now, I know how this works. I am willing to give up a few crates of silver, so you must be willing to give up some men. A ship this size must have more than two dozen at least at the oars—"

"Three dozen, we captured a Dutch trader a few months ago, which added to those ranks," said the Spaniard. "But as you have seen, they die like flies, so it is barely enough."

Isaak had to control his ire at the Spaniard's callousness about his captives and act nonchalant. "Granted. But you can spare the eight men I need, for certain."

The Spaniard stroked his jaw, considering. "Five crates, seven men, then. I am being more than generous. How much silver in each crate, would you say?"

"Filled to the brim," Isaak said. "Now I will signal my ship to pull alongside, so we can transfer the silver. It will make us lighter to unload all that silver, so we shall get by with only seven extra men."

The Spaniard's smile was smug with his belief he had gotten the best of Isaak. He barked an order to two of the men behind him to go below to retrieve the seven galley slaves.

Isaak's eyes darted to each side, evaluating the men on the bridge and on deck. He did not want to attack until after the grappling hooks had been attached but did not want to wait to secure the hatch to lock in the Spaniards below deck. First, he signaled to his man beside him, whose fingers went to his lips, issuing a sharp, loud whistle. An answering whistle came from the bridge of the *Pelican*, and Isaak was relieved when the *Pelican* angled closer.

Isaak whispered to the man beside him, "Move into position above the hatch."

Then, removing his helmet and fanning himself with it, Isaak drew the captain over to engage in a private conversation. "Come, tell me, have you encountered any of those notorious pirates one hears so much about?"

The Spaniard snorted. "The cowards do not approach a galleon such as ours. We carry fifty guns, and they cast a deep shadow over these waters."

"No doubt." Isaak had his pistol in hand, hidden under his helmet. The men he had brought with him had a devilish glint in their eyes as they circulated between the bridge and the ladder leading down to the hold. They were ready to pounce on the Spaniards, but timing was important, since they could not take the ship without the added help of the attackers from the *Pelican*.

The *Pelican* was coming alongside, and as soon as Isaak heard the clank of the grappling hooks, he gave another sharp whistle.

The Spanish captain eyed him with suspicion, but it was too late for that; Isaak had the pistol pointed at his head, as his men on deck secured the latch on the hold and drew swords and clubs. Within minutes, their comrades from the *Pelican* had positioned gangplanks to connect the two ships, and men were swarming over the Spanish galleon's deck.

The Spanish Captain's neck and arm muscles bulged as he was forced to restrain himself due to Isaak's gun at his temple.

Shouts of attack and victory, curses of pain and anger, and the clang of swords filled the air.

It was Isaak's turn to sport a triumphant grin. "Well, *amigo Capitan*, as you can see, we have you at a disadvantage. With a pistol to your head, the best chance of survival is to call to your men to lay down their arms."

Cursing in Spanish, the captain had no choice and surrendered. Without having to fire a single cannon, a prize Spanish galleon had fallen into Isaak's hands.

Chapter Twenty: Belladonna

ON BOARD THE SABATO, SAILING TO CURACAO, The tenth of DECEMBER, 1614

Now settled into the vacated captain's cabin aboard the *Sabato*, for the first time since she had arrived in the New World, Belladonna allowed herself to dream of Venice. The bright sun and never-ending heat of the Caribbean had suppressed her spirits and tamed her ambitions, and she felt diminished. In Venice, she had worn high shoes and elaborate dresses like armor, but here in the heat, in thin gauze and light shawls, she felt so very vulnerable.

She endured life in these climes for the love of Isaak, and without him, life here would be unbearable. Rough living, feeling coated with dirt and recoiling from the pawing of coarse company. Educating herself in art, music and literature had been her forte, but were utterly useless skills in these pirate-infested lands.

Mariella seemed consumed by fear, even aboard the *Sabato*, and clung to her son fiercely, not letting him out of her sight. Perhaps Mariella's behavior reflected her experience of dangerous men she had encountered in Jamaica who came from pirate ships? They both learned to rely on their instincts to survive.

On this ship, at least, Belladonna felt more in control, as there were rules enforced that she could depend on. Isaak had instilled values among his men; including the commitment to protect and defend the honor of women.

Belladonna had confidence in Isaac's crew and felt safe among them.

A persistent knocking shook her from her reverie. "Who is it?"

"Mariella."

"Wait, I will unlock the door." Belladonna rose reluctantly and admitted her sister-in-law.

Mariella took a seat at Isaak's table, with its neat piles of maps and instruments for navigation. With her hair cleaned and tamed and in her fresh clothing, Mariella's beauty was more evident than it had been on the island.

"Where are we going?"

"To Curacao. There are no Spanish soldiers there, and it is in the control of the Dutch, so it should be the safest place for us," said Belladonna. "It had been Isaak's destination before the storm. He may have gotten there, already finding allies among the Dutch."

Mariella lowered her eyes, but Belladonna could sense her sister-in-law's skepticism. "It is what I would do, were I in his place. Besides, we have no other choice. You surely do not wish to stay in Hispaniola with these savage men."

Mariella looked at Belladonna as if what she had said was incomprehensible. "You are convinced we should go?"

Belladonna nodded. "I hope with all my heart we will find Isaak, but I am a practical woman. You were ready when the Spanish came, because you had planned an escape route from Jamaica. Isaak and I had planned on going to Curacao if Jamaica should prove too dangerous for us. Now it is. However, there is one other option for us to consider."

"And that is?" Mariella clasped her hands together, as if she were afraid to release them.

"Venice. I have resources, friends, and a home there. Here, I have the men on this ship as our only friends and this leather sack of jewels as our emergency fund. Once, a long time ago, I was a homeless refugee, and it is an experience I vowed never to repeat."

"Venice?" Mariella repeated, and her voice and the look on her face softened. "What would it be like in such a place?"

Belladonna smiled and took her sister-in-law's hands, cradling them in her own. "It is like no other. It is a city on water that glimmers, reflecting sunlight from the canal waters through the great windows and the mirrored walls of palazzos on the Grand Canal. My palazzo is such a place, and it sparkles with chandeliers of colored glass."

Belladonna paused, her eyes tingling. She blinked repeatedly to keep them from tears. "It is so far away it seems like a dream, while the hurricane and all we have been through in the past few days seems to be a nightmare."

Mariella straightened her back, and her eyes flashed at Belladonna as if she had been infused with a new spirit. "I would go with you to Venice. Moises, too. We have nothing left in Jamaica, and we only face instability and death here in the Caribbean. In Venice, will we be safe?"

There was no true reassurance to provide to Mariella. If they were to settle in Venice, they would not be able to live in a palazzo but would be forced to move to the Ghetto, where the destiny of Jews was always precarious.

"Safer than in Hispaniola." Belladonna believed it was the most truthful answer.

Moises burst in, struggling to free his hands from the overlong arms of the coat he had been given. He was gesturing wildly for them to follow him, and giving each other a wary glance, Belladonna and Mariella followed him on deck.

Hernando's face was solemn as he greeted them. "We have word of Isaak."

"Confirmation he has been taken by the Spanish?"

Hernando nodded. "He was taken aboard the Spanish galleon *El Conquistador*. It is bound for Spain, but we shall try to overtake it when it stops for provisioning at Havana."

"Havana?" Mariella's voice was filled with alarm, "That is like walking into the lion's den. There are forts with many guns pointed at their bays. You will not be able to rescue Isaak; you will only treat his eyes to the sinking of his ship."

Isaak's closest friend and confident Ahmad, the Moor, answered, "Have no fear, we are not fools. We will intercept the *El Conquistador* before it reaches Havana, remove its prisoners, and sail out of these waters for good."

"And we will not be troubled if a Spanish ship is sunk in the process," added Hernando with a wink. "The captain of that ship is said to be as cruel as the Devil himself."

Belladonna twisted her hands into the folds of her dress. "I see you are ready to do battle, and we will do all we can to help."

Ahmad shook his head. "No, my lady. There will be a battle, and it is no place for passengers. We will arrive soon in Curacao, where you will depart this ship. There you can arrange passage from Curacao to Amsterdam aboard a Dutch ship."

Mariella's frown eased, and her shoulders relaxed. Moises looked at Belladonna, his eyes wide as he awaited her response. How could she leave without Isaak?

As if reading her thoughts, Ahmad added, "We will find Isaak, and he will return to you in Venice."

Venice. Belladonna's hand instantly rose to her chest, as if to contain the thumping of her heart and the rush of heat to her throat. Venice was home, where she would no longer be a refugee.

Chapter Twenty-One: Isaak

*IN THE BAY OF WESTERN HISPANIOLA, The twentieth of
DECEMBER, 1614*

It was dusk when Isaak sailed the *Pelican* and his new prize, the Spanish galleon, into the bay of Hispaniola. He was gratified to see two other Spanish ships moored there, a faint light shining from their bows, its silhouettes missing a mast or two, probably as a result of their confrontation with his pirate colleagues.

"Prepare to launch the boats," he ordered.

"Aye!"

He put his fingers to his lips and blew a sharp whistle. He was answered in kind by his first mate, who had captained the Spanish prize and brought it into the bay. Shortly, they both stood opposite each other, astern in the long boats lowered from their respective ships, headed towards land.

"We have been expecting you," said Captain Williams as Isaak and his men entered.

"I hope I am on time," Isaak answered with a confident grin on his face. "Oh, wait, you did not specify a time or a date, now, did you?" He glanced around the room. "Perhaps Captain Olivante has already been and gone?"

Captain Glover cleared his throat. "He has not arrived, but he, too, is expected shortly."

"If the fool has done as he was charged and is not lolling around in his cups," muttered the Dutch Captain.

"Ross is tarrying as well," added Glover.

Far be it for me to say why, thought Isaak, though he suspected both Ross and Olivante had taken a detour if they had been successful in waylaying the Spanish ships from Cartagena. He could imagine each gloating over their treasure as they navigated their way to whatever remote island they hoped to stash their private spoils of war.

"How fared you? What have you brought us?"

Isaak took a seat on a rickety chair and propped his feet against the bench where Williams was sitting. "Aye, as good a prize as any. She's got eleven guns, all ready for firing on El Moro."

"And we took her without firing a shot," added Brockton, the first mate.

The other captains prompted Brockton to elaborate, and he described Isaak's ruse with the Spanish captain and how it led them to easily take the ship.

Hendriksen smacked a fist into his palms. "This I like! A warship delivered to us pristine, with no cannon holes in the hull to be patched, no broken masts to repair, complete with a crew of newly freed galley slaves eager for revenge. I salute you, Captain Isaak!"

Glover clapped him on the shoulder. "Well done, man."

Only Williams held back. His attention seemed to be on the pipe he was attempting to fill, though he glanced up at Isaak when he made the opening shot. "What kind of cargo was she carrying?"

Isaak pressed a finger to his chin. "Let me see now, Brockton, what was it we found? Was it four or five crates filled with silver plate?"

"Five, sir. And do not forget the cones of fine sugar. And chocolate." Brockton tucked his thumbs into his belt and puffed out his chest. "There should be enough to be made from our haul to keep everyone in grub and grog for a year."

Glover eyed Williams, who seemed to take the signal, and added his congratulations as more drinks were brought, and they toasted the accomplishment of Isaak and his crew. Then Glover filled Isaak in on the other two galleons moored in the bay.

"Williams encountered this Spanish brigand not far from here. From the angle of her sails and the path of the wind, it seems she was headed to Havana."

Williams had gotten his pipe lit, and puffs of smoke escaped his lips as he spoke of his conquest.

"It was still dark, only a hair of light on the horizon, when we came upon her on the other side of the island. She was sailing low and slow, so we knew she was fully loaded. I ordered them to bring up the rear and come alongside, thereby unleashing the cannon from the angle they would least expect to aim for the main mast. One glorious shot took it down right on top of their bloody captain."

"Captain Hendriksen came upon his prize sailing from Jamaica, although lacking her usual booty because there was not much left on that poor isle after the storm," said Captain Glover.

Isaak put down his feet and stood. "Jamaica, you say. Had they any prisoners on board?" His stomach clenched with fear Belladonna had been taken during the Spanish invasion, if she had survived the storm.

"None from Jamaica, but a few poor devils they had picked up from atolls after the storm."

"Much like your story, eh?" said Williams, casting a malevolent eye at Isaak.

Ignoring the jibe, Isaak said, "I would like to interview these men before we set sail again. I should like to see what they know of my own ship, the *Sabato*."

"The *Sabato*, you say?" said the man who was refilling their cups. All eyes shifted to him, and he explained apologetically as he backed carefully away from the scowling Glover. "so...so many ships pass through here, it has become our habit to pass along news from one to the other." He looked at Isaak for approval, "and there was a ship of that name that passed through here not long ago."

Isaak could not help himself and immediately grabbed the man's arm. "Where were they headed?"

The man freed his arm from Isaak's grasp and shrugged. "I do not know. They did not say." Despite his denial, he gave Isaak a meaningful look, which

Isaak interpreted as an invitation to be followed up later.

The thuds of boots, accompanied by the clanking of swords, announced the arrival of another pirate captain and crew. Captain Ross doffed his hat as he entered and managed to wink at Isaak before he took his tankard of grog from the server. "Ah, just what I need. We have worked up a mighty thirst after today's battle, am I right, men?"

The three men behind Ross gave their loud assent and demanded their grog in turn. The server escaped into the other room, promising to return with more refreshments.

"Well, well," said Williams, "better late than never, eh, Ross? Three of us have already delivered our quota. What have you to contribute?"

"Only the Viceroy's largest warship. With twenty-five guns ready and loaded." Ross took a large gulp of grog and smacked his lips.

"Any cargo?" asked Glover.

"Enough gunpowder and arms to capture a fort." He turned to Isaak, "Are you ready for the next part of the plan? We have just obtained all you need for your assault."

Chapter Twenty-Two: Belladonna

IN THE BAY OF TOBAGO, THE LEEWARD ISLANDS, The twenty-first of DECEMBER, 1614

After heading north from Curacao, the seas had been stormy, and the rise and fall of the ship among the waves had left Mariella and Moises retching in their cabin. They no longer enjoyed the same comfort and freedom from worry as they had on the *Sabato*, but Belladonna's gold had obtained decent quarters for them all on the Dutch ship. Faring better than her companions, Belladonna managed to go on deck for fresh air whenever there was a temporary lull. It had taken them longer than expected to reach the Leeward islands, their last stop before they began the ocean crossing to Amsterdam, which would take at least two months.

Belladonna and her companions ached to get off the ship and onto dry land before such a long journey, but the Captain did not want them to disembark, claiming it would delay their departure. Mariella convinced him to send them along with the cook to obtain better provisions for the ocean voyage, pointing out Belladonna's thinness as a consequence of the poor food to be found on board.

When they arrived on Tobago, Belladonna spotted her reflection in the glass of a darkened window. Her face had thinned to gauntness, for she had no stomach for the victuals aboard ship. Mariella fared no better, since seasickness had taken its toll on her appetite as well. Mariella managed to find yams and potatoes in the stores on the island, as well as guava and other fruits she recognized from Jamaica that could be cooked into tasty meals. Belladonna encouraged the cook to purchase dried fish and shellfish for a Christmas stew, and when their sacks were full, they returned to the ship, satisfied.

* * *

On Christmas day, God calmed the ocean, and the captain allowed the men to enjoy a quiet day and their holiday stew. Mariella had managed to find another lute-like instrument to strum as she sang songs of the sea. The captain watched them from the bridge but made no move to join them. He seemed preoccupied by ever-present storm clouds and kept his glass on the horizon, alert for stormy seas and high waves.

The lull persisted through the next day, and Belladonna was confronted by the captain as she took a walk around the deck.

"We have hardly had time to get acquainted thus far."

Belladonna wore one of Mariella's shawls, and she pulled it closer across her chest. "There is still time. How long will it take to reach Amsterdam?"

The captain looked up at the sky before answering, "If the wind holds, we should make it in nine weeks. If the clouds foretell a big storm, we might never arrive at all."

"Comforting words."

The captain moved closer, and his arms snaked around her back. "If it is comfort you want…"

Belladonna pressed her hands on his chest to free herself from his grip. "Nine weeks will give us plenty of time, so there is no need to rush, is there?"

A crack of thunder prevented him from taking the conversation further. Instead, he ordered her, "Go down below."

She managed to reach the stairway down to the hold as the sky flashed bright with lightning, and it began to pour. Peacefulness was at an end; they were in the path of a storm.

Chapter Twenty-Three: Isaak

IN THE BAY OF WESTERN HISPANIOLA, The twenty-first of DECEMBER, 1614

The next day, Olivante had not returned, and Ross urged them to set sail regardless, to put the final steps of their plan into action. Hendriksen seconded Ross's call to arms, declaring it unlikely the French captain could capture a Spanish ship and return with it in any useful condition.

Isaak was not ready to depart and reminded the other captains of the need to unload the cargo from the ship they had captured, and to make the necessary repairs so they could sail into the waters of Havana without raising suspicion. The others agreed to the logic of his argument, which bought Isaak a few more days to discover what he could about the destination of the *Sabato*. He had volunteered to take a small boat to lead an attack by land, hoping to later use the same boat as a means of escaping his newfound comrades during the pandemonium of battle. If the *Sabato* was nearby and he could discover its path, his escape would have a much greater chance of success.

After sending his men off to see to the unloading of the newly captured ship, Isaak lingered at the tavern, hoping to catch the server alone. However, the crews of newly arrived pirate ships with newly freed prisoners crowded into the tavern, ready to celebrate their victories over the Spanish.

It became evident there would be no chance to interview the server until very late, and Isaak wandered away from the tavern, taking the path deeper into the trees and away from humanity. Or so he thought, until he tripped over a pair of legs extending across the path.

"Hey, watch your step. Can ye not leave a fellow alone to enjoy a bit of privacy?"

Isaak bowed and stepped over the man's legs. "Not one to join the crowd, are you?"

The man took a long swig of his bottle and gave a satisfied burp. "I been here long enough to know I had enough of them. I doubt any of them captains will take ol' Flash here with them, so I will probably be 'enjoying' their company for a great deal longer."

His assertion perked Isaak's interest, and he seated himself next to the man. "You have been here a long time, you say? Seen many a ship pass through here, I will wager."

"I was dumped here over a year ago, after being liberated from one of them Spanish galleys. I thought to set sail again, and offered my services, but the only one who would take me up on my offer was that rogue of a French captain. I am not desperate enough to sail with *him*."

"And why is that?"

"He is a drunk and takes way too many chances. He takes a prize, but too often, it's at the expense of his crew. Those who come back missing a limb or two, or maybe not right in the head after being clunked doing battle. Captain Olivante is not one to grant extra coin to those who sacrifice an arm, a leg, or an eye. So, no thank you, I will stay right here, until the right ship comes along."

"Tell me, in all this time, has no good ship come through for you? Think of all these ships you have seen—perhaps the Dutch, or some other?"

"I am a good Englishman all said and done, and I will not sail on a Dutchman's ship nor another of those Frenchman."

"Have there been no others from some other strange land?"

The man brushed away stringy hair from his face, revealing his sunken grizzled cheeks and bloodshot eyes. "Hey, there was one such as that, just a few weeks ago. Came out of nowhere, they did, and an odd crew at that.

Some of them sported strange coverings on their head, and others had skin as dark as the earth. They were all right fellows and treated me to a nice dram of grog, plugging me for news of someone they were searching for."

Isaak's neck muscles tensed, and he massaged it to relieve the stiffness. "Did they say where they came from, or where they were headed?"

For the first time, the man pulled back and regarded Isaak through eyes narrowed with suspicion. "Why do you ask so many questions?"

Isaak slapped him on the back, causing the man to cough. "Testing your powers of observation, my friend. I am a captain in need of some crew, and as luck would have it, you have come across my path. I am getting a sense of what use you could provide, that is if you are interested in joining my crew."

The man lowered the bottle and peered more closely into Isaak's face. "Of course, I am interested. And there is none as observant as I am. I have won the prize many a time for spotting a first ship on the horizon."

"Well, besides your powers of observation, tell me of your perceptions. I may ask a man on deck what he thinks as well as what he sees. What were your perceptions of these strange men? Perhaps they are worth pursuit?"

The man laughed. "They said they had come from Jamaica and that they were bound for Curacao. But you would not hesitate to pursue that lot had you seen them. They took with them those women, the most beautiful women I had seen in these parts in a long time, and those women went with them without a peep."

Isaak felt a heat rising across his chest as he had little doubt that he had missed Belladonna and the Sabato by only a few days.

Chapter Twenty-Four: Isaak

*THE CARIBBEAN SEA, OUTSIDE CUBA, The twenty-third of
DECEMBER, 1614*

"Land, ho!"

True to his promise, Isaak's grizzled confidant from beneath the tree on Hispaniola, whose name was Hawkins, had called down from the crow's nest at the first sight of land. Isaak raised the spyglass and focused on a rough smudge of brown and green in the distance and then surveyed the seas to the east and west. No other sails in sight.

"Take her in, Brockton. I want to check on the boats and make sure they are ready to be launched." The burly first mate nodded and took Isaak's place beside the man at the wheel.

Isaak hoped luck was with them as much as the weather seemed to be. The sun was high and bright, and the wind gusted with enough strength to fill the sails and keep it sailing towards its destination. The waves were choppy but not overly high and would carry them towards shore, so they should not have to tax their strength with too much rowing.

Isaak had surreptitiously stocked one of the landing boats with extra food, water, and weapons, so it would be ready for him to make his escape from Cuba. It was a great distance to Curacao, but he hoped to find his ship, his crew, and Belladonna along the way. It had been frustrating to learn he had missed them at Hispaniola, but he was thankful to learn they were still alive and heading to Curacao, just as he had intended.

As they drew nearer to land, his doubts and worries grew. His chances of reaching Curacao from Cuba in a small ship were slim, but nevertheless, he was determined to make it, and if there was a God, he would appreciate His help to arrive there alive. The distance was great, but he had plotted his path and knew how to navigate by the stars. If he could avoid Spanish ships, ration his food and water, and stay on course, he could possibly make it. And if God smiled on him, perhaps the *Sabato* would find him on his way.

He ordered the men to lower the sails to slow their progress. He wanted to wait for the cover of darkness, even though they were to land on the southwestern side of the island, which was mostly unpopulated, filled with woods and swamps. He did not worry about the *Pelican.* If it was seen by a patrolling gunship, since it was flying the Spanish flag, it would be assumed by the Spanish to be one of their own and would not instigate a challenge.

As the current and the wind pulled them closer to Cuba, Isaak raised the spyglass and swept it across the horizon, searching for signs of the other ships. Though the light was fading, he could see no sign of them. They should wait until his fellow pirates appeared. His ship was to be a decoy, but he would not allow it to be a sacrificial offering. If the other ships did not appear, he would have his excuse to order the men to abort this mission and, instead, set sail for Curacao and be done with this perfidious band of pirates. The safety of Curacao should be more appealing to the crew than a suicide mission in Havana.

Various scenarios played through Isaak's head as the skies darkened into night. "Ship ahoy!" came Hawkin's voice from the crow's nest. Isaak raised the spyglass and tried to make out the flag and the bow of the ship, but it was still too far away. Friend or foe, he must be prepared for either scenario.

"Shut all the lights or keep them covered!" Isaak ordered. It was better to be as invisible as possible until he could identify the ship.

"Ship ahoy!" Hawkins called out again. He would not have called out the same ship twice; was it another? Isaak raised the spyglass and set its sights on the approaching ships. The moon had risen and illuminated the ship's prow as they crossed the sea. Extending his arm and the scope as far as possible, Isaak struggled to make out the defining details of the prow, then shifted to focus on their flags. Both ships flew the Spanish flag, and from what he could see of their prows, he could not be certain his fellow pirates had arrived.

Isaak instructed Brockton to take command, and, to keep to the southwest coast and avoid the other ships. The *Pelican* lowered the landing craft. Isaak and ten men climbed down into one boat while twelve men boarded the other. Armed with long swords or cutlasses with daggers and pistols sheathed in their belts. Gunpowder and loading pins dangled from pouches.

As they rowed towards shore, Isaak stood on the prow. Glancing back at the *Pelican*, he tracked its silhouette as it followed their path north along the coast.

The men kept quiet as they rowed, their eyes focused on land, their jaws stiff with tension. The gentle rhythmic sound of the oars splashing into the sea helped Isaak to focus his thoughts on the path ahead.

After studying the map of the island, he was confident they were landing due south of the fortress. Coves along the shore would lead them north, deep into the swamp, and would save them from a long, dangerous trek from the beach. Isaak did not know many of the men who rowed beside him, but their faces were rough and seasoned by the hot climate, and the strange caws of birds and animals in the brush did not seem to perturb them. The course to the cove was very dark, and though they could have used more light, Isaak kept the lanterns covered as an extra precaution. He could not imagine any human would see the light from the swamp, but he never underestimated his enemies.

He had supposed they would sail as far as they could through these waters, but the cove had narrowed, and as their oars began to scrape against rock, it became evident it had become too shallow to continue. Isaak whistled, signaling to the other boat to stop, and he and his men vaulted over its side, sloshing through the murky waters. They guided the boat towards the brush, where they pulled it onshore, folded its sails, and stashed its oars inside. After removing weapons, food, and water, they covered their boats with branches and large green fronds. Isaak had the men mark the nearest twisted tree with a knife so they could find it on their return.

The men gathered around Isaak, and using hand signals, he directed them forward. They proceeded cautiously, in silence, as the night faded into dawn.

Chapter Twenty-Five: Isaak

ON THE SOUTHWEST SIDE OF THE ISLAND OF CUBA, The twenty-seventh of DECEMBER, 1615

They progressed through the swamp, swatting at the mosquitoes attacking their sweating faces, muttering curses whenever something either crawled or slithered across their booted feet. The clicking of bats flying through the trees and the whacking of their cutlasses as they cut through the brush were the only sounds to accompany the noisy sloshing of their boots through the wet ground.

With the coming of the dawn and growing light, they were able to move faster through the brush. It had been a few hours since they had left the boats, and the end of the swamp should be near. The forest faded away to gnarled, thick trees populating fields of wild vegetation and scrub. As the ground became firmer beneath their feet, the sky was brightening with the ever-present sun. Isaak gave a low whistle, his signal for the men to stop and rest.

Gesturing without speaking became the norm out of necessity since Isaak feared there might be hidden sentries squatting in the area. They needed to ensure their attack would come as a surprise to the fort was the one key to success.

The men slaked their thirst and broke off pieces of dried food, shoving it into their mouths. Eyes met Isaak's, but they did not look away. They were an odd assortment of Dutch, native Indians, Moors, English, and Irish, bound by their common hatred for the Spanish. They were sizing him up as a leader and would follow him as long as his orders made sense. There was tension, as if they were a coiled serpent ready to spring. He must take care not to trigger their blood lust too soon, or they would rampage without direction.

Too many different languages would make conversation as a group unproductive. He must command them by signals, as he had until now.

It took another few hours before the sand-colored towers of *El Moro* could be seen in the distance. The men did not seem the worse for the journey and he whistled and pointed to their destination. Faces glistening with sweat, their eyes narrowed, for they were ready in anticipation of a battle.

A welcome breeze of cooler air signaled they had come closer to the fort, which overlooked the bay. From their current position on a nearby hilltop, the walls of the fort seemed massive, with towers commanding a crows-nest view of the sea. The fort was still under construction, and scaffolding masked half-built walls that would provide access into the fort.

The plan had been carefully mapped out before they had been set ashore. Their comrades were in position in the bay, waiting under their camouflage of Spanish flags. At nightfall, the workmen climbing up and down the scaffolding would be gone, and they would have only a few sentries to contend with. Facing the sea, the fort paid scant attention to its exposed land side.

Isaak was a cautious man. He would not place himself or his men in the belly of the beast unless he confirmed his allies would be ready to send their cannon shot at the fort as planned. He gestured to the Moor, instructing him in Arabic to creep up to the crest of the hill, to spy out the ships in the bay. The man nodded and disappeared into the scrub. The other men remained ignorant of Isaak's request and kept to their places, waiting for the order to attack.

It did not take long for his scout to return, but it was with unsettling news: the only ship in the bay of Havana was a French ship—Olivante's *Beau-Marais.*

Now Isaak understood why he had not appeared at the rendezvous on

Hispaniola as planned. As Captain Glover had predicted, Olivante must have been captured by the Spanish. Isaak's thoughts raced. Besides disarming the cannons, they had another task to perform now—to free Olivante and his crew, most likely imprisoned within the stockade. Once freed, they would add to his force and provide an advantage. He informed the other men about Olivante's capture. "We will have to split into two. One group will head to the stockade to free the prisoners, and the other will go to destroy the cannons."

It seemed like a good plan, and odds were it would work, but as his father, the rabbi, always warned, 'Man plans and God laughs.'

Chapter Twenty-Six: Isaak

*OUTSIDE EL MORO, AT THE PORT OF HAVANA, The
twenty-eighth of DECEMBER, 1614*

The hooting of the owls accompanied the fading light into darkness. Isaak and his men kept to the perimeter of trees below the fort, tense and ready to attack. He held back, waiting for his Moorish scout to return from scanning the horizon for sails. If there was still no sign of the other pirates, Isaak would make the decision on whether to attack.

Torches cast flickering shadows along the walls of *El Moro*. Through the spyglass, the steel helmet of a lone sentry was visible as he walked the perimeter of the walls. Isaak had been monitoring the sentries, noting their circuit took them to the scaffolding every twenty minutes. Timing was essential and had to be used to their advantage.

The Moor had returned. He held up two fingers. Two ships. Isaak was taking a gamble by supposing they were the same galleons he had spotted along the coast, and manned by his pirate comrades. Like Trojan horses, they would be entering the bay with Spanish flags flying. Once they increased their force by freeing Olivante's men, odds were they could disarm the guns and set fire to the fort, leaving the door open to Havana for the waiting pirates.

They crept closer to the edge of the trees, waiting until the sentry passed, ready to run to the scaffolding, climb it, and launch themselves over the side before the sentry returned. The minutes ticked by too slowly, and his hands were sweaty as they raised the spyglass to the walls once again.

At last, the helmet of the sentry had disappeared, and Isaak raised his arm. As soon as he dropped it, the men were off, scrambling up the incline. Isaak slammed the spyglass back into its place on his belt and raced after his men.

The scaffolding shook at their onslaught but held their weight. Launching themselves over the side, they descended into the fort. Isaak gathered his men in the shadows as he quickly surveyed the area.

Lights and laughter came from the open window of a long, low building off to one side. The barracks. Another lighted building must be alongside it, which must be the officers' quarters. The largest one must house the fort's commander.

Along the walls facing the bay, massive cannons were silhouetted against the dark blue sky. Opposite the barracks was a low building with a few doors and windows crisscrossed with bars. Only one radiated a dim light.

The stockade would be there. Isaak pointed out their target, and the men raised their weapons. Isaak signaled to the Moor to block the barracks door. It would not be strong enough to hold the soldiers in for very long, but it would buy them some time, possibly enough to free Olivante and his men.

The courtyard was empty and silent. They clung to the shadows as they advanced. Isaak gestured to one group to climb up to the cannons. They were the gunners and knew how to dismantle the firing mechanism without revealing their work. Once they were done, if the Spanish attempted to fire these cannons, they would explode.

The door to the stockade creaked loudly as Isaak pushed it open. They heard the guard curse as he ambled over, and they marked his path by the trail of his flickering candle. As soon as the guard stepped out the open door, a hand went over his mouth and pushed him inside. Once they rendered him senseless, they confiscated his candle to light their way to the cells.

They encountered no other guards on their way, and when they reached the cell doors, they understood why. The cells were empty.

Olivante and his men were not prisoners of the Spanish, but their guests.

After trussing the lone guard and depositing him in a cell, Isaak exited the stockade, leading his men towards the commander's quarters.

They moved in the shadows, careful not to make any noise. As they passed the barracks, where they had barred the door, it rattled as someone inside tried to exit. More shouting and banging followed.

There was no time to lose. Isaak and his men ran and took the guards lounging outside the commander's door by surprise. Leaving his men to fight off more soldiers arriving to defend their commander, Isaak skidded across the polished stone floors to the double doors at the end of the hall. He kicked them open and found himself in the commander's dining room.

The room was bright with the light of torches, their flames dancing in the reflections of the glassware and silver plate spread across the table. Isaak's intrusion may have startled them but occasioned no panic. A pistol barrel was shortly pressed against his side, forcing him to lower his swords.

Olivante prodded him forward, closer to the table. "Welcome, *mon ami*, we were expecting you."

"Olivante," said Isaak, as two soldiers relieved him of his weapons, "I had not expected *this*."

Suddenly, one of the officers slammed his fist down, causing the plate and silver to clatter and wine to spill.

"Kasai!"

With that one word, Isaak feared he was doomed.

Chapter Twenty-Seven: Isaak

EL MORO, AT THE PORT OF HAVANA, The twenty-eighth of DECEMBER, 1614

The officer pointed at Isaak. "Captain Kasai, the devil take him! He and his Berber demons boarded our ship and set it aflame."

The fort's commander, a thickset man of middle age, stood and made a short bow to Isaak. "The notorious Captain Kasai, a pleasure to make your acquaintance. It is not every day a man with a bounty of a million pesetas on his head walks into my parlor. A gift from heaven, eh?"

Isaak inclined his head. "Well, you must give credit to your friend Olivante."

Olivante, pressing the pistol harder into him, said, "You are very gracious, *mon capitan*. I had warned my friends here to expect you, and I was hoping I should have the personal pleasure of killing you. But even I have heard of the great Captain Kasai. I did not expect him to be *you* and to be taken so easily."

"When I sailed with the Berbers, I never had to worry about treachery from one of my partners."

Olivante snickered. "Not treachery, but loyalty. To my country, to France. We are now the allies of Spain and at war with England."

Isaak raised his eyebrows. "Friends one day, enemies the next. How fortuitous for you, as I expect our Spanish friends have rewarded you handsomely for your 'alliance."

"That is not your concern."

The clanging of swords and cries of pain from the open door distracted them. The Moor and the Indian were fighting five helmeted guards. Swords clanged as they dispatched each of them, and panting, they turned towards Isaak, their swords raised and ready to strike.

"Tell them to put down their arms, *Kasai*," ordered Olivante, emphasizing the name.

Isaak, assessing the chances of overcoming Olivante's pistol, sighed and signaled to his men. Their swords clattered to the floor.

The officers rose from the table, and the commander waved them towards the open door. "Go and see to the rest of this rabble. Then, ready the cannon. We can expect more company and must be prepared to greet them."

The Commander's orders were fortunate. If Isaak's gunners had done their job, once the Spanish tried to fire their cannons, they would explode, providing the distraction he needed to get free.

"Commander, I demand the honor of killing him. It should be my reward," said Olivante.

"Kill him?" said the Commander, leaving his place at the table and circling Isaak as if taking his measure, "kill the golden goose? This man is worth more than a thousand ducats! Does a man such as he deserve to die here, in a half-built fort on a mosquito-infested island! No! He deserves a glorious execution, perhaps in an auto-da-fe' in the Plaza del Arraba in Madrid."

"Ah, but first, you have to get me to Spain."

"Easily done. Captain Olivante's ship is quite swift, and none of your pirate friends will attack a French ship. It is unlikely they have heard of Olivante's change of heart."

Olivante smiled, "I shall be sure you are quite comfortable on my ship, *mon capitan* Kasai." He looked at the other two men. "And perhaps we will tie these two to the mouth of the cannons before firing them."

The Commander chuckled. "Excellent idea. They will rejoin their friends in pieces, eh?" He gestured to the soldiers who held the two men. The Moor cursed in Arabic and spat at Olivante, who ignored him.

Their exit was delayed by a succession of booms, which made the room shake and the timbers in the ceiling fall. The cannons had been fired!

Isaak jumped away from Olivante and launched himself across the table, pulling a knife from his belt as he grabbed the commander by his collar. He held the blade to the Spaniard's throat. "Tell them to back off, or I will carve my smile across your neck."

The Commander called out the order, and the soldiers stopped their advance.

"Drop the pistol, Olivante."

Before Olivante could react, there was another loud boom, and the ceiling collapsed. Olivante was caught in the rubble.

A soldier burst in shouting, "We are being attacked!"

Smoke was billowing into the room from all sides. Isaak still held his knife to the Commander's throat, and he called out to his two men. Those soldiers who had not fallen in the explosion, had already run away. His men promptly picked up their swords and followed Isaak as he dragged the Commander along through the smoke.

Outside, pandemonium reigned. Helmeted soldiers raced from one side to the other, putting out flames. Bodies were strewn across the walls and poked out of the debris. His men ran to join their comrades in fighting off the remaining Spanish and Olivante's crew.

Isaak still held the fort's commander but felt hampered by him. Maneuvering their way through the fighting, Isaak steered the Commander towards the stockade. Isaak did not remove the knife from the Spaniard's throat until he had pushed the Spaniard inside and bolted the door.

"How dare you?" shouted the Commander, "Let me out of here this instant!"

His cries were ignored by Isaak and everyone else, who were either fighting, running, or falling. Cannon fire from the ships in the bay whistled through the air above their heads and shattered windows and walls and shook the ground. Isaak climbed up to the top of the wall to get a better view of the bay.

Three Spanish galleons now flew the pirate flag, and Isaak recognized one of them as the *Pelican*. Olivante's ship, the *Beau-Marais* rested at its anchor, unmolested. Isaak gripped the edge of the walls. The *Beau-Marais* would be perfect to take him away from here, to Curacao and to Belladonna.

115

Chapter Twenty-Eight: Isaak

*EL MORO, AT THE PORT OF HAVANA, The twenty-eighth of
DECEMBER, 1614*

Isaak had to get out of the fort amid the clashing swords, spreading fires, choking smoke, and the onslaught of cannon balls. He looked around for the best means of escape. His eyes traveled up to the rooftops, some of them in flames, to the walkway along the walls. Damaged on the bay side where the cannons had exploded, the walkway was untouched along most of the perimeter. If he could follow the walkway back to the scaffolding, he could exit the fort just as he had entered it.

The explosion left piles of stones and bricks which made climbing up to the walkway easy. Crouching, Isaak scurried away from the fighting, taking shelter whenever a whistling noise above his head warned of an approaching cannonball.

"KASAI!" a shout came from below him. It was the same officer who had first pointed him out. Waving his sword, the officer was up on the walkway and running towards Isaak.

No good to run, for this man was in a frenzy and launched himself at Isaak, his rapier swirling and slicing the air a hairsbreadth from Isaak's ear. As if demonically possessed, the officer thrust the point of the sword at him again and again, and Isaak barely managed to parry his thrusts. With only a short sword, Isaak was at a disadvantage against the speed and reach of the Spaniard's longer rapier. His mind racing for a way to improve his odds,

Isaak swung to one side, but not fast enough for the rapier to take a slice of his cheek.

Emboldened by the sight of Isaak's blood, the officer flashed a triumphant grin as he slashed the rapier back and forth, making a whooshing sound. He kept advancing, forcing Isaak backward in retreat. Isaak could not risk taking his eyes off his opponent for even a second to see what was behind him. He felt trapped, until he caught sight of the Moor creeping up behind the Spaniard. Just before the Moor reached the Spaniard, the officer lunged at Isaak. As Isaak raised his sword to parry the Spaniard's thrust, he reached back to gain leverage from the wall, but nothing was there.

Isaak felt himself falling, his body hitting tree branch after tree branch, until his head hit something, and the world suddenly went black.

* * *

Isaak awoke with terrible nausea. He wanted to vomit, but raising his head sent a surge of pain, so he fell flat on his back again.

"He *is* alive."

Isaak moaned as he recognized the voice. "Commander, am I dreaming, or did someone release you?"

"I am glad you still have your wits," said the Commander, "it would be so disappointing if the blow to your head reduced you to an imbecile. You must be at your best, at full strength, when I present the formidable Kasai for execution. It must be impressive, eh?"

Isaak pressed a hand across his eyes to shade them from the light, which made his head hurt more. He took a deep breath, hoping it would keep him from vomiting. "I understand your dilemma. But please, illuminate me. Commander, I assumed you were secured in the stockade. How has everything changed?"

"The Commander and you, *mon ami*, owe your rescue to me."

Isaak moaned before adding, "I thought we had seen the last of you, Olivante, when the ceiling fell in on you."

"I am like that cat, you know, the one with nine lives. It will take much more to get rid of Olivante." Olivante lifted a booted leg and put it right beside Isaak's face. Leaning in closer, the Frenchman added, "And you are now aboard the *Beau-Marais*, as my guest."

"No doubt in your very best cabin." Isaak felt gingerly around his head and was surprised when his fingers encountered a bandage.

"You see, Captain Kasai, we are taking very good care of you. You are in the doctor's quarters, and here you shall stay until you regain your strength. Then we shall have some quiet little talks, where you will share so many things with me. Like where your pirate friends like to hide when they are not attacking Spanish ships, for instance."

Isaak hated the smugness of the Commander's voice, and he moaned again, because he did not have the strength to rage.

The Commander patted Isaak's leg. "Rest up now and regain your strength. It is quite a long ride back to Spain; we will have plenty of time to talk."

Olivante leaned over once more. Isaak shut his eyes, gagging at the smell of the Frenchman's wine-scented breath. The Frenchman laughed and passed him a clay pot, into which Isaak promptly vomited. When he was finished, Isaak wiped his mouth and managed to croak for water.

Immediately cool liquid was passing down his throat. Isaak relished its coldness and asked for more. After drinking his fill, Isaak dropped his head down again, carefully minding the sore part.

"Get well, *mon ami,* I will not enjoy tormenting a man who is already half dead."

Chapter Twenty-Nine: Isaak

ABOARD THE BEAU-MARAIS, THE CARIBBEAN SEA, The second of JANUARY, 1615

Isaak awoke suddenly, finding himself in darkness. He was on the floor against a wall, and the floor was at an angle, so he assumed he was on the high seas. Likely in the midst of a storm. He raised himself on his elbows, but the pain in his head made him swoon, and darkness enveloped him.

When he opened his eyes again, it was lighter, and he was back on the bunk. Light blazed into his eyes, and he raised his arm to block it.

"Ah, the prince has awoken."

Isaak moaned, recognizing Olivante's voice. "Do you hear me, Captain Isaak, or maybe you prefer to be called Kasai?"

Isaak tried to speak, but his throat was dry and all he could manage to say was, "Water."

His request was granted, and not only did his voice feel restored, but so did his wits.

Olivante leaned over, his face very close to Isaak's. "Now, *mon ami*, you have rested long enough. It is time for us to have a little talk."

"Tell me first, how many days have passed since we left Havana?"

"A reasonable question to begin our discussion. Five days."

"We have not gotten very far from Havana, then," Isaak tried again to raise himself, but he was too weak and lay back again.

Olivante corrected him. "We had to make a detour south to avoid our friends Captain Glover and Williams. But now, we are headed northwest, and if the wind holds, we should see the coast of Spain in eight to ten weeks from now."

Isaak raised his hand to block the lantern light. "Perhaps we can have our discussion with the light a little bit lower? I like to be able to see the face of the man I am talking to."

The light was lowered, and now Isaak could make out Olivante, dirty but not drunk, with a rough-looking crewman behind him.

"Although you angered me when you interfered with that girl on Tortuga, I am a benevolent man, and I have forgiven you. Besides, you are worth a pot of gold. But before I turn you over to my Spanish friends, there are many questions I would like to put to you."

"Things change so quickly in the world. How long can your alliance with the Spanish last? One never knows when an ally becomes an enemy."

Isaak was stalling as much as he could to avoid being questioned by Olivante. Isaak kept many secrets; of pirate lairs in the Mediterranean, of signals used among allies, and of caves used to store booty. Olivante could learn much from him, and Isaak did not have enough strength to endure the Frenchman's interrogation.

How could he distract Olivante from prying the secrets of the Jewish Brethren out of him? A greedy man would desire more than secrets. Though his head ached, Isaak suddenly remembered Captain Ross's little sideline.

"*Ecouté*, I was not able to collect my share of the loot, and my men are not happy. Whether my country is at war or peace, if the Spanish are willing to give me 100,000 pieces of eight for you, *eh bien*, they will have you." Olivante smoothed a lock of hair that had fallen out of place.

"What if I have more to offer?" Isaak said, lifting himself onto his elbows.

Olivante's nostrils flared, and he gave a bark of a laugh. "More than 100,000 pieces of eight? What could you have to match that?"

"Emeralds, worth a fortune. A very lucrative endeavor I engaged in with Captain Ross. We captured one or two Spanish ships fresh from Cartagena, with a cache of emeralds collected specially for the Spanish Queen. We would capture the ships, store some of the loot on an uninhabited little island in the Caymans, then head back to Tortuga to meet the others. I can direct you to the place where I was to meet Captain Ross. We were to retrieve the emeralds after the attack on *El Moro*. If Ross survived, he will be sailing towards the Caymans now."

Did Olivante buy his story? Olivante's eyes ignited as he asked, "And you are certain you know where to find these emeralds?"

"I put my stash there myself before we set off for Havana. I suppose Ross did the same with his. He may already be there, or he may be dead. It would be a short detour, and once you have the emeralds, why, perhaps, there should be no need to go to Spain."

If he sounded confident and unafraid, then perhaps Olivante would buy his story. His goal was to delay the voyage to Spain as long as possible and remain in these waters for the *Sabato* to find him. Once the *Beau-Marais* sailed into the great ocean, he would be out of reach and at Olivante's mercy. A trip to the Caymans was his best chance.

Olivante snapped his fingers. "I will take you at your word, since you are bargaining for your life. My men will prefer to be rewarded now instead of having to keep you alive for so many weeks until we get to Spain." He pushed the crewman towards the door. "Go now and tell the navigator to change our course. We sail to the Caymans."

Before he departed, he glared at Isaak and issued a warning. "You had better hope Ross has not gotten there before us."

Chapter Thirty: Isaak

ABOARD THE BEAU-MARAIS, THE CARIBBEAN SEA, The third of JANUARY, 1615

The French ship was quiet, and the men had been allotted extra grog for the first days of the New Year. Isaak felt well enough to come out of his bunk and was given permission to take the air above deck. Wind filled the sails, and the helmsmen navigated with ease across relatively calm seas.

The men lolled about on deck, ignoring Isaak, who had to hold on to the side rails as he walked. He squinted into the sun blazing across the deck from the starboard side and surmised they were sailing due south. There was no sign of land on either side, and therefore, they must have passed Hispaniola and probably had another two-day sail to the Cayman Islands. No sign of a ship on the horizon. Isaak could only hope one would appear before they reached the Caymans, or he would have to come up with a very clever ruse to escape Olivante's wrath.

Isaak breathed in the sea air deeply after so many days inside, while he considered his possibilities upon reaching their destination. The Caymans were composed of multiple islands, had no permanent settlers, but was regularly visited by pirates, refugees, and runaway soldiers for short periods of time. The larger island was where the taverns and traders were found, while the small uninhabited islands would be the likely spot for pirates to hide their spoils.

Rumors that the islands were home to creatures with sharp teeth and man-eating appetites, or 'caymene,' made escaping into the swampy interior seem fraught with danger. If the emeralds were not found, Isaak represented the only reward for his crew, so Olivante could not afford to let him get away. Being fooled would make Olivante even angrier, and he would make certain Isaak would not be in any condition to ever attempt an escape.

Until they reached the islands, Isaak had to regain his strength and plan his escape carefully.

* * *

THE BAY OF A SMALL ISLAND IN THE CAYMANS, The fifth of JANUARY, 1615

Desperately, Isaak looked towards the horizon for a sign of the *Sabato*. No sails were in sight as they lowered the long boats and rowed towards shore.

He had devised a rough plan, but it had a slim chance of succeeding. Olivante's leadership over his men always hung by a thread. They suffered from his brutality and drunkenness, and Isaak had picked up the crew's grumblings on his recent excursions above deck. Not only Isaak, but Olivante stood to lose if there was no treasure on the island. Isaak's opportunity would be to turn the crew against Olivante, unseating him as their leader.

It was still early, but the sun blazed with heat, while the wind was cooling, and the air was fresh with the smell of the sea. Isaak pulled at the oars and cursed along with the men at Olivante, who posed on the prow, his beaked nose pointed towards their destination.

As Isaak trudged through the wet sand of the beach, his spirits revived when he glanced over his shoulder and saw the faintest hint of a white sail on the horizon. A glimmer of hope to lighten his dim prospects. He estimated the ship would be close enough by nightfall, so if he could stall Olivante and his men until then, his chances of survival would improve significantly. It would be best if he led Olivante and his men deeper into the interior so that they would not see the ship until it was too late.

Olivante waited for him, hand on hip, before a sandy path leading through thick foliage. "Well, *mon Capitan,* it seems as if someone has been here most recently. Are we headed in the right direction?"

"Follow me," said Isaak, brushing by him, steeling himself to move forward. The captain assigned a man alongside Isaak to slash at vines and fronds that crossed their path. The ground became drier, the vegetation thornier, as the chirping and clicking of bugs and bats grew stronger, assailing his ears.

There was a sudden scream from behind, and they all turned to see the coils of a large snake winding itself around the neck of the first mate, Legrand. His comrades sliced at the snake with their blades until the coils loosened, and Legrand fell to his knees, spitting curses. Eyes still bulging, he massaged his reddened neck. Now, they moved forward with their swords drawn and in hand.

The path became muddier and softer, with more creatures crawling and crunching underfoot. Then abruptly, it turned and came to hedge oftall grass. Making their way through it, the men cursed at their feet sinking, insects buzzing in their ears, and trees blocking the sunlight. They all stopped when the path came to an end at a forest of closely knit trees, with no sign of where to go forward.

Isaak leaned over, studying the ground for a sign of another potential route. Olivante jerked him up by his hair, tilting Isaak's head back and putting a blade to his throat.

"Are you certain of where you are taking us? Do not play games with me, *mon capitan,* for these men, they are losing patience."

Luckily, Isaak spotted a notch carved into the banyan tree ahead of them. "There is a mark for us to follow."

Olivante lowered the knife, and Isaak cleared the brush beside the tree to reveal another path. This path led them through waist-high reeds surrounded by foul-smelling swamp water. Red eyes blinked at them from the rushes, a reminder they were surrounded by the crocodile-like caymenes that proliferated these islands. He had no idea where this path might lead, but acted as if he recognized his surroundings when they emerged from the swamp into a rock-strewn field. Another banyan tree with the notched mark seemed to point into anotherthicket bordering an open field. Somehow, he had led them into what might be a pirate hideaway.

Pirates liked to boast of their conquests but were notoriously secretive about where they stored their loot. Hiding places were usually found on uninhabited islands like this one, deep in the island's interior, but easily accessible for a quick departure. They would be sure to leave signs to find their way to their stash and back out again. Two trees marked one path.

With no idea of whether they were about to find gold or nothing at all, Isaak still needed to plan for every possible reaction from Olivante and his crew. If they ended up empty-handed, Olivante and his men would certainly turn their wrath on him. In either case, whether they found gold or not, Olivante's desire to kill Isaak might overcome his greed for the reward.

There was movement in the trees. Perhaps it was the wind rippling through the grasses and thrashing the branches. Isaac squinted into the thick foliage, but it was impossible to make out whether there were men or beasts moving among them.

"We should search here," said Isaak, figuring they would be more likely to find something in this flat area versus the marsh. He hoped to make his exit while they searched.

Olivante barked orders at the men, and they spread out, eyes on the ground. Isaak caught more movement in the brush out of the corner of his eye. He headed in that direction. If there was someone there, whether friend or foe, it would be best to confront them head-on.

Olivante must have thought Isaak was trying to run off and started after him. A flash and then a boom, and Isaak instinctively fell to the ground and rolled away. When he raised his head, he could have cried out in happiness.

"Captain Isaak, fancy meeting you here," said Captain Ross, lowering his pistol.

Isaak stood and brushed the dirt from his breeches. Then he spotted Olivante lying face down, his blood spreading through the dirt.

Chapter Thirty-One: Isaak

"I cannot lie; I am glad to see you," said Isaak as more of Ross's men came out of the woods with pistols in hand. He gestured towards Olivante, "I have been his prisoner since *El Moro*."

"He deserved to die in the dirt, the traitor," said Captain Ross, prodding Olivante's body with his boot. "He sold our secrets to the Spanish and then came here to steal from us."

"The Commander informed me that France is now allied with Spain and at war with England. If we had not sabotaged the cannons, Olivante would have been joining the Commander over a toast to our deaths."

Ross's men had gathered Olivante's crew before their captain's corpse. They looked at Ross expectantly. "What say you, Isaak? Should we leave them here to fend for themselves?"

Though Ross seemed to like him, Isaak was planning his exit from this pirate brotherhood and hoped the *Beau-Marais* would be his means. "I believe they suffer from a lack of leadership. Let them back aboard the *Beau-Marais* under my command, and I will redeem them."

Captain Ross replaced the pistol in his belt. He tilted his head back and regarded Isaak through narrowed eyes. "I suppose I shall have to honor your request. God knows you have earned a reward for what you did at *El Moro*."

"How did Glover and Williams fare at Havana?"

Captain Ross smiled, "Once the fort was overtaken, and all the ships in the bay were ours, we sent the Commander to the governor with a message. The governor promptly capitulated and paid our fee for sparing the city."

"I am glad you were able to put the Commander to good use."

Stepping over Olivante's body, Isaak joined the crew of the French ship opposite Ross's men. "If you do not mind, I would like to take these men and be on my way."

Captain Ross's crew still had their pistols raised and pointed at them. "Where are you headed?"

Isaak grinned. "Curacao. I have learned that a very beautiful lady whom I thought I had lost awaits me there. Once I find her, we will head home—back to Venice, where we both belong."

Captain Ross nodded, and his men lowered their guns. "I wish you well."

Pulling a small pouch from his doublet, he tossed it to Isaak. "Here. Your share of our venture. It may help you keep those French rogues happy."

Isaak gave the English captain a mock salute. He did not have to open the pouch to know what it contained. Emeralds.

* * *

With the markings on the trees to guide him, Isaak was able to lead his Frenchmen back to the beach before nightfall. They did not challenge him as they rowed back to the *Beau-Marais* but eyed him from under scowling brows as they bent to the oars. He stood facing them in the prow, as he would not dare to turn his back on them.

As soon as they were back on the *Beau-Marais*, Isaak called 'all hands-on-deck' before they weighed anchor.

"You sailed under a drunken tyrant, and I have heard your grumblings. If you are to sail with me, it must be under different terms. I will lead, but I will not dictate. Should any man challenge me, he will have to prove himself worthy of such a challenge. He must know how to navigate through storms, how to run circles around galleons, and how to fill your pockets with more riches than I can." Isaak took the pouch out of his doublet. "With Captain Olivante, you have not prospered, but I will bring the winds of change to improve your fortunes." He pulled one of the emeralds out of the pouch. A collective gasp came from the gathered men. They were mesmerized by the emeralds, which sparkled with reflected torchlight. "Behold! The finest yield of the emerald crop from Cartagena. It is ours, and each one is worth 300,000 pieces of eight, which shall be divided, according to the Articles, among you."

The display seemed to accomplish his goal of dazzling the crew, and Isaak returned the emeralds to his pouch. Leaning forward from the rail of the bridge, he called out to the men, "Now I ask you, are you with me?"

Unanimous cries of "*Oui!*" brought a satisfied smile to his lips. He gave the order to weigh anchor and directed the navigator to plot their course for Curacao.

Chapter Thirty-Two: Isaak

Isaak had arrived in Curacao filled with expectations of finding a ship allied with the Brethren or gaining some news of Belladonna. Though Curacao was once a Spanish colony, its population was predominantly native, and its newest settlers were pirates of many nationalities. Ships of all sorts entered and exited the port and frequented the many coves and inlets along its shore.

The *Beau-Marais* had found a cove with adequate depth to sail into the interior of the island. Isaak ordered the ship to lay anchor and encouraged the crew to go ashore to find food, drink, and entertainment. He was glad to be free of the French crew, the very worst he had ever commanded, comprised of a mix of cutthroats, thieves, and drunks, like their former captain.

There were so many coves, all safe harbors for ships flying different flags. Sometimes, a cove or inlet led to the port's town, others to a cluster of huts and shacks, a tavern or bathhouse, and occasionally, a smithy. Most businesses, from the transfer of goods to trading in cash, to buying provisions and hiring a crew, were conducted at the tavern. Then there was gambling, drinking, and wenching, where the crew of each ship could spend their share of their loot and forget they would soon be setting sail again.

Isaak made his way from one tavern to the other, drinking with crews from each ship moored in nearly every cove. He was careful not to reveal too much, as he gossiped and shared tales with the hope of catching news of a Dutch ship which might be one of the Brethren's, or tales of a beautiful woman who might be Belladonna.

As he clasped the rough wooden cup filled with rum, he could close his eyes and imagine the last time he held Belladonna in his arms. He had bid her farewell, promising a short return. *Man plans, and God laughs.* His father's favorite saying had proved to be more prophetic than he had ever imagined. How long his journey had become!

The island was not as he expected. As rough and raw as Tortuga, it was another pirate haven and no place for a lady such as Belladonna. Though the waters to the south, near the town, were clear and filled with bright-colored fish, it was hot and arid, the vegetation dominated by rough thorny plants and bushes. On the north side, the waves crashed furiously into rocky inlets and were too wild for human settlement.

If he could not find any means to the Brethren, he was unsure of what to do. He had no desire to continue to be the captain of the late Olivante's surly crew, but it would not be easy to rid himself of them. The Frenchmen needed a leader, and it seemed he had won them over for the time being, to follow him, but under their own conditions. He would be their captain, but in a sense, he was also their captive. Not a good formula for survival.

Isaak looked around the tavern. The hour was late for supper and too early for serious carousing, so it was relatively empty. He despaired of discovering a Dutch ship sailing for the East India Company or manned by Dutch pirates, who would likely be allied with the Brethren.

A thick hand fell across his shoulder. "There you are, *mon capitan.* We have been looking for you," said Legrand, a thick-headed thug easily angered and eager to throw his fists into his fellow man.

Isaak swiveled to face him. Legrand had not come alone; three other grumbling and bad-tempered crewmen were with him. "Well, you have found me at last. Now, to what do I owe this honor?"

"We want more gold. Let us go capture more ships. More ships, more gold. You are our captain, so you must come," said Legrand, his nostrils flaring along with his temper.

"What, have you spent all that I gave you from the sale of the emeralds?" Isaak asked in mock horror, knowing full well that these men had been drunk for more than a fortnight, and their share of the emeralds must have paid for it.

The other men looked down at their feet, but Legrand raised a fist. "Not your business. You are our Captain. Your job is to help us get more gold."

"I see," said Isaak, wrapping his own hand around the raised fist and forcing it down. For all his bravado and bulk, Legrand was not as strong as he looked. "And you are here representing the crew?"

Again, eyes dropped, and the shuffling of feet. Isaak took it to mean the rest of the crew was still carousing. "Well, then, round up the crew and get the cook to bring in the provisions, and then we can be on our way."

The other men looked at Legrand, confused. Legrand shook his head. "No, you must round up the crew; they will listen to you. You are the captain."

Isaak surmised the man had used up all his cards and was not up to a continued conversation. With a wave of his hand, he dismissed them, "Tomorrow. We will talk of this then."

This caused Legrand to raise his fist once again and snarl, "No, you come now, with us."

Isaak stood and faced Legrand eye to eye. Raising his own fist, Isaak glared at the ruffian. In a threatening tone, he conveyed his message, "I am the captain, and you do not command me, understand?"

As he supposed, Legrand backed down. "Tomorrow, then."

Isaak resumed his seat and took up his cup of rum, waving off his crewmen. They stomped out. As soon as they were gone, Isaak began to plan. He had to find either another crew, or another ship. He glanced around the tavern. There was a group of sailing men in the corner, not as ragged as the others, speaking and not shouting, keeping to themselves. Maybe it was time to make some new friends.

Isaak carried over a bottle of rum and stood in front of these men. "May I buy you all a drink?"

The four men at the table turned towards their comrade with the large hat, who responded on their behalf. "What for?"

Isaak spoke in Spanish although he was certain they had been listening in to his conversation in French. "I find I am in need of friends to share a drink, and you seem to be the only ones here sitting upright at present."

"Are you celebrating something?" asked Big Hat, in the same language, although from his accent, Isaak surmised he was not Spanish.

"Just enjoying the spoils of battle, friends. My ship is resting in the cove, my men in taverns and brothels scattered across this fair land, so it leaves me with some time and coin to indulge myself." Isaak offered the bottle to the man sitting opposite Big Hat. After a quick glance at Big Hat, who gave a short nod, the man accepted it.

Big Hat invited him to pull up a chair and poured each of his comrades a drink. "You are a lucky fellow then if you still have a ship and have come here equipped with spoils. From where do you hail?"

Isaak sighed, "Originally, I came to the Caribbean from Venice after a woman. A long story."

"A long story that sounds interesting, considering it involves a woman," said a fellow with a bandana tied around his neck. Upon closer look, it covered a nasty scar, one which may have been made by a rope.

"First, let me test my assumption. I take it you are not Spanish?"

"We are not. Our crew is from many places, but English is the language we usually speak."

"Then we should have much in common," said Isaak in that language, "and I can share my story."

As the four men leaned in, Isaak did.

Chapter Thirty-Three: Isaak

CURACAO, The twenty-fifth of JANUARY, 1615

The four men in the tavern were English pirates whose ship was damaged from an encounter with two Spanish warships during a raid on Port of Spain. After more than two months moored in a nearby cove, the repairs were nearly complete. They were interested in the attack on Havana, and were grateful for being apprised of the new alliance between the French and Spanish.

"A crew of thieves and murderers and Frenchmen to boot, eh? You will need to be looking over your shoulder day and night with that lot," said Penner, the man with the big hat. "A few allies aboard are what you need."

Isaak subdued his eagerness at the hint they would be interested in joining his crew.

"Amen to that, good friend. Now, if only I could find such men…" he said as he raised his eyebrows and opened his eyes wide, "why, if I could find men such as you to sail with me, my worries would be over."

The three other Englishmen looked to Penner, who said, "That is very generous of you to invite us aboard, but we are committed to another, so to speak." Quick looks passed between the four men before Penner added, "However, there is an interesting coincidence I see happening here. You have got a fast ship ready and able to sail, but a crew you cannot rely upon. And we have got a ready crew, but a ship we do not have faith in can take us far out to sea. It presents possibilities, yes?"

Isaak stroked his chin and said, "Gentlemen, when opportunity presents itself, it is up to each of us to seize it. I suggest we do not hesitate so we both benefit. The only thing standing in our way is that cursed French crew. Perhaps if we put our heads together, we can find a way to be rid of them?"

Penner smiled and shook Isaak's hand. "Now, this is the way our partnership begins. Where it takes us, God only knows."

Penner was the ship's navigator, Oliver was the head gunner, Silver was the first mate, and Jones was the second mate. Their captain, Thomas Bloodwell, had been sorely wounded and was being tended to on shore. The men had little faith he would recover any time soon.

"A switch, that would be ideal. Put the failing crew aboard the faulty ship and the stellar crew on the stalwart ship," said Isaak.

Oliver, the gunner, raised his cup in salute. "Cheers! Looking forward to blasting cannon again."

Jones added, "At the Spanish, of course."

They all raised their glasses and downed the contents of their cups. All but Isaak. He could not afford to indulge in drink. He needed to keep his wits about him. It seemed he had found allies, but he was always suspicious. It had kept him alive so far.

They arranged to meet again in two days. By then, the Englishmen would be ready, and Isaak would have enough time to engage the interest of the French pirates in another ship to loot. He expected the opportunity to attack a captainless ship loaded with precious cargo would appeal to his greedy crew. Besides the prospect of lining their pockets, there was the added pleasure of tossing Englishmen over the side of their own ship.

He had once considered Curacao as a possible refuge if they had to leave Jamaica. Abandoned by the Spanish and now a stronghold of the Dutch, it could be a safe place to settle. New Christians, once-secret Jews, had emigrated to the island from Spain, hoping to live openly as Jews as far from the reach of the Inquisition as possible. With the growing dominance of Dutch ships, they were bound to attract more Jewish settlers, and Isaak had hoped he and Belladonna could become part of their community.

The Brethren had made it known to all its captains that there were Jews on

Curacao who could be counted on for support. Isaak still had a few emeralds left to sell, and there was a man in the Jewish quarter who specialized in the trade of fine stones. If there was news to be shared for the Brethren and by the Jewish pirates of the Caribbean, it would be delivered through the Jewish quarter.

Isaak had been directed to a strip of houses backed onto a high hill overlooking the bay. He stopped in front of a yellow building next to another house painted in sky blue. This must be the place, though it did not look like a shop, but a residence. Isaak stepped inside, blinded momentarily by the bright sun. A voice called out from the shop's shadowy interior, "Just a moment."

As his eyes adjusted, a grey-haired man appeared, like a specter. "May I help you?"

Pulling out the pouch of emeralds from his doublet, he spilled a few into his palm. "What can you give me for these?"

Taking one, Grey-hair went to the window and held it up to the light. "Mmm, these are of excellent quality. I would say they are Cartagena emeralds, no?"

Isaak shook the emeralds in his hand. "Could be. But you know I did not come here to discuss their provenance, but their worth. How much can you give me for them?"

"How many?"

Isaak opened the man's hand and poured the stones into his palm. The grey-haired man glanced from the stones to Isaak's face. "Seven stones. Five hundred pieces of eight for each."

Isaak grinned. "They are worth far more. But I will accept it. Consider the difference as my personal donation to the Jews of Curacao."

"Where are you from, sir? You speak Spanish but I warrant you are not from Spain."

"Allow me to introduce myself; I am Isaak, son of Rabbi Leone di Modena of the Republic of Venice. You may not know me by the name of my birth, but rather by what name I took on. Kasai." Isaak gave a short bow.

"Kasai?" the word came out with a gasp. "You are Captain Kasai?" A hand shot out and clutched Isaak's arm. "You rescued my brother outside of Algeciras, from death as a galley slave at the oars of a Spanish warship. You must come with me, inside. I am Julio—Yehuda Mendez. I am one of the leaders of the community here. Come, I am honored to help you."

Isaak followed him down a shadowy corridor and up a flight of stairs to the upper floors. In contrast to the shop below, the room at the top of the stairs was filled with light and air. There was a large table and a cabinet, both of dark old wood, and a few stools and chairs scattered around the table. The windows were long and wide open, and seated beside one of them was a middle-aged woman sewing, dressed in a mix of fabrics, her head covered in a matching wrap.

"Devorah, we have a most important guest," Isaak's host called out to the woman, who Isaak supposed was his wife. "Please give him some food, something to drink."

The woman rose and began to open drawers and cupboards, arranging fruits and nuts on a tray. Yehuda Mendez assured Isaak that all food and wine he would be served were prepared according to kosher laws.

Isaak ate the food offered him, and both Yehuda and his wife peppered him with questions about how and why he had come to Curacao. When Isaak finished his bread and his story, he leaned back and asked his host about the Jews of Curacao: *how big is the community here? Have you been here long?*

Every time Yehuda opened his mouth to speak, Devorah would cut him off, asking to allow her to tell their story her way. "Our families, like many others here, were in Recife, but escaped before the Inquisition arrived. Curacao was settled by other New Christians, who considered it a haven because it was too small, too overrun with natives to captivate the interests of Spain."

Yehuda was able to cut in when his wife took a breath. "That was ten years ago. Jews have been arriving here ever since, so our community is growing. We should soon have enough permanent Jewish settlers here to warrant the construction of a synagogue."

Isaak took out his pouch and upended the emeralds onto the table. He pushed a few emeralds to Yehuda. "Please keep a few of these emeralds to finance your efforts for the community. I need only a few hundred ducats to support me until I can find my ship."

"Your ship?"

"It is called the *Sabato*, and I was separated from it in the storm. It is why I sought you out in case you might have seen or heard of it in the past few weeks. If I cannot find it, I will have to risk sailing to Europe in a French ship, with my choice of either the roguish French or the untrustworthy English for a crew."

Chapter Thirty-Four: Isaak

CURACAO, The twenty-fifth of JANUARY, 1615

Yehuda Mendez crinkled his forehead. "There was a ship here not many weeks ago, claiming to be allied with the Brethren. I do not recall the name of the ship, but I clearly remember their passenger. A beautiful woman spoke to me in Spanish and said she had come from Jamaica. She came to me with the most extraordinary necklace to sell."

Isaak's pulse quickened, for he had no doubt the woman described was Belladonna. Of course, she would have escaped the storm and the Spanish with her leather sack of jewels. "Thank you, Yehuda, you have given me hope. That woman seems to be the person I have been searching for. Do you have any further knowledge of the woman or where she was bound?"

Yehuda shook his head. "I do not know that ship's destination, but the woman wanted to sell the necklace to pay for her passage aboard another ship, a Dutch ship sailing to Amsterdam."

Isaak's tense shoulders relaxed. Amsterdam! Belladonna was gone, but at least he knew she would be safe. If the ship that had brought her to Curacao was the *Sabato*, perhaps it was still in these waters?

His thoughts were interrupted by a tinkling of the bell, signaling a new visitor at the shop. Yehuda excused himself to see to his customer, while Devorah hovered with food and offers of more wine, which Isaak refused.

Time to return to the French devils. He would wait for Yehuda before departing since he still had a few more questions for his host.

Many footsteps thudding on the stairs meant Yehuda was not alone. Instinctively, Isaak's hand went to the dagger at his belt. He glanced about for a potential route for a quick escape. Isaak was ready to bolt when Yehuda reappeared with a younger man by his side. Isaak released a deep breath, for the young man looked so much like Devorah. There could be no doubt he was her son.

"A blessing of welcome on you," said the young man, "I am Menachem, son of Yehuda. My father told me he had a visitor and that you were seeking information about a ship that was here recently. I am honored to meet you, Captain."

From the Menachem's deferential bow, Isaak surmised Yehuda had revealed Isaak's identity as Kasai.

"I am pleased to meet you, Menachem. I am seeking information about a ship, the *Sabato,* *a* brigantine that is part of the fleet of the Jewish Brethren. Your father seems to recall the ship being here but remembers most distinctly its woman passenger. Had you come across either the ship or its passenger?"

The young man stroked his chin, which, unlike his father's, was clean-shaven. "I trade in hemp and ropes, and I am often called in to help provision ships when they make their repairs. I had visited the ship of which you speak, which had much need for new rope after losses during a great storm near Jamaica. I do not recall the name of the ship, but it had a most diverse crew, speaking many different languages. They did seem to be men of a better caliber than many of the ships which sail without a country's flag and are frequently moored here."

"They refitted their ship, and they let off their passengers. Did you get any sense of the ship's next destination or what they were after?"

"Come, boy, you must have overheard something," said his father as he gestured for both Isaak and Menachem to be seated.

Menachem knitted his brows. "I did overhear an argument between the woman and the first mate. She wanted to stay on board and go with them to continue searching for something. He was trying to convince her that she would just be an impediment to them, and that they needed her to go to Amsterdam to the Brethren. I did not hear for what they were searching, and what support they needed. But the woman must have lost the argument, because the next day, she and the other two passengers disembarked."

"Others?"

"Another woman, dark-haired, and a young boy, who looked to be her son. I am not certain they all traveled together, but they did leave the first ship together."

"Did you see them board another ship, then?"

Menachem nodded. "There was a Dutch merchant ship bound for home, and I believe they boarded it. I have not seen them here since, so they must have gone."

"And the first ship, do you have any guesses as to where it was bound?"

Menachem shrugged. "They never mentioned their destination the whole time I worked on their riggings. Wait, one thing they asked me, about the Leeward Islands, and whether they were controlled by the Spanish, or open to pirates."

"And what did you say?"

Menachem glanced at his father, who nodded. "I mentioned the most welcoming island for ships unaffiliated with Spain was Tobago. It is an island nobody seems to care about and is only populated by a few natives."

Menachem seemed to have more knowledge of the ships and crews than his father, so Isaak thought to ask him about the Englishmen he had recently encountered.

Menachem's mouth twisted as if he had eaten something unpleasant at the mention of the four Englishmen. "That lot! I suppose they spoke of some treasure they could lead you to if only you would put your trust in them. Or maybe they have volunteered to bring you a new crew?"

"It sounds like what they had offered me," said Isaak, explaining how he ended up with a French crew who he did not trust.

Yehuda cleared his throat to add his voice, "I do not know much about these Englishman, but it may be your interests are aligned. They are after your ship for certain, but they still hate the Spanish. If your French crew knows you are Kasai and that there is a bounty on your head, if I had to choose between them, I would choose the English devils over the French ones."

Menachem was stroking his chin with one eyebrow raised. "I have another thought. I can raise some more men to join you and your Englishmen, which would give you additional allies aboard ship."

Time to go. Isaak drank down the last of the wine and rose, asking Menachem, "How long will it take?"

Menachem grinned. "We shall be ready when you need us."

"Wait," said Devorah, "this will be dangerous, and you must have protection," she waved her hands at her husband, "Yehuda, you must give them an amulet."

Yehuda did not hesitate or challenge his wife's direction, but held up a hand, signaling they were to wait as he left them. When he returned not long after, he held a small parchment scroll, which he unrolled before Isaak.

A golden menorah had been painted on the parchment, which in turn was overprinted with Hebrew words. Isaak recognized it from his father's books. The words were protective incantations from the Kabbalah, which promised the bearer God's oversight and a greater likelihood of survival during battle. A life-saving memento.

"Thank you, " Isaak said, taking the scroll from Yehuda gently.

Chapter Thirty-Five: Isaak

CURACAO, IN A CAVE, NEAR THE BEAU-MARAIS, The seventh of FEBRUARY 1615

From the sale of the emeralds, Isaak had enough gold to keep his crew motivated to do his bidding. Isaak nailed one gold piece to the main mast, offering to double it to the first man who sighted their next ship to be captured. With big grins, elbows, and chucks at each other, each man pointed to the doubloon and swore they would be the one to win it.

Isaak had met twice with the Englishmen, who swore they were ready to put their plan in motion. Isaak's job was to get the Frenchmen off the ship and into the tavern. Let them drink, curse, laugh, and boast with the Englishmen until they were in the best of spirits, but not at their sharpest. By twelve o'clock, Isaak should prod them to return to the ship, leading them straight into the trap being set by the Englishmen.

Menachem was true to his word. Several young men were eager to sail with Captain Kasai. They were hiding among the caves near the cove where the ship was anchored, ready to advance at the signal.

Getting the French crew off the ship was not difficult. Isaak offered to pay for their drinks, an offer none of them could refuse. The Frenchmen drank with him, but Isaak felt prickles at the back of his neck as he caught the glances between Legrand and Benoit and the snickers which appeared on each of their lips.

At half past midnight, Isaak rose and stretched. "Time to get back to the ship for the night. We want to be off in the morning, yes?"

Again, the shifting eyes, the secret smiles, as the crew rose from their places, making loud grunts and yells. Isaak noted which men were drunk and who had remained sober since an attack would likely come from the latter. He suspected Benoit and Legrand had their own plan for him—to keep him on board the *Beau-Marais* as prisoner, not captain.

They followed the path towards the cove. The Englishmen should be in position at the point where the path abruptly turns, before a large clearing near the cove. Because the brush was filled with prickly bushes and brambles, Menachem's friends were hidden among the large rocks by the shore. Isaak kept one hand on his sword, his ears open and his eyes shifting from right to left, wary of an attack from any side.

They were nearing the turn of the path, and Isaak was ready when the Englishmen pounced. Benoit, Legrand, and several others had pulled out their weapons, but the path was dark, and they did not know it as well as the Englishmen. The Englishmen had increased their force with several natives brandishing clubs. Wine had dulled most of the French crew, and they had little chance against the natives, who came at them swinging and shrieking. Those Frenchmen who managed to avoid getting smashed turned and ran. Benoit was already dead, face down in the dirt, while Legrand was stabbing at Penner with his rapier, with Penner parrying his every thrust.

Oliver and Jones had dispatched many of the French crew and stood by Penner until he managed to score a final thrust at Legrand, who fell, clutching a wound at his chest. The English force lowered their weapons when it was evident there was no more resistance.

"It takes a good Englishman to put those French rogues in their proper place," said Penner, panting from the exertion of the fight. "Now let us get on to the ship, so we can throw the rest of those Frenchies over the side."

Isaak saluted the fallen men with his sword. "And so ends an association that never should have been."

As they proceeded towards the cove, Isaak's spirits rose, for the most difficult part of the plan was accomplished. Menachem would be joining their party at any moment, and they would soon be in control of the *Beau-Marais*.

The four Englishmen and their equal company of natives sheathed their knives and swords and wiped their faces as they descended down the rock-strewn path towards the water. As they reached the boats, a torch flared to life, revealing Menachem and six other men blocking their way.

Immediately, swords were out in both parties.

"Who goes there?"

Isaak turned around to face Penner. "They are my men."

"They are not French. They are local. I recognize that one," Jones said, pointing to Menachem with his sword.

"I have invited them to join our crew. You know we cannot manage a ship like the *Beau-Marais* with only a few men. I would rather sail with these men than any others on board." Isaak gestured with his thumb to the *Beau-Marais*.

"We will not sail with them," said Penner, raising his sword and taking a menacing step forward.

"And why is that?" asked Isaak, folding his arms and standing between Menachem's men and the Englishmen.

"Because they are Jews, you fool. You cannot trust them," Oliver chimed in.

"Oh?" Isaak raised his eyebrows. "Have you known many Jews? I have heard there have not been Jews in England for six hundred years. How do you come to know so much about them?"

"We know of them. The Spanish brought them over here, calling themselves 'New Christians.' But I tell you, they are no Christians. They have strange rites, and I will not sail with them. They bring bad luck."

Isaak touched his hat in a mocking salute. "Well, then, gentlemen, our association is at an end. I will go my way with my new crew, and you shall find yourselves another ship."

Penner snarled, "Rogue, you choose to sail with Jews rather than good Englishmen?"

In an instant, Isaak had his sword tip under Penner's chin. "Any day.

First, because I do not consider you and your friends good Englishmen, and second, since I am myself a Jew, I would consider it very bad luck for you to sail with *me*. Now, drop your sword and go, and I will not run you through."

Isaak pressed the sword deeper into Penner's flesh, enough to draw a trickle of blood. Penner lowered his sword and took a step back, as if accepting defeat. But it was a feint, and dodging round Isaak, he charged at Menachem with his sword, calling for his men to attack.

Isaak went to his knees and slid forward under Penner's charge, parrying his blade and tripping him. Penner fell and scrambled to recover his sword and resume his attack, but Isaak was on him, his sword clanging against Penner's. He caught sight of Menachem and his men fighting off the other three Englishmen. The natives held back, refusing to defend the English or get into the fray, and soon it was over. The four Englishmen lay in the dirt, clutching at their wounds.

"I wish you death, Captain," gasped Penner. "and I am certain my wish will come true. If the French do not get you, the Spanish will. Besides, you cannot sail that ship without us."

Isaak saluted him. "I have been known to cheat both death and the Spanish several times. I appreciate your offer, but I am afraid this is goodbye, Penner, and I wish you a speedy recovery from your wounds. We will trust our luck and the wind to help us sail the *Beau-Marais*."

A tramping of footsteps coming from the path. Someone was approaching. Isaak lifted his sword, but once the moonlight illuminated the faces of the new arrivals, Isaak lowered it.

"Your luck has just improved, Captain Isaak. We have found you at last," said Hernando.

Isaak rushed forward to embrace Hernando, but a sudden pain in his hip caused him to double over. Pulling aside his doublet revealed a red stain spreading across his shirt, along one side. One of Penner's thrusts must have penetrated, and in the frenzy of battle, he had not noticed it.

Hernando did. "Captain, you are hurt?"

"No matter, it is not deep, but it does bleed."

Hernando tore the bottom of his own shirt and insisted Isaak allow him to wind it around his middle. "We must show this wound to Ahmad. He has the talent to fix it, and you will be back to fighting soon."

It did not take much for Isaak and his large party of men to secure the *Beau-Marais*. The night rang with French curses, as the handful of sleeping Frenchmen onboard were flung into the cool waters. As Hernando took the helm and steered the ship out of the cove, the sky was fading from deep black to dusky blue. Only a few more hours until dawn.

"We go now, to the *Sabato*."

"Your timing, Hernando, is always perfect. Tell me, how did you know where to find me?" Isaak said. His wound ached, and he had to lean against the rail.

Hernando shrugged, but his eyes were merry. "No big secret, Captain Isaak. We come to Curacao, and where do we go, but straight to Yehuda. Well, we were looking for Menachem, because we needed more repairs, but we did not find him, so, of course, we go to Yehuda. And then his wife tells us this story about a great captain who had come to Curacao, looking for a ship called the *Sabato*. And here we are! Yehuda, he told us where you were and where Menachem and his men were going to meet you, and so again, here we are. No big secret, eh?"

Isaak smiled. "It was lucky you returned. God willing, let us hope such luck continues to follow us. We could certainly use it." He waited a few minutes before asking, "Now, what about Belladonna? Yehuda tells me a woman came to him to sell some magnificent jewels. Belladonna?"

Hernando nodded enthusiastically. "Yes, we bring her here on the *Sabato* from Hispaniola. She wants to go look for you, but we heard you were taken by a Spanish ship. We are determined to find you, which means taking many Spanish ships, and for this, we cannot have a woman with us. We take her here to Curacao, where there would be a Dutch ship sailing to Amsterdam. We tell her to go to the Brethren there, in case the ship you were being held in had already sailed for Spain."

If Belladonna had returned to the Old World, he had no doubt she would have to return to Venice. Isaak stared at the horizon as if he could see beyond it, across the great seas to the Aegean and the waters of the lagoon, back to Venice. The city still tugged at his heartstrings, no matter how long he had been away from it, and it would certainly affect Belladonna in the same way.

Hernando had steered the *Beau-Marais* into another cove. This one was bordered by thick banyan trees and large outcrops of rock. Ahead, the silhouette of his ship, the *Sabato,* stood out against the dusky blue of the sky.

The main mast was missing, and the *Sabato* seemed to lean on the starboard side. He turned to Hernando with eyebrows raised. "How bad?"

Hernando sighed and explained. "We got into a tangle with a Spanish ship we thought you could be on. We did not do so well, but we did escape and managed to come here, where we could make repairs without the Spanish breathing down our necks."

Isaak repeated his question, adding, "Can she sail?"

Hernando tightened his grip on the rail. "Not for a while. Maybe not ever. The main mast, she snaps in two pieces, and one piece go into the sea."

Isaak nodded as a new realization was dawning. "God has sent us the *Beau-Marais.* On this ship, we shall sail for home."

Chapter Thirty-Six: Belladonna

CROSSING THE GREAT OCEAN, The seventh of FEBRUARY, 1615

They had already been at sea for more than a week, and Belladonna suspected she would not be able to fend off the Dutch Captain any longer. That night, she came with Mariella to the Captain's cabin wearing masks. They had fashioned them from scraps of lace torn from their most tattered skirts. The storms and choppy seas had kept the captain occupied for most of the voyage, but there were days when the skies were clear, and the ship sailed on smooth waters, and the captain and his men seemed to leer at them more and more.

Mariella retreated to the cabin, barricading the door, but Belladonna recognized they needed a better strategy. "There are still many days to this journey, and the men want to be entertained. They are under the captain's orders and must be respectful of us as long as he orders them to do so. Therefore, we must keep the captain happy."

Mariella's eyes widened. "You cannot mean we are to seduce him?"

Belladonna smiled and patted Mariella's hand. "In the way Judith entertained Holofernes. We will engage the captain, entertain him, and ensure he has a deep, restful sleep. Unlike Holofernes, he shall keep his head."

Mariella smiled back, and Belladonna continued, "We shall engage him with flirtations and ply him with wine laced with a small amount of poppy oil. Then you shall lull him with the softest ballads and the most haunting music. We will creep out after he sleeps, and he will remember only a most enjoyable evening."

"Where did you get the poppy oil?"

"On Tobago, from the Moor who traded in medicines and herbs, remember?" Belladonna added, "I am glad you were able to convince the captain we had to go ashore."

First, the captain's eyebrows rose when he saw their masks, and then his white teeth flashed amidst his beard, and he opened his door wide to admit them. The table was laid with silver goblets, and Belladonna made note of the knives, which she decided they should take with them after they had put the captain to sleep.

"We are here to celebrate Carnevale!" Belladonna announced.

Mariella began playing a lively Spanish tune, and Belladonna danced. The captain fell into his chair and clapped in time to the music. Belladonna spun and laughed and soon fell down breathless. When the captain reached for her, Mariella immediately filled a goblet with wine and placed it in the captain's outstretched hands.

"A toast!" she ordered, "while Belladonna regains her breath, you must make a toast for our celebration."

The captain stood and raised his glass. "To the lovely ladies who bring joy to a long journey."

"And a tired captain," Belladonna murmured to herself as the captain downed the wine in a few gulps. Belladonna hastened to refill his cup, adding a few drops of poppy, as Mariella took up her guitar and began to sing her choice of a lullaby.

Chapter Thirty-Seven: Isaak

SOMEWHERE IN THE CARIBBEAN, NORTH OF CURACAO
The fifteenth of FEBRUARY, 1615

Isaak leaned against the rail for support before raising the spyglass. Though there was a brisk wind blowing through his hair and filling the sails, he felt uncomfortably hot. He swiped at the sweat beading his forehead and grasped at the rail for support as a wave of dizziness overtook him. As he did, a sharp ache reminded him to be careful not to put pressure on his side. The wound had not healed properly despite Ahmad's immediate cauterization and careful ministrations. It was swollen and tender and continued to ooze, which Isaak was certain was not a good sign, but he did not want to derail their progress towards home. He feared every day spent in these lawless waters, they were at great risk of an attack by English, Spanish, or pirates.

He raised the spyglass and peered first across the prow and then to starboard. Nothing but blue sea and sky. No ships or land. He exhaled deeply and put down the glass. Why was it so hot? Closing his eyes, Isaak raised his face to the wind, letting it cool the sweat. When he opened his eyes, the horizon seemed to be tilting, and a wave of nausea overwhelmed him before all turned to black.

Isaak awoke feeling cold, his body shivering. He was no longer on the bridge, but in his own cabin, which was dimly lit by a few candles. He heard voices nearby and shook his head from side to side to clear his muddled ears.

"Look, he is awake!" Hernando's voice.

"A good sign." The solemn tones of Ahmad's words frightened him.

He opened his mouth to speak but could not get a word out.

"He needs water," said Ahmad.

Rough hands lifted his head tenderly, and cool water trickled into his mouth and his parched throat.

Another hand, cool and smooth, was on his forehead. "The fever is gone. Another good sign."

Ahmad's hand and pronouncement were comforting.

"How long have I been here?" Isaak managed to croak.

Hernando cleared his throat, annoying Isaak with his delay in answering. "Several days.

Now, how are you feeling?"

"My head pounds like the beat of a galley drum, but I can pray to God once again for restoring my soul to me," said Isaak. Silently, he recited the short prayer his father had taught him to say every morning upon waking.

"It is right to pray to Allah to restore your soul after such a fever. You collapsed suddenly on the bridge, and we feared… but it seems Allah was not ready to take you away from us yet," Ahmad pointed to Isaak's wounded side. "Though that wound was not deep, it turned dangerous as bad humor around that island infested it and brought infection. I have given you all my most potent remedies, but to regain your strength, you must rest and have proper nourishment."

Isaak sighed, "Well, the voyage to Amsterdam should give me ample time to rest as long as we do not encounter any pirate ships."

He caught a quick look from Ahmad to Hernando. Hernando treated Isaak with a wide grin. "So true, my Captain. But one little suggestion. With your permission, we propose to sail directly to Venice."

Isaak's eyebrows rose, along with his concern. "Why is that?"

Ahmad, patting his hand, gave him an answer that thinly veiled his concern and made Isaak realize his collapse was not a minor setback. "You need to rest, and your full recovery may take longer than expected. Though the cut did not go deep, it went deep enough to pierce an organ. The organ has leaked more bad humor into your body, and there may be more medicines and care needed. Your father has the most knowledge in such matters and has studied the books of the great physician Ibn Said. Therefore, we feel it would be best if your care was supervised by him. Hence, I recommend going directly to Venice."

Isaak exhaled. He barely had the strength to lift his head, much less challenge their recommendation. His eyelids felt very, very heavy, and he just wanted to close them and sleep. So, he did.

When he awoke later, there was a strong shaft of light breaking up the dark shadows of his cabin. The ache in his head had subsided, and tentatively, he tried to lift it from the pillow. There was no pain, so he became bolder and tried to lift his upper body to rest on his elbows, but a sharp pain in his side forced him to collapse flat on his back again. He took a few deep breaths and was conscious of great thirst. He was alone in the cabin, and if Hernando and Ahmad were on deck, they would be unlikely to hear him if he called out.

He turned his head, and there was salvation at hand. A clay cup he usually used for water. If he could sit up and stretch out his arm, it would be his. *If he could sit up.* This time, he lifted his head and tilted himself to his unwounded side, propping himself on one elbow. No dizziness, no pain, but the cup was on the other side of him, the same side as his wound. He could not stretch out his arm, or he would resurrect the pain. Could he manage to swing his legs out and onto the floor and attempt to stand? He decided to try but first had to get himself to a seated position before he could attempt to rise. He put all the strength he had into pushing up from his elbow but could not manage it. He lay back down and closed his eyes. He had never felt this helpless before.

He did not want to return to Venice like this.

The bunk shook, and Isaak was slammed against the wall, feeling a jolt of pain. Hernando flung open the door. "Why have you changed course so suddenly?" Isaak challenged him.

"Sails on the horizon, many sails. We are not far from the French island of Martinique. Our best chance of escaping notice is near a French island, raising a French flag, no?"

"A sound suggestion, Hernando, I thank you. One more request."

Isaak pointed to the cup of water, and quickly, Hernando was at his side, slaking his thirst. After drinking his fill and satisfied with Hernando's strategy, Isaak gave in once again to his fatigue and was asleep in an instant.

Chapter Thirty-Eight: Isaak

OUTSIDE MARTINIQUE, IN THE CARIBBEAN, The sixteenth of FEBRUARY, 1615

"There is not much on this island, but it does have what we need—fresh water, fruit, and goats for milk and meat," said Ahmad to Isaak, who still lay flat on his back in the bunk. His head had begun to ache again, and when he tried to rise, he was struck with dizziness.

Ahmad placed another cool hand on Isaak's forehead and then handed him the clay cup, half filled with liquid. "I fear your fever is rising again. We have not been able to free your body of the bad humor which threatens it. Here, you must drink this. I was able to obtain willow bark from the island. It will dissipate the fever. When I return, we shall see if there is an improvement. Now rest."

Isaak drank the willow bark, then lay back and closed his eyes. The bobbing of the ship on the soft waves lulled him to a peaceful sleepiness. If only they could be left alone to pursue their journey without threat of attack. But the odds were against that—the Spanish fleet would be prowling to mete out retribution for the attack on Havana, and the pirates would attack just for the sheer opportunity to obtain more booty. He exhaled and shifted his body on the bunk. He must regain his strength; he must be ready for the next attack. In the meantime, he would sleep.

He dreamed of Jamaica, of palm fronds shifting in the wind, of the hodgepodge of colors and languages and cargo being loaded onto waiting ships. Belladonna's face rose like the moon in a world of darkness, shining its bright beauty like a beacon to guide him home. In his dream, he was aboard an undamaged *Sabato*, ready to sail with the masts intact and its sails billowing with wind. He took the helm himself and steered towards the bright light, which flashed between the moon or the oval of Belladonna's face. He felt the swells of the sea beneath his feet, lifting the ship and pushing it forward. But no matter how high the swell or how fast the ship traveled through wave after wave, their goal never seemed to grow closer and remained remote on the horizon. A sudden jolt and the wheel beneath his hands was spinning out of control. It was too fast for him to grab, and the horizon tilted, and he heard the crack of the mast. He raised his arms to protect himself, and as its shadow fell across him, he screamed.

"Captain!" Isaak opened his eyes to Hernando, who crouched beside him. "You cried out. Have you great pain?"

Hernando held a sea sponge that dripped, and Isaak felt the tingle of cold wetness on his forehead.

"No, it was not real pain that wrenched that cry from me, but the phantom terrors of a dream." Isaak raised his head, but Hernando firmly pressed Isaak's shoulders to keep him supine.

"Not yet, Captain. You must rest."

Isaak could feel the rocking of the ship. "Have we set sail?"

Hernando nodded. "At dawn. It is still early, but the wind and weather were fair, and we thought to take advantage of it. We sail north and then east across the great ocean."

Isaak nodded. "Very good. But Hernando, you cannot keep me in this bunk forever. I must move my arms and legs to regain my abilities."

"Very soon, Captain, I promise. Ahmad must first see to your wound, and then he says you will be on your way to recovery."

Isaak did not like the sound of that. "What does he plan to do?"

Hernando looked away. "I shall not speak for him. You know Ahmad has the knowledge and training from Moorish physicians. Rest now, and he will come soon and tell you all you wish to know."

There was little for Isaak to do but follow Hernando's advice. From the gentle rocking, he surmised they were still in the Caribbean and had not entered the rougher great sea that stretched from the New World to the Old. If Ahmad wished to perform some surgery upon him, it would have to be within the day, since he would not want to conduct such a procedure with the ship tilting more than necessary. It was best to rest now and preserve his strength for the surgery, which he assumed would involve much risk and great pain.

Isaak was awakened by a gentle shake and Ahmad's voice. "Isaak, it is time to awaken. I must drain the wound so the bad blood does not build up inside of you and damage your organs further."

"I am awake, but I cannot say I am looking forward to your ministrations," said Isaak in an attempt to sound more positive than he felt. The dread of pain and the fear of death filled him so effectively that he could not even attempt to turn his head in Ahmad's direction.

"Lift his head and help him to drink," Ahmad instructed Hernando. Isaak took heart that Ahmad did not have other strong men beside him to hold him down. Perhaps the procedure would not be as dreadful as he anticipated. He drank the cool liquid, which tingled on his lips and tongue. "What is it?"

"A derivative of poppy seed, which will relax you and make you feel no pain."

Isaak nodded. "I have seen it in my father's *Book of Medicines* from the great Ibn Said. He, too, has used it to subdue pain."

Ahmad put a hand on Isaak's chest. "We will give you enough to put you into a twilight sleep, which will dull your senses so you will not feel anything as I cut into your wound. I will use a thin reed of bamboo to drain the bad blood out, and then I will clean it and cauterize it again. If my efforts are successful, you shall improve and soon heal."

Ahmad's voice was growing distant, and Isaak felt as if he was growing lighter and drifting above Ahmad and Hernando's heads. Hernando was drawing back the blanket, then his shirt and finally removing the bandage around his wound. He felt nothing as Ahmad's fingers pinched the oozing, puckered gash, nor did Isaak feel the slice of the gleaming knife into the tender flesh or the insertion of the thin bamboo into the opening he had made. As if in a dream, a black viscous stream poured out, a river of blood and vileness which Hernando directed, like a demigod, to flow into a clay basin.

Isaak felt a loosening, as if a pressuring vise on his insides had been unlatched. There was still no pain, only the revulsion at the vile fluids draining from his body. When it seemed as if the flow was ebbing, Hernando removed the dirty basin, soaked the sponge in another, and gently applied it around the perimeter of the wound. After removing the bamboo, Ahmad covered the open wound with a clean white cloth. Red dots of blood were forming rapidly into blots on the white. Hernando pressed the cloth to the wound, and after wiping the knife's blade clean, Ahmad held it to the flame. He kept it there until its edges glowed red, and then in a quick swipe, pushed aside the white cloth and pressed the hot blade to the wound.

Isaak heard a sizzle and smelled the odor of burning flesh but still did not feel any pain. Ahmad regarded his work and leaned back, giving Hernando the opportunity to see it as well. Isaak looked over their shoulders from above. The skin had been seared and puckered once more over the smaller gash Ahmad had made. There were no more red spots of leaking blood, nor the yellow of pus, or the black oily substance that had infested him. Hernando widened his eyes when Ahmad removed a hunk of old bread from a pouch popped it into his mouth, and began to chew. *Had the operation made Ahmad hungry?*

Isaak felt as surprised as Hernando by Ahmad's next act. Though he chewed for some time, his throat did not seem to swallow the masticated bread. Instead, Ahmad spit the chewed bread into the palm of his hand. After dipping a finger into the mess, Ahmad spread it completely over the newly pink puckered flesh of Isaak's wound.

"It is finished. I will bandage you now, and you will rest. You must be feeling very sleepy by now," said Ahmad to him.

Strangely, Isaak suddenly felt very heavy, and his body no longer seemed to float, but to sink. His side now had begun to throb, but he had already allowed himself to succumb to the heaviness of his eyelids and sleep.

II

The Old World

Chapter Thirty-Nine: Belladonna

AMSTERDAM, The twenty-first of MARCH, 1615

By the time the ship arrived at its dock, the three passengers were already on deck, their belongings in hand. As soon as the gangplank was put in place, the two women stunned the captain by giving him an appreciative hug before scurrying to shore, making certain to disappear from view by mingling with the crowd.

Belladonna secured Mariella's hand and ordered her to do the same with Moises.

"You must stay close," Belladonna warned as she navigated their way through throngs of seaman, officials, porters, and merchants eager to meet the arriving ships. There was a tavern Isaak had mentioned, and she assumed it would be frequented by the Brethren. Therefore, it was her destination.

As soon as they had cleared the crowds by the docks, Belladonna singled out a middle-aged man wearing a modest but spotless ruff who had paused to light his cheroot pipe. Approaching him with her two companions trailing behind, she asked, "Please, sir, can you direct me to the Golden Goose?"

The man raised his eyebrows, looking the three of them up and down. He removed his pipe to answer. "That is a tavern not known to be frequented by ladies."

"It is where we were told to find news of our husbands," said Belladonna, lying easily, "they are employed by the Dutch East India Company, and we were told to go there to receive word of when we are to sail to the New World."

The eyebrows settled down, and the man nodded. "You were well informed. The tavern is frequented by the men of the Dutch East India Company." He leaned over and pointed ahead with his pipe towards a busy street lined with shops. "Walk to the end of those shops and turn to your left. You will see the sign swinging above your heads."

Mariella gave him a courtesy.

He nodded at them absently and turned his attention back to his pipe.

The Golden Goose appeared to have seen better days. Its interior had sunk into a dim brownness from the clouds of smoke that stained the windows and the walls. Belladonna had not anticipated so much smoke. It hung like a halo above many a patron's head and collected like a great rain cloud beneath the low ceiling. Mariella and Moises could not stop coughing, and she debated which would be more hazardous– inhaling the smoke inside or encountering ruffians outside.

There was a great deal of murmuring as the trio made their way towards the barman. The man and the woman behind the bar sneered at them while filling their patrons' cups.

Belladonna took a deep breath and readied herself for an unpleasant encounter. She had done enough work for the Brethren in the past and knew their pass-phrases. But she did not know who to approach, and her instinct was that the couple who ran the Golden Goose were not the ones.

Turning away from the bar, she quickly took stock of the patrons, looking for a familiar face. Then, at last, she found one. A large man in a black velvet doublet and matching hat. A small mustache, pointy beard. He looked prosperous like most of the other patrons. Dutch merchants all looked the same, but this man had a large bulbous nose it would be difficult to forget.

She saw a flicker of recognition in his eyes, but he did not gesture to her or provide any acknowledgment he knew her. From his behavior, it was clear to her that the Golden Goose was no longer a place to connect with members of the Brethren.

"Let us go; there is nothing for us here." She put a hand on both of her companion's shoulders to urge them forward. Eagerly, they hurried out and took deep breaths in the cool open air. They stood before the tavern, watching horses and people pass by, at a loss of which way to turn. "Go to Holger's coffeehouse just over there," said the large man, who appeared beside her, pointing.

In a voice so low she could barely catch his words, he muttered, "I will meet you there shortly."

He tipped his hat to her and strode off in the opposite direction. "This way," she said to her companions. At last, they were making some progress.

The coffeehouse was a sharp contrast to the smoky, dismal tavern. Bright and lively, with sparkling glass and polished brass, filled with men and women, and the inescapable but enticing aroma of strong coffee. Moises and Mariella found seats at a long table. A pleasantly round young woman greeted them warmly and asked whether they would be having any food along with their coffee. They had not eaten in a while, and Belladonna ordered bread and cheese, but Mariella and Moises settled only for coffee. There was an occasional glance from the patrons in their direction, but no one scowled at them or inquired who they were.

When the large man entered, a path was cleared for him, and he made his way straight to their table and came directly to the point. "Why are you here?"

Belladonna boldly met his stare. "We bring a message from the *Sabato*."

His eyebrows rose, and his large hands clenched. "You bring news?" He looked around. Their encounter had engaged an audience. "Not here. Come."

Belladonna rose, as did Mariella and Moises. The large man pointed at them. "Not them."

Belladonna's nostrils flared. "They will come with me. They are the family of Roderigo, of Jamaica."

The large man squinted at Mariella and then nodded. "Come." He repeated.

He led them to a door at the far end of the room. Rapping on it twice in rapid succession and then pausing and rapping again caused the door to be opened, and they were admitted inside.

It was dim in the corridor, which was lit by candles burned low in their sconces. The bulk of the large man blocked their view of whoever had opened the door, and they followed him to the end of the corridor and another closed door. After a repeated sequence of quick knocks, the door opened into a large, bright room lit by the many candles in the chandelier above their heads. There were a dozen men seated around a polished wooden table. From their leather doublets to the brass earrings many of them wore, it was evident they were men of the sea and not of the drawing room.

The large man who had been their escort gave a slight bow as he faced them.

"Who are they, and why are they here?" came the demand of a grey-haired man at the head of the table.

"We bear a message from the *Sabato*," said Belladonna, coming to the end of the table with her eyes focused on the man at the head.

"How is it you are familiar enough with the crew of the *Sabato* to deliver messages for them?" asked the grey-haired man. All heads swiveled from the man at the head of the table to Belladonna at its foot.

"I have sailed with the *Sabato,* most recently, to the New World. I have come from Jamaica by way of Curacao to enlist the Brethren's help to rescue Captain Isaak from the Spanish."

"The Spanish!" the large man exclaimed. "Isaak cannot have been taken by the Spanish; he is far too clever."

"Rafael, how do you know these people can be trusted?" asked one of the seated men at the table.

The large man pointed to Belladonna. "I recognized her, even if you lot did not. She has done much for us in the past. Belladonna of Venice."

"Isaak's Belladonna?"

"The very same," she answered. "Which is why I have come all this way—to ask your help. Isaak needs you. We cannot let him fall into the hands of our enemies."

Her name seemed to be known to these men, as it caused them to whisper among themselves. Rafael's brows furrowed. "You must tell us everything. How he came to be captured, and what you have learned from his crew on the *Sabato*."

Belladonna took the chair offered to her. While seats were brought for her companions, Belladonna shared the events of the past few months and what had happened to Isaak.

When she finished, there was a momentary silence; her tale had made for deep thought.

Rafael was the first to speak. "The *Sabato* will continue to search for their captain in the Caribbean while we have been asked to watch in these waters. It will necessitate more ships and more weapons, so we have the firepower to waylay any Spanish ships from the New World headed to Spain. In the meantime, what can we do for you and your friends?"

Belladonna had noticed the droop of Moises's head. Both he and Mariella must be hungry and exhausted. "We need to find somewhere to stay for a few nights until I can arrange transport to Venice."

The grey-haired man waved a hand at one of the men, who promptly left through another door. Belladonna continued, "Before we go, I wish to know what else I can do. Isaak is in captivity, and I am filled with dread that he will be taken to Spain."

Rafael put a meaty hand on her shoulder. "You have done all that could be done. It is up to us now, with our ships and our guns, and up to the Almighty to keep him alive."

Chapter Forty: Diana

VENICE, The fifteenth of APRIL, 1615

Swatted by large rolls of fabric carried by a servant, Diana nearly fell down the large marble staircase as he sprinted past her. What could Mattia want with so much fabric? His studio was already littered with swaths of dark-colored satin to drape around his models. She regained her footing just in time; another tradesman in clacking silver-buckled shoes nearly knocked her down, muttering 'pardon' before continuing his rapid descent.

Mattia did not care if tradesmen brought their wares and deliveries up the main staircase instead of the back entrance meant for such commerce. Belladonna, the owner of this palazzo and one of the most powerful and influential courtesans of Venice would have been appalled at such liberties. The once elegant palazzo had suffered great indignities since Belladonna had allowed the artist to take up residence. Mattia did not manage the servants and in return, they ceased being vigilant for dust and dirt. As a result, the floors were were not polished, and the crystals in the sconces grew duller than they had ever been.

Diana, a rabbi's daughter who rarely stepped outside the walls of the Ghetto, had been dazzled at her first visit to the courtesan's palazzo. From the great polished marble staircase to the blazing torches in their crystal sconces, it had made her head spin as she strove to take it all in. The great French doors had not been streaked with dirt as they were now, though they still managed to let in a pleasant cool breeze on a temperate spring day.

Diana recalled her initial view of the elegant salon with its strategically placed divans and tables, which allowed for an easy flow between guests and conversations. Now, it was littered with tables, canvases, jars of paint, powders of pigment, piles of clothes and fabrics, and a variety of abandoned props and screens. At the far end of the room stood the artist, Mattia Correr, before canvas and easel, positioned to capture the best of the outside light from the long windows. He wore a linen shirt dappled with splotches of paint and was contemplating his canvas. He stood with one hand on his hip, and his brow was furrowed. He seemed to be scowling at the painting before him, which he picked up and tossed to the ground. It was then he looked up and noticed her.

"Diana. You have caught me as I leave this place," he said, as he gestured to the cluttered room, "It is good for me to leave. I have been too distracted here."

"Leave? Where are you going?" Diana asked, admiring how the sunlight highlighted the gold in his long brown hair and accented his handsome profile. She swallowed down a lump of panic at the thought of his departure from Venice.

"You have not heard? Everything must be packed up and moved within the next few days. Luckily, I was able to reclaim my former rooms at Ca' Vendramin."

"Why? What has happened?"

"Belladonna has sent word that she is returning to Venice. All must be made ready for her." He looked around the room again and laughed. "Her poor servants! They certainly will have quite a time cleaning and restoring this place to meet their mistress's expectations."

Diana agreed and now understood the flurry of fabrics and the visits of tradesmen. "She has been gone so long; I had hoped it would be for good."

Mattia ran a hand through his hair and shifted his eyes to a large canvas against the wall. "It has been more than a year. I am glad of her return, for it will provide me with the chance to finish her portrait. I warrant it is one of my best works."

Diana wanted to ask how he felt about her own portrait, but instead said, "I was not aware you had painted her."

Without responding, Mattia had been shifting canvases until he selected a larger one and placed it onto his easel. He gestured for her to come see.

There she was, Belladonna. The woman who had once been her benefactor and had become her friend.

Mattia had captured Belladonna's poise and elegance, and her painted image was dazzling. Honey-colored hair glinted with gold, piled high and threaded with pearls. Long white fingers, bedecked with multiple gemstones, held the edges of a fine veil as if she had just lifted it. In a three-quarters view, with her body twisted away, her head was turned back, her eyes looking straight at the viewer, fierce and defiantly green. There was a hint of a smile on her rosy, pink lips, as if she had just learned of someone's indiscretion.

"It is extraordinary. Whenever did she pose for you?"

Mattia studied the painted image of the beautiful woman on his canvas. "She could not sit for very long. It was before the Englishman and the envoy from the New World arrived in Venice, and the Spanish assassin began to stalk her. But her image and her music were so clear in my mind, I did not need to see her in my studio to paint her."

"It looks complete. What is unfinished?" Diana did not see any sketchiness in the brush strokes.

"It is the eyes and the face that need a few touches more. Then there is her gown. I have not captured its lavishness; it does not bedazzle you, does it?"

Diana cocked her head and squinted at the painted face. "It does not seem unfinished. You have captured Belladonna's self-assuredness in the tilt of her head and her sense of irony in the playful expression of her lips. I cannot imagine how you have made her so without having her in front of you as you painted."

Diana, as much of a scholar as her late husband, believed the artist could capture the essence of his subject's soul and pored over her father's kabbalist books to learn more about it.

She had desperately wanted to experience the mystical connection for herself, which is why she accepted Mattia's invitation to be painted as one of the 'beauties' in a visiting English lord's collection of portraits of beautiful Venetian women. Though Mattia had spoken of hearing 'her music' as he painted her, and the portrait was astonishingly like her, she had felt nothing like the transference of souls the kabbalists described. Instead, she experienced stirrings of another kind with Mattia—and it shamed her to admit they were romantic and not spiritual in nature.

Mattia fell in love with the subjects of his portraits—but only while he painted them. Diana's portrait had been finished nearly two years ago and hung in the morning room of Belladonna's palazzo. Now, she and Mattia had a friendship born of an alliance against their common enemies, though she could not help her heart fluttering at any glimmer of romantic interest from him.

Snapping out of her reverie, Diana asked, "Who informed you of Belladonna's return?" She wondered why Belladonna had come back to Venice and whether she was alone.

"Jacob Sullam. He had received a letter from Belladonna from a merchant who had just arrived from Amsterdam. By this time, Belladonna is expected to arrive within the next week or so."

Diana gestured to the mess on the floor. "There is a lot to do. Perhaps she will not mind how you have cared for her palazzo when she sees the portrait."

Chapter Forty-One: Belladonna

VENICE, The second of MAY, 1615

Belladonna's first sight of Venice after so many months brought tears to her eyes. The glimmer of golden sunlight basked the city in a warm, amber glow. The past few weeks had been frustrating; she had been forced to review her story over and over again with so many different captains, delaying her departure from Amsterdam.

Nightmares were frequent and deprived her of sleep, while every day, thinking of Isaak sent a wave of longing that swept through her, leaving her desolate. She had to muster her strength and determination to keep up the polished façade she had cultivated.

Once again, she was arriving in Venice as a refugee from the New World. When she had been rescued by Isaak from the Barbary pirates so long ago, she had no family, and the people of the Ghetto had taken her in. This time, she was a wealthy woman with friends and influence, and she was not alone. Mariella and Moises were her family now, and though she could not acknowledge them publicly, they would find a warm welcome from her friends in the Ghetto. For the time being, until she could arrange for their settlement, they could stay with her as guests in her palazzo on the Grand Canal, outside of the Ghetto.

With each step she took up the large marble staircase, her spirits lifted, for she was returning to her palazzo; she was home.

"Belladonna!" came a cry from above her. A patter of rapid footsteps, and

Diana appeared, nearly toppling her with an enthusiastic embrace.

"I appreciate you being here to welcome me," said Belladonna, and she disengaged herself from her friend, "especially since you had no inkling of my return."

Diana flushed. "Your departure from Venice was sudden and came to me as a surprise. You and Isaak…but I suppose not everything occurs as planned."

Footsteps approached, which temporarily ended their conversation. Mariella and Moises held their belongings clutched to their chests. Ironically, her sister-in-law was taking tentative steps up the staircase to a sumptuous Venetian palazzo while she had marched boldly into a dangerous swamp. Though it was a mildly warm day, Mariella shivered and clung tightly to the brightly colored shawl she had wrapped around herself. Moises peeked out from behind Belladonna, and Diana granted the young boy a welcoming smile.

Belladonna led them into the large entry hall, where she made the introductions in Spanish.

In Venetian, Diana asked, "Do they speak our language?"

"Not really. They speak mostly Spanish, but they speak and understand a little Italian and English."

Moises jumped up, seeming to have understood the dialogue. "I have also studied Hebrew and can read it and speak it a little bit. When I turn thirteen, the age of *mitzvah*, I will put on *tefillin* and read from the Torah in Hebrew." He raised his chin proudly.

"*Kol hakovod.*" Diana said in Hebrew. From the boy's grin, he understood her congratulations.

"How have you been able to master our Venetian language so quickly?" asked Belladonna as they were all seated in the salon.

Moises's smile was so wide he seemed to beam. "I learned from Isaak on Jamaica, and then I kept practicing on the *Sabato*."

"Isaak's ship," Belladonna explained to Diana as she summarized their journey from Jamaica. "The waves of a great storm swept Isaak off the deck, and his crew on the *Sabato* have been searching for him ever since.

We, too, had escaped the storm and sailed from Jamaica to a small island populated by men of many nationalities who could turn from friend to foe in an instant. We were relieved when the *Sabato* found us and took us to Curacao under their protection. In Curacao, we separated from the *Sabato* and found another ship which sailed from there to Amsterdam."

Mariella had not uttered a word and seemed entranced by the figures on the painted ceiling. Belladonna had to nudge her with an elbow to gain her attention when she introduced Diana as the sister of Isaak. Mariella gave Diana a graceful curtsy and murmured a greeting in Spanish as Diana curtsied back.

"I could not imagine it would be so beautiful." Mariella spoke as if she were in a dream.

The servants entered the salon waving their hands and making a fuss over Belladonna's return. She had always been generous to her staff, and I was moved to see she had been missed. Shooing the footmen off with requests for hot tea and food, she ordered the maidservants to prepare baths for herself and her guests.

As soon as Mariella and Moises were ushered to their rooms, Belladonna took the opportunity to recount all that had happened to her since she departed from Venice more than a year ago.

"We sailed to England first with Sir George Villiers, who promised to rally support at the English Court for the annexation of Jamaica. Then we set sail for Jamaica to inform Roderigo's wife and child of his death. We stayed in Jamaica for several months, but with no sign of the English in the bay, Isaak feared for the future. Spanish control seemed imminent, and so he boarded the *Sabato* for a fortnight's excursion to Curacao to see if we could settle there."

"Then came the storm?" asked Diana.

Belladonna nodded. "The Jews of Jamaica had prepared a refuge, a secret cave hidden high in the tallest mountain, rumored to be the hiding place for the lost gold of Christopher Columbus."

Diana's eyes widened. "Did you find the gold?"

Belladonna shook her head. "We did not search for it, but if it is still there, its location has been lost. We kept huddled around a brazier for warmth with many others, sharing food and our fear as the winds and waters raged outside. Once the storm passed, we returned to the plantation with the hope of making it habitable after the ravages of the storm, but Spanish soldiers arrived. While they were busy looting the fallen house, we escaped through a swamp. Boats hidden by the Jews were our means of departure for a nearby island controlled by pirates."

Diana was studying her face, and Belladonna wondered whether the hardships of the New World had marked it. Diana took both her hands and clasped them in her own. "Pirates! I know you do not want to dwell on what you have endured, especially when I am certain the most devastating has been the loss of Isaak. I admire you—you have the instincts for survival that have helped you overcome the ravages of nature and thwart the evil designs of men."

Diana's words brought tears to her eyes, but she blinked them away. "Fate had intervened in the course I had planned, but for once, I was not alone. If not for Mariella, I would not have escaped the storm nor the swamp, and Moises—in him, I recognize Roderigo as a young boy..." Belladonna had to stop, or she would not be able to hold back her tears.

Diana waited until Belladonna had regained her self-control before asking, "If not for the storm, you would have remained in the New World?"

Belladonna understood what Diana was asking. "Isaak and I had wanted to stay together, and in the New World, we had a chance to wed without laws to separate us because of our origins." She lowered her eyes to hide her grief over the impossibility of that dream. "Every time Isaak has sailed away, I feared it would be the last time I would see him. It is difficult to accept, but this time, Fate seems determined to keep us apart."

Tears dripped down Diana's cheeks, which she wiped away with her hand. "You cannot believe Isaak is—is—?"

Moises, who had returned, interrupted Diana by answering, "Isaak lives; the crew say he has always survived!"

The servants had returned, along with Mariella and Moises. Plates of food and steaming carafes of coffee were arranged on small tables beside them.

Inhaling the aroma of strong coffee strengthened her, and she straightened her back and sniffed back her emotions. Taking a sip, and in a calmer tone, Belladonna added, "The men of the *Sabato* had heard talk of survivors of the storm captured by the Spanish. They believe Isaak is now aboard a ship bound for Spain."

"Isaak falling into the hands of the Spanish? Whatever shall I tell my father and mother?" Diana's words did not end as a question, but as a moan.

"That is why we set off from Curacao towards Amsterdam. The Brethren needed to be told of Isaak's capture, for only they had the firepower to find and free him. The Brethren will send word to all their captains to stop every galleon approaching the coast of Spain."

She bit her lower lip hard before continuing, "But that is not enough. I must do something, and I have the resources to do more. First, I plan to enlist the help of the Turk."

Diana agreed. "The Turk seems to have great loyalty to Isaak."

Belladonna's nostrils flared. "To ensure his loyalty, I will give him enough gold to make it worth his while. I plan to visit him tomorrow."

Chapter Forty-Two: Belladonna

VENICE, The fourth of MAY, 1615

Belladonna was seated comfortably in her gondola, enjoying its journey up the Grand Canal. The facades of the palazzos were warmed to pleasant pastels by the morning sun and reinforced the beauty of the city that had become her home. It was only her greater love for Isaak that enabled her to tear herself away from it.

The gondola was turning into the Misericordia, which would lead to the *Campo di Mori,* the area of the Moors. Stepping carefully up the stone steps from the canal, she caught sight of the familiar statues of the two Moors holding up the building that had given the *campo* its name. She proceeded across cobblestones glistening with moisture, holding up her skirts. She had not worn her high *chopines,* but simple leather slippers, like those worn by Diana, for the cobblestones were uneven and often slippery from the refuse of vegetables and fish tossed to the ground by vendors in the *campo.* Belladonna was no stranger here; she had visited the Turk when she had been hiding in the Ghetto and had sought his assistance on other matters. Belladonna smiled to herself as she recalled how Morosini, Isaak, and the Spanish assassin Antonio, had come to the Turk then in search of *her.*

The blue door in the long wall that surrounded a tall house was her destination. When she rang the bell, it was opened by the Turk's daughter, who ushered her into a little Garden of Eden. The scent of the new blooms and a gentle breeze finding its way through lush leafy plants were soothing to the senses. She followed the fluttering veils and tinkling bracelets of the Turk's daughter through the lovely garden, past a three-tiered fountain into a courtyard.

The Turk seemed to have designed the courtyard for intrigue. One side had a covered trellis, perfect for listening unobserved to the conversations in the nearby courtyard. Beyond the trellis was where the Turk's guests would share their plans, often in lowered voices. Belladonna suspected the Turk hid behind the trellis to take measure of his guests before meeting with them, since he always seemed to have a ready response to any request they made.

"Belladonna returns!" The Turk greeted her with a wide-toothed smile and open arms.

She let herself be embraced as he continued in his way of flattering her appearance before coming to the point. He had not asked about Isaak; he was being discreet, supposing the courtesan and the pirate had parted ways. "What can the illustrious Belladonna want from me?"

"I have come to talk to you about Isaak."

The Turk was a large man, and now he shifted his bulk, as if his garments were suddenly too tight for him. "I have sailed with Isaak; we have been comrades in arms. My loyalty to him is unshaken."

"Good." Belladonna seated herself on a high divan that would make it easier to manage her voluminous skirts. "Isaak has been captured by the Spanish, and I am relying on you and your resources to help me rescue him."

The Turk's eyebrows shot up to the edge of his turban, and he sat back and slapped his knees. "Of course! If Isaak needs my help, he has it. Tell me more."

Belladonna complied, telling her tale of the storm and how Isaak had been lost and captured. Then she described how she had mustered the help of the crew of the *Sabato* and traveled to Amsterdam to enlist the Brethren.

"But it is not enough," Belladonna concluded, "you understand why we cannot let Isaak be taken into Spain. For a start, you must enlist the help of the Barbary pirates you once sailed with. Then appeal to your friends in Constantinople, those with the swiftest ships so adept at waylaying Spanish galleons."

The Turk raised his eyes heavenward and folded his arms over his massive chest. "Allah preserves you, Isaak, my friend. If he is recognized as Kasai, he is doomed."

"Kasai?"

The Turk took a deep breath. "Isaak commanded a ship of Barbary Pirates and was known as 'Captain Kasai, the Scourge of the Seas'. The Spanish put a high price on his head, a king's ransom for his capture. For Kasai not only captured their ships but destroyed their forts in Algeciras and other key points along the trade route. Captain Kasai's exploits were legendary, and he was summoned to the Sultan of Morocco, who wished to reward him with command of his fleet. Isaak refused the honor and, as a result, had to contend with the Sultan's displeasure. Eventually, he discontinued his exploits for the Kingdom of Morocco, took up with the Brethren, and so, Captain Kasai disappeared."

As Belladonna smoothed her skirts, her hands trembled. "Will Isaak be recognized as Kasai?"

Chapter Forty-Three: Belladonna

The Turk sent her off with promises of his support and asked her to return in a few days for a report on his efforts.

When she returned to her palazzo, Belladonna found Diana with Mariella by the window in the grand salon, the red damask draperies in her hands. Mariella raised the fabric to her cheek and caressed it. "Beautiful!"

Belladonna was grateful for the distraction from Isaak after her conversation with the Turk.

"I shall have a new dress made for you in just such a fabric," said Belladonna in Spanish to ensure her sister-in-law would understand. Mariella's immediate embrace surprised and nearly toppled Belladonna from her seat, but she did not mind. Mariella had provided her much happiness in Jamaica, when Belladonna was sick with longing for Venice. She was eager to provide any small joy to this woman, who had suffered both the loss of home and husband.

Her eyes followed her sister-in-law as she caressed the fabrics and raised her eyes to the painting's inset in the ceiling. Though Mariella was the daughter of a wealthy trader, the lavishness of the Old World had not reached the New. Moises also had his eyes on the ceiling.

"Who painted those pictures?" Moises asked after finishing the last crumb of the biscuits that had been placed before him.

"The artist Tintoretto. It was commissioned by the previous owners decades ago. I have many other paintings by Venetian artists in the library," Belladonna said and pointed to the doorway on the left side of the salon. "You may discover something to inspire you."

Immediately, Moises was out of his seat and on his way to the library. Belladonna was pleased with his enthusiasm for art. With his solemn nature and intellectual curiosity, Moises should not find any difficulty living in the Ghetto.

"You are changed," said Diana to Belladonna as soon as Moises left the salon.

Self-consciously, Belladonna smoothed her hair. "In those first few days after discovering Isaak was lost, I could not find solace or hope at all. If not for Mariella and Moises, I would not have had the will to survive. And had it not been for the good sense of generations of Jews of Jamaica, the cave would not have been there as our refuge."

"Do you believe the treasure exists?" asked Diana. "I am afraid Morosini must still have hopes that it does."

Belladonna winced as she recalled how the tale of the lost treasure in Jamaica had convinced the Venetian nobleman to be a part of their plot with Villiers over a year ago. "I am afraid the treasure is a myth, or its location has not been passed down from generation to generation of Jamaica's Jews as we had assured Villiers. It seems the promise of lost treasure was not enticing enough to the English king to exert any effort to take Jamaica from the Spanish."

"What happened to the English?"

"The English never appeared, and the island has been turned into a Spanish dominion. We had to leave. Since I am considered a New Christian, I would become a prime victim of the Inquisition."

Diana grimaced. "Like your parents. Despite all our efforts and your brother's mission to save the Jews of Jamaica, the Spanish prevailed."

Belladonna pressed the corner of each eye to prevent tears from escaping. She had been reunited with her brother Roderigo after supposing he had been murdered by the Inquisition, like her parents, in Recife. Their discovery of each other had come too late, and Belladonna had lost him once again.

Now, the one man who was the love of her life had also been taken from her. Conscious of Diana's eyes upon her, Belladonna inclined her head towards Mariella. "I thought it best to resettle my brother's family among their people in the Ghetto."

"Of course. We have a special fund to help refugees—"

Belladonna, frowning, interrupted her. "Even though I cannot publicly acknowledge my kinship I shall assume any costs necessary to make a suitable home for Mariella and Moises." She could not change her life to live in the Ghetto, and unless they converted, Venetian law would not allow Moises and Mariella to remain outside of it. Nevertheless, though they could not continue to live with her, with Diana's help, she was more confident her brother's family would not feel abandoned when they moved to the Ghetto.

Their eyes shifted towards Mariella, who had moved on from the draperies to running a hand across the damask fabric of the settees. Diana tilted her head towards Mariella. "She is certainly a beauty, and if it is known she is financially secure, she will not lack for suitors."

Belladonna had not considered Mariella's intentions to remarry. Mariella had been devastated at the news of Roderigo's death, and she had been true to the thirty days of mourning required by Jewish law for a widow. It was more than a year since they had brought the news of her husband's death, and Mariella seemed to have moved on from her grief. Perhaps it was the nature of the instability of living in the New World that kept her so resilient. If so, it would do her well in the days to come, for acclimating to the challenges of the Old World were much more complicated than they had been in the New.

Chapter Forty-Four: Belladonna

VENICE, The fourth of MAY, 1615

A strong smell of paint wafted into the salon, heralding the arrival of the artist, Mattia Correr. He rushed into the salon, his hair loose and flying in all directions, his doublet missing, and only wearing his white linen shirt over his breeches.

"Belladonna! At last, you have returned. I feared you would not," said Mattia, sitting beside her.

Belladonna did not admonish the artist for his familiarity; they had developed a level of trust between them that allowed for a diminishment of usual protocol. She tilted her head to accept his welcoming kisses on each cheek. "I hope your residence here inspired you to produce a prodigious body of work?"

Mattia grinned and replied, "The light was superb for an artist's studio." He glanced around, "but I see your staff have transformed it rather quickly to its former grandeur."

Mariella had caught Mattia's eye. "Ah, who have we here? Have you a new protégé?"

Mariella, who was not very fluent in Venetian, gave Belladonna a puzzled look, though she seemed to recognize Mattia's admiring gaze, and her cheeks pinked to a rosy olive.

Belladonna sighed, realizing the longer Mariella remained in her palazzo, the greater the chance her sister-in-law would be perceived as a new courtesan she was grooming.

"She is not a courtesan, nor will she ever become one. She is Roderigo's widow from Jamaica, staying with me temporarily after losing her home as a result of a terrible storm."

Diana, who had clenched the fabric of her skirt as soon as Mattia's attention had shifted to Mariella, now added, "They will be settling in the Ghetto as soon as arrangements can be made."

"The Ghetto?" Mattia repeated, his eyebrows raised.

"My brother Roderigo not only represented the Jews of Jamaica but lived openly as a Jew with his family there. I am certain it would be his wish they settle in the same community here."

Mattia appealed to Diana. "I must paint her. I already hear her music in my head."

Belladonna refrained from rolling her eyes at Mattia, but instead, responded firmly with her wishes. "It is not possible at this time."

Diana interrupted Mattia before he could protest, "What of the portrait of Belladonna? You must show it to her."

Clever of Diana, deflecting his attention from Mariella.

"Yes! Belladonna, your portrait is nearly complete," the artist perked up, his eyes alight with excitement, "come, I will show you. I have kept it in the small salon, awaiting your return."

Belladonna was eager to retire to her private rooms to enjoy a heated bath, but she followed Mattia, with Diana and Mariella trailing behind them.

The portrait stood on an easel, veiled from view, in the smaller room, which was filled with the strong odor of wet paint. With a dramatic sweep of his arm, Mattia lifted the drape, and his painting was revealed.

It took Belladonna's breath away. She had not seen herself in a very long time as magnificent, but in Mattia's rendering, the woman of the portrait glistened with an other-worldly light. Her hair looked gilded and was studded with pearls, which also graced her long neck. True to life, her elegant fingers were entwined with an iridescent strand of pearls that cascaded from her neck, usually played with while deep in thought.

What she loved most about her portrait was the face. The eyes were merry and intelligent, the lips contributing to the expression of mild amusement at the gaze of the viewer.

Mattia had truly captured her as the elite courtesan she once was, and though she had no wish to resume that role, she wished to appear just as dazzling as she had been before.

Chapter Forty-Five: Diana

Mattia was rambling on about Mariella as they took their seats in the gondola. Diana listened sporadically, catching only snippets, such as 'savage beauty' and 'Judith with the head of Holofernes.' When he finished his monologue, he banged the side of their boat with his fist for emphasis while declaring, "I must paint her. I must!"

Diana bit her lip to prevent herself from unleashing an angry retort. When she did not respond, he asked, "Do you agree with my vision for Mariella?"

"I am a widow like Mariella, who lost the man I loved with all my heart and soul. It took me a long while to overcome the pain of his loss. Perhaps now is not the right time to prevail upon Mariella."

Mattia ran a hand through his hair. "I beg your pardon; I had no intention of being insensitive to her loss. But you understand what inspiration means to me. I hear her music, Diana! I have not heard such music so clearly since the days I painted those portraits for the Englishman's Gallery of Beauties."

"Your portrait of Belladonna is magnificent."

Mattia sighed. "That was the last of my good work. Despite the light in Belladonna's palazzo, the work I have done there has not been my best. Come, be truthful, you have seen those paintings, do you agree?"

Diana averted her eyes, shifting in her seat. "I have not seen your finished paintings, so I cannot say."

"The music. You know I must hear music when I study a subject for a portrait. I have posed other women, beautiful women, in various tableaus in my studio, but I could hear nothing from them, and the paintings are lackluster because of it."

Mattia pounded again on the edge of the gondola, forcing the gondolier to turn around and mutter a warning.

Diana tried to reason with the artist. "Mariella and Moises are refugees. They must find a home and regain their moorings. I will speak to my father, and perhaps the Sullams will help them to find a new home. They have the means, unlike most others in the Ghetto, to help them as they once helped Belladonna." Diana patted the artist's arm. "You must be patient. Once Mariella is settled, she will be more inclined to pose for you."

The artist seemed to acquiesce, but Diana did not believe he would give up on his pursuit of Mariella so easily. But he surprised her by asking, "Do you still think of your husband?"

She turned away from him, facing the horizon beyond the lagoon. "I will never stop thinking of Yaakov."

"What of your brother Isaak? Do you believe Belladonna loves him in the same way?"

"I am certain of it."

No more questions from Mattia. She assumed her acknowledgment of Belladonna's true emotions had triggered introspective thoughts in the artist.

Diana's eyes glazed as she stared at the blue horizon, wondering at the dangers that Belladonna and Isaak had faced in the Caribbean. Instead of peaceful waters gently bobbing with small craft, she tried to imagine vast walls of water overwhelming a ship and sweeping men out to sea.

Diana dropped her head in her hands, as if she was overwhelmed by such a wave. The warmth of a hand across her back seemed to break the spell. She lifted her head, and Mattia's hair brushed her cheek as he pulled her close. "There, there."

Comforted by his warmth, she wanted to remain in his arms, but forced herself to pull away. It was dangerous to engage in this kind of closeness in public, as such relations between Jew and Gentile were against Venetian law. With an eye to the gondolier, who, luckily, had not turned around, she added, "I am sorry. I lost myself in thinking of Isaak."

Mattia caught her gaze and fell back in the seat. "Isaak is a seasoned sailor, and there is every reason to believe he has the skills and stamina to survive."

Diana clasped her shawl tightly and looked towards the horizon. "That is what I shall tell my parents."

Chapter Forty-Six: Belladonna

VENICE, The fifth of MAY, 1615

Belladonna felt refreshed after a long, hot bath, and once her maid had tamed her honey-gold hair into civilized submission. She descended from her private quarters into the smaller of her dining rooms. Mariella had been dressed by the maid in a yellow gown salvaged from a cupboard and looked very different with her dark hair fashionably braided and coiffed.

There had been a less successful transformation of Moises, who wore breeches and a shirt one of the younger footmen had outgrown. Moises was a much smaller boy, and some quick adjustments had been made to the breeches so they would not fall beyond his knees, and the shirt sleeves had been rolled up to free Moises's fingers. Belladonna had already sent for the best tailors to fit her brother's son properly.

Belladonna entered the room with the gentle swishing sound of silk and the scent of a tantalizing perfume. Her fingers reached for the strands of perfect pearls that cascaded from below her neck to her waist. They made a clacking sound as her fingers played with them. She took her seat at the head of the table.

"I trust you feel better now," she spoke in Spanish for Mariella's benefit.

Her sister-in-law nodded. "It is so beautiful here; everything glistens like morning dew."

"How very poetic. Now, let us enjoy our first civilized meal together in so many months. I had it prepared in the Ghetto, so the food complies to your kosher laws."

Belladonna's pronouncement seemed to overcome any hesitation from Moises. He filled his plate from the trays of fish and vegetables presented to him by the footmen. Mariella, displaying more of an appetite since their flight from Jamaica, also ate with gusto.

Belladonna had too much on her mind to have any desire for food. There was a meeting scheduled with Jacob Sullam on the morrow. She had entrusted all her possessions and holdings to his management, and she proposed to visit Jacob at his home in the Ghetto. It would also provide her with the opportunity to introduce her sister-in-law and nephew to Sarra and life in the Ghetto. She would instruct Jacob to settle an ample amount for their support and hoped he could find a new home for them.

Belladonna decided to broach the subject. "I hope to take you to visit the Ghetto tomorrow. It is where we shall find you a home."

Mariella looked up from her food, frowning. "Please, what is this Ghetto that you speak of?"

How could she explain? "It is the area where the Jews live in Venice."

"Why?" asked Moises, "why do they live in this area?"

"It is the only place where Jews are permitted to live. It was originally designated for Jews as a means of protecting them."

Moises looked from his mother to her, his brow furrowed. "How is it that you do not live there?"

Mariella's eyes narrowed as she waited for Belladonna's answer. Belladonna cleared her throat. "I do not belong in the Ghetto."

"Perhaps neither do we," Mariella said, raising her chin defiantly.

Ignoring Mariella's comment, Belladonna took a gentle tone to allay their fears, saying, "There is so much to be learned from our friends in the Ghetto. Rabbi di Modena, Diana's father, has many books of Jewish learning and mysticism, as well as books about herbs and medicines."

Moises's eyes opened wide. "Would I be permitted to look at them?"

"Diana or her father will be glad to share their knowledge. I shall be sure to mention your interest."

Mariella leaned forward, interested. "They have books of medicine?"

Belladonna remembered Mariella's use of herbs and willow bark as remedies in Jamaica. "Diana has developed great skill in healing from her study of these books. Though they are normally forbidden books, the Council of Ten has given special dispensation for their study by the rabbi and his daughter."

The conversation was at an end, and with no desire to eat or drink anything more, Belladonna rose. "Tomorrow, I shall bring you with me to the home of Jacob Sullam, and you will be paying your first visit to the Ghetto. I bid you both a good night."

Afterwards, as she undressed, Belladonna reflected on Mariella's remark. Though Moises was eager to live among other Jews, perhaps Mariella no longer wanted to be identified with a persecuted people. The young woman could question such a future as Belladonna once did when, as a refugee, she was welcomed into the Ghetto by the Sullams. She had chosen to live as a Christian, a decision she did not regret, though she was conscious of the hurt she had caused to the Sullams by rejecting a life with them.

There was a quiver of doubt in the pit of her stomach as she remembered her promise to Roderigo. How could she encourage his wife to disengage from her people after Roderigo had died trying to protect them?

Chapter Forty-Seven: Diana

VENICE, The fifth of MAY, 1615

"Are you telling me Isaak is dead?" Her father blinked several times after hearing her news.

It was late, and the lines around his eyes and mouth deepened with sorrowful shadows in the flickering candlelight. They kept their voices low since her mother was already sleeping, and they did not want her to wake up and hear their conversation.

"It is not certain. During a terrible storm in Jamaica, Isaak was swept out to sea."

"Has he drowned?" The hand that stroked his grey beard trembled.

"He was alive when he was last seen and was taken aboard a Spanish ship, according to what Belladonna had learned from his men. There were witnesses to Isaak being taken by the Spanish."

Her father slapped a hand on the table. "Then we will not sit *shiva* for him, for there is no evidence of his death and good reason to hope he is still alive."

Diana frowned, mentally reviewing the many pages of the Talmud with discourses about the *Agunah*, an abandoned wife. The rabbis had agreed that without an eyewitness's confirmation, there could be no conclusion of death, and the woman could not transition to the status of widow. A great problem, especially after wars and pogroms and now, with storms and ships sinking so far away in the Caribbean.

After a mournful sigh, her father said, "So, without the evidence of his death, as stated in the Talmud, there is no need to sit shiva, and we will not need to discuss Isaak at all with your mother. Is there any hope we will receive news of him soon?"

Diana cleared her throat to continue, "While his crew searches the Caribbean, Belladonna has been to Amsterdam to enlist the help of the Jewish Brethren. They are both committed to Isaak's rescue."

Despite the hopeful news, the rabbi pursed his lips as if he had tasted something sour at the mention of Belladonna's name. "With God's help, may he be found unharmed. What happened in Jamaica? I thought the English were going to wrest the island away from Spain."

Diana updated her father on the failure of Roderigo's mission, and that Spain was now in full control of Jamaica.

The rabbi released another deep sigh. "What you say is disheartening. Sir Henry Wotton, as their ambassador, can find out what has happened at the English court. It is a shame that after all of our efforts and Roderigo's sacrifice, the Jews are forced to flee oppression once more." He sighed again with more depth of emotion. "And now, Isaak—"

Diana interrupted her father, placing her hand over his. "Though it has been several months since the great storm, Belladonna and I are convinced Isaak will find some way to survive. He always has."

* * *

Belladonna awoke suddenly, drenched in sweat, her head and arms dangling over the edge of her bed. Another nightmare, her body tossed in sleep as if it were a dinghy wrestling with stormy seas. In her dream, Isaak had appeared in the waves, and she had reached out for him. Nearly in her grasp, she leaned more and more out of the boat. Then a crash of a great wave and she was no longer in the boat but desperately paddling to stay afloat. And Isaak had disappeared.

She tried to settle herself back to sleep, reassuring herself it was only a dream and she was safe in her own palazzo, with servants and friends around her. But she could find no peacefulness, and so she yawned and stretched, throwing off her thick bedclothes to face the chill of a misty dawn.

Cool air was welcome after so many months of awakening to the relentless heat of the Caribbean. She ran a hand along the fine linen of the sheets, relishing their softness in contrast to the many places she had recently laid her tired body down to rest. Reluctantly, she forced herself out of the comforting nest of soft pillows, sheets, and coverlets.

She inhaled deeply and exhaled, preparing herself for all she had to do. She hated ringing for her maid so early, but she needed a cup of steaming chocolate to banish the damp chill inside of her from her dream.

Much later, dressed and coiffed, a cultivated image of sophisticated beauty, Belladonna greeted her sister-in-law and nephew. The servants had already brought in the trays of steaming coffee and rolls. After scrounging for so many months, Moises's eyes lit up whenever prepared food was offered. However, Moises would not partake of any of her food until she reassured him that she had made the cook prepare it in accordance with kosher law and in separate utensils and pots. Mariella did not seem to have the same concerns as her son and seemed eager to sample everything. It made Belladonna reflect once again on whether Mariella would take to living in the Ghetto.

"The gondola is waiting, and there is a chill this morning, so there are cloaks available for you both," said Belladonna.

Both of her guests put down their cups at her announcement.

"Is it on another island?" asked Moises, getting to his feet.

Belladonna smiled at him, "Yes, but it is not a far journey like it was from Jamaica to Curacao. Venice is really composed of many little islands, all connected to each other by footbridges. In essence, traversing this city is literally going from island to island."

Moises raised an eyebrow and said, "How very curious."

Mariella caressed the silky fabric of the settee. "Tell me, do the Jews in the Ghetto live like you do?"

"Some do, and some, like most other Venetians, live simply. Come,

Mariella. It is best you see for yourself."

Chapter Forty-Eight: Diana

VENICE, The sixth of MAY, 1615

Diana arrived at the Sullams just as Belladonna and her family were being admitted. The footman did not have the temerity to ogle Belladonna, but he leered at Diana and Mariella. Diana silently commended Mariella for ignoring him, wondering how much the dark beauty was used to receiving such attentions.

Inside the Sullams' home, Mariella's head swiveled left and right at the sight of the fine tapestries and the glittering chandeliers. Diana recognized the clomping sound of Belladonna's chopines, the platform clogs that gave her the additional height and proclaimed her status. Although many found it difficult to navigate in such high shoes, Diana had seen Belladonna dance gracefully in them. Mariella was tall for a woman, but even with her glossy black hair contained in plaits piled on top of her head, she seemed small in stature in comparison to Belladonna. Beside both of these women, Diana felt diminished and plain.

Diana's insecurities melted away with the warmth of Sarra Sullam's welcome and her invitation for Diana to sit beside her in a place of honor.

"Belladonna! We are happy for your safe return and welcome your new family," said Sarra, taking the courtesan's hands in her own.

Belladonna gave Sarra a warning look. "My *guests*," she emphasized the last word, conveying a clear message that her relationship with Mariella and Moises was not to be publicly acknowledged. "Mariella and Moises have arrived from the New World after losing their home in a terrible storm. I assured them they would be welcome in the Ghetto among their own people."

Sarra turned a bright smile to Mariella and reached out to clasp her hands. "Of course! Though nothing can compensate for your losses, be assured you have found a community and friends who will support you here."

Bowls filled with a savory stew were placed on the long table, and they were invited to be seated. Moises had his eyes glued to the stew as it was placed before him. "Please, is the food kosher here?"

Jacob smiled. "It is. Please, take, enjoy. All have been prepared with the strictest adherence to the laws of *kashrut*."

Without delay, Moises was filling his mouth with the stew. Plates of other savories were placed on the table. Moises reached for a pickled olive, which popped between his lips before answering Jacob. "I do know about these laws. We must only eat fish with fins and scales, and we do not eat fowl or meat with cream. But I have never had the chance to *study* them."

"Can you read Hebrew?" asked Diana.

"A little." Moises's response was somewhat garbled since his mouth was so filled with food.

"I can share my father's books with you, and both my father and I can teach you how to read them. It is how I learned."

"Diana is a respected Talmudic scholar," explained Jacob, which caused Mariella to regard her with a new intensity, "and her father is a chief rabbi of the Ghetto. A better teacher you could not find."

Mariella had kept quiet, but at this turn of conversation, she asked Diana, "How is it you have been able to learn so much? On the island, most women cannot read and are too busy with chores and children to make time to learn how to do so."

It was Sarra who answered. "Venice is a city of great thinkers, authors, and poets, and neither Jews nor women are excluded from being a part of it. Those of us without children or with servants to do their chores can find purpose in study."

Diana reddened at Sarra's frankness. Both she and Sarra were childless, and Sarra was a wealthy woman with servants, allowing for more time to study. Besides, the rabbi had cultivated Diana's interest in books, while her brothers had no desire to study.

Moises had finished chewing and wiped his mouth. "Would I have the opportunity to study in a school?"

Jacob answered, "There is a *Cheder,* a boy's class for studying the Torah. Diana's father would be very pleased to help you discover what you would like to study."

Mariella's next words were an appeal to Belladonna. "It has been one disaster after another since Roderigo left us. We have just arrived in a strange city, with customs and food and clothing so unlike anything we have ever known. Can we have some time before we must confine ourselves behind these grey walls?"

Belladonna's mouth opened to answer, but she closed it again without speaking. It was Moises who interrupted the uncomfortable silence with his plea, "But I want to stay here. I want to study and go to school. Please, mother, may I stay?"

Jacobsmiled with true happiness, and he made his offer to Mariella. "Of course, we would be very happy for you and Moises to be our guests here until you are ready to find a place of your own."

Moises's eyes lit up, but his mother did not look pleased. "Moises, we should stay together with Belladonna—"

Appreciating Jacob's offer, Belladonna interrupted Mariella since she did not want it ignored. "I see no reason why Moises cannot remain here now. The Sullams have graciously volunteered to care for him, and living with them should make for an easier transition."

Mariella opened her mouth to protest, but promptly closed it again. She had the good sense not to contradict Belladonna's decision. Belladonna spoke to Diana quietly, out of earshot of the others, "Perhaps you can take Moises and Mariella to the *campo* of Ghetto Nuovo and then to your father's study while I meet with Jacob about my finances."

Diana rose, inviting Mariella and Moises to follow her out. Before they left, Belladonna promised to have Moises's belongings sent to the Sullams.

Sarra hugged Mariella and promised they should become friends. Mariella sighed dramatically but followed Diana and her son out of the salon to explore the Ghetto.

Chapter Forty-Nine: Belladonna

After Mariella and her son departed, Jacob ushered Belladonna into his study. Belladonna admired this room, which was lined with bookshelves and featured a large and elegant dark wooden desk as its centerpiece. Both behind and before the desks were comfortable-looking chairs, and she and Jacob took their places to discuss their business – the status of Belladonna's finances.

Jacob did not waste words but came straight to the point. "All said, your fortunes are in good order. Your income from the vineyard in the Veneto is ample enough to cover the expenses of maintaining your palazzo, and the investments in the silk trade have paid off handsomely."

"Yet, I sense there is a threat to my prosperity?"

Jacob pressed his lips together tightly, pausing before delivering unpleasantness. "There is a great pressure to make a large investment in a highly speculative enterprise."

"From whom?"

"Morosini."

Jacob shifted his eyes away from her, as if he did not want to bear witness to her discomfort at the name. Bardon Morosini was one of the most prominent leaders of the Council of Ten, men of nobility and fortune who controlled most everything in Venice. Morosini could be a dangerous enemy, though he had been an equally powerful ally to Belladonna and the

Jews of Venice.

"Bardon has always been wildly speculative in his enterprises, and nearly all have paid off handsomely. Why are you so concerned over this one?"

Of all the leaders in the Council of Ten, she had always counted on Bardon Morosini as an ally, and he had proved his loyalty. Unlike many of the other scions of old Venetian families, Bardon Morosini had intelligence and daring and was not afraid of using unorthodox means to achieve his ends.

Jacob cleared his throat, again delaying his answer. "This time, I know how shaky is the ground on which he hopes to build his fortune. He has a partner in this venture, with a merchant from the Ghetto, who has been gathering funds to build a new harbor for trade to the East."

Belladonna's eyes widened. "How very…ambitious. Quite an undertaking, and one that challenges the fortunes of other powerful men on the Council of Ten."

Jacob exhaled deeply, as if he was relieved she had perceived the heart of the matter. "Need I say more? It strains many of us merchants of the Ghetto in two ways: one, the mastermind of this affair, Avigdor Margulies, is a leader of the community, and two, it places us directly between the competing interests of two powerful families—the Morosinis and the Contarinis."

Belladonna gave a sharp intake of breath at the latter name. Niccolo Contarini had once been her lover, but in the past few years, the nobleman had become her nemesis. He was as clever and ruthless as Morosini and had no love for the people of the Ghetto. "The Contarinis have interest in many enterprises, but I suppose this new harbor will somehow circumvent his centers of profit?"

When Jacob nodded, she asked, "How so?"

Jacob clasped his hands resting on the table and leaned towards her so he could lower his voice.

"Every ship that comes in to dock in the harbor must receive a license from Customs. Inspectors make their rounds of the docks and check that such licenses are in hand, and then verify payment of the docking fee with a stamp. Those who do not have the proper paperwork are fined. The

Contarini family is well represented by these inspectors and toll takers."

"And a new wharf will have new inspectors. The friends and family of Morosini." Belladonna gave a deep sigh. "An investment in the new wharf places us both in a precarious position. Investing with Morosini may be risking a great deal of money and certainly results in becoming an enemy of Contarini. On the other hand, Morosini is our ally, and Contarini has always cast himself as our enemy. Therefore, the most we can lose is our money."

"A great deal of money," said Jacob, stroking his well-groomed beard. "And another matter of concern. Most of the funding comes from Constantinople, from an advisor to the sultan, which could lead to charges of treason leveled against us."

"Contarini would not dare make such a charge against Morosini! Their rivalry is well known, and it would be seen as a wild and personal accusation and only turn the Council against him."

Jacob shook his head. "For Morosini, maybe the charge would seem ludicrous. But against the Jews of the Ghetto? There would certainly be more supporters of that."

Belladonna bit her lip. Jacob had made a valid point, and what was left unsaid was whether she, who had departed Venice under mysterious circumstances, could also be vulnerable to such charges.

Chapter Fifty: Belladonna

Mariella had returned from her first visit to the Ghetto with a scowl on her face. Belladonna had ordered her servants to pack Moises's meager belongings and send them to the Sullams. She did not feel capable of alleviating her sister-in-law's gloom, but nevertheless, Belladonna felt it was impossible to ignore it.

"I have sent all Moises has required to the Sullams. I am certain they would accommodate you if you would like to stay with them until you find a suitable home." Belladonna hoped Mariella would agree to her proposal.

"I prefer staying here instead of retreating behind the Ghetto walls." Mariella held her arms across her chest and pouted like a child. "The buildings there are so tall, they seem to suck the life out of the sky. I am used to so much air, so much sky, I feel I should wither within those gates."

After living under the bright sun and vast open fields in Jamaica, Belladonna could well understand Mariella's dismay at the sight of the grey walls of the Ghetto. Nevertheless, Mariella did not belong in the salons of Venice, with the jaded and the cynical. She must go to the Ghetto to live with her son and her people. To live otherwise would mean hiding her origins and creating a new identity.

Diana once found the temptation to live under a new persona particularly appealing. Now, she realized it could make things become more complicated. Morosini had taken to Diana at their first encounter at Belladonna's salon when she, like Morosini's wife Therese, had been one of the subjects for the Englishman's Gallery of Beauties. Diana had the intuitive skill to parlay her rejection of the nobleman's attentions into a grudging respect for her.

Mariella did not have the same cleverness and would no doubt find the attentions of noblemen like Morosini or charmers like Mattia Correr irresistible. This was not what her dead brother would want for his widow.

Ignoring what Mariella had said, Belladonna continued, "The Sullams' mansion is quite as lavish and as comfortable as any palazzo on the Grand Canal. Many women of the Ghetto dress to the envy of many a woman in Venetian society, with access to the finest and most colorful silks and gemstones. It is a far cry from your life in Jamaica, but you will be accepted there and will have a home, a place, and a community—all of which you could never have outside the Ghetto. Believe me, though there are walls around the Ghetto, life outside of it can be more restrictive,"

Mariella lowered her arms and raised one eyebrow. "How so?"

"You have not heard of the sumptuary laws that govern Venice. There are laws about how a Venetian citizen may dress, how much fabric to their clothes, gold thread, and pearls about a woman's neck. There are laws as to how lavish a party may be, how many women are in attendance, what manner of decoration, and how many gilded furnishings. Such restrictions do not apply *within* the Ghetto, where women of means, like Sarra, are able to wear all the gems and satin they wish behind its walls. Had Sarra's parties occurred outside of the Ghetto, she would have been denounced. All it takes is a note placed in the *Bocca di Leone*, the Lion's Mouth, adjacent to the magistrates' offices in the ducal palace."

"You seem to live in defiance of such rules," Mariella's mouth curved into a knowing smile.

Belladonna raised her chin with pride. "I have earned status, which gives me some latitude. Certain members of society can obtain exemptions from specific rules."

Mariella did not retreat, and the color rose in her cheeks as she brushed her errant curls away from her face impatiently. "If you have earned such an honored place in society, I should like to, as well."

"What do you mean? You have a son and a people—"

Mariella interrupted her and waved her hand dismissively, "I am your brother's wife. My people are yours, are they not? If you do not have to join them behind the walls of the Ghetto, why should I?"

Belladonna bit her lip to withhold the retort she wanted to make, and instead, answered, "You were born a Jew and raised a Jew, and I was not. Roderigo chose to be part of the Hebrew community, while I did not. Though we find ourselves connected through Roderigo, we are not the same, and our paths are destined to go different ways. It is best for us both for you to accept that truth."

Mariella's face fell, and she seemed to crumple into herself, falling onto a settee. Belladonna was at a loss. She had not meant to hurt Mariella, but only to make her face the reality of their situation. She did have Mariella's best interests at heart. Mariella was brave but did not have the guile to survive in a society that always wore a mask of its true intentions.

Mariella looked up at Belladonna, worry on her face. "What shall become of me?"

Belladonna put her arms around her sister-in-law, who rested her head upon Belladonna's shoulder. "Do not worry, I shall not abandon you. We may walk on different paths, but we will find a way to stay together."

A footman appeared. "A visitor, madam, is at the door, demanding to see you."

Belladonna hoped it was not Bardon Morosini, for she felt unprepared at this moment to deal with him. Mariella had upset her, and she must have her emotions completely under control before engaging with the nobleman.

"A nobleman?"

The footman shook his head. "No, a young man," he cleared his throat, "and I would venture, not one of a noble background."

Belladonna's curiosity was aroused. Mattia Correr? It could not be, for then the footman would have recognized him and admitted him without question. Who could this be?

"Belladonna, I have returned!" the dark curls bounced free as the young man removed his cap, and Belladonna's eyes widened as she recognized her guest.

"Zebulun."

Chapter Fifty-One: Belladonna

Belladonna's visitor had made himself comfortable in the salon. He sprawled across a divan, booted feet outstretched, as one hand meandered through his black curls.

Belladonna clasped her hands and held her breath, hoping Zebulun, also a member of the Jewish Brethren, had news of Isaak. Her hopes were dashed when she received a blank stare at her questions about Isaak.

"You have not come from the Jewish Brethren?"

"No, I have come from Constantinople."

Belladonna swept a hand across her brow. Whenever Zebulun returned, there would be trouble. Unlike his two siblings, Diana and Isaak, Zebulun never gave himself a moment to think before he jumped into action. Now, disappointment shifted to concern. "You had earned yourself a ship from the Englishmen, so I had imagined you sailing around the coast of England. What happened? Are you now in the service of the Sultan?"

Zebulun placed a booted foot across his knee and gave a short laugh. "Not the Sultan, but one who is highly favored by him. A woman, in fact."

Belladonna raised her eyebrows, and Zebulun continued, "A very wealthy woman, one of two sisters originally from Spain, a New Christian. Her family had become wealthy enough to attract the attention of the Inquisition, and so—they came to Venice. The Sultan hears of this woman's remarkable trade business and invites her to Constantinople to establish a trade route and build a business for him. She decides to accept his offer because the Sultan also assures her that she can live as a Jew or Christian, whatever she wishes. And she wishes to be a Jew."

"I have never heard this story. Who is this woman?" Belladonna was skeptical; Zebulun was often taken in by the stories of adventurers who professed to have great wealth.

"Her name is Dona Elena di Martinez, but she is an old woman. I am on a commission for her nephew, Joseph di Azzura from Constantinople. He has come to Venice with great plans, and that is why I have come to you."

Standing in front of Zebulun, Belladonna folded her arms across her chest and tapped her foot. "And what are these great plans?"

Zebulun jumped to his feet, his eagerness unable to be contained. "A new port, much larger, on the other side of Venice, facing the Aegean. It will be able to receive so many more ships, especially from the East."

"That is a big plan and one fraught with trouble. You do realize that by creating a new port you are compromising the revenues of the masters of the old one. The Contarinis rely on the docking fees collected by the officers of the Punta del Dogana."

Zebulun waved his hand, as if he could eliminate the opposition easily. "With the new port, their revenues could double—even triple. Why ever should they oppose it?"

Belladonna sighed. "Morosini is involved in this plan?"

"He is, but he is not the only one. There is a very important man from Constantinople who I work for now. It was Morosini who advised me to come to see you with the plan."

Morosini was very clever—and very persistent. She must learn more of these plans, and it would be best to hear of them from Zebulun, who did not have the guile to shadow its faults or conceal its risks.

"Morosini must have shared his plans with you and your patron. How does he plan on circumventing the Contarinis? They will find every means to oppose this plan."

Zebulun launched into a long story of how this port, because of its proximity to the Arsenale, where the ships were built, was directly facing the Adriatic Sea. By the time Zebulun ended his discourse, his eyes were shining, and his lips were parted with excitement.

"This will provide Venice with expedited access to the shipping routes to the East and help block rivals like Genoa, who will stop at nothing to thwart us."

The machinations of Morosini, true to script, calling out the need for protection against the evil Genoese.

"This plan will cost a fortune."

"A short-term investment, which will make you very wealthy."

Belladonna rolled her eyes. "I am already wealthy."

Zebulun would not desist. Morosini had trained him well. "You will be so much wealthier. Morosini is convinced this port will upend the current power structure. What is more, it will ensure we will never have to live with a Contarini Doge."

"Zebulun, I am tired. You are filled with big ideas that will likely cost me trouble and a fortune. Right now, I do not have the strength to entertain such plots. I have only just returned to Venice after a long and arduous journey from the Caribbean. I have survived a colossal storm, the ransacking Spanish, and the company of pirates. What is most terrible, is that Isaak is lost, swept overboard in the storm, and taken by the Spanish. I had been wishing for news, but not of the kind you have brought."

Zebulun's mouth dropped. "I-Isaak has been captured by the Spanish?"

Belladonna pressed a hand to her eyes. "It is difficult to even think of him in the hands of those brutes. If they find out who he is…"

Zebulun clenched his hands into fists. "Isaak is smart enough to find a way out. He always has. What of the *Sabato*? His men?"

"They search for Isaak in the Caribbean, sailing under the noses of the Spanish. The Spanish have colonized most of the islands, but they face strong opposition from the pirates, the English, French and Dutch, many who have been liberated from Spanish galleons."

Zebulun collapsed onto a divan, his velvet cap in hand, his enthusiasm deflated. "I did not know. I have been in Constantinople for many months with no word of the world outside. Isaak…I feel…helpless."

Belladonna put her hand on his shoulder. "It was difficult for me, too. I have searched with pirates in the New World and have briefed the Jewish Brethren in Amsterdam. The response is always the same: as a woman, I must stay out of it. Be patient. 'A ship is no place for a woman during battle.' Now, you bring me more troubles with this new port brought to us by Morosini. Perhaps you, too, should follow the advice I have been given and stay out of it."

"But—"

Belladonna gestured for him to rise. "Go home and see your family. They will give you the same advice, and please be cautious and stay out of trouble. We do not need any more than we have already, I assure you."

Chapter Fifty-Two: Diana

VENICE, The eighth of MAY, 1615

"My boy!"

Her mother's cry awoke Diana. She wondered which of her brothers had returned and hoped it was Isaak, freed from captivity.

Quickly, she fastened her bodice and skirt over her muslin shift and tidied the thick featherbed, a remnant of her marriage, before exiting the alcove.

"Zebulun."

There must have been a note of disappointment in her voice since Zebulun asked, "Are you not happy to see your younger brother?"

Diana threw her arms around Zebulun in response.

"Have you come from England? Are you a member of that lord's household?" asked his mother, eyeing her son's clothing, which appeared to be made of rich fabrics and looked barely worn.

Zebulun did not answer his mother's question but pointed to the kettle warming on the newly lit fire. "Is there anything to eat? I am starving."

Their mother immediately took up the ladle and began filling a wooden bowl with steaming stew from the kettle. Zebulun closed his eyes as he inhaled the smells coming from the bowl in front of him.

"Your famous chickpea and lentil stew. I have dreamed of this stew, Mother, many a night."

Their mother's grin stretched wide across her face. Wiping her hands in a cloth, she arrested his hand as he lifted the spoon to his mouth. "Wait. Have you washed? This is still a civilized household, and we do uphold the proper customs, even if you have come from the fancy palazzos of the English. Take the bucket out to the well, you know where it is, and bring water for washing. Diana could use a wash, too."

Diana took the bucket and exited, stopping to touch the *mezuzah* on the doorpost. She signaled to Zebulun he must follow, and he did after casting a longing look at the bowl of stew.

The well stood in the large *campo* in the Ghetto Nuovo. It was still very early in the morning, and the *campo* was empty. Only the beadle was about, tapping his long cane across the shutters, calling the men to go to the synagogue for early morning prayers.

"It is so early, yet Father is already at the synagogue."

It sounded accusatory to Diana, and she responded defensively. "Of course, he is. He is the rabbi, and he must be there for prayers, morning, afternoon, and night. Besides, it is not a terrible thing to greet the dawn of a new day with a prayer."

Zebulun snorted, and Diana gave his arm a light punch. "Did I push you to join him at the synagogue? You do as you please, just as you always have, regardless of the cost to the people who love you."

Zebulun grabbed her hand and held it in his strong grip. "What about you? Ever consider the embarrassment you may cause Father by your association with a courtesan?"

Diana's nostrils flared, and she felt like upending the full bucket over her brother's head. "I should not have to defend myself to *you*, of all people. Now, before we have to go back inside, tell me what news you have of Isaak?"

She wiggled herself free of his grip and looked at her brother expectantly.

Zebulun took the bucket out of her hands and filled his sister in about his recent travels. "I have been in Constantinople, so I have heard nothing of Isaak."

Diana stamped her foot. "You have dashed my hopes! Ugh, it is so frustrating to know he has been taken but to hear nothing and be able to do nothing about our brother!"

"Our parents know of this?" he asked and gestured towards their home.

"I have told Father, but Mother does not know anything, and I am sure you will agree it is best it remains so."

"We should not talk of Isaak when we go inside," she added, "Tell her of your adventures and your visit with the English lord." She tugged at the dark velvet of his doublet. "Regale her with the story of your new clothes. Then, once she goes off to the well to share your success with her cronies, we can have our own talk."

"Agreed," said Zebulun. He picked up the full bucket, and the two siblings went back inside to face their mother.

***

"I have been to see Belladonna," said Zebulun in a low voice. He had finished two full bowls of stew, and their mother had taken the bowls outside to clean and dry. "She is not the same woman."

Diana looked at her brother with a tilt of her head as if she was noticing something new about him. "How could she be the same after what she has been through? Besides losing the man she loves, she now bears responsibility for her brother's widow and orphan."

This, too, was news to Zebulun, and Diana told him of the arrival of Roderigo, Belladonna's lost brother, and how he met his death in Venice. She touched on the intrigue with the English lord Sir George Villiers and how they had dangled the prospect of treasure to be found in Jamaica if he could persuade the English king to take the island from the Spanish.

Zebulun gave a low whistle at the conclusion of the story. "I have heard that name! Villiers was my Lord Arundel's nemesis at Court. Everyone hated him except for the King. Villiers has used his position as the Royal Favorite in any way that could line his pockets."

"Is Lord Arundel at Court then? You helped him escape from Venice, and he had made great promises to you. Has he been true to his word?"

Zebulun shifted from one foot to the other and was unable to meet her eyes. "Lord Arundel's offer of a commission, a home within his estate, had one requirement. I had to give up my birthright and convert to Christianity. To Church of England, I believe, but there were two rival churches, so I am not quite certain which one I was to join." He raised his eyes to meet hers. "I thought I had no ties to our traditions, but when it came to giving up my heritage and my history for another religion I do not believe in, I could not comply. And with that, I was forced to take my leave. Jews are still banned from living in England.""

"I am so sorry, Zebulun." She took his hand and clasped it between both of hers. They tilted their heads towards each other until they touched. Then Zebulun freed himself of her hands and placed his hands on his hips. "Well, not all was lost. Arundel outfitted me at his own cost, and he did let me sail away on the ship he had purchased for his escape from Venice. So now I look like a success and even command a ship. But once again, the course of my life has changed, and I have a new mission."

"Is that what brings you back to Venice?"

Zebulun nodded vigorously. "I have met a most unusual man, and it is he who commands me now. You shall meet him; he is here with me in Venice."

"He is wealthy then, your new patron. And he is a Jew? I suppose you both are staying at the Mitudela Guest House?"

The Ghetto had a variety of guest houses for Jewish merchants and traders who sought a safe place to stay where they could eat the food prepared according to Jewish traditions. For the most part, the hospitality was offered at a nominal charge, for the houses were supported by the Jewish community, as other guest houses were in other cities. The Mitudela Guest House was different; it catered to the wealthiest merchants and required a lodging fee to compensate the owners for providing such luxurious quarters.

"He is the equivalent of a king. The Sublime Ruler of the Golden Door has granted him dominance over the small island of Naxos. His aunt sits on the right hand of the Sultan and builds great wealth for herself and the kingdom. She has ambitious plans, which she has entrusted to her nephew, and he has enlisted me to help him accomplish them."

"Your father will be home shortly, and he shall be so glad to see you." Their mother had returned, and their conversation, therefore, had come to an end.

Zebulun rose from the table and gave his mother a kiss. "Time for me to go."

His mother pouted, and began to protest, but Zebulun put a finger to her lips. "I have not returned home alone, but with my employer. He is at the Guest House, and I cannot leave him so long to fend for himself. He has never been to Venice."

"Oh, ho, my son is now with a *G'vir**. No wonder you are dressed in such fine clothes! You see, Diana, the great success your little brother has become?" Her mother placed both hands on either side of her grown son's face and treated him to a series of kisses.

Zebulun, once freeing himself from his mother's embrace, immediately made his escape.

** a very important person*

Chapter Fifty-Three: Belladonna

VENICE, The tenth of MAY, 1615

The mauve silk was just right for Mariella's golden-brown complexion. As Mariella turned sideways to admire her profile in the mirrored walls, Belladonna recognized what a beauty Roderigo's wife was. Her most recent images of Mariella as a bedraggled woman with wild hair were banished after seeing her now, resplendent in silk, her glossy dark hair curled in the latest fashion.

"This dress is very complicated," said Mariella as she held out the underskirt. "In Jamaica, I could never wear such a thing. And these shoes! How am I supposed to walk in them?"

Mariella had been fitted for a pair of high platform shoes, and she lifted each foot tentatively while raising her skirts to view them.

"One of my greatest pleasures is wearing *chopines*. I truly missed living without them in the New World. With them, I am as tall as most men, and I walk through the room with power. You shall see, once you are used to them, you too will enjoy wearing them."

"I am not certain I wish to be on the same level with men. I feel better keeping my thoughts and my powers hidden beneath a cloak of meekness and submission."

Belladonna nodded slowly. "That is certainly one strategy and one I have never been able to adopt. In your case, Mariella, it is best you do not attract too much attention—which will be difficult since you have such great beauty."

Mariella shifted her neck in the high lace collar. "I am not in my element in such attire, but in a drawing room such as yours, filled with others similarly dressed. The outdoors is where I feel my power, not in high shoes." She gazed out the high windows. Laced with falling rain, the view was blurred. "There are barely any gardens here, and I miss the scent of the fields and flowers."

"That is why I have planned for you to settle in the Ghetto. You will feel more natural there. In this palazzo, you will be forced to accept the formalities of dress expected of Venetian society."

Belladonna waved the fan to stir the air about her face. It had been one of her favorites, crafted from peacock feathers with a handle of ivory, and had been stored away with a few of her favorite shoes and gowns when she had gone away. Though they were a year out of date in style, Belladonna's clever maid had been able to inflate the sleeves and lower the lace collar so they could still pass muster until her new gowns were finished.

Though it was only May, it was unseasonably warm, and she had chosen lace gloves rather than the leather ones to cover her hands, which had suffered from the months of rough living. Belladonna was just as uncomfortable in the layers of shifts, underskirts, overskirts, and bodices, but she had trained herself to be oblivious to the heat and discomfort. She had been gone more than a year, and she had yet to reclaim her status. With Isaak, she had thought she was done with creating such a facade, but without him, she needed power to protect herself—and her new-found family.

Now that her return was common knowledge, she expected society would come to call, and she had to refashion her impenetrable façade that served her so well before. It was a great risk to present Mariella to the outside world. She did not want her sister-in-law to garner the amorous attentions of any nobleman, as had happened with Diana. Diana's origins were unknown when she first appeared with an English nobleman and Mattia Correr at her salon, and Morosini had become an admirer.

However, even if Mariella was not known to be of the Hebrew faith, she was different and would be considered her protégé, which is not how

Belladonna wanted her sister-in-law to be perceived. Nor could Belladonna acknowledge their relationship without revealing her own origins and secrets. Her intuition was warning her to send Mariella away immediately, but she did not have the heart to force Mariella to leave.

The footman appeared and announced a visitor, which made her thoughtful meanderings futile, so she gathered her skirts and forced herself to stand stick straight to greet Bardon Morosini.

At first glance, Belladonna almost did not recognize her old friend and business partner. His face and body had thinned, and his cheekbones and chin seemed sharply chiseled from granite. He was dressed as immaculately as ever, though the new fashionable shorter pantaloons showed his stockinged legs had also lost their fullness.

He took her gloved hand and raised an eyebrow. "Well, it is good to see you are as well accessorized as ever." He did not release her hand and did not raise it to his lips. As he studied her face, his lips curved into a knowing smile. "Perhaps your sojourn from Venice has made its mark on you."

"Alas, time has a way of making its mark on us all."

"Perhaps it does," he acknowledged, having the grace not to specify how. His gaze had shifted beyond her, and she realized she had forgotten about Mariella.

"As you can see, I have not returned alone. May I introduce Mariella, who I have brought with me from Amsterdam."

Mariella, ignorant of society, did not tilt her head at Morosini coquettishly. After a brief curtsy, she stared at him for a few moments and then nodded as she would to a sailor on the *Sabato*. Morosini surveyed the younger woman from head to toe. Belladonna suspected that he was taken with her beauty and that her lack of courtly polish would intrigue him.

"Ah, a most enchanting visitor. I suppose she has some understanding of our language."

Belladonna gestured towards the divans, and they all took their seats. Mariella kept her eyes down on her skirts, trying to arrange them on the divan, avoiding the steady gaze of the visitor.

Morosini addressed Belladonna instead of Mariella, "She looks quite exotic. What language does she speak?"

Clever way to discover Mariella's origins. "Her native language is Spanish, but she is from the New World. She has some understanding of our language but is far from fluent." Though Bardon Morosini had been an ally to her and Roderigo, Belladonna hesitated to reveal that Mariella was Roderigo's wife. Morosini's assistance on behalf of her brother's mission had been based on the promise it would deliver a share of lost treasure. Belladonna suspected it was why Morosini had not wasted any time to find out the status of his investment.

"I predict you will find great success in Venice," said Morosini in Spanish, nodding to Mariella.

"Thank you for your confidence in me," said Mariella, "but I am curious as to why you have it?"

Her face was tilted at a becoming angle and took the sting out of her forthrightness.

Morosini's response showed that though he looked strained, his wit was as sharp as ever. "How refreshing, a woman whose tongue is as bold as her good looks. That will be the key to your success, my dear, along with the intelligence I see in your eyes."

Mariella smiled; it was the first sign of amusement on her sister-in-law's face in many long months. Morosini seemed to have awakened Mariella's spirits.

He surprised her with his next comment, which he delivered with his eyes locked on Mariella's. "Much as I am confident I would enjoy your company very much, I must beg your pardon, as Belladonna and I have business to discuss."

Mariella, taking the hint, rose. However, the look she gave the nobleman as she departed worried Belladonna. Morosini's regard for Mariella was equally evident.

As soon as she was gone, Morosini leaned forward to Belladonna with a confidential air. "I eagerly await to hear of your adventures, and I am agog with excitement to hear of the treasure in Jamaica."

Belladonna's fingers migrated to her pearls, fondling them as was her habit to calm her racing thoughts. "All did not go as planned, and the Spanish have overrun Jamaica."

Morosini's lips compressed into a hard, straight line. "And the treasure?"

Belladonna would never admit there was no treasure, other than in legend. "Though we located the cave, we did not have the chance to search for it, before a great storm came, followed by the invasion of the Spanish."

Morosini's jaw tightened, and his voice held menace as he said, "That is unfortunate for both of us, though it makes your investment in my new endeavor even more necessary."

Belladonna had to flutter her fan to cool her face. "I have spoken with my investment advisor. Highly speculative and very ambitious. Not your usual style." Her best position was to challenge his.

Morosini scowled. "I am sure you will recognize, as I did, the immense opportunity this presents. One neither of us dare refuse."

Belladonna treated him to a stony gaze. "I should like to know more, especially how you hope to see it pass the rulings of the Council of Ten without challenge from the Contarinis. I would think that all who promoted this plan would become their sworn enemy."

"Do not fool yourself, Belladonna. Both you and I can already count ourselves on the Contarini's list, especially from our past activities. Have you forgotten the poison that was meant for you but took the life of your unfortunate maid instead?"

"Before I left Venice, we had reached a détente. There are lines that should not be crossed with Niccolo Contarini, and this will be one of them."

"You will have my protection," said Morosini, rising, signaling their meeting had come to an end. "You will need it more than you suspect. You have been gone for a long time, and in the interim, other stars have ascended."

"Perhaps I have no wish to return to my former status." She fluttered her fan for emphasis.

Morosini shrugged. "Your decision. The competition will be fierce for the most influential woman in Venice, since Isabella has successfully claimed it. Beware of her, she can be formidable, as I can personally attest."

Like Belladonna, Isabella was a *cortigiana onesta,* an elite courtesan known for her wit and talents as well as her beauty. Isabella had been Morosini's mistress until he severed ties with her upon the murder of his wife, who, as he discovered too late, had been the love of his life.

Before Belladonna left Venice, Isabella had been hotly pursued by several young noblemen. "It is fortunate Isabella has had success even after you had tired of her."

Morosini gave her a knowing smile. "You shall see. However, I may venture to say that with your new protégé, you should present an interesting challenge to Isabella. Do not say I did not warn you, because now I have."

Chapter Fifty-Four: Diana

VENICE, The tenth of MAY, 1615

Zebulun had departed before the rabbi returned from morning prayers. Father and son did not see eye to eye, and their reunion would invariably lead to digs at each other, culminating in loud protests. Diana could not understand why her father, a broad-minded, tolerant, and modern man, could not accept his son's life choices. Diana agreed with her father that Zebulun was far too impetuous and did not make good decisions. However, she believed chastising him at every opportunity would not be of any benefit to either of them.

Delivering the news of Zebulun's return was the main purpose for Diana's visit to her father's office when morning services were over. His reaction was the very opposite of her mother's. First, he moaned, then he placed his head in his hands. "Oy, this I need now? Whenever there is a thundercloud of trouble hovering over the Ghetto, and Zebulun blows in, somehow, it turns into a great storm."

Diana took a seat. "What trouble?"

The rabbi sighed. "It involves Avigdor Margulies. He is stirring the pot once again, working with an agent from the court of Constantinople."

"I know."

The rabbi raised one eyebrow and prompted her. "Yes?"

"It is some great scheme to develop a new port, instead of relying solely on the existing one near the Punta del Dogana. Zebulun has returned as the escort of an important man from Constantinople."

Before the rabbi had a chance to reply, the door was flung open by a red-faced, portly little man, Avigdor Marguiles. Shaking with rage, he pointed a stubby finger at the rabbi.

"Where is your son? The funding for this project was all but assured. He had but a simple assignment: to deliver the investor and his capital. I will not face Morosini nor the Council of Ten on my own. If Zebulun does not appear by tomorrow, *you* will accompany me, dear rabbi. With your silvery tongue, you have managed to escape their censure before. And believe me, if I am blamed, the entire community of the Ghetto will be painted black with the same brush. This will not end well for any of us."

"Calm down," Diana said, "Zebulun is here in Venice."

Avigdor lowered his hand and shifted his attention from the rabbi to her. "How would you know?"

"Because he came to our rooms. I have just come here to advise my father of his arrival."

The steamed-up expression on Avigdor's face seemed to cool, and he muttered, "Well, why did you not say so at the start? Well, then, where is he? I have checked the guest houses, and he is not there."

Diana had an idea of where Zebulun would be found if he was not staying at the fancy Mitudela Guest House. At the home of the Turk. Particularly since the man he had brought with him was from the Court of the Sublime Ruler of Constantinople. But she did not offer this intelligence to Avigdor.

The rabbi stood behind his desk and leaned forward, his eyes fiery and his nostrils flaring. "How dare you barge in here in such a manner! My son is a grown man, and I do not answer for him, nor do I take responsibility for his actions. If he has angered you, it is his business and yours, but not mine. So, if you will, please take yourself out of my study..."

Both Diana and Avigdor were speechless. They had never seen the rabbi react with such anger to a congregant. The rabbi raised his hand and pointed to the door. "Go!"

Astonishingly, the belligerent Avigdor Margulies turned on his heels and left, slamming the door behind him.

Chapter Fifty-Five: Belladonna

VENICE, The fifteenth of MAY, 1615

"Good morning, Madama. Shall I send for the dressmaker to fit you for your dress for the *Festa della Sensa?*" asked Belladonna's maid as she pulled open the curtains surrounding her bed.

Belladonna had just awoken and paused in mid-stretch. "Oh, I had forgotten. When is the festive day?"

"On the twenty-fifth day of this month, Madama."

"That does not give me much time. Thank you for reminding me, and yes, please send for my dressmaker."

As if she were conscious of time wasting, Belladonna launched herself from the bed. Her bare feet, enjoying the chill of the terrazzo floor, took her to the large windows, which the maid had opened to let in the cool morning breezes from the canal. It was late, the sun already high in the sky, the fishing boats were already gone, taking their noise and circling gulls along with them.

As Belladonna washed, the maid returned with arms filled with her clothing and an eagerness to gossip. "This year, the festival should be even grander. The Gonzaga Duke, from Mantova, has already arrived, and the Duchess and her ladies shall join him before the Ascension."

"The Duke of Mantova? How long has he been in Venice?" Belladonna said as she raised her arms to allow the maid to pull on the gossamer-thin linen chemise. She gave a deep sigh, relishing its softness against her skin.

Rough living on the island of Hispaniola had given her a new appreciation of the luxuries of her life in this palazzo.

"A few weeks," said her maid as she adjusted the brocade bodice to Belladonna's form. "We are fortunate you have returned now. We were afraid the Provost would allot this palazzo to the Gonzagas for their stay, and we would be without a place until they decided to leave."

"Why would you think that?"

"Such a grand visitor would certainly have his own retinue of servants and would not have need of us," answered her maid, as if such a conclusion were common sense.

The maid's gossipy familiarity was becoming annoying. Besides, a woman of importance should not receive news of Venetian society through her maid.

"Can you tighten the bodice? It hangs too loosely," Belladonna said, changing the subject as she regarded her reflection in the mirrored wall.

The dress did not suit her as it should due to her considerable weight loss. Along with the roughness of her hands, both were the result of the difficulties of the past few months. Belladonna decided she needed the dressmaker as soon as possible. She could not reclaim her status, looking too thin and less than perfectly attired.

There was much to attend to, and Belladonna would not waste time. She had already decided to announce her return to Venice with a grand entrance at the *Festa della Sensa*. But besides the dressmaker, she needed to know more of the Duke of Mantova's agenda to develop her own.

She knew just where to go to retrieve such information. "Send for my gondola and advise Mariella that I will not see her until later in the evening."

* * *

The gondola rounded the curve of the Grand Canal, and upon seeing the familiar façade of Isabella's residence, Belladonna smiled. Feeling she could rely on her long-standing friendship with Isabella, she was suspicious of Morosini's motives in warning her away from his former mistress.

Isabella, elegant as a statue in her usual all-white ensemble, greeted her with kisses on each cheek in the entry hall of the *piano nobile*. Taking Belladonna's hand as if she were a child, Isabella brought her friend into the great room of her salon.

Belladonna had to admit, the room was breathtaking; from the cream on white patterned wall coverings with their matching draperies to the white columns holding up a balcony for musicians. Wall sconces of crystal reflected their candlelight onto the large gilt-framed paintings of idyllic landscapes. All in all, the room was a perfect setting for Isabella's serene beauty.

"You must have found a new patron since Morosini," said Belladonna.

"More than one," said Isabella, with a close-mouthed smile, not elaborating.

"I assume your salon must be the most sought-after destination in the city," said Belladonna after making herself comfortable on a settee opposite Isabella.

"You flatter me. I could never achieve what you did with your salon, I do not have the imagination."

"You certainly have the flair and good taste." Belladonna tilted her head back to view the paintings on the ceiling. "Tintoretto?"

"Peter Paul Rubens. He had been here to study with classical artists years ago, and these paintings are from that period. He is now a court painter in the Netherlands."

Why did she feel as if Isabella was tallying some secret score? "I am familiar with Rubens. I was quite taken with him when we met in Amsterdam. Perhaps you have some coffee?"

"Of course, how silly of me. We have been friends for so long that I neglected to offer more formal hospitality." Isabella flagged her lingering servants to bring in some refreshments. Belladonna could find no fault in the swiftness in which her request was honored, nor in the quality of the coffee she was served.

After placing her now-empty cup back in its tray, Belladonna spoke her mind. "I have come to you, Isabella, to learn in a nutshell what I have missed.

Is Contarini still in power? Is he still at odds with Morosini? And why has the Duke of Mantova come to Venice?"

Isabella replied to her questions with simple answers. "Contarini has been named Provost and is still active on the Council of Ten. Morosini opposes him at every opportunity, including how and where to entertain the Duke and his Duchess during their visit. As to why the Duke has chosen to visit Venice, he claims it is to pray at the feet of the Virgin in the chapel of San Christiano, which he credits with restoring his sight. He was supposedly so moved by the experience he decided to extend his stay and wishes to purchase his own residence in Venice."

"Have you made the Duke's acquaintance?" Belladonna noted that Isabella did not shrink from her gaze, though she did sense not all the information in her possession was being shared.

"Not yet. Although I will be attending the elaborate banquet at the Arsenale. One hundred ladies have been invited and are expected to be dressed as lavishly as possible, all at the expense of the *Officiali alle Rason Vecchie*. I have arranged for Gaspara and Cassandra to perform one of their compositions." There was no mistaking the self-satisfied smile that accompanied Isabella's announcement.

In Belladonna's experience of Venetian society, there had not been so extravagant a banquet. With so much investment in the fabulous attire of so many ladies, Isabella was shrewd enough to use it as her chance to establish herself as the leading courtesan of the city without having to lay out a ducat from her own coffers.

Well, let Isabella claim the crown of Queen of the Courtesans. Belladonna was no longer a courtesan but a woman of power who could dazzle any jaded Duke and thereby demonstrate the superiority of Venice in art and beauty.

"How fortuitous. I shall be glad to renew my acquaintance with the Duke then." Belladonna lied, and continued in her fabrication, noting her words caused several creases to appear in Isabella's unusually smooth forehead. "Oh, perhaps you did not know the Duke and I are old acquaintances? But I applaud your initiative. I expect the Duke will enjoy listening to a performance by Gaspara and Cassandra."

Isabella's frown deepened as she muttered, "No doubt."

"Now, I must run, but I shall see you at the banquet." Belladonna rose and patted Isabella's shoulder. She planned to secure her invitation to the banquet at the Arsenale from Morosini.

Isabella escorted her from the salon but did not hesitate to launch a little dig at Belladonna. "I am so glad to know you are one of the hundred ladies. With you being gone so long, I feared you had been forgotten."

Morosini was right; Isabella had changed, and she had just dropped the gauntlet before her.

Chapter Fifty-Six: Belladonna

Morosini would not be eager to supply her with an invitation to the banquet unless she provided her assurance she would invest in his enterprise. She decided to pay a visit to Jacob Sullam to instruct him to set up the funding. She would bring Mariella along with her. The more her sister-in-law was exposed to the Sullams' life in the Ghetto, the more appealing living there should become.

She found Mariella alone and looking as melancholy as she had aboard ship. "Is there nothing in my palazzo to bring you joy? Or are you sad without Moises?"

Mariella brushed an errant curl from her cheek. "Of course, I miss Moises, along with blue skies and the windswept fields of Jamaica. I still dream of it."

Belladonna took Mariella's hand. "I understand. You feel like a stranger here and cannot see how you will fit in. Take comfort; I felt the same way when I first arrived, and."

Mariella continued her sentence. "You dreamed of Venice all the while you were in Jamaica. Tell me now, if Isaak were to be found, would you abandon this place and sail away with him again?"

"Do not ask me such a question, for I am not sure how I would answer it."

Mariella hung her head. "I am sorry, I just feel so very lost. I know I do not belong in this palazzo with you, but I do not know how I will survive enclosed behind the walls of the Ghetto. I am used to my freedom."

"I had once seen the Ghetto as you do, but more recently, I found behind its walls a place of refuge and friends I can trust." Silently, Belladonna contrasted her friendship with Diana with her relationship with Isabella. "Come with me now to the Ghetto. We will see how Moises fares."

Obediently, Mariella accompanied her to the gondola. "One request I have of you: allow me to stay with you but a little bit longer so I may experience this city as you do. Perhaps then I, too, will grow to love it."

Slowly, Belladonna nodded. Morosini's observation about Mariella came to mind. If Mariella were to accompany her to the banquet at the Arsenale, she would be a sensation. She could sing and play her guitar and entertain the audience as well as Gaspara and Cassandra. Belladonna was competing with Isabella for status, and Mariella wanted to experience the best of Venice, so the Banquet of One Hundred Ladies would serve both purposes. After the *Festa della Sensa*, when the festivities would end, normalcy would be restored, and Mariella could retreat to the Ghetto.

She tapped a finger to her chin. It might even be wise to let Mattia Correr paint Mariella's portrait as he so desired. Her own portrait and Mariella's would be a suitable gift to make to the Duke, as it was the custom of such nobles to assemble a 'gallery of beauties' for their palazzos. Inspired by her plans, Belladonna bid the gondolier to pole faster towards one of the two bridges that led into the Ghetto.

* * *

A visit to the Sullams would allow Belladonna to cross more than one task off her list. Besides Jacob's ability to facilitate the investment in Morosini's project, he was an importer of silks and magnificent fabrics from the East. She would choose the fabric for her dresses for the *Festa della Sensa* today and work with the dressmaker to ensure her gowns for the banquet would surpass anything Isabella might wear.

As soon as they entered the salon, Moises ran to them, engulfing his mother in his arms and nestling his head against her chest.

As if awakened from a stupor, Mariellacovered her son's face with kisses. "My great big boy! How are you faring? Have you been drawing more beautiful pictures?"

Moises politely greeted Belladonna and disengaged from his mother's grasp. "Better than that! I have been learning to write the Hebrew letters. The rabbi and the scribe are teaching me. Then, I will be able to create beautiful *ketubot* for weddings. Perhaps even for you?" He winked at Belladonna.

Belladonna's hand strayed to her pearls, and their clacking helped her swallow down a bitter surge of sorrow over the loss of her future with Isaak. Mariella's face reddened, and she pulled her son away, asking him to show her his work.

Belladonna left mother and son to their reunion and headed towards the study. Grateful to find Jacob reviewing documents at his desk and without Sarra, Belladonna waved aside the usual pleasantries. "I have decided to invest in Morosini's scheme."

Jacob put down the papers and frowned. "I must recommend against it. The Jews are being forced to invest in this scheme, but there is no reason you, too, should take such a risk."

Belladonna placed her hands on the edge of his desk and leaned forward. "You continue to have misgivings about the new port?"

Jacob cleared his throat before answering, "Something is not right; there are too many coincidences."

"Such as?'

"The arrival of Josef di Azzura offering an investment from his patron in Constantinople, once our sworn enemy. Then the Gonzaga Duke of Mantova arrives, the brother-in-law of the Holy Roman Emperor in Austria, another enemy, who also expresses an interest in investing."

Belladonna shifted her position and perched herself on the edge of the desk. "I see. I, too, do not believe in coincidence. But I need Morosini's help, and he is pressuring me to invest."

"What type of help? Perhaps I can be of assistance. My network of merchants make it their business to know what intrigues are brewing behind the scenes."

Belladonna's fingers played with her pearls. With Morosini, who was aware of her rivalry with Isabella, she could find out more about Gonzaga's proclivities and preferences in women and entertainment. Not the territory of traders and merchants. However, any information about the hidden agendas of either Gonzaga or the emissary from the East would be useful.

"What have you heard?" she prompted.

Jacob looked around to ensure no servants lurked or eavesdropped. In a lowered voice, he said, "I fear a plot is about to hatch, centering around the new port. Avigdor Margulies has been tasked to find the resources and architects, which is unusual. Have you ever heard of a project of such magnitude being entrusted to a Jew from the Ghetto?"

"A fair point. What can you tell me of this man, Margulies?"

Jacob took a deep breath. "I cannot imagine bestowing such an official role on a man like Margulies or how he gained the confidence of a shrewd character like Morosini. Avigdor may be successful as a merchant, but he is plagued, like your father, with the urge to gamble. Not at the tables, but in highly speculative schemes that have cost him and his fellow investors dearly."

Belladonna tapped her lip. "I agree with you; there is something going on here. Your people have been placed in the center of two opposing enemies, effectively positioning the Jews to take the blame for any disaster that may occur."

She sighed. A consultation with Morosini was necessary. Only he would be privy to the true agenda behind this new port.

But first, she had another purpose. Jacob was an importer of fabrics from the East, and so she asked to see some of his samples. Grateful for the change of subject, he offered to escort her to the storeroom where they were kept.

Chapter Fifty-Seven: Belladonna

VENICE, The seventeenth of MAY, 1615

The late afternoon sun cast long shadows across the *campo* but cast warmth on her shoulders as her gondola turned towards the Grand Canal. The air was mild and breezes aided her hair in escaping from her coiffure. The playful shouts of children vied with the cries of vendors hawking their wares. Women clustered around both groups, gossiping and negotiating deals. Exotic music came to her ears as she merged into the bustle of the *Campo di Mori*.

Women in veils, and men in turbans, colorful carpets hanging from balcony railings, and vendor stalls rich with the aroma of coffee and spices nearly distracted her from her purpose. Skirting along a brick wall, she came to the distinctive blue door and pulled the chain to ring the bell. The Turk's daughter admitted her and led her through the fragrant garden to the courtyard where visitors were received.

She had not expected to encounter Zebulun here, and he was not alone. The Turk welcomed her with his usual enthusiasm. "Ah, the beautiful Belladonna has graced us with her return. Gracious lady, I am at your service."

Zebulun rose and made the introduction to a bearded and turbaned man at his side. "May I present Josef di Azzura from Constantinople."

"Pleased to meet you." The bearded man gave her a small bow.

"Please, sit." The Turk gestured to the cushioned divans and signaled to his daughter, "Bring refreshments for all my good friends."

"Your visit has been much anticipated," said Belladonna to Josef. "I understand you plan on making a substantial investment in the construction of a new port."

Josef smiled, revealing strong white teeth. Steely blue eyes held her in their gaze. "You are surprisingly well informed."

Belladonna inclined her head towards Zebulun, and Josef understood. "My young friend has been promoting my agenda, as well he should."

Fiddling with her pearls, Belladonna said, "It seems there are so many interested in this new port. Bardon Morosini encouraged me to invest, and now I understand the Duke of Mantova may stake an interest."

Would he take the bait?

Zebulun opened his mouth, but the steely blue eyes shot a warning look, and he closed it. It was the Turk who responded to her question. "The Duke has already arrived *incognito*, but in the company of the Venetian gentleman Pietro Foscarini. When Foscarini came to me to arrange for certain specialties, he confided that the Duke wished to negotiate the possibility of opening a new water-borne trade route that would extend on land to Mantova. I assumed this would be of interest to my friend Josef."

Turning his blue gaze back to Belladonna like a weapon, the man from Constantinople said, "The Turk wisely passed this information along the proper channels until it reached my patron, a great lady who has the ear of the Sultan. Hence, I made haste to arrange for a guide," he waved a hand towards Zebulun, "and the funding for claiming a significant stake in this project."

"My financier considers this a highly speculative investment. Is your patron one to take great risks?"

Josef di Azzura gave her a smug smile. "The Duke also made it known that he was willing to act as an intermediary between Constantinople and the emperor, his new brother-in-law. So, I consider the investment well worth the risk."

"Perhaps that is why Bardon Morosini is so convinced of its success. But I did not come here to learn more about the plans for the new port."

The Turk's eyebrows rose as if he wondered what she was talking about.

Belladonna continued, "If someone wants to throw a lavish entertainment, they are likely to come to the Turk to provide the luxuries needed. You must know what entertainments and sumptuous banquets are being prepared for the Duke's visit and whether the Duchess will also make an appearance in this city."

The Turk leaned back, placing both hands on his belly. "You have come to the right conclusions, my dear. And I will be happy to share what I have learned about the preparations for the celebrations over the next few days for the *Festa della Sensa*."

"I, too, shall be interested in hearing of the plans. I plan on staying in Venice until after the Ascension, and my patron will want to know all about such activities," said Josef.

Zebulun, who had been quieter than usual, spoke up now, "The Jewish traders have been tasked with supplying all the fabrics for the barges and gondolas of the Duke's processions. They have already gathered large swaths of red velvet to be draped across the Duke's gondola and across the path in the Arsenal where the banquet in his honor will be held."

"The Jews always must bear the brunt of the cost of a visiting dignitary. You are fortunate to have men of means to supply the necessary capital," said Josef, but he looked off into the distance, as if he was not speaking of Venice but his own land.

"Is it the same in Constantinople? Jews are taxed and forced to finance the luxuries for the state?" asked Belladonna.

"Yes."

There were a few moments of awkward silence until he seemed to recover himself and continued, "It is slightly different in some ways, but the same in others. As the Inquisition gained power in Spain, it forced the migration of Spain's Jews. They came to Amsterdam and Venice, where they prospered. The Great Sultan of the Golden Door is no fool, recognizing that Spain's loss could be of benefit to his empire. Invitations and promises of the Sultan's protection were issued to many of these refugees, such as my patron, a widow of Don Isaac di Martinez. Dona Elena di Martinez is a clever woman and has amplified the fortune of the Sultan as well as her own."

"She lives openly as a Jew in the palace of the Sultan, in a section of her own, more lavish than any palazzo I have ever seen. Her dinners are lavish and served on golden plates, with goblets of the finest crystal."

When Zebulun paused to take a breath, Josef interrupted him. "But just as anywhere in this world, it can all be gone in an instant." He snapped his fingers. "If the Sultan's fortune suffers a loss, Dona di Martinez must make it up. And if the Sultan should die…So you see, as it says in the *Pirkei Avot*, The Ethics of Our Fathers, *Good fortune is a lie, and beauty is nothing, for only good faith should be admired.*"

The strong aroma of fresh coffee warned them of the appearance of the Turk's daughter, which put a pause to their discussion. Instead, Zebulun spoke of the different competitors in the upcoming regatta, a key feature of the *Festa Della Sensa*. As the men compared the merits of the various teams, Belladonna closed her eyes, savoring both the aroma and the flavor of the coffee. When she opened her eyes, a few moments later, she encountered Josef's steely gaze.

"You are looking at me quite intensely, sir," Belladonna saw no harm in confronting him.

"You present quite an unusual picture," Josef said. "such a gentle loveliness, yet there is no serenity in your eyes. In fact, I would say there is great pain hidden in their depths."

"Are you a mind-reader as well as a businessman?" Belladonna's hands flicked over her pearls; their clicking was music to her ears. "Perhaps you can satisfy my curiosity. If you are a master of the trade, you must have many ships at your command, am I correct? If the need arises, you could call on such ships to Venice, and they would heed your commands?"

Josef eyed Zebulun before nodding.

"I am certain Zebulun will vouch for the need to liberate his brother Isaak, a man who has dedicated his life to the rescue of Jews from slavery and death and who is now imprisoned on a ship bound for Spain."

Chapter Fifty-Eight: Diana

VENICE, The seventeenth of MAY, 1615

When Diana returned to the Ghetto Nuovo, she was surprised to find Mattia Correr there, spinning to the right and left, searching for something, and running a hand through his long hair. As soon as he spotted her, he hurried over. "Diana, I need your assistance."

Diana looked around the busy *campo*. An acquaintance waved to her from a group of young women gossiping by the well. She gestured towards the bridge and walked towards it, expecting Mattia to follow.

Across the bridge was the Sullam mansion and, a few buildings away, her father's office. Mattia caught up to her in front of the Sullams as she was knocking at their door. Instead of a maid, it was Sarra herself who admitted them.

"Diana! How good of you to visit. And you have brought the portrait painter," said Sarra, curtsying to Mattia.

Mattia bowed, "Sarra, so good to see you once more! You are still as lovely as the day I first painted you."

Sarra gave the artist a half smile. "Come now, it was only a year ago, so I should hope I have not changed. Now, join us in the salon. I have guests, but I shall introduce you."

Taking the artist's arm, Sarra escorted him through the great hall and into the salon. Diana followed, peeved that Mattia seemed to have forgotten her.

Her fears were confirmed when Mattia cried out, "She is here!"

Mattia rushed forward and bowed dramatically before Mariella. "I have been looking everywhere for you. I must paint you, and there is no time like the present."

Mariella looked puzzled and repeated. "Paint me?"

"Your portrait." Sarra informed her, "He is an artist, quite an accomplished one. He has painted Diana's portrait and Belladonna's as well as mine. Would you care to see it?"

"A true artist! Please, please, I should so like to see your portrait!" cried Moises, leaping up, forgetting the cluster drawings he had on his lap, which scattered across the floor.

Sarra gestured for them to follow her into a small parlor furnished in pale greens and gold. A small writing desk stood before the large window, and beyond it, above the white marble mantlepiece, hung the portrait of Sarra. The painting was filled with pale pinks and blush tones that fit well with the green and gold coloring of the room.

"How lovely!" said Mariella, her eyes raised to the portrait in admiration.

"Goodness, I should very much like to know how to paint like that," said Moises, and he shifted his adoring gaze from the painting to Mattia.

Mattia seemed to warm to the young man. "I always appreciate someone's desire to learn more about art. I would be very happy to instruct you." He snapped his fingers, as if an idea had just come to him. "And you will have the perfect opportunity to observe my methods when I paint the portrait of your mother."

"Do you think that is wise?" Diana jumped into the conversation. "Mariella wishes to establish a new life here in the Ghetto. It would not bode well for her reputation to have her portrait painted now."

"I painted your portrait and Sarra's. Why should it be a problem for Mariella?"

"Sarra is a married woman, and no one in the Ghetto knows about my portrait."

Mattia ran a hand through his long hair. "I do not see the difficulty then. Mariella is still living with Belladonna, so no one in the Ghetto needs to know of it. I left some of my supplies in the palazzo, and it should be no matter to set up a little studio. Mariella will pose for me there." Mariella could not follow much of what Mattia was saying, but Moises quickly translated for her. Her son took her hand and implored her, "Please, Madre."

Mariella looked at Sarra and Diana, but only Sarra nodded. With a great sigh, Mariella smiled at Mattia and said, "I will do it."

Mattia looked pleased enough to dance and clapped his hands in enthusiasm. Diana pursed her lips and was about to protest once more, and then she stopped herself.

Why was she so disturbed by Mattia painting Mariella's portrait?

Chapter Fifty-Nine: Belladonna

VENICE, The thirteenth of MAY, 1615

Zebulun jumped up. "Isaak could not allow himself to be captured by the Spanish. He is far too clever! You must be mistaken."

Ignoring his outburst, Belladonna turned to the Turk. "Have you learned anything new?"

The Turk adjusted his turban and cleared his throat before answering. "I have just received news from a Moroccan who sailed with Isaak a few months ago. He had just arrived from the New World and had quite a story to tell."

"You see! Isaak is alive. The Spanish could not get the better of him." Zebulun raised his chin high and folded his arms across his chest.

"This Moroccan, he talked about an attack on a Spanish fort," continued the Turk, "he was part of a small force that landed unobserved on another side of the island, making their way through swamps and snakes to El Moro, the formidable fort guarding the bay of Havana. They manage to get inside the fort and do something to the cannons. The pirate ships arrive and attack by sea, but when the Spaniards push their canyons into position and then light them…BOOM! They explode in those Spanish faces."

"You believe this is Isaak's work?" asked Belladonna.

The Turk nodded. "The Moroccan tells this story, but no one believes him. No one but me. Why? Because I have seen Isaak do this before, at the fort in Algeciras. It was glorious! Yes, I know this is Isaak."

"Well, what happened then? Where is Isaak?" asked Belladonna, clenching and unclenching her hands.

The Turk sighed, "There, the Moroccan could not say for certain. He saw Isaak fighting a Spaniard on the walls and then topple off."

Belladonna took a sharp intake of breath and raised a hand to her temple.

"No! It cannot be!" cried Zebulun, sinking into his seat.

The Turk held up his hands. "Wait! I have not finished. The Moroccan climbed down from the walls to see if Isaak still lived. Allah preserve him, the trees had broken his fall, and he seemed to be alive, but before the Moroccan could come to his aid, some French men appeared, they found Isaak and evidently took him aboard the French ship."

"A French ship?" asked Josef, who had been listening carefully. "A French ship would have the opportunity to slip away while the other pirates were focused on the Spanish."

"Yes, my man was clear on that. The French ship sailed off while the other pirates went on to take Havana."

"If Isaak is a captive aboard the French ship, perhaps he is safe now from Spain?" Zebulun looked to the others for confirmation of his wishful thinking.

The Turk shook his head. "With Isaak aboard their ship, their destination is Spain. There is a hefty reward for Isaak's capture."

Belladonna's fingers flew to her pearls, and clicking them calmed her. She had two disturbing realizations. "The Frenchmen must have discovered who Isaak really is, which is why they took him along. A French ship would be able to sail unmolested away from the scene." She stared at Zebulun. "Do you see the implication? I had begged the Brethren in Amsterdam to overtake every Spanish ship from the New World, assuming Isaak would be found on a *Spanish* ship. A French ship could sail right by with Isaak inside without being stopped. Zebulun, do you have a way to reach the Brethren and alert them about the French pirate ship?"

Zebulun got to his feet. "Yes, but I must set off immediately. The usual rendezvous is tonight at midnight."

Josef also stood, placing a hand on Zebulun's shoulder. "We must not allow this French ship to slip away from us. Isaak cannot fall into the hands of the Spanish inquisitors, for he knows too much about the Brethren. If he were put under torture, he would be forced to provide dangerous intelligence to the Spanish of secret drop-off and rendezvous points used by the Brethren and the routes of my patron's ships. The Sultan's benevolence towards all the Jews who reside in his lands is dependent on the success of our trade routes. We cannot take any chances. The Turk and I will see to messaging our collaborators to send the swiftest ships to intercept these French pirates."

Belladonna's forehead beaded with sweat as she imagined how Isaak would fare aboard the French pirate's ship. If his fall had left him severely injured, would he be cared for? If Isaak was worth gold, they would not allow him to die on the journey. But in what condition would he be in by the time he was brought to the Spanish court?

She raised a hand to her head, momentarily dizzy. She must force her thoughts away from this, or the anxiety would overwhelm her. She sensed Josef's eyes upon her. Had he something else to offer?

She addressed her next comment to Josef. "I appreciate that you feel the same urgency to rescue Isaak. As a woman, I cannot do much more to help him. But you are not without resources and influence. What can you suggest?"

Josef did not hesitate to answer. "I have access to the swiftest ships under the command of the Sultan. They can join the Brethren, and together, we shall have a force no French ship can slip through."

Belladonna felt like embracing him, but instead, she presented a solemn nod of approval. She rose, ready to depart, but Josef raised a hand, signaling her to wait. "There is another matter I would like to discuss that could be the first sign of trouble for us all. For the festivities of the *Festa della Sensa*, the Gonzaga Duke has demanded the Jews supply the fireworks to set off after the regatta. Their agent, Foscarini, has been plaguing Avigdor Margulies for the fireworks, insisting they must come from the Ghetto."

Belladonna raised an eyebrow. "The Ghetto? That makes little sense. As Foscarini knows, the Berlandaos of Chioggia are the suppliers of fireworks, and the skies of Venice are always lit from their supply. Why would he expect to receive them from the Ghetto instead?"

Zebulun nodded. "That was my reaction as well. Something is not right. I advised Avigdor to tell Foscarini it would be ordered from Chioggia, which he did. But it did no good. Avigdor says Foscarini said the Duke expects the fireworks to come from the Ghetto and not Chioggia. Every day, he sends the same message about the fireworks, and we have been delaying until we can find a way out of this."

Josef added, "The Gonzaga Duke must have planned quite a show for the *Festa della Sensa* and the regatta, but I fear for the role he wishes the Jews to play."

Chapter Sixty: Diana

VENICE, The fourteenth of MAY, 1615

Diana, with Moises in tow, silently chided herself about her misgivings about Mariella's portrait as she mounted the stairs to the *piano nobile* of Belladonna's palazzo. Moises's face was so eager as he clutched a folio Sarra had given him to hold his paper and charcoal; it made Diana appreciate how much each session with Mattia meant to Moises.

She found Belladonna first, in the great salon, amid a cluster of tradesmen, presenting rolls of satin, lace, and gilded trim for her perusal. Belladonna looked up at their entry and, treating them both to a warm smile, gestured to an open door behind her. "I have allowed Mattia to set up his easel and supplies in the small salon, which has the best light."

Diana was relieved that Mattia had not begun his painting. Mattia was known to rage at anyone who interrupted him when his brush was in his hands and while in the throes of his inspiration.

Mariella never looked more beautiful. Mattia had dressed her in saffron satin, its bodice loose and low across her shoulders. The color offset the coppery tones in her hair which cascaded down her back in rich, glossy waves.

A cloud of annoyance passed over Mattia's face as Mariella reached for her son, who embraced his mother. "Careful, my boy, I must not anger Mattia by shifting my position. He was very particular to arrange my hair and skirts just so."

As Moises pulled away, his hold on his folio slipped, and several sheets of his drawings fell from it to the floor.

Sketches of his mother, Sarra, and scenes from the Ghetto in black charcoal were revealed. Mattia picked up the drawing of Sarra and studied it carefully. "You have a natural talent. You have captured, in a few sure strokes, the essence of your subjects."

He clapped Moises on the back, adding, "I would be happy to help you hone your skills. If you apply yourself with diligence, you may become one of the great artists of our city."

"That is kind of you to say," said Mariella.

Diana hoped Mariella was not succumbing to Mattia's charm, like so many others who posed for him. It was not a jealous observation, but a real concern. Any relationship between Gentile and Jew could merit harsh penalties—on the the entire community of the Ghetto.

"It is not out of kindness, but appreciation of the quality of your son's work." Mattia was saying, as he handed the sketch back to Moises. The young man was busy collecting his work and shoving it quickly back into the portfolio.

Mattia beckoned to the boy. "Take a place over there, behind the easel, where you will be able to see how I paint."

Moises followed the artist's direction after putting away his sketches. He took a chair and placed himself in the best spot to observe the artist at work. Diana was dismayed Mattia had not paid her any mind and was wholly focused on Mariella. *Should she say something?*

She cleared her throat to catch Mattia's attention. As if he had just noticed her, Mattia treated her to a most charming smile. "Diana, I am sorry. You know how absorbed I have become in my work. Especially when I hear my subject's music. It has been playing in my head incessantly."

Mattia had confided his secret in capturing the essence of his subjects to Diana. He claimed to hear the music of their souls in his head, beginning when he raised his brush to the canvas at the start of the painting and concluding when it was done. His explanation was similar to the Kabbalah's description of the transmigration of souls. It was why she had consented to have her portrait painted, to find proof of this premise by her first-hand experience.

"How lucky for you that you have not even begun to paint, and you hear the music." Diana hoped there was no sign of her disappointment on her face. When Mattia was endeavoring to capture Diana's likeness on canvas, he could not hear her 'music' at first and had delayed painting her portrait until he could. Diana folded her arms and regarded Mariella's pose. *What makes her different?*

After tilting Mariella's head slightly in the direction of the waiting canvas, Mattia seemed ready to begin. With Moises watching him, Mattia began to mix paint in jars and then dabbed a prodigious amount onto his palette. Choosing a wide brush, he swirled it into the paint and raised it to the canvas.

Mattia described his actions out loud for the benefit of his pupil. "First, the canvas must be covered completely in a very dark base color. I have chosen a rich dark umber since it will enhance the colors of the skin tones and dress as they emerge from its darkness."

The sounds of paint being smoothed over canvas were interrupted by the swooshing of silk as the scent of gardenias wafted through the odor of oils.

Belladonna had entered the room, and she was not alone.

Chapter Sixty-One: Belladonna

VENICE, The eighteenth of MAY, 1615

Josef of Constantinople surprised Belladonna by appearing at her palazzo. Zebulun had already departed the city to contact the Jewish Brethren. Josef, too, was about to depart to rally more support from his fleetto capture the French ship. Before going, he was paying Belladonna a visit to deliver some important messages. Belladonna believed Josef also wanted to assess *her* and the extravagance of her palazzo.

Belladonna led him through her grand entry hall into the elegant salon. Josef stopped short, his eyes staring and his mouth agape at his first sight of Mariella posing for her portrait. Belladonna was pleased with his reaction and hoped Mattia's painting would elicit the same response from the Duke of Mantova. She intended to unveil it at the Banquet of One Hundred Ladies during the *Festa della Sensa*.

When Mariella shifted slightly to see Belladonna's guest, Mattia threw down his brush and stood up. Stretching his arms above his head, he called out to Mariella. "I have not yet outlined your form, so you may relax your pose—but do not rise from the divan."

Diana must have noticed the visitor gazing so intently at Mariella and positioned herself in between them. Belladonna introduced her to Josef. "Zebulun's sister. With her, you can entrust your messages."

Giving her a short bow, Josef asked Diana, "Is Avigdor Margulies a man you would know?"

Diana nodded. "Yes, I do. He is a merchant who involves himself in all kinds of intrigue. I saw him yesterday when he barged into my father's office, demanding to know the whereabouts of my brother Zebulun."

Josef clasped his hands together, as if in prayer. "Perfect! Please give him this message: the fireworks will be placed in a warehouse near the *Campo di Mori*, courtesy of the Turk. Tell him Zebulun is gone for now but will return before the week is over."

"But where—"

Belladonna put a finger to Diana's lips, interrupting her. "Wait. I will inform you of the reason for Zebulun's departure and all I have learned from the Turk."

Gesturing for Josef and Diana to follow her, Belladonna headed for the door. Josef lingered his eyes once again on Mariella.

Mariella met his stare with her own. "Why do you look at me so?"

"I wonder if we have met before?"

Mariella gave a short laugh. "I have but recently arrived from the New World. Have you been there?"

"No, though I have traveled extensively from Spain to Constantinople, I have not gone that far. I assumed you were from a sunbaked land. You are unlike the women in this city who take great pains to keep their skin pale."

As their eyes remained locked on each other, there was no mistaking an instant attraction between them. The spell was broken when Mattia called out, "Resume the pose, please, I am ready to outline."

* * *

After Josef departed, Belladonna briefed Diana on what she had learned about Isaak. Diana let out a deep breath. "It was fortunate you had contacted the Turk. We now have confirmation that Isaak is alive and an idea of where to find him."

Belladonna clasped her hands together tightly. "If only we were men and could go after him ourselves!"

Diana did not disagree but could think of no course of action the two of them could take to bring Isaak back. They sat in silence, their eyes on each other, listening to the gentle ticking of the French clock on the mantlepiece. Belladonna sighed and took Diana's hand. "We must be patient. Time will determine whether they shall succeed. Now, find this man, Avigdor Margulies, and relay Josef's message. These fireworks worry me. In the meantime, I will invest some time and money to learn what I can of the Duke of Mantova."

"I suppose you are planning something spectacular for the *Festa della Sensa*. It will be your first appearance in Venetian society since you returned."

Belladonna fingered her pearls. "I shall certainly do my best to overshadow Isabella."

"Has Isabella become your rival instead of your friend?"

"Isabella is an ambitious woman. I suspect she has set her sights on the Duke of Mantova, to secure the position as his Favorite. Such a position comes with land and a magnificent palazzo that befits a Gonzaga Favorite. I imagine it would suit Isabella well."

Inclining her head towards the small salon where they had just left Mariella and the artist, Belladonna said, "I hope Mattia will complete the portrait in time for the Banquet of One Hundred Ladies. Mattia's skill can transform Mariella's image into a mythical creature, as he did with my portrait and yours. I am also planning to serve something special for the Duchess, also thanks to Mariella. Chocolate."

"Chocolate? Though it is a new beverage I am certain they must have sampled it before."

Belladonna beckoned to her. "Come with me later to the kitchens, and you shall have your first taste of chocolate morsels. It is a common treat in the New World, but a rare delicacy in Europe. Mariella has shared the secrets of its preparation with my cook."

Belladonna's fingers strayed automatically to her pearls. Click, clack. The sound of them knocking together was like a balm. She closed her eyes for a moment. "Come, let me show you the fabrics I have picked for my gown for the *Festa della Sensa*."

Placing an arm around Diana, Belladonna escorted her friend into the great room, where the rolls of colorful fabrics were draped across several divans. Peacock blues vied with royal purples while gold satin shimmered among them. "I must make an impact, and my dress must be spectacular. Which do you think will serve my purpose best?"

"I prefer the peacock blue with your coloring. But it will be up to you to discover more of what interests the Duke and what he is after here, in Venice."

Belladonna gave Diana's hand a squeeze. "I agree with you on both counts."

Chapter Sixty-Two: Belladonna

VENICE, The twentieth of MAY, 1615

Only a few days remained to complete all the arrangements for the Banquet of One Hundred Ladies and the many outfits necessary for her to shine at every event of the *Festa della Sensa*. At her visit to the Turk, the iridescent veils of the Turks' daughter had caught her eye. She was able to acquire the fabric for her gown for the ceremony of the marriage of Venice to the Sea. With its subtle greens and golds, it would shimmer like the sun on the lagoon, and she envisioned herself with veils aflutter, seated on a shell-like throne fitted into her gondola.

It was quiet in the salon; no murmurs of conversation drifting in from the smaller room adjacent to it, where Mattia should be hard at work on Mariella's portrait. Belladonna had not seen either of them yet this morning and preferred they stayed out of her salon until after her new guests departed.

With promises of investment, Belladonna had succeeded in motivating Morosini to invite Pietro Foscarini, the Gonzaga duke's designated escort, to Belladonna's salon this afternoon. Checking her reflection, Belladonna decided she liked the loose arrangement of her hair, which the unrelenting Caribbean sun had lightened to a golden hue. Despite having faced storms and swamps, her face had retained its smooth elegance and did not look weatherbeaten. Belladonna wore her pearls wrapped around her neck and, because this was an informal afternoon visit, did not wear a stiff lace collar but let the bodice alone frame her bare neck. A pale green silk dress adorned with silken flowers complemented the room's décor and enhanced the green coloring of her eyes.

Yes, she was ready for her performance. She did not know Foscarini well, but he was not known to have possessed great wit or savviness. With Morosini as her foil, she should have no trouble extracting all the information she needed about the Gonzagas—their agenda, arrangements, and predilections. Belladonna patted her hair to reassure herself it was neat and smoothed her skirts after arranging them around her on the divan.

The last effort was to plaster a welcoming smile across her face when her guests arrived. Morosini was the first to cross the threshold, his silken shoes leaving soft taps with each step he took across her terrazzo floor. The nobleman's face had sharpened, and his eyes narrowed, making him look more foxlike than ever. He was suited to accommodate the mild May weather, fashionable in a pale blush-colored doublet paired with beige pantaloons, stockings, and shoes.

Morosini bent down to kiss her hand. *He, too, is performing.* Morosini's bored, lazy manner was contrary to his highly strung, ambitious true self. In contrast, Pietro Foscarini was precisely the type Morosini disdained, with the weak chin and shuffling gait more suited to a servant than a noble. Though still in his prime, Pietro's eyes were pouchy, and his cheeks becoming as jowly as an old man. He was a man born to suffer indignities and knew it—the perfect escort for demanding visitors like the Gonzaga Duke.

Morosini immediately took a seat at the pianoforte and began to play. His long fingers flew over the keys, and he played like a virtuoso. Pietro sighed. "Bardon would have been a much better companion for the Duke than I. The Duke is obsessed with music, and such playing would keep him entertained, at least for a while."

"If so, it is no wonder why he would want to stay in Venice. Our musicians and composers are superior to any in Mantova."

Belladonna hoped to steer the conversation to the purpose of the Duke's visit, but instead, Foscarini took her comment as a prompt to list all the entertainments on the Duke's agenda. A visit to the convent choir of San Sebastian, a tour of the treasury of St. Marks and the chambers of the Council of Ten, and the church of San Doni to hear a nun sing.

Pietro concluded with a summary of the Duke's background and expectations. "It was only two years ago Fernando Gonzaga passed away, may God rest his soul, and Alviso, his brother, inherited the title. Alviso was a great patron of the *Accademia degli Elevati* of Florence and was himself a composer, filling his court with musicians and beautiful ladies with golden voices. He expects the Duchess to arrive before Ascension Day with an entourage of these ladies for the Banquet of One Hundred Ladies."

Belladonna smoothed her skirts, keeping her eyes lowered and away from Foscarini's. "Ah. It would seem the Duchess approves of this pastime. Is there one whom the Duke prefers among all others?"

Perhaps interested in Foscarini's answer to her question, Morosini concluded what he was playing with a long lingering note and joined her. "Has he brought one of his golden-voiced ladies along with him?"

Foscarini cleared his throat. "Well, ahem, there is one soprano, Adriana Comaneci, who has been singing for the Duke for the past few months. But then again, the Duchess has an entourage of ladies who dance the ballet, which the Duke also enjoys immensely." He wiped his brow, saying, "Have you heard of this dance?"

Not wanting to admit she had not, suspecting Foscarini was aching to give her a full description and history of it, Belladonna directed a desperate look for help to Morosini.

Morosini waves his hand, exposing an intricately designed lace sleeve. "At least the man has a passion for something more enduring than horses. I loathe those noblemen who can talk of nothing but their hunts and their horses. Come now, Pietro, we do not believe for a moment Gonzaga has come to Venice solely to listen to music. You are clever enough to have learned something of his true agenda."

Foscarini glanced at the mirrored walls and, straightening his back, fluffed out his chest, saying, "Well, the Duke did confide two things to me." He paused, clearly relishing how he was captivating their interest, "First, to buy a palazzo and his intention to stay in Venice for some period of time, and second, to cultivate a new singing lady to add to his entourage."

Morosini snorted and said, "Come now, Pietro. Do not tell me that is all he is here for. Alviso has the entire Academy of Florence at his beck and call and a veritable army of beauteous and talented women singers. He barely leaves his palace to visit his own lands; there must be more to inspire him to come to ours."

"Well…" Foscarini's forehead was beaded with sweat, and he pulled a lace cloth from his sleeve to wipe it away. "You know his new brother-in-law is the Holy Roman emperor? Well, Gonzaga has been given buckets of gold from the emperor to serve as his go-between in Venice."

"Ah, now there is a tune I could dance to. For what purpose?" Morosini's nostrils flared, and Belladonna imagined he had picked up the scent of profit.

Foscarini rolled his eyes. "That is beyond me. I did hear some talk of investing in the development of a new port of trade or something from Venice to some city in the emperor's dominion. I cannot be bothered with remembering such intricacies of policy while trying to keep on top of the Duke's schedule."

"You are right; now is not the time for us to talk of such things," said Belladonna. "Tell us more details of the entertainments planned. You mentioned the ballet? And what of the banquets and dinners being prepared in his honor?"

For once, the light of mischief appeared in Pietro's dull eyes. He leaned forward and lowered his voice as if they were conspirators engaged in a plot. "Isabella has prepared some kind of secret banquet with those two fabulous sisters, Gaspara and Cassandra, to perform. There are to be ice sculptures of nymphs and other sea creatures. No expense spared, I hear."

Belladonna's eyes narrowed to cat-like slits. "Yes, I am sure. Has he met Isabella, or was the banquet arranged, and gifts were sent to encourage his attendance?"

Foscarini folded his hands together and rested them on his lap. "Of course, he has met Isabella. She is trying her best to become his new mistress."

The sound of music and the soft voice of a woman singing made the visitors turn their heads towards the far side of the room where Mariella was posing for her portrait.

Pietro heaved himself to his feet and said, "Spare me from the sound of women singing! It is all I hear, day and night in the Gonzaga court. I must go and see to tonight's banquet and musical accompaniment."

As soon as Pietro Foscarini had departed, Bardon Morosini headed into the small salon, and Belladonna followed.

Mariella had stopped singing, startled by the visitors. She was on the divan, posing with the guitar on her lap. They stood in the doorway, gaping at her, while Mattia paid them no attention, his hand loaded with his paintbrush, flying with fervor over the surface of the canvas. The odor of paint was so strong, it overwhelmed the visitors and drowned out the omnipresent scent of Belladonna's perfume.

"Do not stop playing, please. I need you to continue," Mattia called out, his voice edged with impatience. "I will let you know when I am ready for you to break."

Obediently, Mariella's fingers stroked the strings, and she continued her song, a Spanish ballad Belladonna had heard sung by the workers on the plantations in Jamaica. Her voice and the music seemed to mesmerize Morosini. Belladonna tapped him on the shoulder and motioned him to come away. Reluctantly, he complied.

"You have just seen the surprise I had planned to unveil at the *Festa* at the Banquet of One Hundred Ladies."

Bardon grabbed her by the shoulders. "Do not expose that woman to the Duke of Mantova."

Belladonna looked pointedly at his hands on her arms, and he released her. "I am not *offering* her to the Duke. I am unveiling her portrait and having her play at the banquet. After that, she will disappear."

Morosini straightened his doublet. "You are playing with fire, Belladonna. But then, you always do."

Chapter Sixty-Three: Belladonna

VENICE, The twenty-sixth of MAY, 1615

There was great excitement everywhere as the gilded barge commandeered by Foscarini for the Duke and his entourage slowly progressed along the whole length of the Grand Canal. The public gathered along the shores and raised their arms and their voices in a show of enthusiasm. Trailing behind were the forty young nobles pulling on the oars of their craft for the regatta which generated more cheers from the crowds as they passed.

Wearing a gown of diaphanous iridescent veils, Belladonna was seated on the top of her gondola, which had been specially fitted for the occasion. A throne had been mounted on the top of the cabin, gilded, and shaped like a giant shell. Belladonna was framed by the shell-like back while Mariella, dressed in a new gown of saffron silk, stood just below her. Mariella seemed to marvel at all the pageantry around her as the gondoliers poled their craft along the Grand Canal.

"What is that?" Mariella pointed to a *peote*, a flat-bottom gilded boat festooned in white and crimson. There were several men dressed in white doublets with short red cloaks which flapped in the wind.

"Those are the seven Senators who have been appointed to officiate at the banquet after the *Festa della Sensa*. They will lead the Duke's flotilla to the Arsenale, where the banquet will take place."

"Is that where we are going?"

"Eventually. First, there will be the ritual of the wedding of Venice to the Sea. The Doge's *Bucintoro* will come into view soon. Wait until you see it. It is a wonder."

Despite the warm day, the wind on the canal was whipping at her hair, and Belladonna unfurled a scarf and wrapped it around her head to protect her coiffure. Mariella's hair, naturally curly, blew in many directions but seemed to always settle into a billowy fluff that suited her.

Mariella turned from side to side, taking in the liveried gondolas in their bright colors on one side and the pastel-colored palazzos on the other.

Laughter and calls from a craft filled with merry young men came alongside them. "Wish us luck, Belladonna! We aim to win."

Two of the young men, dressed in green edged with gold, stood up to blow them a kiss, but lost their balance and nearly toppled into the canal, causing jeers and more laughter from their comrades.

"Careful," called out Belladonna, "I have bet good money on you winning!"

The men waved and then pulled at their oars as if demonstrating their skill, and their boat quickly shot forward of Belladonna's.

"Look!" cried Mariella, pointing ahead, "is that the Doge's barge?"

It was the *Bucintoro,* the largest gilded craft on the Grand Canal. Its oars were raised and lowered rhythmically, moving it at a fast pace through the water. Red and gold banners adorning its sides fluttered in the breeze. At one end was the canopy that shaded the Doge on his throne-like gold chair, with the Dogaressa by his side. The men of the Senate dressed in scarlet and gold stood in formation across the deck.

Clustered around the *Bucintoro* were smaller vessels of similar design, with golden frames and red curtains. There were so many boats of all kinds coming alongside them, from the sleek oared boats of the regatta to the ornate *peotes* bobbing beside black gondolas draped with banners in a wide array of bright colors.

Two *peotes* approached, one bearing footmen dressed all in white and the other all in gold. They were the forerunners of the gilded Ducal *peote*, adorned with banners of gold and silver and draped with festoons of white satin. The gilded frame at the center was canopied in white gauzy curtains that fluttered around its occupants, making it difficult to see the face or features of the Duke.

Belladonna's gondolier was able to navigate his way through the *peotes* to bring them alongside the *Bucintoro*. Belladonna stepped onto the deck of the *Bucintoro*. Marching up the red carpet that ran the length of the barge, she curtsied before the Doge and Dogaressa. Once, Belladonna had influenced their son to abandon his libertine lifestyle and take a wife, earning her the everlasting gratitude of the Dogaressa. Therefore, the Dogaressa had warmly granted her request to be a part of the wedding of Venice to the Sea, and the Doge was forced to agree.

Belladonna then turned and headed to the end of the red carpet, stepping onto a small balcony that jutted out to the sea. The Doge followed, traversing the length of the *Bucintoro* on the red carpet to meet her on the balcony. He raised his arm, summoning a footman in gold and white livery who presented a small pillow of red velvet with a golden ring resting on it to Belladonna. She, in turn, presented it to the Doge, who removed the golden ring from the red velvet. Raising his hand high, as cheers rose from the boats and the crowds and facing the sea route upon which the fortunes of Venice rested, the Doge threw the wedding ring into the sea reciting:

"I wed thee, O Sea, in token of true and lasting dominion."

Then the Doge turned to Belladonna and took her hand, escorting her back along the red carpet to stand beside the Dogaressa. As sun and wind played with her diaphanous veils, heads turned, and the Dogaressa gave her a conspiratorial nod.

Chapter Sixty-Four: Belladonna

Now that the ceremony was complete, Belladonna returned to her gondola since the regatta was about to begin. Barges, *peotes*, and gondolas had been cleared to the side. Forty-two of Venice's finest young men in seven *caorlinas*, stood face forward in their colored liveries, their oars held in readiness. Bright smiles as they posed over their oars, jeering at the competition, awaiting the signal to begin. It was difficult, with the pull of the currents, for all seven boats to line up at the same point. Prior to beginning, they had drawn lots for their lanes, since some were more favored by the currents than others. The competition was good-natured and friendly, but there was a handsome purse to be awarded to the winners, so the ambition was high.

The glorious visitor from Mantova was given the honor to signal the start of the race. The Duke wore a long robe of golden brocade and a white doublet with white hose and shoes. He came forward onto the deck of the *peote*. The crews in each *caorlina* leaned forward over their oars when the Duke raised his pistol and fired. The boats shot forward amid the raucous shouts and cheering of crowds along the *fondamenta*.

Mariella clapped her hands and bounced up and down on her toes, which caused the gondola to rock. Both Belladonna and the gondolier warned her to curtail her enthusiasm, and she apologized, saying, "Such excitement! It is unlike anything I have ever seen before."

Belladonna smiled. "Wait, you have not seen the women's regatta yet."

Mariella's dark eyebrows arched. "They allow women to compete against the men?"

"No, not against the men, but against each other. In smaller numbers, usually four boats, with two women in each. Unlike the male competitors, they are not required to be of the noble class. Most of them are young and work or own businesses, which is necessary to contribute to the hiring of the boats and liveries." Another shout and some cheers, and Belladonna added, "It seems they have gotten to the pole that marks the turning point. The sun is in my eyes, so I cannot see which color is in the lead, but we shall know soon, as they are now on the final course."

Mariella placed a hand over her eyes to shade them and said, "I think I see the green is in the lead. Which team is that?"

Belladonna tried to make out the colors as well. "I think you are correct. That is good, the green team is captained by Mocenigo's son. He is an able youth and of good spirit. He will make a good winner."

The boat rocked once again from Mariella's clapping and enthusiasm when the winners were declared. Belladonna decided to descend from the throne and take a safer seat in the interior of the gondola. As the men's team raised their oars to the sky, honoring the victorious team in green, Belladonna instructed her gondolier to pull into a better spot for viewing the women's regatta.

Four teams of women, wearing shirts and breeches like men, in the four liveries representing the bakers, the glassmakers of Murano, the norcinos, and the glovemaker's guilds positioned their boats at the starting line. Once again, the gold and white-clad Duke of Mantova shot his pistol into the bright blue sky, and they were off.

Belladonna cheered the team in blue and gold in which her friend, Miretta, the talented woman glassmaker, was pulling ferociously at the oars. Miretta's rippling golden hair had been tied up to keep it from whipping into her face and interfering with her progress.

Shouts and whistles rang out as four sleek boats rounded the pole that marked the course's end. The blue and gold boat was in the lead. Now, it was Belladonna who rocked the gondola. She clapped enthusiastically for her friend Miretta's boat, which rapidly pulled ahead of the others and merited the prize.

Mariella's face was flushed, and her eyes glittered as she clasped her hands before her face and said, "Truly, Venice is a wondrous place!"

"Just wait until darkness falls and the fireworks are launched in honor of the winners. We shall now dress and prepare, and we will be getting the chance to view the fireworks before it is fashionable to appear at the Banquet of One Hundred Ladies."

Mariella clapped her hands again, "I can hardly wait!"

* * *

Mariella's portrait had been packed for transport to the Palazzo Barbaro for the Banquet of One Hundred Ladies. Mattia fussed about its care on the journey, since the paint was not yet fully dry. Mattia had high hopes for the display of his painting, expecting to get many requests for portraits

Mattia had managed to gain an invitation to the evening's festivities, and Belladonna suspected he was hoping to secure a commission from the Duke of Mantova. "He has arranged a vocal performance by his protégé, Adriana, at the banquet. Once he sees Mariella's portrait tonight, I am certain he will decide I should paint Adriana next."

Belladonna wished the artist the best of luck, secretly hoping the Duke would give Mattia the commission, hastening his exodus from Venice. Diana harbored feelings for the artist since he had painted her portrait, and Belladonna feared the same might happen to Mariella.

While Mariella strummed her guitar, Belladonna's maid was putting the final touches on her coiffure, weaving pearls and rubies into its crown of braids. This evening, Belladonna had chosen gowns of rich, iridescent claret silk for both of them, with stiff, high collars of ecru lace that nearly touched her chin. At the 'v' of her neckline, she had pinned a brooch with a large ruby set in gold studded with pearls.

Mariella was not used to such collars, so Belladonna had the dressmaker create a lace collar that fell loosely around her lovely neck. Belladonna had added a gold and ruby necklace to her sister-in-law's ensemble, which sparkled provocatively in the candlelight. They were ready to go.

It was late May, and the night air was warm, but both women wore hooded cloaks to protect their hair and skirts from breezes and splashes as the gondola headed towards the Arsenale. Scaffolding for the construction of the new port would serve as the launching site for the fireworks. She hoped, for Avigdor Margulies' sake, that the required boxes had been delivered as requested by Josef or there would be consequences for the Jews. Belladonna was still curious and suspicious of why the fireworks had been demanded of the Ghetto instead of the experts who created them on Chioggia.

The gondolier was merry like most everyone in the city today and sang old ballads as he navigated the craft among a forest of bobbing gondolas and *peotes*. The winners of the regatta had hosted big feasts in their *sestéres*, so the city was awash in wine and good cheer. The fireworks would be the culmination of a festive day for most Venetians, as only a select group were invited to the banquet for the Duke.

Belladonna imagined Isabella's face after her appearance at today's ceremony. Would she feel threatened, as Morosini warned? Though Isabella had set her sights on the Duke, Belladonna had no desire to cultivate an acquaintance with him; she had no more need of patrons. But she did need to re-establish her position of influence. The passion for power was not the same for her, as her dreams revolved around finding Isaak. Nevertheless, a small voice niggled at her consciousness with the question, *what will happen when Isaak returns?*

It was a question she could not address until they found Isaak, and it depended on his status when they found him. So why make this great effort to shine at the *Festa Della Sensa*, to regain her power, if when Isaak returned, she would relinquish it all again for him?

It gave her a headache to think of this now. The sky had darkened to a deep blue, and the moon was full, presenting a shining golden path across the waters of the lagoon.

"Shall we stop here, lady?" asked the gondolier.

They had passed the pillars of the lions, and the Doge's palace, and the riva degli schiavoni. The entire shoreline was filled with crowds awaiting the drama about to begin in the sky.

"Yes, let us wait here. The fireworks should begin any moment."

Mariella sat very straight beside her, head tilted back, eyes raised to the skies. Short popping blasts and the whistling of fireworks left a trail of color high above them. A large boom and the rockets exploded, showering cascades of pink and golden yellow which lit up the sky.

Grabbing Belladonna's hand at the first boom, Mariella clutched it tight as her eyes were fixed on the colorful lights. At the popping of more rockets exploding, Mariella gasped and squeezed her hand. "Truly amazing! How is it done?"

Belladonna did not know. At this moment, she missed Diana, whose scholarly interests would assuredly have provided some informed answer. The bangs and whistles of the fireworks continued, but it was the screams that drew Belladonna out of her reverie.

This was not part of the show, and it meant something had gone wrong. Belladonna swiveled in her seat as the gondolier pointed behind her at the dock under construction by the Arsenale.

"Fire!"

Chapter Sixty-Five: Belladonna

VENICE, The twenty-sixth of MAY, 1615, Night

The scaffolding for the construction of the new port was on fire. Immediately, men and boats were dispatched to put it out before it could spread to the wooden ship-building areas. There was a great deal of shouting as flames shot out and sparks flew. The black gondolas of the Men in Dark Cloaks had arrived to help subdue the fire, along with the soldiers of the Council of Ten.

"Onward," commanded Belladonna to the gondolier. The smell of smoke and pieces of ash was in her eyes and nose. She pulled the hood of her cloak close and instructed Mariella to do the same. Boats moved past them, some towards the fire, some away from it. The *peote* of the Gonzagas and their entourage had gone. Belladonna searched for the gondola with Morosini's colors, but it, too, had departed. It was time they got to the banquet and took their place among the other ninety-eight ladies.

Two long tables ran the length of the great hall of the Barbaro palazzo. The hall was bright from the dozens of candles in the many wall sconces and the two large chandeliers of Murano glass. After the servants had taken their outer wraps, Pietro Foscarini was at the threshold of the grand salon to greet them. Belladonna glanced at the head of the long tables where a dais stood, with seats for the Duke and the senators and the other important persons in the Duke's entourage.

Foscarini was frowning. "The Duke will be arriving soon, and there is so much to see to! Look up there," he pointed to a balcony above their heads, "do you see the musicians there? No! Where are they? Who knows. What shall I do if they do not arrive, I ask you? Adriana is to sing, and she must have accompaniment."

"It is early yet, and I am sure they will be there. It was probably the fire that detained them," said Belladonna.

"Fire?"

Belladonna waved her hand, as if it were of no importance. "A fire from a firework that had gone awry. It caused a bit of chaos, but I am sure it is being addressed. The Council of Ten will see to it. It is far enough from here; we should not even smell the smoke."

Before Foscarini could ask more, Belladonna excused herself, explaining she had to see to the surprise she had arranged for the Duke. Beckoning Mariella to follow, she proceeded into the salon, where the attendees were milling around while goblets of dark red wine were served by an army of footmen.

The large windows had been left open, and breezes cooled the crowd so that no one felt the need to use their fan. At the far end of the room was a section that had been curtained off, from which Mattia Correr emerged, dressed in a black high-collared doublet embroidered with golden thread. Though he was well-attired, the perfection of his appearance was disrupted by his unruly hair loose about his shoulders. In a few quick steps, he joined them, raising each lady's hand to his lips in a gentlemanly manner.

"All has been made ready?" asked Belladonna. "Both the portrait and Mariella's guitar have arrived in good condition?"

Mattia ran a hand through his hair. "There was but a tiny smudge, where the paint was still wet, but it was in the background and did not affect the image."

Mariella frowned. "My guitar is there?"

"Yes, yes, "said Mattia, his head turning from side to side, his eyes searching those around them for a face he recognized. "All is set. The portrait sits upon an easel, which is now standing behind those curtains. When you come out to present it, you need only to pull the cord," he indicated a gold rope hanging among the red folds and continued, "and the curtains will open to reveal the portrait. Mariella will be seated behind the second row of curtains with her guitar."

"Shall I go there now?" asked Mariella as she glanced nervously at all the elegantly dressed women around them.

Belladonna took her arm. "Not yet. I will let you know when it is time."

With her arm still locked in Mariella's, Belladonna began a tour of the room. A servant offered her wine, but she refused, as did Mariella, while Mattia accepted a glass. The banquet was supposed to be attended by one hundred of the most prominent women in the city. Professional beauties, courtesans like Isabella, entertainers like Gaspara and Cassandra, and the wives, sisters, and daughters of the most prominent families of Venice.

The sumptuary laws had been relaxed in honor of the Duke's visit, and the women were permitted to wear any color except gold and silver and to adorn themselves with pearls and precious stones to their heart's content. As they paraded about the room, the loveliest of Venice did not disappoint. There were dark-haired beauties in gowns of rich yellow and coppery brown and the Titian-haired women in gowns of pale blue and green. There were those in bright saffron silks and richly embroidered deep greens and lilac. There were high, stiff collars and necklines draped with lace. Diamonds, sapphires, and emeralds twinkled in decolletages and in braided hair, while pearls glowed with iridescence in the candlelight.

Belladonna spotted Morosini to her left, his head bent to listen to a man dressed in a doublet of white-and-silver. His back was to them, but Morosini must have advised his companion of their approach, and he turned around. Belladonna stopped in her advance, and Mariella gasped. It was Josef of Constantinople, without a turban and dressed like an affluent Venetian. His eyes locked on Mariella's, and his lips curved into a smile.

"May I present Josef di Azzura of Constantinople," said Morosini, his eyes on Belladonna. "Josef, may I present Belladonna, the most powerful woman in Venice."

Belladonna acknowledged the introduction with a curtsy to Josef, as if they were meeting for the first time. She, like Josef, did not want to reveal their prior acquaintance to Morosini. Belladonna introduced Mariella, who seemed stunned by Josef's appearance.

Morosini asked Mariella, "I hope you will consent to play for us this evening. Our illustrious guest has brought us his personal marvel, the singer Adriana. How like a Gonzaga to be haughty enough to assume we need a gift of music in Venice."

"Now, Bardon, please, you know His Excellency the Duke considers himself a connoisseur of the musical arts," said Josef as he pinched the bridge of his nose. "He has cultivated this woman to be his own private nightingale, and now he wants to share his protégé's accomplishment with the world. If we wish to do business with him, we should show some appreciation for his efforts. He should have no need to add any more women to his collection," said Josef, his eyes on Mariella. With Josef's attention to Mariella, Belladonna decided she must keep her eye on the attraction growing between the two.

Morosini was speaking low, close to her ear. "The fire has been blamed on the Jews, accusing them of sabotaging the fireworks. There is talk of an arrest and a fine to be levied on the Ghetto to pay for the damages caused to the new port and the Arsenale."

Belladonna straightened. "Who instigated this, Contarini? He is the Procurator, and he must have been responsible for demanding the Jews supply the fireworks?"

"Keep your voice down, and believe me, now is not the time to make accusations. There is more to this than you know."

Belladonna stared at Morosini. Niccolo Contarini, a prominent leader of the Council of Ten, had intrigued against them both as well as the people of the Ghetto. Why would Morosini defend Contarini now?

As if reading her thoughts, Morosini said, "The enemy of our enemy can be our friend. Contarini has no love of the Duke of Mantova."

Before she could challenge this statement, Pietro Foscarini was calling the assembly to attention.

The orchestra had arrived and began to play a march at the entrance of the Duke of Mantova and his entourage. The Duke was slim and of average height, dressed in a white and black doublet edged with silver, snug against pantaloons of black satin. His white hose met his black shoes, which sparkled with diamonds inset into large silver buckles. Thick eyebrows emphasized deep-set eyes under an impressively large forehead. His mouth was bracketed by a black mustache, and his pointed chin was edged by a well-trimmed beard. He appeared every inch the aristocrat, with a demeanor and expression fitting for a visiting dignitary.

Belladonna took her place among the other ladies who had lined up in two long rows along the length of the room. She had sent Mariella to take her place behind the curtains. Isabella faced her in the opposite row. Pietro Foscarini escorted the Duke down the aisle, introducing each lady, who then lowered her eyes and curtsied deeply.

The Duke stopped at Isabella. Isabella did not lower her eyes and held her head high, like a queen. The Duke gave her a slight bow and continued down the row until he came to Belladonna.

"Ah, so we meet at last. The bridesmaid of the sea, Belladonna?"

Belladonna curtsied. "Your Excellency honors me by your recognition."

"You would be very difficult to forget."

Pietro tapped his shoulder and whispered in the Duke's ear. "Ah. I have been told you have planned a surprise for me. I am touched by your thoughtfulness."

"I hope you will be satisfied with my contribution to this evening's entertainment."

The Duke nodded and moved on. Though he had been perfectly civil, Belladonna was repelled by the coldness of his eyes.

After the Duke completed his tour, a chair was brought for him, and he took his seat before the red curtains. Isabella took center stage to announce Gaspara and Cassandra, who carried her lute.

"Your Excellency. We are honored by your presence in our city, and your visit has inspired us. This is the Banquet of One Hundred Ladies, and you are about to hear a musical composition by the beautiful Gaspara and Cassandra, who shall play their music in your honor."

She bowed away gracefully, and the Duke's eyes rested on the two sisters.

Dressed in black, with a white stiff collar, Gaspara's golden hair cascaded over her shoulders. She kept her hands clasped before her, as if in prayer. Cassandra picked out chords on the lute, and then Gaspara began to sing. The sisters had performed at Belladonna's palazzo in the past, and their performances were always a marvel. But tonight, the music of Cassandra's lute and Gaspara's clear voice was haunting. She was tempted to close her eyes and savor the beauty of the music, but when she glanced at the Duke, he seemed unmoved. As the last notes faded away, the Duke clapped enthusiastically, and the two women curtsied and hurried away.

"Astonishing, are they not?" Foscarini asked, his eyes eagerly awaiting the Duke's nod of approval.

"Of course," said the Duke, "although you have not yet heard my Adriana."

Foscarini swallowed and conceded. "We anticipate that honor."

The Duke brushed an imaginary speck of dust from his pantaloons. "Now, what is next?"

Foscarini nodded to Belladonna. She went to the red curtains and reached for the golden cord. "Your Excellency, Venice is a city of beauty, and known for its beauties. Titian and Tintoretto's paintings of such beauties have gained fame throughout Europe. Over a year ago, a visiting English nobleman commissioned the portraits of our most beautiful women to be displayed in his Gallery of Beauties. Those portraits were painted by Mattia Correr, and your patronage of music and the beauty of Venice has inspired him to create this portrait."

She pulled on the rope, and the curtains parted, revealing the portrait of Mariella. It was an inspiring image of Mariella, with lips parted and shining eyes, posed as she leaned over her guitar. Then, as if the portrait had come alive, a woman began singing a Spanish ballad to the accompaniment of a guitar.

The Duke raised his definitive eyebrows, and he glanced at Foscarini, who tilted his head and gave his superior a tentative smile. But as the song came to its close, the Duke began to clap, slowly at first and then with great enthusiasm.

A smile of satisfaction appeared on Belladonna's lips.

"I appreciate the magic of the mystery, but perhaps you can pull aside the second curtain so I may meet the subject of the portrait?" The predatory look on the Duke's face sent a chill up her spine.

"Perhaps it is best to keep to the illusion," she said, adding, "the reality rarely can compete."

The Duke rose, and Foscarini's eyes widened with alarm. "Oh, but I insist."

It seemed Belladonna had no choice. She pulled the golden cord, revealing Mariella.

Carrying her guitar, her face flushed from the pleasure of playing, Mariella hesitated before coming to Belladonna's side.

The Duke seemed to be assessing Mariella as if she were a prized mare, walking slowly around her to view her from every angle. "In this case, reality does not disappoint. What is your name, my dear?"

"Mariella."

He lifted her chin and raised her face, looking directly into her eyes. "You do not speak like the others, and your singing—you are Spanish?"

"Yes."

"Ah." The Duke, glancing at Belladonna, clasped his hands behind his back. "You will join us at the banquet. You both will sit beside me."

It should have been a triumph for Belladonna, but instead, she felt dread.

Chapter Sixty-Six: Belladonna

VENICE, The twenty-sixth of MAY, 1615, Night

A long and lavish table was set with towers of fruits and flowers in ornate silver vases. Large platters of gleaming silver rested alongside colorful porcelain from China. Crystal goblets sparkled, filled with ruby red wine, and liveried servants were depositing platters full of the fruit of the sea before a large glass sculpture of Neptune with a raised trident.

Foscarini directed everyone to their seats. Belladonna and Mariella were seated to the left of the Duke at the center of the table, while Isabella, Gaspara, and Cassandra were on his right. Morosini was seated directly across from them, with Contarini beside him. A more lavish chair awaited the Doge and Dogaressa, who were placed at the head of the table.

After the Duke took his seat, Foscarini escorted a dark-haired, slim young woman, proudly wearing a silver-embroidered bodice over skirts of gold satin. Either the Duke or the famous singer had chosen to ignore the sumptuary laws of Venice, which specifically forbade most women to dress in gold and silver.

"And where am I to sit?" said the young woman, standing behind Belladonna and casting fiery looks at Foscarini and the Duke. Arms folded and foot tapping, she awaited to be shown to her seat. The Duke ignored her, and Foscarini gave a small shrug, which did not appease the proud woman.

"Tell this woman to give me her seat." The demand had been voiced.

Belladonna took a sip of the excellent wine and smiled at the Duke. She had no intention of moving.

The Duke raised his eyes from his plate, his glance cold, but his words more chilling. "Adriana, you are not to be seated, nor are you invited to eat. You are here only to sing."

Adriana stamped her feet so hard, the pearls around her neck jumped. She opened her mouth to respond, but seemed to think better of it and spun on her heels and marched out. The Duke watched her go and then seemed to notice Mariella's glass and plate were empty. He pointed to her, "You see, this woman knows you cannot sing effectively on a full stomach. The churning of digestion ruins the voice, does it not?"

Mariella looked up at the Duke, but Belladonna squeezed her hand, so she did not respond. The Duke then pointed to Gaspara and Cassandra, who also had not taken food or wine. "You see?"

Most women would not eat at a banquet since it was a messy proposition that could ruin a façade so carefully crafted. Besides, Gaspara and Cassandra were naturally shy, and their lips trembled every time the Duke glanced in their direction. They would not have the courage to raise a single morsel to their lips in his presence.

"Unlike these lovely women, or the Duchess, Adriana needs a lesson in comportment. Her voice should be heard in song, never in complaint," said the Duke.

Whatever the Duke believed about singing, his prized soprano did not seem to receive either kindness or respect from her patron. Belladonna did not like to imagine what 'lesson' the Duke had in store for Adriana.

From across the table, Morosini's eyes were eloquent in their suggestion for her to change the subject. So, she did. "Venice is famous for its beauties, both its setting and its women. Has our city lived up to its reputation in your eyes?"

The Duke wiped his mouth and fingers with a fine white napkin and cast an appreciative look at Mariella, Isabella, Gaspara, and Cassandra before smiling back to Belladonna. "I always enjoy the company of beautiful women, and this city has much to commend it. The music, the art, the palazzos have all worked their charm on me so successfully, I am now determined to purchase a residence here. The Duchess will be arriving shortly with her entourage, and we will rely on the services of the Procurator and Foscarini to help us find a suitable palazzo."

The rumors were true, then. Belladonna was glad her palazzo, though lavish, would be too small for the Duke and Duchess of Mantova, or there was a chance, especially with Contarini as the Procurator, for it to be requisitioned and offered to a potential new noble resident.

At this turn of conversation, Contarini found his opening. "Your brother-in-law, the Emperor is also interested in paying a visit to our city?"

A momentary grimace crossed the Duke's face, which he quickly covered by wiping his lips once more with his napkin. "The Emperor is in favor of creating a new trade route to the East, and my residency in Venice will bring it to fruition."

"I see," said Contarini, and his lips hardened into a straight line, which Belladonna knew well was a sign of his displeasure. Niccolo would not appreciate the involvement of the Emperor in Venetian affairs.

"Your excellency has certainly been supportive of the project to build the new port at the Arsenale," said Morosini, to which the Duke inclined his head in affirmation. "We can only hope that tonight's faulty fireworks did not cause any damage to its construction."

The Duke frowned, and his nostrils flared. "Faulty fireworks? And who was responsible? If there is damage to the port, we expect speedy repair or restitution."

Foscarini sniffed, as if an unpleasant odor had wafted by him. "The fireworks came from the Ghetto, as per your orders."

The Duke treated Foscarini to a look that would shrivel fruit and reiterated. "Responsibility and restitution, I say."

Tension was escalating, and Belladonna, a practiced hostess, knew how to diffuse it. "It grows late, Excellency, and the ladies await the music and dancing." She looked pointedly at Foscarini, "Is it not time for the dancing to begin?"

Foscarini cleared his throat and rose to address the assembled guests. "Ladies and gentlemen, the music and dancing are about to begin. Please take your places in the ballroom." He gestured with a white-gloved hand to the adjoining grand hall. A chorus of scraping chair legs and the rustle of silks accompanied the murmur of conversations and flapping fans as those dining rose to follow Foscarini's direction.

As Belladonna passed Morosini, he managed to convey another word of advice. "Best if Mariella were to disappear before the end of the dance."

Bright colors, flashing gems, the clacking of pearls, and the tread of *chopines* accompanied the one hundred ladies who tittered as they sought partners on the dance floor. Adriana glittered on the balcony where she was poised to play harp to the accompaniment of violin and lute.

Belladonna whisked her skirts before her as she stepped up to the curtains behind the portrait. To Mariella, who hurried alongside her, she whispered, "Slip behind the curtains and escape as quickly as you can. Instruct the gondolier to take you to the Turk's home. He knows where to go. I will be in touch with you there."

Mariella gave a short nod and looked around. Neither the Duke nor Foscarini were in sight. Without another word and holding her skirts in both hands, Mariella disappeared behind the curtains.

Belladonna sauntered to the center of the hall, where she could see Isabella's head, with its crown of ebony braids above the others. *Isabella must be wearing the highest chopines.*

Gaspara had partnered with Cassandra, and Isabella was alone. Belladonna approached her and asked, "Will you be my partner?"

Isabella's smile was enigmatic, but she nodded, and Belladonna took her raised hand and a position by her side. The violins toyed with sample arias, and a cascade of notes tinkled from the harp. All were awaiting the entrance of the Duke.

Isabella, in a barely audible whisper, said, "I am not your enemy."

Belladonna did not hesitate to reply, "I did not so accuse you."

"Trust me, and not Morosini," were Isabella's final words before the music swelled, and Adriana began to sing.

Belladonna trusted neither of them, but they were at least aligned on the potential danger from the Duke of Mantova and the Emperor. The Duke reminded her of a snake waiting for the opportunity to strike. With his sponsorship of Avigdor Marguiles's new port, she worried her friends in the Ghetto were set up to be his first target.

Isabella and Belladonna moved in perfect step, despite the height of Isabella's shoes, and they swiveled and turned as the dance demanded. Belladonna was aware of the Duke's eyes following them as they danced. Adriana's voice reverberated throughout the hall, rich and strong, carrying the tune and inspiring her feet to follow along. Up and down as they curtsied to each other and stood on their toes, then bowing and turning, extending a graceful arm.

She caught sight of Morosini standing beside Contarini. A footman approached them, but Belladonna was forced to turn away and did not see anymore. After traversing through the outstretched arms of the other women, Belladonna surveyed the clusters of onlookers, searching for a flash of Morosini's elegant white satin or Contarini's stern face. Neither were to be found.

The dance seemed to go on forever, but at last, Adriana ended on a lingering high note, and the music quieted. Belladonna and Isabella curtsied to each other, and Belladonna hurried towards Foscarini, who was being harangued by the Duke.

Foscarini, his face red and sweating, invited the men to join the ladies on the dance floor, and then headed towards the exit. Belladonna lifted her skirts and hurried after Foscarini.

"Where is Morosini?" she called out to Foscarini, who was still mopping his forehead as he was surrounded by several footmen, awaiting his orders. *Why had Morosini run away?*

A peevish expression filled Foscarini's face. "That is what I should like to know. This is *all* Morosini's doing, and *he* should be the one to see to it, not I."

It was unlike the two noblemen to leave an event such as this, unless there was a crisis. She felt the tremors of panic inch up her spine. Morosini and

Contarini seemed fiercely united, and that can only be because Venice is threatened.

"Whatever can you mean?"

"We have received word that though the fire was subdued, the dock is beyond repair, and several houses are damaged. What is more, Avigdor Margulies, the Jew responsible for the faulty fireworks that led to this disaster, has been found dead."

"Killed when the fireworks exploded?"

"He was supposed to check the fireworks before they were lit," said Foscarini, the twang of complaint in his voice. "The Jews must be made to pay. That is what the Duke keeps repeating. Restitution, restitution, restitution. It has become his chant. One would think he is glad of the damages to justify the collection of this 'restitution.'"

At last, the plot was revealed. Extortion now and perhaps expulsion later, if the Duke has his way and becomes a permanent player in the power structure of Venice.

"And the cause of the explosion, was it the fireworks?"

"What happened is not my affair, nor yours. It is a matter to be addressed by Contarini and the Council of Ten."

"This Margulies may also be a victim. I assume he would not have been there to see to the lighting of the fireworks if he knew they were set to explode," said Belladonna, hoping to shift blame away from the Jews.

Foscarini's eyes narrowed as he regarded her. "What are you implying? And why are you seeking Morosini?"

Belladonna gave him a charming smile and ignored his first question. "Morosini and I have…an arrangement."

Foscarini nodded. This he could understand. He opened his mouth to say more but was interrupted by the pounding footsteps in *chopines* across the terrazzo floor. Flashing silver and gold in the candlelight, Adriana stormed by, shaking a fist in the direction of the salon.

"That man is a beast! How dare he? After my performance, he dares to ask for another. And he does not let me eat! Pshaw! I shall not be returning to Mantova, Foscarini. I have decided to stay in Venice."

Foscarini wiped his face with a bit of lace he pulled from his sleeve and headed back towards the salon, muttering, "I must see to the Duke."

Belladonna caught Adriana's arm before she stomped away. "Who has the Duke asked for?"

Adriana glared at her and disengaged her arm. "The Spanish girl with the guitar. An amateur. *That* is who he prefers to Adriana." Chin raised high as if challenging the air, and Adriana stormed off, leaving Belladonna alone and disturbed.

For Belladonna, the festivities were over, and her plans to upstage Isabella now seemed so petty and beneath her. She recalled the words 'the Jews must pay' and did not like its implication. There always seemed to be the willingness to ascribe every societal ill to the Jews, to validate an injustice or atrocity being inflicted on them.

On her way to depart, Mattia crossed her path. "Belladonna! The Duke is calling for Mariella. Where is she?" He glanced towards the portrait on its easel before the curtains. "Do you think he will keep the portrait?"

Belladonna glanced at the painting. "That is all he can have of Mariella, for she has gone. I must find Morosini, and then I, too, must go."

Mattia ran a hand through his unruly hair and exhaled. "I will go with you. Morosini has departed, along with Contarini. He asked me to warn Diana, for there is trouble in store for the people of the Ghetto."

Chapter Sixty-Seven: Diana

VENICE, The twenty-seventh of MAY, 1615

Her father was still at morning prayers when Diana entered his study, intending to search among his many piles of papers for a sample *ketubah,* an illuminated Jewish marriage contract, to show Moises. The door suddenly banged open, which made her drop the sheaf of papers she had been holding, scattering them. Looking up at her father as she crouched down to gather them, she was alarmed to see his eyes were wild, and his hair stuck out in tufts from under his hat, as if he had been pulling at it with both hands.

Still crouched low behind his desk, the rabbi did not see her until she rose, holding an untidy bundle of paper to her chest. "Diana, terrible, terrible news!"

Diana felt her stomach clench as fear seemed to reach inside of her and twist. "Tell me."

"Avigdor Margulies has been murdered! The Chevra Kadisha retrieved his body, which I have been able to examine as they were preparing for the burial."

"Murdered, how?"

"Stabbed through the heart. A single, accurately placed wound, the work of a professional," said the rabbi as he collapsed into the chair.

Kneading her hands, Diana thought of Zebulun. As a known associate of Margulies, was he now in danger? She did not reveal her fears to her father, but asked, "Do you believe Margulies was murdered by assassins of the Council of Ten?"

The rabbi rubbed his forehead, as if her question made his head ache. "We have received a demand from the Council of Ten. The Jews are ordered to make restitution for the fire, which caused the ruin of the unfinished dock and several adjacent houses. They blame the explosion on faulty fireworks, which they say came from the Ghetto."

"If that is the case, then why kill him? It seems it would be more profitable to imprison Margulies in the *Pozzi*, and then demand a ransom from the community for his freedom. The Council of Ten always seeks the most lucrative solutions, especially when they can assign the blame to us."

The rabbi dropped the hand from his head and stared at his daughter. "It seems you have learned a great deal about political intrigue from your friend, the courtesan."

Diana bristled at her father's tone, which always took a derogatory turn when referring to Belladonna. Did he resent Belladonna for her rejection of Judaism, her profession, or for her relationship with Isaak? She brushed such thoughts aside, the pressing issue now to discover why Margulies had been murdered and whether Zebulun might also be a target.

"Margulies must have been at the dock when the fireworks were launched. If someone had tampered with the rockets to cause them to explode and Margulies was witness to it, he would have to be silenced. But why would the Council of Ten order the fireworks and then have them sabotaged?"

"Why order the fireworks from the Ghetto in the first place? That is the first clue, as we are not known in the Ghetto for our expertise in rockets. For medicines, for amulets, for imports, yes. Fireworks no. That comes from those brothers on Chioggia who long ago mastered their use." Her father stroked his beard and hummed, a sign he was deep in thought.

Diana rose and grabbed her shawl. "We have only suspicions, but no definitive answers. Meanwhile, you must go to Jacob Sullam for help in raising the gold necessary to satisfy the Council of Ten. I will go to the Turk because it was he who obtained the fireworks for Margulies."

The rabbi raised an eyebrow. "You will also find out if Zebulun is involved in this somehow and how we can ensure he is not arrested."

Diana did not respond, but marveled at how well her father knew her.

***

It was a quick walk over two bridges from the Ghetto to the *Campo di Mori* to the blue door of the residence of the Turk. Inhaling deeply the intoxicating aromas of herbs and flowers, Diana followed the Turk's daughter to the courtyard, where the Turk was still enjoying a late-morning coffee. She was surprised to find he was not alone, but entertaining Mariella, Belladonna, and Mattia.

Diana seated herself next to Belladonna while the Turk offered her coffee, which she graciously refused. Belladonna described what had happened at the banquet and Mariella's need to escape.

Mattia added a moan over the loss of Mariella's portrait. "It was truly my best work."

"Maybe the Duke will not want it," Diana said, regretting her words, which were spiteful and unlike her. She tried to qualify her intent. "It may only serve to remind him of something he could not have."

Mariella raised her head in a defiant pose. "I am not a possession."

Belladonna patted Mariella's knee. "Gonzagas considers everyone and everything a possession. But have no fear. I will ensure you never have to contend with men such as he."

Diana changed the subject. "I have news. Avigdor Margulies has been murdered. Stabbed precisely through the heart."

The Turk placed a hand on his chest, and Belladonna put down her glass, saying, "Stabbed! I thought he had been killed by the explosion."

Diana explained how the body was claimed by the Jewish burial society, giving the rabbi the opportunity to examine it as it was prepared for burial. "My father suspects an assassin committed the crime since there was only one wound, delivered with a professional's practiced accuracy to find its way directly to the heart."

"The Council of Ten," said Mattia, giving voice to everyone's suspicions.

"Morosini is on the Council of Ten and an investor in the new dock. Though it had not been fully complete, I cannot see him sacrificing his investment. Although…" Belladonna said that the image of Morosini and Contarini clustered together at the banquet came to mind. She turned to the Turk. "What does the Duke of Mantova expect out of the construction of the dock? Why has he sponsored it?"

"You flatter me, my dear. I am not privy to the plans or projects of the Duke," said the Turk, although there was a glimmer in his eye that hinted he was not revealing all he knew of the Gonzagas investments.

She would have to coax it out of him. "Perhaps the Gonzaga family has engaged you to help set up a new trade route through Mantova?"

A smile curved through the thick black mass of the Turk's beard. "Perhaps."

Belladonna tapped a finger to her lip before adding, "The Contarinis would not want a new port, since they have full control of the Punta del Dogana, the collectors and administrators are all under their 'management.' Morosini was trying to convince me to invest in the completion of the dock, and he was pressing Jacob Sullam for an investment, too. So why would Contarini and Morosini, usually at odds and seemingly antagonists on this issue, suddenly be aligned?"

"The enemy of my enemy is my friend," said Mattia, as if her review had just clarified the situation for him. "Regardless of their conflicting interests in Venice, they both seem united in their dislike of the Duke."

"Evidently," said Belladonna, annoyed that Mattia's suggestion was so blatantly obvious. She had ignored the signs of a deep intrigue because she had been too absorbed in her rivalry with Isabella. Isabella had warned her not to believe Morosini, an insight she should not have ignored, having come from a trusted friend who had also been the nobleman's mistress for several years. It was Morosini who had put suspicion of Isabella in her mind, and perhaps it was purposeful—to keep her distracted from observing his new alliance with Contarini.

Belladonna revealed her suspicions. "Morosini and Contarini must have hoped to discourage the Duke's continued stay in Venice by sabotaging the dock. However, their plans went awry, for the Duke had a greater interest in remaining in Venice than the construction of these docks—his love of music and his interest in beautiful women."

Picking up on the thread of her argument, Diana added, "The Jews would be the perfect scapegoats, which is why Foscarini ordered Margulies to supply the fireworks. Perhaps Avigdor may have been instructed to tamper with them. Either Margulies must have learned too much or complained too often, and they determined Margulies had to be eliminated."

Belladonna, Diana, and Mattia all turned an accusative eye at the Turk. He threw up his hands and shook his head. "I was not involved in Margulies death."

"Avigdor could not get the fireworks from Chioggia; they would not sell directly to a Jew," said Diana. "if not from you, how else could he obtain them?"

The Turk frowned and pursed his lips before sighing. *"Personally,* I did not supply Margulies with the fireworks he needed, but I may have directed him to someone who could."

"And who would that be?" asked Belladonna.

"I would rather not reveal my source, as he knows how to procure items that are hard to find—for a very steep price, mind you. He can procure it from Chioggia, but not from the usual channels."

Belladonna understood. The Turk's channels sometimes took irregular paths that risked arrest by the Council of Ten. With adequate coin, however, a few boxes of fireworks could be missing from the Chioggia warehouses where they belonged. A dead end.

"Besides," the Turk continued, "those who procure for me would not deliver goods that are tainted or had been meddled with. Believe me, it would be bad for their business."

Another thought occurred. "Wait, it was Foscarini who ordered the fireworks from Avigdor, not Contarini, who is supposedly the official Procurer. Why? Unless we assume Foscarini was secretly acting under Contarini's orders. Or, it could have come solely from the Duke of Mantova."

"The Duke of Mantova?" repeated Diana, "why should he want to orchestrate this disaster to a project he is rumored to have invested in?"

"Two possible motives. One, it was not the Duke's money, but his brother-in-law's. The investment in the new docks may have been only to provide a rationale for his continued stay and interest in Venice. Or he must play to his brother-in-law, the Emperor, who may have decided he did not want another new port in Venice after all. Two, the Duke stands to collect a great deal of gold for himself, claiming it as restitution for the damage caused by 'faulty fireworks'."

The Turk leaned forward and, in a softer voice, said, "There is another possibility. The construction of a new port is more expensive than was originally thought. The dock alone cost more than was expected. Therefore, Marguiles had reached out through certain channels and was to receive funding by my Sultan. Josef di Azzura was sent here to personally see to it. A new port in Venice would serve as an important port-of-call for trade with the East and provide a route with less exposure to the patrolling Maltese pirates."

"But the Emperor is not at war with the Sultan," said Diana, "and neither is Venice."

"For now," said Mattia, with a frown.

The four of them fell silent, and Belladonna supposed they were sifting through all these factors just as she was, trying to sort them out.

Diana was the first to offer a new hypothesis. "Perhaps the purpose of the explosion and the destruction of the new dock was first to blame it on the Jews, then accuse them of acting for the Sultan, to escalate the situation to a war."

"Who would want a war?" asked Mattia.

"Perhaps the Duke of Mantova," Diana said. "If there was an arrest of the agent of the Sultan..." Her forehead creased with worry as she asked the Turk, "Has Zebulun returned?"

The Turk shook his head. "Not yet."

"But Josef is here," offered Mariella, who had been silent so that Belladonna was unsure how much she had understood of their conversation.

All eyes shifted to Mariella. "He was at the banquet. Remember?"

Chapter Sixty-Eight: Belladonna

VENICE, The twenty-eighth of MAY, 1615

Belladonna decided it was time to confront Bardon Morosini about the explosion, the murder of Margulies, and his warnings about Isabella.

As the anxious excitement of the banquet receded, exhaustion began to soften both her pose and her resolve as she stepped out of the gondola and onto the landing of Morosini's palazzo. She was aware it was unfashionably early to be calling upon a nobleman, but patted her hair into place and smoothed her skirt so Morosini's staff would recognize she was a visitor they should not dare turn away from his door.

The tinkling of musical notes from a pianoforte signaled Morosini's presence in the salon. He did not look up nor shift his attention from the keys as he continued to play. Belladonna stopped in mid-step to listen, tilting her head. When the last chord echoed, and all was quiet, Morosini said, "I have been expecting you."

Belladonna took a seat beside him and placed a hand on his satin-clad shoulder. "We used to rely on each other a great deal to further our mutual agendas and to alleviate the boredom that permeates so many of the salons in Venetian society. Where has our alliance gone awry?"

"You have forgotten the laws that govern Venice—expediency and self-interest," he shook her off as his fingers danced across the keys in a trill, ending on a high note. "You have been gone far too long and are not privy to where both may currently lie."

Belladonna felt stung by his words but kept her back straight and her voice even as she challenged him with, "I cannot have been gone long enough for a Morosini to consider his best interest lies with a Gonzaga duke or his Contarini Procurator."

He stabbed his pointer finger on a deep-toned key. Its sound was enough to put her teeth on edge. He sighed deeply before answering her. "Never a Gonzaga, but alas, times are difficult enough that I find my interests this time align with those of Niccolo Contarini. Hence, as you may have noticed at the banquet, we seek each other's company more than we ever have before."

"Is it under your orders or Contarini's that Margulies was murdered?" she would be relentless with her questions until she pried the truth from his sneering lips.

First, he played a discordant chord, then he answered, "The responsibility for that deed lies with the Duke of Mantova."

"Why ever would the Duke of Mantova sabotage the fireworks and lose his investment by destroying the docks when they were nearly complete?"

"It is a long story, and quite complicated," so saying, Morosini rose from the bench and reached for her hand to accompany him. "Come, let us sit so we can face each other eye to eye, and I can provide you the insights you seek."

Belladonna took his hand, all senses on alert, and took a seat opposite him in one of a pair of facing settees. She folded her hands in her lap and looked up at him expectantly. Morosini reached for a small bottle of brandy and poured a bit, which he promptly drank down. After giving a satisfied sigh, he began to explain. "The Duke of Mantova has designs on the trade route from the Far East to Europe, now controlled by Venice and Constantinople. His purpose here is not to invest but to disrupt and to destroy, to sow the seeds of havoc and dissent and weaken the mastery Venice has established in trade to the East. The irony was his appearance at the *Festa della Sensa* and the wedding of Venice to the sea! How the Duke must have secretly snickered, with the knowledge he was here for the sole purpose of putting an end to it."

Belladonna tapped her cheek with one finger and narrowed her eyes. "Are you saying the Duke gave Avigdor Margulies his support for a new port, all the while planning to destroy it?"

"Of course. The Duke excels at duplicity. Margulies, who has a history of trading for the Gonzagas, must raise funds from his fellow Jews to augment what he received from the Duke and Emperor. The Duke knows a new port would kindle the interest of both the Jews of Venice and the Jews of the Levant, who would jump at any opportunity to circumvent the heavy tariffs leveled by the Punta del Dogana against their trade. Then Margulies comes to me to garner support from the Council of Ten, playing upon my rivalry with the Contarinis and my own self-interest to develop an alternative to the docks at the Punta del Dogana."

"You never like to be anticipated or manipulated, no matter how advantageous it could prove to your interests."

"Precisely," agreed Morosini, smoothing his mustache with one thumb. "And of course, I was immediately suspicious when I was approached by this Marguiles. Why would the Duke rely on a Jew from the Ghetto to lead such a project for him?"

Belladonna nodded. "A fool's errand, bound to stir up trouble and little else. Then you put pressure on my agent, Jacob Sullam, to wrest an investment from me. You thought I would be eager to reclaim my status and, therefore, would be an easy dupe. Bringing the Duke another substantial investment would convince him of your gullibility. Then, to be sure of my insecurity, you instigated a rivalry with Isabella. You are as much a master of deceit as the Duke."

"You know me well. I thought I knew you as well, but you are no longer the jaded woman of the world to whom I once allied myself." His eyes bored into hers, as if challenging her to shift them away. He continued, "No longer convinced of your infallibility, you appeared vulnerable, and being the man that I am, I sought to exploit this to my advantage. You ended up serving a purpose, to distract the Duke, most admirably."

Belladonna pressed her lips into a flat line. "And Margulies served his.

Had he become aware of your deception or the Duke's?"

Morosini lowered his eyes to his long, elegant hands, concentrating on the flexing of his fingers, avoiding giving her his answer. "Margulies had the misfortune of discovering the fireworks had been tampered with and shared his alarm with Foscarini, who dutifully reported it to the Duke. I suppose the Duke did not want the alarm to spread and could spare an assassin or two from his entourage to ensure that it would not."

"Foscarini knew. Why did he not raise an alarm?"

"Because Niccolo Contarini asked him not to, at my suggestion. Niccolo and I find ourselves more in agreement than ever, especially about the true purpose of the Gonzaga visit. We wanted to force the Duke to show his hand so we could choose the appropriate plan to be rid of him."

Belladonna suddenly remembered another point. "At the banquet, you were with Niccolo, which was surprising, but I also recall you conferring with Josef. How does he fit in?"

"I was trying to confirm what I suspected, which is that his patrons were not a part of the Gonzaga plot but were to be another of its victims. You see, the second part of the Duke's plan went awry, thanks to Margulies. The fireworks were to cover the sabotage not only of the new dock, but of the existing port and the Punta del Dogana. Contarini does keep a very thorough control of the Punta del Dogana and discovered a cache of gunpowder set to explode in time for the fireworks. That is what Margulies stopped; the launch of the second round of rockets aimed to cover the destruction of the Punta del Dogana."

Belladonna frowned. "A very comprehensive plan. End Venice's control of the trade by destroying its ports and ensure the blame is placed on the Jews and their allies in Constantinople."

Morosini nodded. "This Duke may have noble tastes, but his mind works like a brigand—what he wants, he seizes. Which reminds me, your gift of the portrait has instigated the Duke's acquisitiveness. Take care to keep your protege hidden away from him."

Belladonna scowled at him. "If it were not for your hints and warnings about Isabella's intentions, I would never have had it painted."

Morosini grinned and poured himself another drab of amber-colored brandy. "My apologies. I did not enjoy deceiving you."

"Do not lie, Bardon. You very much did enjoy the deception. It shall be difficult to forgive you, but I must." Belladonna rose. She had obtained the information she was seeking, and there was no need to remain.

"Ah, I see my ploy has worked its wonders. Expediency and self-interest have been restored. Now, once again, you are one of us."

Chapter Sixty-Nine: Diana

The solemn procession departed in hired gondolas for the Lido. Rabbi di Modena was in the lead with the family accompanying the coffin of Avigdor Margulies. Diana and her mother were present but trailed far behind. Sobbing, faint murmurs, the rustling of skirts, and the shuffling of feet were the only sounds along the way. Weeping willows on the perimeter of the old cemetery emphasized the sadness of the occasion, while bright beams of sunlight were persistent in breaking through, as if there was happiness still to be found outside its gates.

The funeral for Avigdor Margulies took place before his open gravesite after the coffin had been lowered. The rabbi began his eulogy, speaking to lowered heads as those assembled peered down at the plain pine box which held Avigdor's remains.

"Avigdor had been given the gift of vision and the blessing of hope, both of which he dedicated to the purpose of increasing the fortunes and the stability of the Jews of Venice," the rabbi looked to Avigdor's widow, "his family should be proud of his dedication to the community, and how much he wanted to give. Like many of our forefathers, the Prophets, who had visions of what could be, Avigdor had the persistence to pursue his vision despite the criticism and the personal danger involved. The loss of Avigdor's family is a loss to us all."

He beckoned to the *Chazzan*, a young man with a deep booming voice, to recite the prayers of Tehillim, each prayer that begins with a letter from Avigdor's Hebrew name. The mourners were able to follow the recitation, knowing the words by heart. After they finished, the *Chazzan* recited the *Kel Maleh Rahamim,* the final prayer of mourning. Then, the rabbi gestured for the widow to pick up a small shovelful of dirt and toss it into the grave. The mourners formed a line behind the widow, and each one was handed the shovel in turn and threw their shovelful of dirt. The men at the end of the line took turns tossing in more dirt until the pine box disappeared from view. The crowd began to disperse, heading to the waiting boats to take them back to the Ghetto.

Diana knew the rabbi would be the last to leave, so she lingered with her mother in the shade of a weeping willow. Besides his widow, Avigdor had left two grown sons, who would never have the joy of their father dancing with them at their weddings.

The presence of our parents in our lives is a blessing to be appreciated every day. Though her mother nagged and complained, she did not like to think of how life would be without hearing her voice in the morning as she prepared the mid-day meals or in the evening as she recited her prayers before going to bed.

The rabbi had been cheated of love by Death, and ironically, so had she. Her father had been betrothed to a woman he loved, but she had died before their wedding, and he had married her sister. Diana had found her soul mate in Yaakov, but he had been taken from her so early in their marriage. Until she met Mattia Correr, she had not been interested in a relationship with any other man. But Mattia's mystical talent and dedication to his craft attracted her in a way that made her redden to acknowledge.

Mattia was much on her mind, and Diana had a desperate urge to see him now after being surrounded by death. The blue skies were billowing with grey clouds that blocked the warmth of the sun, and the swish of the wind through the willows fueled morbid thoughts.

Diana left her mother to her father's care and her father to the usual barrage of her mother's tongue and headed towards the boats. With her eyes lowered to keep her feet on the path without tripping over roots or rocks, she did not see the figure blocking her way until she was almost upon him.

"Zebulun!" She threw herself into his arms, nearly knocking them both off of their feet.

Zebulun's face looked tired, and there was a thick grizzle of whiskers over his usually clean-shaven face. His eyebrows and lips curved upward at her welcome. "You have missed me, and I have only been gone a short time."

"I have so much to ask you and so much to tell. Have you any news of Isaak? If you have come here, you must have learned that Avigdor Margulies has been murdered." Without allowing her brother to answer, Diana grabbed hold of his arms. "You, too, may be in danger from the same assassins. You should not go back to Venice. Sail away with Josef of Constantinople. You will be safe under his protection."

Zebulun gently freed himself from her grasp. "Calm yourself, sister, and listen to me. I did come here because I learned of Avigdor's death. Josef has warned me of the danger to us both, and we sail tomorrow. I also bring news of Isaak, and for this, I need your help with our parents."

Diana stopped short, her knees weakening so that she clung to Zebulun's arm to prevent herself from falling. She must get off the Lido. She believed only ill winds blew here, bringing only death and disaster.

"It would be safest for us to go to the Turk, and he can send a message to Belladonna. She must hear your news of Isaak."

Chapter Seventy: Diana

VENICE, The thirtieth of MAY, 1615

The skies had faded from blue to grey, and a mist had risen as their gondola followed the turns of the Grand Canal towards the *Campo di Mori*. Diana would not permit Zebulun to speak of Isaak until Belladonna was present, but she held his hand and listened to his stories of the wondrous ships he had seen in Amsterdam and Constantinople.

Diana always relished the short but fragrant walk through the Turk's beautiful garden to the courtyard, but now there was the added accompaniment of the music of a guitar. Mariella was seated on a cushion-strewn divan, singing softly as she played the guitar. Mariella's voice was haunting and sorrowful, and Zebulun was mesmerized. He had stopped in his tracks to listen. The Turk's daughter had disappeared into a shadowy corridor, promising she would return shortly with her father. Diana took a seat among the colorful cushions arranged in a corner and folded her arms as she waited for the song to end and Zebulun to come out of his reverie.

"Oh, I did not hear you arrive," said Mariella, putting aside the guitar and giving them a small curtsy.

"We have not been here for very long," muttered Diana.

"But long enough to enjoy the beauty of your music," said Zebulun, making a courtly bow. "And your singing," he added.

Mariella lowered her eyes, and color flared momentarily in her cheeks. Diana gave Zebulun a look to signal he should not press her more. Zebulun seemed to have gotten her mental message and took a seat, reaching for a ripe-looking plum from a bowl of fruit on a table nearby. None of them spoke for several minutes until Diana, feeling guilty for her gruff behavior to Mariella, spoke of Moises.

"Your son and I have much in common." When Mariella's eyebrows raised, Diana quickly clarified, "We both enjoy the study of Torah. Though he has not had much formal training, he is quickly grasping the fundamentals and is advancing at an extraordinary pace."

Mariella smiled. "That is good. His father would be proud."

In conjuring Roderigo, who had lost his life in Venice, all of them fell silent once again. Before Diana could speak again of Moises, the Turk joined them, arms akimbo, rings flashing, and a wide smile cracking through the thickness of his beard.

"My friends, the children of the most honorable Rabbi Leone di Modena, it is so good for you to visit me once again. Tell me, to what do I owe this pleasurable visit?"

Zebulun said, "I have returned with a message from the Brethren," he paused to raise an eyebrow at his sister.

"Isaak is safe?" The Turk's eyes were wide. No matter what his agenda may truly be, he seemed to be invested in the welfare of their brother.

Zebulun glanced at Diana again, as if weighing how much he could say before Belladonna arrived. "Yes, Isaak is safe, but there was no need for a rescue. As I always said, Isaak is clever enough to defeat any Spaniard." A searing look from Diana made him stop. "I should wait for Belladonna's arrival before I say any more."

The Turk nodded. "Yes, I understand. A message has been sent, and we must be patient. In the meantime, you will enjoy some coffee?"

The Turk's daughter had appeared once again, her veils fluttering, bearing a tray with an urn and glasses. Zebulun inhaled the rich, strong odor and did not hesitate to drink it as soon as it was poured for him, though both Diana and Mariella declined.

"Would you play some more?" Diana asked Mariella, "It is beautiful, although so sad."

"I sing of home, which is why it is sad," said Mariella, "a place where I can never return."

"You will find a new home. Here. You will be welcomed in the Ghetto. You shall see."

Mariella shook her head. "Thank you for saying that. But I do not belong here."

Diana chided herself for being jealous of Mariella and not putting enough effort to make her feel welcome. She reached out and took Mariella's hand. "I understand how you feel. I, too, have lost a husband. But you are lucky. You have Moises. He seems to be very happy here."

Mariella stared at Diana, with her eyes misting. "It is true I feel bereft without Roderigo. But I was also torn from the island, which had always been my home, and it was so different from here. Here, it is cold and damp, and the sun…the sun can barely lighten the greyness inside the Ghetto. I cannot feel at home there."

"Then what will you do?"

"Josef has offered to take me with him to Constantinople and then to the island of Naxos. He says there, I will be able to build a home. With him and Moises."

Diana was speechless. She had imagined Mariella was in love with Mattia, but she had been wrong. Josef had captured her heart.

Zebulun jumped at the mention of his patron. "Josef has a vast house and many ships—"

"Zebulun, I would rather you did not speak about me," said Josef, who had just arrived. He bowed to Mariella and Diana but gave Mariella an additional nod.

Mariella raised her chin high, and color flared in her cheeks. "I have just informed them of my plans to leave this place and go to Constantinople."

"A wise plan," said the Turk. "The Duke of Mantova has already sent inquiries about both of you, though I suspect for different purposes. How soon are you to set sail?"

"As soon as possible," answered Josef, but turning to Zebulun, he asked, "unless there is other news you bring from the Brethren?"

Zebulun jumped to attention. "I do. They have given us a warning about the Maltese pirates. The Duke of Mantova promised his support to Malta to attack any ships leaving from Venice or Crete and bound for Constantinople. He means to end Venetian control of the Eastern trade in order to establish his own."

Josef's eyebrows raised, and he clenched and released his fists. "This is indeed worrisome news. The Duke is moving fast. I must warn my captains. The Maltese pirates are fierce fighters and have challenged us greatly in the past."

Diana said, "Zebulun has news of our brother, Isaak."

"That is precisely what I have come to hear."

Belladonna had arrived.

Chapter Seventy-One: Belladonna

Zebulun launched into the story of Isaak's escape from the Spanish and his alliance with the pirates of the Caribbean, which he claimed had come directly from Isaak's lips. At last, his story came to an end, and he conveyed the news they had been waiting for. "As we had suspected, Isaak was aboard the French pirate ship instead of the *Sabato*, which had been too damaged to sail. However, his capture of the French ship was not without consequences, and Isaak was wounded in the process."

Belladonna gasped, and a hand flew to her chest, and her heart felt as if it would burst. "Where is he? How severe is his wound?"

Diana, too, was now standing. "Who cares for him? Take us to him immediately."

Zebulun pulled back his shoulders and scowled. "Wait! Isaak has been treated by Ahmad, the Moorish physician who sailed with him on the *Sabato*. I have seen him. Isaak is recovering from his wound, which he assures me was a minor cut on his side. He is weak, however, and does need time and care to fully recover his strength—especially if there is a need to fight off the pirates of Malta."

"Where is he?" repeated Belladonna. She gestured to Diana to join her as they faced Zebulun with determination. "We must find your father and go to Isaak. I trust you and your father can restore him."

"Isaak is still aboard the same French ship, moored beyond the Lido. His ship was escorted here by two vessels of the Brethren. They will not dock here."

"It might be best for us to take him to Giudecca," said Diana, "Considering neither the Ghetto nor Belladonna's palazzo would be the best place for him to recover. I remember the excellent care Roderigo received at the convent. The nuns were knowledgeable in medicines and were kind, and the premises were very clean."

Belladonna agreed to Diana's plan; she, too, had been impressed by the care provided by the convent for Roderigo. "I accept your recommendation. Diana and I will go there to see that they are prepared to receive him. Will you arrange to have him brought there?"

Zebulun nodded.

"Can I do anything to help?" asked Mariella.

Belladonna had forgotten about her and the need to keep her from the Duke. "It is not safe for you to be seen. I will have to arrange somewhere safe for you to go."

Josef took Mariella's hand. "I will keep her safe. We sail on the morrow. There is no need for delay."

Mariella turned to Diana. "I know you have helped make Moises happy here, and I am grateful. But I cannot leave without him. Will you bring him to me here?"

Diana readily agreed and hurried away, first to the Ghetto to retrieve Moises to go with his mother and then to bring her father with her to see Isaak settled on Giudecca.

Belladonna inhaled, taking a deep breath. So much had changed, so quickly! Isaak had been restored to her. The very forces of nature had tried to separate them, but they had managed to survive and find each other once more. There was not just relief but triumph at the thought of holding Isaak in her arms again.

She glanced at Mariella, who she caught regarding Josef with admiring eyes. She was glad Mariella had found happiness with Josef, though she ached at the thought of losing her. She had become accustomed to a feeling of kinship with Mariella and Moises, even if she had to keep their relationship to her asecret.

They had become a family she cared about, and she had seen the extent of how much they had cared about her. Mariella had welcomed her into her home and led her through the swamps of Jamaica, then helped her charm the men with her singing on Hispaniola and aboard the Dutch ship. Moises's enthusiasm and spirit reminded her so much of his father, Roderigo, before the Inquisition had taken their parents and changed the course of their lives.

She would miss them both greatly.

* * *

Though the day was warm, by late afternoon, the wind was high, and the waters of the lagoon were choppier than usual. The trip seemed to be eternal to Belladonna, although it was only a few minutes before the gondolier pulled into the dock at Giudecca.

Diana helped her father out of the gondola as the rabbi held on to his hat and his bag to keep both from blowing away. Though the convent was knowledgeable in many herbal remedies and grew many herbs themselves, he insisted on bringing several of his own concoctions to share. Belladonna hoped the same nun who had taken such good care of Roderigo last year would be available to care for Isaak. Sister Maria had been kind and capable and would not ask too many questions about her patient's wounds.

It took several rounds of persistent knocking until the door was opened by a younger nun, who dutifully led them to Sister Maria at their request. Belladonna was relieved to see the nun's kindly face, which broke into a smile as soon as she recognized them.

"I hope you have brought good news of my former patient."

Belladonna arranged her skirts to allow herself to control her emotions before responding. "Unfortunately, he did not survive. But we appreciated the care you gave him. That is why we have returned. We have another patient for you."

The nun's eyes widened, and her back straightened. "Not—"

Diana responded before she uttered the word for the illness that everyone feared. "He is in no mortal danger, but he is weak and needs time and care to recover his full strength."

Sister Maria's posture relaxed, and her smile returned. "We are certainly capable of aiding in his recovery. When the weather is this fine, we have fewer patients, so he will have our full attention. When shall we expect him?"

"Shortly, and we will wait."

The rabbi and Diana took the opportunity to share his cache of herbs with Sister Maria, describing how they worked and how they should be used with her patients.

Belladonna paced the entry hall where Sister Maria had directed them to wait. Belladonna hoped her prediction of Isaak's arrival was true, as she could barely contain her excitement. After so many months, Isaak would arrive shortly, and she would hold him again after fearing for so long he would be lost to her forever.

Within the hour, when her patience was at an end, there was the tinkle of a bell announcing the arrival of another guest. Belladonna clasped her hands together to contain her desire to spring into a run. She chided herself that it might be another visitor, and she was about to make a fool of herself.

Footsteps echoed on the flagstones. Slow, stopping, and starting. They had reached the threshold. She held her breath.

He was thin, the bones of his face more prominent than ever, his eyes sunken beneath a mop of unruly hair that fell across his forehead. Lids lowered, his attention was absorbed on his feet, which he moved by sliding, not lifting off the floor. Zebulun supported him on one side and Josef on the other.

"Isaak." She released her breath as she said his name.

The red-rimmed eyes looked up at the sound of her voice. "Am I dreaming? Or are you..." His voice faltered, as if he did not have the energy to say her name.

"It is Belladonna." She took his face in both of her hands and gently kissed his lips.

"Belladonna." He repeated, and his eyes began to fill. "So long I have tried to find you."

"I know, my beloved. We are both here, in Venice, and we are both alive and safe." She kissed him again and then released him as she heard the voices of the rabbi and Diana approaching.

He, too, heard the voices and shifted his gaze from her to his father and sister.

"Isaak!" his father cried while Diana ran to embrace him.

"You see, your family is here, and with their help, you will soon regain your strength."

Sister Maria had joined them, along with two other nuns, who each took the place of Zebulun and Josef in supporting their new patient.

Isaak beckoned to his father, and the rabbi held his son in his arms for several minutes, his eyes raised skyward and his lips murmuring a silent prayer.

Belladonna felt the need to say a prayer to acknowledge how grateful they were for surviving, and for being united once more.

Silently, she said the prayer she had heard the little children of the Ghetto say upon awakening: *thank you for restoring my soul to me.*

Author's Note

The Courtesan's Pirate is the third novel in the Venice Beauties Mysteries, following the story of Belladonna, the elite former courtesan of Venice and her long lost love, Isaak, the son of the chief rabbi of the Ghetto and a pirate. Each book in the series can be read on its own, and each is its own adventure with the same cast of characters taking their places either at center stage or as supporting cast.

The seventeenth century was a golden age for Venice, and was the start of the new age of piracy in the Caribbean, as other nations besides Spain made their moves on the riches of the New World. I have always been a fan of pirates, from my first exposure to the series of novels by Rafael Sabatini about a doctor-turned-pirate in *Captain Blood*, and especially after the film with Errol Flynn in the 1930s. I had not intended to write a pirate adventure, and originally this novel began with Belladonna's return to Venice. As I began to imagine where Belladonna had been since leaving Venice with Isaak in *The Courtesan's Secret*, scenes began to play along the lines of a classic pirate movie.

Like my previous novels in this series, the new setting in the Caribbean merited a great deal of research, and I was grateful to have *Jewish Pirates of the Caribbean* by Edward Kritzler as a source, providing the doses of reality for my story. It also necessitated a field trip to Curacao, one of the early pirate havens, before it became an official settlement of the Netherlands (it still remains a Netherlands territory today).

I did take liberties with the timing of the events, since the pirate activities I describe in Hispaniola, Curacao and Cuba were reported a decade or two later than the events of this story. The lack of recorded history of the early 1600s did not stop me from imagining what happened in those lawless years when the Spanish hold was weakening in the Caribbean islands like Hispaniola and Curacao.

I did find some evidence of Jewish pirates in Curacao, in a tombstone recovered from a cemetery now on display in the synagogue there. The earliest recorded Jewish settlers were Dutch, who did not step foot on Curacao until the 1650s. These early Jewish settlers were known to be involved in the seafaring trades, and many of the tombstones had carvings of ships on them. One tombstone with the skull and crossbones of pirate flags, which I've never seen on a Jewish grave in any cemetery in Italy, Germany, Poland or Slovakia that I've visited, supports the possibility that a member ofthe Curacao Jewish community might also have been one of the brotherhood of pirates.

According to Kritzler, many of the early settlers of islands like Jamaica and Cuba were New Christians or secret Jews, who had the most incentive to leave the Old World for the New—to avoid the covetous reach of the Inquisition. Though over 100 years had passed since the banishment of Jews from Spain and Portugal, corrupt leaders of the Spanish Inquisition still launched accusations of heresy against Christians of Jewish descent so they could confiscate their estates. Which is what happened in Recife, Brazil, after the Spanish wrested control of the settlement from the Dutch, and proceeded to target Crypto Jews who had made their fortunes in the silver mines of Brazil. Many of these New Christians who came to the New World decided to revert back to their religious origins and became practicing Jews, but even if they remained Christians, they could still be accused of heresy, like Belladonna's parents, and be burned at the stake for their crime.

As in *The Gallery of Beauties* and *The Courtesan's Secret*, my character's Jewish heritage leads to dangerous encounters and narrow escapes from the Spanish, a shared enemy with the English, Dutch and French pirates.Jews in the New World, for all the dangers they faced, may have had a less precarious existence, as blood libels, expulsions and persecutions were still the norm against Jews in the Old World.

For the *Festa della Sensa* and the intrigues of the Gonzagas of Mantova,

I lucked upon excerpts of a documented record of the Duke of Mantova's visit, enumerating the extravagances rolled out by the city for this holiday. The plot with the fireworks was my own invention, but the description of the Doge's barge and the ceremony of the marriage of Venice to the sea was taken from written accounts of those who witnessed it. The Duke's visit and the special Banquet of One Hundred Ladies held in his honor were also based upon written reports of the time.

I haven't been to Venice since before the pandemic, but I am looking forward to visiting this year to walk along the same pathways as Belladonna and Diana which haven't changed all that much in 500 years.

If you wish to read more about my research of Venice or Curacao, or learn more about the other books in the series, you can subscribe to my newsletter at https://venicebeauties.com.

Acknowledgements

I started out to write this novel solely about Venice, but ended up writing about the Caribbean before returning to Venice. Thanks to the Facebook Group, *Errol Flynn The Legend Lives On*, for reminding me of *Captain Blood*—the original and best pirate movie ever, which provided inspiration to populate the pages taking place in the Caribbean. My trip to Curacao also helped me with the island settings, particularly the north side of the island which is wild and underdeveloped and battered by high winds and choppy seas.

I am so appreciative of the support and friendship of my fellow Curators of Crime, authors Connie Berry, M. A. Monnin and Lane Stone, who additionally make book promotion so much fun. I have found my tribe with Sisters in Crime, where I've found mentorship, friends, support and inspiration. The TriState NYC group published my first short story, and have provided promotional help, guidance, friendship and blurbs that I could not do without. I'd like to acknowledge my historical developmental editor Jenny Q. from Historical Editorial for her ability to find the plot holes and her advice on how to fill them, and last but not least, my editor Verena Rose for her guidance to publication and Shawn Reilly Simmons for her covers of this novel and the entire series.

About the Author

Nina Wachsman is a graduate of the Parsons School of Design, where she studied under Maurice Sendak. She is currently the CEO of a digital marketing agency in New York City. She is also a descendant of a chief rabbi of the Ghetto, a contemporary of the rabbi in the novel. She is a member of Sisters in Crime, Mystery Writers of America, and the Historical Novel Society and has published stories in mystery and horror magazines and anthologies. *The Gallery of Beauties,* her debut novel, was an Agatha nominee for Best First Novel, and along with *The Courtesan's Secret* was a finalist for the Silver Falchion for Best Historical.

AUTHOR WEBSITE:

  https://venicebeauties.com

SOCIAL MEDIA HANDLES:

  https://www.instagram.com/thegalleryofbeauties/
  https://www.threads.net/@thegalleryofbeauties
  https://www.facebook.com/GalleryBeauties
  https://www.facebook.com/curatorsofcrime

Also by Nina Wachsman

The Gallery of Beauties, Level Best Books, July 2022

The Courtesan's Secret, Level Best Books, August 2022

Short fiction:

"The Deadly Portrait" in *Feisty Deeds: Historical Fictions of Daring Women*, anthology of the Women's Fiction Writers Association, available June 8 2024

"The Assassin's Portrait" in *Mystery Magazine*, August 2022.

"Good Help is Hard to Find" in *Night Terrors Scare Street 23* – Short Horror Stories Anthology

"Off the Wall" in *State of Matters*, online magazine, March 2022.

"Laundry at Midnight" in *Justice for All: NY, Tristate NY Sisters in Crime Anthology*, September, 2022

"The Right Spin" in *Curators of Crime*: Holiday Sketches, December, 2023

www.ingramcontent.com/pod-product-compliance
Lightning Source LLC
Chambersburg PA
CBHW021501110726
47899CB00001BA/250